THE HIDDEN

Kathryn Mackel

WESTBOW
PRESS

A Division of Thomas Nelson Publishers
Since 1798

visit us at www.westbowpress.com

Published in Nashville, Tennessee, by WestBow Press, a division of Thomas Nelson, Inc.

WestBow Press books may be purchased in bulk for educational, business, fund-raising, or sales promo-
tional use. For information, please e-mail SpecialMarkets@ThomasNelson.com.

Library of Congress Cataloging-in-Publication Data

Mackel, Kathryn, 1950–
   The hidden / Kathy Mackel.
     p. cm.
   ISBN 1-5955-4037-7 (trade pbk.)
   I. Title.
PS3613.A2734H53 2006
813'.6—dc22   2005031040

Printed in the United States of America

06 07 08 09 10 RRD 6 5 4 3

Praise for *The Hidden*

"With imaginative plotting, depth of detail, and strong dialogue, Mackel shows great promise as part of the new and improved wave of faith fiction."
— PUBLISHER'S WEEKLY

"Kathryn Mackel's *The Hidden* is read-in-one-sitting good! Mackel's consummate skills have created an unforgettable story."
— ANGELA HUNT,
author of *Uncharted*

"I make it a point to read everything Kathryn Mackel writes and *The Hidden* is her best book yet. This novel doesn't just yank at your spine (as a good thriller should), but it also tugs your heart and grips your soul."

"Kathy Mackel [...] series and [...] early day tomorrow, don't [...]"

"[*The Hidden* is] [...] ng insight into the unseen [...]"

"*The Hidden* giv[...] between good and evil wr[...]"

"*The Hidden* is w[...] battle of good verses evil.

[...] award-winning author of *Finding Christmas* and *Michigan*

"Wow! *The Hidden* is Kathryn Mackel's trademark Christian Chiller with all the stops pulled out. An amazing, riveting read not to be missed!"
— COLLEEN COBLE,
author of *Alaska Twilight*

"I enjoyed every minute of *The Hidden*. I highly recommend it!"
— LINDA HALL,
award-winning author of *Dark Water*

OTHER BOOKS BY KATHRYN MACKEL

The Surrogate

The Departed

Outriders

For more information, visit

www.kathrynmackel.com

and

www.birthrighters.com

To Harry and Evelyn Mackel

This is what the Sovereign LORD,
the Holy One of Israel, says:
"In repentance and rest is your salvation,
in quietness and trust is your strength,
but you would have none of it."

— ISAIAH 30:15

ONE

A RAUCOUS SCREECH WOKE SUSAN STONE OUT OF HER REST-
less sleep.

Not her own screams, for once. The phone next to her bed buzzed.
She fumbled for her glasses, checked the clock. Three in the morning.
She pressed the talk button. "Dr. Stone."

"Susie?"

Her father's wife. Another stroke? Or perhaps a heart attack this
time. "What's wrong, Jeanette?"

"Your father didn't want me to call."

The knot in her stomach loosened. Pop was alive, at least. "I'm glad
you know enough not to listen to him. What's happened?"

"He's in a lot of pain, but he won't take anything. I need you to talk
to him."

Susan switched on the lamp, tried to get her bearings. "Sure. But I
need you to tell me what I'll be talking to him about."

"Oh, sorry. My nerves are shot." Jeanette exhaled. "Sarraf threw him."

"Sarraf's been dead for forty years."

"This is a new one, a wild horse that your father says looks like his
old favorite . . ."

Susan took a long drink from her water bottle. Late-night calls were
routine—mostly overdoses and suicide attempts. And sometimes suicide successes, but she couldn't go there, had to focus on what Jeanette
was saying.

". . . wandered in from the hills. Your father thinks he's still a cowboy, can jump on any horse anytime and anywhere."

"Where is he, and what's his condition?"

"Hardesty Medical, down in Steamboat. His leg is broken."

"Which leg?"

"Um. I'm not sure. Sorry, my head is fuzzy. I need some coffee. Which leg . . . does it matter?"

"His right hip is arthritic. That could complicate things."

"No, let me think. I'm in the lobby, on my cell. He made me leave the treatment room, said I was a bigger pain than his broken leg. Okay, the left leg, that's it."

"Not the femur?"

"Is that the thigh bone?"

"Yes."

"No. It's the lower leg."

The femur would have required a cast up to his hip. Lower leg, he'd be hobbled but able to get around. "Did the doctors say anything about internal injuries? His spleen or kidney?"

"Just the leg. This is one nasty horse, tossed your father hard. I don't care how beautiful that stallion is—Charlie shouldn't be messing around with wild horses, not at his age."

"Can you tell me exactly what happened?"

"I was in the upstairs bathroom, getting ready for bed. I thought your father was still downstairs, watching that cop show of his. Then I heard the cry from out back. It cut right through the wall, like the coyotes' howls do sometimes. I ran outside, found Charlie in the far paddock. Bouncing on his backside along the ground, every bounce setting off a yelp of pain. He was going to drag himself back to the barn, can you believe him?"

"I sure can."

"The fool horse followed him, head hanging low like a kid who knew he'd gone too far."

"Did they set it?"

"Not yet. They need to do surgery, put pins in to hold the bone together. But his heart is acting frisky. And of course, Charlie is refusing to cooperate. Saying to throw on a cast and let him go home."

Susan rested the phone against her cheek, took another deep breath. "What's his doctor's name? I'll have him paged, see what can be done."

"The orthopedist left for the night. He won't do anything until the heart lady comes in. Meanwhile, they got your father in a blow-up cast.

He's the color of pea soup. And all sweaty, but it's cold sweat. I hate to see him like that. You need to make him take the pain medication."

Susan got up, went to the window. The lights of Boston glittered like fireflies in the fog. Rain coming again. So far, May had been a washout. "This happened tonight?"

"Ten our time. It was one of those magic nights, the kind you get only in Colorado. Moon rising up out of the mountains, air so clean it feels like it's washing you inside and out. Even the birds quieted, like they just wanted to sit back and enjoy it." Jeanette paused. "My battery's low, I've got to go."

"I'll call him, try to talk some sense into him."

"No. You'd better just get out here. We need you—"

The phone went dead.

Eighteen hours later, Susan touched Charles Robinson's shoulder as he dozed. His eyes opened, blinking. "Vannie?"

Susan bit the inside of her lip to keep from snapping at him. "Papa, it's me. Susan."

He shook his head. "For a moment there . . . your hair, cut like that. The way you hold your head, your chin up . . ."

She kissed him, keeping her face next to his while she let the moment pass. The stubble on his cheek was soft.

He pulled away and squinted at her. "What are you doing here?"

"Checking up on you."

"Jeanette put you up to this?"

"Don't you go giving her a hard time. Jeanette did the right thing."

"I didn't want you to be worried. 'Cause there's nothing to worry about."

"Maybe not. But I had to see that for myself." Her clinical eye took in his condition—surgical splint, morphine drip, heart monitor. His color was good and his pulse strong, but his eyes were still dimmed from anesthesia.

"I read your chart. The surgery went well."

"This morning. They brought me back to this room. Tucked me

into bed. I was sweet-dreaming for hours, but they woke me up, forced some Jell-O down my throat, and then made me get in this chair. Something about blood clots. Can't leave a body alone for one minute. Trying to justify the outrageous charges. Probably costs five bucks just to flush the toilet."

Susan glanced at her watch. "Why don't I get you back into bed? They won't bother you again, except to check your temperature. You can get a good night's sleep." She wrapped her arm around his waist and helped him up.

His skin was loose and silky, his muscles knotty.

"Don't put any weight on that leg," she warned. After a month, they'd replace the splint with a fiberglass cast. He'd face days of being in a wheelchair, weeks on crutches, months of physical therapy.

"I know, I know. They told me five times. I'm old but not deaf."

She set the IV pole so Charlie could reach the button on the morphine drip, then pulled up the side rails.

"Don't do that. I'm not a baby that's gonna fall out of bed."

"This way you can get at the call button."

"They did their blasted surgery. Why can't I go home now?"

"They need to monitor the swelling in your foot overnight. Also, give you some therapy to teach you how to use the wheelchair."

"Wheelchair! Just give me crutches, I'll get about. Or tell them to put on one of them walking casts." His pout was almost comical.

"You'll get that in a few weeks. Just relax and get better. Don't rush it."

Her father shifted in bed, his brow creased with worry.

"Are you in pain, Pop? Just push the button on the IV. You'll get the right amount of medicine."

"No, that's not it." He rubbed his face. The back of his hand was spotted and the skin translucent. "I don't remember the last time I used the bathroom. Maybe I'd better get in there before I hunker down for the night."

"No need to. You're catheterized."

"What?" He lifted up the blanket. "I didn't even feel this. Why did they do that? I don't need—"

"Whoa, hold on there." Susan grabbed his hand before he could tug out the tube. "This makes things easier for you overnight. Plus it lets them monitor your urine, make sure there's no blood in it. You took a nasty fall."

"I hate being like this. When I'm an old man, don't ever let them put me in those diapers. I'll jump out a window before I let them—"

Like an electric current to her spine, it struck Susan.

. . . the radio said there was a jumper, a young man, right outside your apartment building. I worried it was one of Christopher's friends, but he's still in Colorado, right? Dr. Stone, are you all right . . .

Charlie fumbled for her hand. "Gee, oh Susie, I didn't mean to say . . ."

Susan turned away, hand to her mouth. Focus on something, anything. The drapes were an institutional beige, with nine folds each. The tile was grouped in diagonals, blue squares alternating with black. She counted the squares, pushing the pain deep, clinging to her methodical breathing and meaningless counting. Six tiles, seven tiles, eight tiles.

"I'm sorry, baby. I just . . ." Charlie's hand brushed her back.

"Shush. You didn't do anything wrong."

Oh Christopher, I was so wrong . . . Oh God, let me take it back.

She smoothed his hair, willing her fingers not to tremble. "Be patient, okay? Tomorrow will be a better day, Pop. I know it will."

He clutched her hand. "Today's good, Susie. Now that you're here."

She kissed his forehead, then sat by his side until he fell asleep.

It was almost midnight when Susan arrived at the ranch. She tossed her suitcase onto the twin bed she had slept in as a child, hoping for nothing more than a better night's sleep than the one before.

But Jeanette had asked her to put on jeans and sneakers and come to the barn.

"Thanks for coming out here," she said.

"I'm so sorry I missed your wedding." Susan cringed. What a stupid thing to say. Her father had remarried almost four years ago. Yet even that couldn't induce Susan to come back to Harken.

"I meant, out to the barn."

"It's almost midnight. Are you sure this can't wait until morning?"

"You should've known before, Susie."

Susan's nerves crackled with fatigue. "Can't you just tell me?"

"You've got to see for yourself."

As they crossed the drive, the size of the blue spruces startled Susan. They had been three feet or less when she left for college, immature saplings. Now they were fully mature and beautifully shaped, a graceful barrier between house and barn. As they passed through them, the yard lights came on.

Susan gasped when she saw the barn—sparkling new and large enough to accommodate at least twenty horses. "When did this all happen?"

Jeanette cleared her throat. "A bit over a year ago. Charlie was planning for the future, something to pass on to his grandson. That was before . . . you know . . ."

Of course she knew.

"He wouldn't let me tell you, and he swore Christopher to secrecy. Knew you wouldn't approve." Jeanette opened the door.

The scent of leather hit Susan first as they passed the tack room filled with harnesses, bridles, and saddles. In the main part of the barn, it was all horse—the clean odor of pine shavings mingled with a sweet, musky smell.

Horses drowsed lazily in the stalls, some on their sides asleep, others curious at the intrusion. A gray gelding pushed against his gate, looking for a treat. Susan instinctively patted her pockets for carrots. *After thirty years*, she thought. *Still a habit.*

She flipped on the stall light and was surprised. "Dude horses. What's up with this? Is my father giving trail rides again?"

Jeanette nodded. "He needs the income."

The all-too-familiar ache of frustration crept into Susan's throat. "After the stroke, he promised. We had an arrangement." She should have known better. Her father's promises were as good as the winter wind. Ever-changing, impossible to pin down.

"He got them at auction two years ago, cleaned them up, fed them well. Don't they look good?"

Susan peered into the adjacent stalls. "They do look good, but that's irrelevant. What happened to the retirement fund I helped him set up? It should have kept you both for the rest of your lives." The crash of the eighties had impoverished her father, almost cost him the ranch. Charlie had barely survived bankruptcy by selling off his stock at pennies on the dollar. With Susan's help, he made it through, switching from breeding to trail rides. When he developed cardiac issues four years ago, he had sold his dude horses, kept one for occasional riding, and was supposed to be retired.

Jeanette looked down at the floor. "The retirement fund is gone."

"Why didn't you tell me, Jeanette?"

"I respect my husband's wishes, even when they're prideful."

Susan wanted to shake her. "What's he up to? He didn't empty out that account to buy some over-the-hill dude horses."

"Come see." Jeanette steered her to the back.

The last two stalls were double-sized. The one to Susan's left was empty, but in the other one a horse lumbered to the gate. Susan's breath caught in her throat. "She's . . ."

"What?"

"Spectacular."

Jeanette shrugged. "Charlie says she is. I pray every night that he's right."

"What's her name?"

"Rayya the Regal. Rayya for short."

Susan kissed Rayya's muzzle, softer than satin against her skin. The horse's breath was sweet from alfalfa. She was a bay, with a rich mahogany coat, and black mane, forelock, and tail. Her eyes were huge, her forehead broad and flat. Her ears were set perfectly atop her crown—small, tight, and beautifully shaped. Her nostrils were huge and her heart would be strong because Arabians were bred for endurance and power as well as grace. Her long neck was set high on deep and sloping shoulders. Balanced and well proportioned, she would be as perfect in motion as she was at rest.

"Where did she come from?"

"Your father's old poker buddy, Ray Field. He got into something so deep he couldn't dig back out with a bulldozer."

"Gambling debts, I assume."

"Las Vegas bookmakers. Charlie said she was a bargain, but more important, that she was special. He was afraid some rich weekend rancher would buy her for his kids to trot about in the show ring, never realizing her true value. So he emptied out the retirement and bought her."

"There was a quarter million in there. She couldn't have cost that much."

"She was fifty thousand. Got her cheap, Charlie said. Most of the rest of the money went for this barn."

A weariness settled on Susan. "He already had a barn."

"Not good enough. Or big enough. I couldn't stop him—it's his money, not mine. He wants things back like they used to be. When the Robinson name was known all over the country for the best Arabians."

Rayya pushed against her, wanting more patting. Susan flicked on the light over the stall and went in. "Oh my. She's in foal?"

"Due to deliver sometime this month. The sire is Magnum Psyche."

"I'm sorry, Jeanette. I haven't followed Arabians for years."

"He's the top horse in the country. Maybe even the world. Charlie bought an entire breeding package. He expects Rayya to produce many champions, restart the industry single-handed."

Susan leaned her face against Rayya's neck. She was a quiet horse, but Susan could feel her well-formed muscularity, could easily imagine what it would be like to ride her, the power flowing from horse to rider, the respect going from rider to horse. "If you emptied out the account, how are you making ends meet?"

"Trail rides. Melissa helps out as a guide, plus she gives lessons."

Susan struggled to keep her expression neutral. "I didn't know Melissa still worked here."

"She believes in what Charlie is doing. Now this—Charlie putting himself out of action with tourist season about to start."

Susan tore herself away from Rayya. "How much do you need?"

"No, no! Your father would die before taking money from you."

"I have more than I'll ever need." Between the nest egg Paul had left her and her own lucrative practice, she had plenty of money. And no future, not anymore.

Jeanette took her hands and looked deep into her face. "You've got your father's eyes. All these years and I still don't know what color that is. Too many gold highlights to be hazel."

Susan turned her face away. "What can I do for you?"

"I know you swore you'd never come back."

"It's best if we leave the past where it belongs, Jeanette. Of course you understand."

"Of course I do. But Susie, could you stay for a while? Maybe until the foal is born. Then everything will settle out like it's supposed to. Just a few weeks. Please."

Jeanette couldn't be serious, couldn't possibly expect her to stay after all that had happened. Ancient history or recent history, it was all the same. Bitter and ugly. Susan would do the right thing—pump some money into an emergency account, hire a manager to run the tourist rides and a good vet for the mare. But to expect her to stay was too much to ask. Jeanette had to know that.

And then Rayya nickered, anxious for more attention.

Thirty years of resolve crumbled. "Of course I'll stay," Susan said. "I'd be happy to."

TWO

RICK SMELLED THE CORPSE FROM A HUNDRED FEET AWAY.

He could smear the Vicks or light a cigar, but burned flesh had a way of clawing into your throat and holding on.

"That must be the guy who called it in." Joyce Freeman pointed to a man sitting at the side of the road, head in his hands. He looked up as they approached.

"I'm Sheriff Sanchez," Rick said. "This is Dr. Freeman."

"Keith Mullen." The man braced himself against the guardrail and tried to stand.

He was in his early thirties, Rick guessed. Muscular, a weekend mountain cyclist by the looks of the expensive bike sprawled halfway up the ridge. Probably a good-looking guy when his features weren't twisted in shock.

"Don't get up," Joyce said, pressing her stethoscope to his chest. "The dispatcher said you took a tumble."

"I'm okay." Mullen rubbed his face. "You need to get up there. That thing—"

She glanced at Rick.

"Go ahead. I'll be up shortly," he said.

Joyce headed up the steep slope. Rick took out his notebook and pen. "What can you tell me, Mr. Mullen?"

His shoulders shook. "I didn't mean to run over it. I mean, it's dead. Whatever it is or was . . ."

"Whoa. Slow down. Take your time, start at the beginning."

Mullen let out a measured breath. "I'm on a weeklong trip."

"Anyone with you?"

"No. I came alone. I'm a process engineer for a chip manufacturer down in Denver. High-tech and high-pressure job, so I need downtime every once in a while. I camped up the Greenville Mine Road, then pedaled a bit more north and went up that peak there—" He tipped his head to the mountain that rose behind them, not as high as the other Rockies, but still rock-faced and studded with pockets of snow.

"Folly Mountain."

"I couldn't get cell reception up where I camped. I have a phone conference scheduled for noon, so I headed out before sunrise."

"That's rough terrain up there. Dangerous pedaling in the dark."

"Sure is. But the sky had grayed enough to give me decent visibility. I came down some sort of a fire road."

"More likely a snowmobile track. They're everywhere these days."

"When I spotted the river, I decided to cut across that ridge—" Mullen motioned behind him, but wouldn't look that way.

Didn't matter—neither of them could ignore the smell. Joyce had scrambled to the top and just stood with her back to the road, staring down at what had to be the body.

Mullen's face went green.

Rick touched his shoulder. "Get your head down a bit. It'll help."

He bent his head to his knees and continued. "I was making good time when the stink hit me—*slammed* me. By the time I realized something was burning, I had to hold steady or crash into those boulders. I thought—okay, it's just a bag of garbage. Even as I ran over it, I was still thinking: no, it's solid, maybe a log.

"It hit me like a punch—*it's not trash, not wood, it's a body*. I come out here for the beauty and solitude, not this . . . this . . ." Chills seized Mullen, chills so violent that his jaw rattled.

Rick grabbed a blanket from his trunk and wrapped it around him. "Can I call someone for you?"

Mullen shook his head.

"I've got to get up there and see if Dr. Freeman needs any help. Some folks are on their way to help out. Don't try to get on your bike, okay?"

Mullen drew up his knees. "No worry there."

Rick was almost to the top before he spotted the charred mass. He sprinted the last hundred feet.

Joyce glanced up and went back to work, occasionally stepping away to get a fresh breath. Rick paced the immediate vicinity, looking for footprints or, more likely, tire impressions from an ATV or dirt bike. He traced Mullen's bicycle track back toward the trail, marking the skid and recovery that had brought him sprawling over the body.

Rick could find no indication of how this body—or its killer—had come onto the ridge. The forensic folks were on their way in from Denver, along with the specialists from the Colorado Bureau of Investigation. Rick called them for assistance even before he picked up Joyce.

The 911 call had made it clear this would not be something a county sheriff was equipped to handle. Life in the Elk River Valley was slow and predictable. Rick's primary duty as sheriff was rounding up drunks on weekends and interceding in domestic incidents. The few murders he had investigated had been straightforward.

Not something like this.

Joyce waved him over. "It's bad."

"Male or female?"

She shrugged. "Don't know. It's that bad."

Rick took shallow breaths through his mouth. Mullen's impression of a burned log was fairly accurate. The mass was about five or six feet long with limbs somewhat discernable if one looked for them. "Can you even be sure it's human?"

"Under all that charring, we've got most of a skeleton, plus plenty of tissue for DNA."

"Did you take a dental impression? We might get a quicker ID that way, especially if we get a missing persons—"

"No teeth."

"Hm. False teeth? Maybe someone with a bizarre fetish who took a trophy? Or was this a quick and ugly way to solve the problem of grandma?"

"No. Not that. There are no teeth because there is no—oh, this is insane even to say this. The head is there, you can see the outline. But Rick—it's like someone dissolved the skull inside the head. It's just not there."

The scene plays out like a movie, more satisfying since he's got a free pass.

The fool on the bicycle, calling for help and puking into his phone. The patrol car pulling up. A muscled stud gets out, hand on his gun, ready to wreak justice. The doctor at his side, striding purposefully as if she could be of any use. He knows these two, has done his homework well, congratulates himself as they play true to form.

The doctor takes the steep climb without breaking a sweat. Her breath doesn't catch until she sees his work of art. The sheriff is fit enough, but given to quieter pursuits. An occasional round of golf or horseback ride up into the hills. He pants, not from exertion, but from dread.

They don't notice him or hear him, though he is not far from them. He envies the doctor her work. Running her hands over the thing of no consequence. *Ashes to ashes*, he wants to whisper, but he suppresses his ironic amusement. Why throw his pearls before these swine?

The sheriff paces around the body, his steps slowing with each cycle. He notes that hesitation, files it away for future use. There's some anger there, a ripple of rage that the fool doesn't even know exists.

Indeed, doors are opening everywhere.

Soon enough, he will go in.

THREE

SOME DAYS WERE EMPTY. SOME DAYS WERE WORSE THAN EMPTY. But not today. As soon as Melissa stepped outside, she knew this would be a full day. The wind gusted across the meadow, ruffling spring-green grasses. Meadowlarks, robins, and finches chattered away in the brush.

Even Charlie's accident couldn't dampen her mood. They'd been through worse together. Melissa would work extra hard to keep things going for him. They'd survive.

Her trailer was set just a bit off Routt County Road 102, but the main house was almost a mile up the dirt road. On cold days Jeanette picked her up, but today was a good day. Maybe even a sweet day. She walked briskly, warming sleep-heavy muscles. When she got her wind, she broke into a jog. It wasn't until she came around the back of the house that she spotted the Mercedes SUV with a rental sticker in its back window.

Only Susan Stone would rent a luxury car to come to a working ranch.

Like that, Melissa thought with an imaginary snap. The day empties out. Maybe she should just go back to the trailer. Call Jeanette and claim she had a migraine. Let Susan Stone do the day's manure slinging. But no—Charlie had entrusted the horses to Melissa's keeping. She'd do anything for Charlie.

Melissa never knew her own father, remembered her mother only in a haze of men, smoke, and booze. Jeanette was her foster mother from kindergarten on. When Charlie married Jeanette, they wanted Melissa to move into the main house, but she kept to the trailer. The distance made them all that much closer.

Melissa kicked off her sneakers and went into the kitchen.

Jeanette turned from the stove to kiss her cheek. "Good morning."

She turned away, angry at the tears swelling in her eyes. "How long is she staying?"

"A few more minutes and the rolls will be ready. How do you want your eggs?"

"Ma . . ."

"As long as she's needed."

"It's only a broken leg. She could have called, sent flowers. She'll only cause trouble. You know that."

Jeanette grabbed her by the shoulders. "Stop it. We've had enough bad blood around here."

Melissa wriggled away. "That's not my fault. You know that."

"Hon, I had to do this. Charlie needs help."

Melissa poured herself a cup of coffee. "He's got me. Don Camara will stop by, do whatever I can't get to. Other neighbors too. There's plenty of help."

"Not the kind she can give." Jeanette's voice was little more than a whisper. "Where are you going? Let's talk about . . ."

Melissa took her coffee and headed back outside. The grass was still too full of water to have any nutritional value, so the horses were being fed hay and grain. She'd get them fed, turn them out, muck the stalls. Hard work was always a good remedy for times like this.

Jeanette followed her out to the porch. "Hon, don't go. You're taking what I said wrong."

Melissa waved her away. It wouldn't be the first time Susan Stone had showed up here, trying to buy off a problem. But Charlie didn't need her—he had Melissa. The sooner Susan went home, the better for everyone.

Susan wandered into the kitchen, rubbing sleep from her eyes. Her mind felt like mush. "Did I hear voices?"

Jeanette went right to the refrigerator. "Sit. Let me make you breakfast."

"Just coffee. I've got to turn out the horses. I didn't mean to sleep so long."

"Melissa does the morning shift. Charlie can't fire on all cylinders until midday, but that girl is like a sparrow. Can't keep to the perch once the sky lightens. Too bad she can't sing. Scratchy little voice, that one. You should hear her in church."

Probably sooner than later, Susan would have to face the girl. But she couldn't worry about that now, at least not until after she had a cup of coffee. They were still using the old tin pot with the dents. The coffeemaker she had sent as a wedding gift was probably in the attic. Or maybe Jeanette took it to her church. Sometimes her father went to service with her, Jeanette said. Susan was glad they'd found some comfort for themselves.

She took a few sips. Caffeine settled her, the stimulant kicking her mind into gear, allowing it to keep those dark undercurrents at bay.

Jeanette had emptied half the refrigerator onto the counter. "Okay, I've got fresh eggs. I could scramble them. Or are you like your father, with the once-over-easy? Got some homemade bread that makes great French toast. Or . . ." Jeanette peered back into the fridge. "I thawed a roast for supper. I could cut off the end for steak and eggs."

Susan laughed. "I'd better stick to coffee before you have me too wide to get out the door."

A worry line creased Jeanette's forehead. "You could stand a little meat on those bones."

Susan turned to the window so Jeanette wouldn't see the tightening in her jaw. Her father's wife would be dismayed to know she had echoed Susan's mother. But only in the words—Jeanette didn't have an ounce of the meanness that Vanessa Robinson had had in abundance.

Too skinny. Tell her, Charles. Men don't like string beans.

Susie's fine, Vanessa. Riders are lean.

She needs a more graceful presence in the ring. Susan, I'm talking to you. Sit up straight. You're like a bag of bones. And don't glare like that. Where are you going, young lady? I'm speaking to you.

I don't know where I'm going. Don't care. As long as I get away . . .

The mountains were visible through the trees, the upper peaks still frosted with snow. Any snow that lingered in Boston quickly browned with street dirt and car exhaust, but up in the Rockies, the snow kept its perfect sheen until it melted away. Susan would only have to step outside and turn to see lofty peaks in every direction. Even back in Boston, she had always known—had counted on—the constancy of the Rocky Mountains. The one thing in her life that couldn't be shaken, couldn't come crashing down on her.

The doorbell rang.

Jeanette padded down the hall. Susan heard a man's voice, followed by the sound of footsteps as they came into the kitchen. The visitor was about her age, with dark brown eyes and salt-and-pepper hair cut short. Clean-shaven and tanned, he wore jeans and a navy button-down shirt.

He smiled at her, both hands extended. "Hello, Susan."

As familiar as the back of her hand and yet she couldn't place him, not thirty years out of context. "I'm sorry. I'm not connecting . . . oh, Ricky!" Susan opened her arms, and he wrapped her in a hug.

He had written last year, a sweet letter that she hadn't mustered the energy to answer. Nothing to be said, not then and not now.

"How are you?" Rick said.

"Fine. But Pop's not, which is why I'm here." Susan leaned back so she could look at him. The lines around his mouth had deepened and one of his front teeth was chipped. He had thickened, as men do—his jaw almost blocky but not unattractive.

Rick smiled, his crooked grin bringing back so many memories. Long rides along the river, into the hills, even sneaking up Folly. Sharing a first kiss in seventh grade, just to help each other get over it. Trudging through high school, she the top student and he the sturdy baseball catcher. Their paths split with Susan going to Harvard and Rick to the Marine Corps. Weekly letters, then monthly. She went to Paris for a semester, he shipped out to Japan, and that was the last she'd heard from him. Until last fall.

"I heard Charlie got tossed. Middle of the night when reasonable people are in bed."

"That's my father . . ." Susan ran out of words, unsure how to keep him from offering condolences that she couldn't bear to hear.

Jeanette rescued her with a clatter of pans. "Sheriff, I was about to make breakfast. I got bacon, I got eggs, I got steak, I got homemade bread. You name it, you got it."

He laughed. "No restaurant compares with Jeanette Robinson's kitchen."

"You're the sheriff?" Susan said.

Rick shrugged. "Guilty as charged. I was an MP back in the Corps. Made sense to keep at it, so I did criminal justice at Colorado State. I've been with Routt County for fourteen years now."

"Good grief, I've got some serious catching up to do. Can you join us?"

"I'm afraid I'll have to take a rain check." He gave Jeanette a warm smile that faded quickly. "I'm here on business. That stretch of ridge on RCR 101—between the town limit and the Advent River? That's Robinson property out there, right?"

Jeanette nodded.

"I'm afraid we've found a body up there."

Jeanette turned, her eyes wide. "A body?"

Susan shifted instinctively into physician mode, her eyes suitably concerned, her face bland and trustworthy. She had seen many bodies in her time, handled it with professional aplomb. Until . . . deep breath, *Think of Jeanette and her hands shaking. Rick's jaw tightening; something eating at him. Anything but that day.*

"What can we do to help?" Susan said. Good words, level tone despite the adrenaline buzzing through her. Fight or flee—but whom to fight and where to run?

Rick pulled out the chair for Jeanette. "Let's all sit down for a minute."

"Is it someone from the valley?" Jeanette asked.

Rick shook his head. Not meeting their eyes now. "Identification will be difficult. The body was burned." He spoke faster, as if to put that ugly fact far behind. "Jeanette, have you seen anyone on your property? Someone who shouldn't be here. Riding or maybe four-wheeling?"

Jeanette smoothed her sleeve, clutched her apron. Her fingers couldn't seem to settle. Susan took her hands, held them. "Were there vehicle tracks near the site?" Susan asked.

"Nothing at the approach except the skids made by the mountain biker who found the body. The folks from CBI are there now, and the evidence techs. It's their investigation—"

"The guys from the state? They don't know us," Jeanette said. "Not like you do, Sheriff."

"I'm just not equipped to handle this kind of homicide, not without specialized help. They'll handle the technical stuff, and I'll take care of local angles. Coming to see neighbors like you, Jeanette. To let you know what's happened, see if we can piece something together."

Jeanette got up and began cracking eggs into a bowl. Rick watched her, his brow creased. Susan squeezed his hand and mouthed, *I'll take care of her.*

Rick nodded. "Has Charlie started up his trail rides?"

"He did a few last weekend." Jeanette had cracked a full dozen eggs.

"Lessons?"

She nodded, intent on whisking.

"I'll need a list of anyone who's been in those hills recently," Rick said.

"I'll ask my father," Susan said.

Jeanette motioned with the whisk. "Melissa knows everyone who comes here, which day they come, even what trails they ride. She's out all the time, riding one horse or another. Ask her, Sheriff."

"Thank you. I'll want to talk to both of them. Susan, when did you get here?"

"Last night. I haven't seen anything but the hospital and my old bed."

"And Rayya," Jeanette said.

"Rayya?" Rick asked.

"My father's latest folly."

"Oh." He got up. "I'll go see Melissa."

Susan walked him to the door. He took her hands and whispered, "Too long, Suse."

She hugged him, holding on tight. "I know."

"You okay?"

"Managing."

He put his face to her hair. "I prayed my heart out when I heard. Is there anything I can do?"

Nothing anyone can do, she wanted to say. Nothing. That's the only reasonable remedy . . . nothingness. Even the mountains will one day succumb to nothingness, because only *nothing* is unshakable.

Susan clutched his shirt, her fingers working into the fabric. "Pray harder, Ricky. Please."

FOUR

HE IS IN A THINKING MOOD AND INCLINED TO SHARE HIS wisdom.

Tonight's lecture, students, is—*cue drum roll*—the animal world.

The first beast specifically mentioned in the Bible is . . . anyone? Come on, children. You've read the press release. *Now the serpent was more crafty than any of the wild animals.*

Condemned to crawl on his belly . . . it is abundantly clear that the snake gets a bum rap. Certainly there are beasts far more manipulative. Consider cats, for example. Why are they elevated to household companionship while snakes are shrieked at, stomped on, driven over? Are sleek fur and twitchy whiskers really more attractive than exquisite scales or those penetrating eyes? *Droll sigh.* I fear that those little ears and friendly purr are cunningly deceptive. The truth is that a cat will rip out a throat simply for the amusement of it. And their inclination toward humans is not to be interpreted as any sort of interest. Indeed, cats are the ultimate narcissists. Their way or the highway, baby.

Perhaps—*cue drum roll and make it a double*—a creature's worth should not be measured in its essence, but in its function. Is not the rat known by the garbage he consumes? Though this is a worthwhile and perhaps enviable contribution, nevertheless folks fling invectives at these creatures when they really should sing praise. Certainly, if one would rat out the truth, pun intended—*self-deprecating chuckle*—it wasn't trash that devalued the rodent, but that he bore the black death. And consider this: why are the two middlemen overlooked in this equation? The flea, which has its own public relations nightmare to contend with. At the bottom of it all—it was bacteria that caused the plague.

We fear what we can see while the hidden persists, undeterred.

And therein lies the beauty of this lesson. Power sometimes comes in tiny packages. And sometimes it is more potent when masked by a bland countenance. You can have your HIV, polio, and smallpox. Give me the common cold any time. Truly now, what decimates a population with as much consistency and equality as the splendid rhinovirus?

So much for that allegedly grand scheme of things.

Modest nod. Thus ends today's lecture. Go in peace, children. Or go in pieces, pun most definitely intended. The choice is yours.

He suppresses a chuckle as his musings fade. In the fullness of time, he will indeed get the last laugh.

For now, there is work to be done. He slips through the shadows in a practiced crouch, moving from manure pile to hay shed to barn. The earlier activity has ceased—stupid people taking stupider lessons to teach the stupidest of animals how to behave. So much for synergy.

He moves along the stalls, ignoring the common beasts that mutter or shuffle in their sleep. The crown princess has her own stable, her own paddock with the choicest of pasture. He approves because royalty demands white-glove treatment.

Of noble lineage himself, he knows majesty when he beholds it. True, this horse shows the strain of pregnancy, her hide stretched to accommodate her burdensome belly. But her eyes are clear, her neck strong, her demeanor superb. That the frail flesh of man can conceive of a breeding program that improves on the grand scheme is something to be respected.

Not that he is of any mind to show respect.

The regal one dozes. There are no fences in her dreams, no saddles, no halters, no bits. *Yes, dear one. Freedom is the true heaven.*

Though he can't see the foal, he knows her well. Surprised by his own fascination with the growing scrap of inseminated ovum, he has stopped by here often. He has taken to speaking to the foal when the mare sleeps, maternal instinct being so strong that it is simply wiser to circumvent it. It is only recently that the foal, now near-term, has responded to what has become her master's voice. Yet the final test lies ahead—a simple request on his part, but a difficult act for this young one. The foal is all neck and legs, nestled face-forward as instinct decrees.

Instinct is a fine thing, he supposes, if one can abide lock-step adherence to genetic slavery. He prefers chaos to chains, thank you.

He slips into the stall and whispers in the mare's ear. She startles, but her pregnancy is so onerous that she is quickly calmed and lulled back to sleep. Pressing his hands to her withers, willing her to be silent, he bends to her belly and speaks to her foal.

Turn, baby. Turn.

FIVE

THE RAIN CAME DOWN LIKE THE END OF THE WORLD, WITH no sign of stopping. A freak storm, the weather folks said, the kind that seldom happens in these mountains. One for the record books. Though it was midafternoon, the sky was as dark as night. Only the flicker of the emergency lights was visible through the haze, except when the lightning split the sky. Sheets of rain obscured the barn.

Melissa's jeans were soaked through in less than a minute, and even her boots started to fill up. The dude horses clustered under an ancient ponderosa pine, the branches providing little cover from the rain. She whistled from the shelter, and they looked her way. Job—the smart one—came first, followed by Jeremiah, Deborah, and Abigail. Jonas meandered behind them, too dense to come out of the rain but hoping for a treat.

They were Arabian-quarter mixes that Charlie had picked up at auction last year. Their owner had been a devout Jew, naming his horses out of the Old Testament. The man was kind and sweet, but old and bent with arthritis. He hadn't been able to properly care for his stock for some time. They came to Robinson Ranch with matted manes, dirty teeth, and hooves badly in need of trimming. After months of Melissa's good care, they frolicked like colts, their coats shiny, their bodies smooth and sleek, their necks proud.

That stupid stallion was in the far field, head high and focused on the storm. He gave Melissa a haughty look as if to say, *Don't even bother*. She wouldn't—Prince Sarraf hadn't let anyone near him since he tangled with Charlie a week ago. Her main interest in him was to keep him away from the others, especially Rayya. She had loved the Arabian from the moment she saw her. She'd better not waste any more time out here—Rayya would be looking for her.

When she returned to the barn, the mare lay on her side, panting. Charlie sat with his head in his hands. Susan stood at the door to the stall, back straight and hands on her hips. She and Melissa hadn't said more than three words to each other in the week that she had been here.

Rayya rolled in the straw, nipping at her side as if freaked by what her own body was doing to her. Heart aching, Melissa would have given anything to go into the stall and soothe her, but Charlie said mares in labor liked to be left to themselves.

"I don't get why this is happening," she said. "That doc—excuse me, that world-famous doctor of world-famous horses—said she wasn't showing any signs of labor. That it could be days or even weeks."

Charlie let out a loud curse. "That blasted expert my genius daughter hired doesn't know his oats from his barley. He's not worth fifty cents, let alone the thousand bucks a day he's getting."

Susan's face was tight, the twitch over her left eyebrow betraying her anxiety. "Dr. Rodgers tends to the dams of Derby winners, Pop. If he said there was no sign of her being anywhere near starting labor yesterday, there wasn't."

"Maybe we should try to load her into the trailer," Melissa said. "Get her to the animal hospital."

"Don't be ridiculous," Susan said. "You don't move a mare in this condition. Besides, our driveway is half washed out by now. If we were foolish enough to put her in a trailer, she'd probably have a broken leg before we even got out to 102."

Susan Stone, the expert on everything from trailering a horse to the condition of the road in a storm, even though she hadn't been back to Colorado since long before Melissa was even born. Melissa pressed her fists into the small of her back to keep from sniping at her. Rayya was in enough distress—she didn't need to sense her anger and frustration.

"We've got to do something," Melissa said. "We can't just let her go on like this."

Charlie slammed his crutch against the wall. "I should be taking care of her. Stupid fool—"

"Stop it, we don't have time for that. She's right, we can't wait any longer," Susan said. "Melissa, get the chlorhexidine and some warm water. Two buckets of it. We'll need the clean cloths and anything else that's in the foaling box. I need to trim my nails before I examine her. Pop, where's the clippers?"

He looked up at her, eyes dull as if the fight had fizzled out of him. "I don't know."

"Forget that." Susan bit down her fingernails while she scanned a book on equine emergency care. Meanwhile, Melissa wrapped Rayya's tail, then scrubbed down her hindquarters, breathing slowly to keep her hands from shaking. She was an experienced groom and rider, but she had never seen a foaling, let alone assisted at one. Charlie had been out of the breeding business when she started up with him. Rayya's was to be her first of many, Charlie had promised. *You and Christopher will carry this on when I'm long gone.*

Melissa and Christopher. Nearly a year ago, they had watched the insemination and whispered about their own plans for the future. Susan's plan for him was some white-collar drudge job, a condo in Back Bay, and a summerhouse on Nantucket Sound. Instead, Christopher had fallen in love with Colorado, horses, and Melissa.

Rayya and her foal were all that were left of last summer. How Melissa's heart ached for the mare. She knew what it was like to have a baby stuck inside, not able to find her way out.

Jeanette came in, soaked to the skin.

"Did you get through?" Charlie asked.

"No answer at the hotel or his cell phone number. RCR 102 is probably washed out. That would explain why Dr. Rodgers hasn't gotten here yet."

"What about Doc Potter?" Melissa said. Dave Potter had been caring for Rayya since the insemination. There had been no reason for Susan to hire some Kentucky vet to tend their mare. Except to show off how rich she was.

"He was called out past Clark to care for a colicky horse. Mary said he hydroplaned, flipped his truck."

"Is he all right?" Charlie said.

"He's down at Hardesty, getting a cast on his arm." Jeanette wiped more rain from her face. "What can I do to help here?"

Charlie pulled her to him and whispered something.

She backed away, shaking her head.

"Just in case," Charlie said.

"What? In case what?" Melissa said.

"Nothing." Jeanette went out again, returning in a minute with more water streaming down her face and slicker and something wrapped in a towel. Charlie took whatever it was and stuffed it under his shirt.

Susan stripped off her shirt. Underneath, she wore a tank top. She scrubbed her arms to the shoulders. As she shook off the excess water, she glanced at Melissa. "Do you think you could coax Rayya to stand? She'll be easier to examine that way."

It took some effort and a lot of pleading, but she got Rayya up. The mare shuddered as a contraction seized her, pressing her muzzle into Melissa's chest. Rain pelted the metal roof like a barrage of bullets. The thunder was continuous, but Rayya's universe had shrunk to her womb and nothing beyond. *I'm her lifeline*, Melissa thought. *And I don't have a clue.*

"Jeanette, I'll need you to hold the tail out of the way," Susan said.

Charlie banged his fist against the wall. "I'm useless. Bloody useless."

"Pipe down," Jeanette said.

Susan looked around Rayya's rump. "Is she ready?"

Melissa tightened her fingers in the mare's halter. "I guess."

Susan stretched out her right hand and reached into Rayya's womb.

Warm and roomy, Susan thought. *Too roomy.* If the foal were in the correct position, her forelegs and nose would be pressing into the vagina, a hard bulge under the fluid-filled membrane that would indicate everything was fine.

"Well?" Charlie said.

"Hold on. I feel a bump. Oh no, it's the tail. She's in backwards, Papa."

"Lord have mercy on the little thing," Jeanette whispered.

"I've delivered them like that before. Just do it fast," Charlie said.

"It's not just breech. I can't feel the legs."

"What does that mean?" Melissa said.

"The legs have to come first, or they'll snag on the pelvis. They must be bent under the foal's body instead of extended back." Susan snipped through the amniotic sac. She slipped her hand inside, pushing the foal forward with her left hand and sliding her right hand down the foal's flank, looking for the right leg. The uterus contracted with such raw force Susan had to take deep breaths to keep from crying out. After half a minute, the pain yielded to numbness.

The contraction passed, and the blood rushed back into her fingers. "Okay, I found one of the hind feet. Jeanette, get me the strap."

"Susie, make sure you cup the hoof with your hand. I can't have that foal tearing up Rayya's uterus," Charlie said.

Susan guided the foot out and looped the strap around it so it couldn't be withdrawn back into the uterus. "She doing okay, Melissa? She's so quiet."

"Rayya's a good horse," Melissa murmured. "She knows we're trying to help."

Susan pulled out the other leg, moving quickly before the next contraction hit.

"Now what?" Melissa said.

"The next contraction, I pull the foal out."

"Susie. Once the rump passes into the vagina, it'll press on the cord. You gotta be quick," Charlie said.

"You mean the umbilical cord?" Jeanette said.

"In a normal birth, the forelegs come out, followed by the head," Susan said. "The foal starts breathing even before it's delivered completely. With the rump leading the way, if the umbilicus is compressed, it'll cut off the foal's oxygen. So we've got to get the foal out fast, once we start this."

As if on cue, the next contraction hit. Susan yanked on the straps. The rump slipped into the vagina and then stuck.

"I lost the contraction."

Charlie hopped over to the door of the stall, his face contorted with pain. He clutched the wall for support. "Come on, Rayya. Push that thing out."

Rayya's neck twisted back in such a way that Susan feared the mare would snap her own vertebrae. Her forelegs buckled, and Melissa cried out, trying to brace the 800-pound horse by pure force of will. As Rayya went to her knees, gravity pulled the foal back into the womb. The foal was a time bomb now, threatening herself and her mother.

"What in the Sam Hill is happening?" Charlie shouted. "Is she having a fit or what?"

"I don't know!" Susan said. "Maybe the foal is pressing on a nerve or the aorta."

Rayya's legs gave out. As she went down, Susan braced her foot against the mare's rump and pulled with all her might. The foal was still stuck.

"Don't do that. Stop that," Charlie said. "Don't drag the foal. I can't have her ripping my mare apart."

What did he expect from her? She was a psychiatrist, not a vet. "Pop, we're out of options. I've got to get the foal out."

Charlie unwrapped the towel. Inside was a hacksaw. "Jeanette's already sanitized it. You know what to do, Susie."

Her throat clenched. "No, Pop. I can't do that."

"You need to save my mare. Do you understand? You've got to end this now. Do whatever you have to, but get that thing out of her."

Melissa lay across Rayya's neck, her arms cushioning the mare's head. "Charlie, don't give up on the baby."

"It's been too long. The thing is as good as dead anyway."

"Pop, don't ask me to do that," Susan said. "You know I can't."

"If you don't have the guts to do it, I will."

"You will not." Susan wouldn't let him take the easy way out, not this time. This was so typical of Charlie Robinson. He talked a good game but when the pressure came down, he always chose mother over daughter.

She yanked the straps with all her might. Nothing happened.

Charlie came at her with the saw. "Get out of my way."

"No!" Susan pulled again and, with a quiet snort and a *whoosh*, Rayya delivered her foal.

The newborn lay in the straw, draped in its amniotic sac and streaked with blood. If the beautifully-shaped head was any indication, she surely could have been a champion. Rayya lifted her head, made a halfhearted effort to nip at the sac, but couldn't muster the energy.

Charlie slammed his fist into the wall. "I told you it wouldn't survive."

Susan ripped the sac from the filly's face. "Melissa, help me."

They lifted the newborn's rump high over her head until her neck was fully extended. A rush of fluid stained with fecal matter came out of her mouth.

"You see that?" Charlie said. "She let go while she was still inside Rayya. If there's a tear in the uterus, it'll probably kill my mare because you couldn't do what I told you to."

Susan wiped the filly's nose and mouth with a cloth. She felt something hot and wet through the knees of her jeans—Rayya, left to her own devices, had passed the afterbirth.

Melissa guided Rayya to stand, pressing her face against the horse's neck to distract her from the distress of her newborn. "Susan, she still isn't breathing."

Susan pressed one nostril closed, cupped the filly's mouth, and blew into the other nostril.

"Her chest is moving. Keep at it," Jeanette said.

"You idiots. It breathed in its own manure. That's the kiss of death. Do the smart thing and just let it go."

It. Her father had already depersonalized Rayya's foal. *Thirty years and he still acts true to form,* Susan thought.

The filly coughed, dribbling yellow mucous out of her mouth. Her nostrils flared, and she pulled in a huge breath. Susan gathered her up and put her near Rayya's teat. The filly just lay there, legs quivering and eyes dim.

"I told you, Susan. She's brain damaged. Rayya is probably infected. But would you listen?" Charlie growled.

"Be quiet," Jeanette said.

"So help me, Susan Robinson. If Rayya dies . . ."

Susan lay the filly carefully in the straw and covered her with a towel. Then she wiped her hands and slipped her shirt on. "What will you do to me, *Father*?"

Charlie slammed the hacksaw against the door to the stall. "I'll never forgive you, that's what."

Susan gave her father one last look and walked out into the storm.

"You said, 'No, we will flee on horses.'
Therefore you will flee!
You said, 'We will ride off on swift horses.'
Therefore your pursuers will be swift!"

— Isaiah 30:16

SIX

A SLEEK BLACK STALLION CAME AT SUSAN FROM OUT OF THE rain. This had to be Prince Sarraf, the horse who had injured her father. His eyes burned with defiance—others might flee from this storm, but he would stand his ground.

Susan grabbed the lead rope on his halter and flung herself onto his back.

Sarraf broke into a trot, and she found a good balance, her legs hanging loose, her arms stroking rather than grasping his neck. She let him have his way, and within a few minutes he ran with abandon. How sad that she had left all this behind—riding into the wind, nothing between her and her horse, his raw power surging into her until they were as one. Surely this was how it was meant to be, horse and rider, not separated by saddle and blanket, not hindered by any fence, not fearing anything except that they would run out of room to run.

The lashing rain felt good to Susan, not driving away her pain but stripping her down until that was all she was, every other trapping of civility and society washed away. She knew from too many years that she couldn't outrun the ghost of her mother and from many tears that she couldn't restore the spirit of her son.

At least she could choose the way she would put them—and herself—finally at rest.

The horse didn't slow down until they reached Folly Mountain. He arched his neck, unsure of the course.

Susan patted his rump. *Up. All the way up.*

As they climbed, the sun broke through the clouds even as the rain continued to pelt down. If Susan glanced over her left shoulder, she'd likely see a rainbow. But she would not look back, not turn back for anything. She would ride until she came to the end of herself, fully aware of this one final irony: in her headlong rush to death, she felt incredibly alive.

Paul Stone had loved her, but he had never provoked in her this kind of passion. Yet she was grateful for a marriage that was not marred by the histrionics that she had endured growing up. She would still be married to Paul if an aneurysm hadn't cut him down when he was only thirty-three. Christopher became her world, and the little things of his life became her joy. The first time he pitched Little League and struck out three batters. The violin recital when he brought the audience to their feet. Waving his high-school diploma, earned in sweat and frustration. Each time he had smiled at her, the dimple in his cheek like his father's, his eyes the same hazel as hers and Charlie's.

"Why?" she cried out, but her voice was swept away on the wind.

Prince Sarraf climbed on, as sure-footed as a mule. How the horse could find the trail in the deepening shadows, she didn't know. Why he did, she didn't care. Whatever thrill he had given her had been tempered by the inevitability that joy always dies.

Sometimes you're the one who kills it.

The trail leveled out halfway up the mountain. Susan remembered this long stretch, galloping with Ricky as if they could ride off the top of the world. One last time, one last holler into the sky, and then she'd get on with ending it.

"Hee-ah!" Susan slapped Sarraf's rump.

He took off in a dead run. A cry came from deep inside her, loosed from that vault she had built, brick by brick, from the age of four when she realized something was wrong in her family, from the age of eight when she understood that the *something* was her mother, and from the age of fourteen when she knew that her father didn't have the guts to do anything about it.

After a couple of minutes she leaned into the stallion's neck and said, "Hold up." Ahead was rough terrain where the mountain was slashed by ravines and cliffs. She had chosen her fate, but she would not inflict it on the horse. Not as Mother had.

"Come on, boy. Stop." She pulled hard on the cotton lead. He yanked his head and tore the rope from her hand. She grabbed the crown piece of his halter and leaned back with all her weight. "Whoa, Sarraf, whoa!"

Head down, he galloped on. "Please," she whispered, "let me go on by myself."

Sarraf reared to a stop. Susan flew off, and for a split second hung suspended between the sky and the mountain, between the end of the day and the coming of night.

From pure instinct, she tumbled as her father—*oh, Papa*—had taught her so many years ago, shoulders curled inward, head curved into her chest, rolling with the fall and not resisting. She tumbled down a steep slope, one rocky fist after another slamming against her. She wanted to unwind and be broken, but her body kept tightly curled, overruling her will.

After a few seconds she landed in a mass of brush. She sat up, dazed. Every inch of her body screamed with pain, but she was whole and she was alive.

She had even screwed up dying.

Yet somehow the darkness comforted Susan. At last, between walls of ancient rock, she found quiet. Out of the reach of the wind, the only noise was the trickling of water.

Something moved to her left.

It had to be a rattlesnake, maybe seeking sanctuary from the water that had flooded its den. Her heart thudded—she didn't fear dying, but she was terrified of snakes. Mother had made sure of that.

Always wear long pants and boots because one never knows.

There are no snakes in Cambridge, Mother.

You're not going to Massachusetts. Tell her, Charles.

Susie, you won't leave your old Papa, will you?

Ghosts. Where better than at the bottom of a rocky abyss?

A pebble rolled and sand skidded. Close—too close. The skin on the back of Susan's neck prickled. She poked at her pockets, trying to find the penlight she had carried out to the barn. Rayya's labor seemed a lifetime ago now.

"Is someone there?" Her voice was strong, her id ridiculously driven by the instinct to survive even while her ego argued the opposite.

Metal *clanked*. Was that a round being chambered, a gun ready to fire? Charlie had taught her to shoot, but wisely had kept the guns locked up. Even now, the thought of a gun in Vanessa Robinson's hands was frightening.

Something moaned. Susan's skin erupted in goose bumps. Against all common sense, she crept toward the sound. "Who's there?"

More clanking now. Was some horrible animal chained down here?

She found the penlight clipped to the pocket of her jacket and hurriedly switched it on. The narrow beam bounced as she swept the light in half circles from her feet outwards. She saw trickles of water, cracked rocks, outcroppings, pockets of brush. Steep walls on either side, rainwater creating a moat at the bottom. Slowly, slowly—snaking the light deeper into a darkness of such substance that she instinctively recoiled from it.

The light found the first link of a chain. Susan followed it with the light, link by link, until she saw what was chained under the darkness.

SEVEN

"SHE WENT FOR A RIDE, THAT'S ALL." CHARLIE ROBINSON SAT in the kitchen and nursed a glass of straight-up whiskey.

"That's not all and you know it." Jeanette twisted the dishcloth, the veins on the back of her hands swollen. "She was broken up, Sheriff. The foaling went bad, and she's blaming herself—"

Charlie cut her off. "Sometimes you gotta take drastic measures."

Rick ran his hand over his head. His hair was bristly, still damp. "I don't understand."

Charlie gulped down the whiskey, poured another.

"You think you oughta have more, with you still on the pain pills?" Jeanette said.

"I just need to settle some, that's all."

Jeanette glared at him, turned to Rick. "She ran out of the barn. I tried to catch up with her, but I don't move so well, not with these bad knees. I saw her getting on that horse. The one that tossed Charlie."

Charlie downed the rest of the whiskey. "Just like when she was a kid—jump the fastest horse around and hightail it out of here. I'm going to bed." He tried to rise, the booze making him unsteady.

Rick took his arm. "Wait. Let me get the wheelchair."

The old man yanked away. "Leave me be. Don't need a chair, don't need help, don't need anybody."

Rick stepped back and let Charlie hobble out of the room.

He followed Jeanette out onto the back porch. The air was clear and crisp. Stars studded the sky. She had carried the dish towel with her, wrapping it and then unwrapping it around her hand. "I'm scared. Something in my bones—my soul—tells me she's in terrible trouble."

"She's a good rider," Rick said.

"That's not it. Don't you remember, Rick?" Jeanette grabbed him by both arms, digging her fingers into his biceps. "Don't you remember how Vanessa died?"

A young man was chained under a darkness so complete that it seemed to pull in light even from the stars high above and consume it.

Susan resisted the urge to shine the penlight into his face. If this were a nightmare, then her fevered mind might spit out something horrific. If reality, she needed time to comprehend how anyone could condemn a man to this fate.

His feet were bare, the soles as dark as the dirt. He sat cross-legged, his back against the rock wall. Heavy manacles encircled his ankles and wrists. Dressed only in shorts of a rough weave, he was muscular, his chest hairless.

When Susan shone the light on his face, he raised his arms to shield his eyes, rattling his chains.

"Sorry. I didn't mean to hurt you."

His eyes were deep-set, pewter gray. His hair was dark brown, curling in strands past his shoulders. He showed no obvious injury, had good color, steady respiration. Light phobia had been his only negative response. That—and a lack of communication. "I'm Dr. Susan Stone. And you are . . . ?"

"I . . ." His voice was raspy. From disuse? How long had he been down here?

"You're safe. I won't hurt you. Can you tell me your name?"

"I don't know my name." His voice cracked like an adolescent's.

Something *clanked* behind him.

She swept the vicinity around him with the light, illuminating rocks, brush, and water runoff. The chain stretched into a darkness that was too deep to penetrate farther than about ten feet. A cave, perhaps, but she had no intention of stepping in there simply for the sake of intellectual curiosity. Something was not right, and Susan was not equipped to deal with that something.

"Is someone else in there?"

"Bats. That's all," he said.

She bent down next to him, her fingers finding the pulse in his neck. Blood trickled from his throat, and she pulled back with a gasp.

He hunched his shoulders and covered his head. "I'm sorry sorry sorry . . ."

"No, wait. It's okay. It's my own blood. Look." She took off her jacket, pushed up her sleeve, and showed him a gash in her forearm.

She ripped the sleeve off her shirt, wrapped it around her arm, and went back to her exam. His heartbeat was slow and surprisingly strong, his skin pliable and apparently hydrated. "Can you say *ahh*?"

His throat looked clear, his teeth were straight and white with no fillings. His breath had no odor nor did his body. She should at least smell the sour perspiration of fear. But she smelled only the metallic scent of her own blood and the musty odor of dirt that never sees the sun. He felt warm to her touch, even though Susan was quickly becoming chilled. Even so, she wrapped her jacket around him.

"How old are you?"

He squinted. "Almost forever."

Dissociation was not unusual, given the circumstances. She would have to be more specific. "What is your age in years?"

"I don't know how to count forever."

"Where are you from?"

He shook his head, eyes downcast as if he feared disappointing her.

"Can you tell me who did this to you?"

He shook his head.

"You don't know?"

"No. I don't."

Her penlight flickered and dimmed. She switched it off.

He clutched blindly at her. "Bring it back."

"It's all right. I'm still here." She smoothed his hair as one might a child's. "The batteries are running down. I've got to preserve them."

"Batteries?"

Had he completely lost context? "The batteries make the light work. They last for a short time, so it's best to conserve them."

He clutched at her again. "Put the light back on. Please."

"Do you remember my name?" she asked.

"Susan. You're a doctor."

His memory loss wasn't immediate. "You know what a doctor is?"

"I do. But I'm not sick. I'm—" He rattled his chains.

"We'll need a metal saw or maybe even a blowtorch to cut off those chains. I'll have to climb out of here, go for help—"

"No, don't go!"

"I'll be back as soon as I can."

"No, no. You don't need to do any of that."

"Of course I do."

"No, you don't." He pressed his lips to her ear. "There's a key . . ."

The 911 caller was frantic.

"Can you slow down, ma'am?" Rick said. "I'm having trouble following."

"Right there in the ditch. I thought someone had set a brush fire, but that didn't make sense. Not after all this rain. So I pulled the car over to look."

"What were you doing out at this time of night?" Rick checked the dashboard computer for her name. The dispatcher had patched the call through to the cruiser. "Ms. Latham?"

"I'm a labor and delivery nurse. I'm usually on second shift, but a first-timer begged me to stay with her. The baby was born in the middle of the night."

"Can you tell me the exact location of the fire?"

"On County Road 102, right where it turns off 47. Once I saw what it was, I—" Her voice broke.

"It's okay. I'm on my way out there now. The state cops and forensics folks are coming too."

"CSI is coming?"

Even in a nightmare, pop culture trumped everything. "Colorado's version. I'm still a few miles out. Do you want to tell me more or wait until I'm there?"

"I need to keep talking or I'll go nuts here. So anyway, I grabbed the pepper spray—that's okay that I have it, right? I work odd hours."

"That's fine, ma'am."

"Good, thanks. Anyway, I got out to look, my finger right on that button."

"Good thinking." Rick drove southeast, still five minutes out from her location. The sky was gray, with dawn still a bit away.

"I walked over to the ditch, slowly. Ashamed, because I'm a nurse. I should have gone right to it, seen if there was anything I could do. Thinking it was a car fire, you know. But something held me back." A sob caught in her throat.

"Ms. Latham, if you'd rather wait—"

"No, no. The thing is—there was no car. Just this lump of what looked like a body. Skin scorches, chars, even crackles, but it doesn't flame. I thought, okay, it's a joke, it's a dummy, but I knew in my gut it was human. I prayed it wouldn't move, because if it moved, I'd have to help it. And how do you help someone who has been . . . I'm so sorry . . ."

"You did great. I'll keep the line open, so if you think of anything else . . ."

He drove faster, hands clutching the steering wheel. Another dead body. And where was Susan?

EIGHT

MELISSA WOKE UP TO A FLASHLIGHT GLARING IN HER EYES. "Who's there?"

The overhead lights flickered and came on. Doc Potter, left arm in a sling, stared down at her. Jeanette came up behind him. "Stupid generator was out of gas. Don't know when they'll get our lines back up."

Melissa adjusted the heating blanket over the filly. "What time is it?"

Doc Potter's eyes were bleary. "Four in the morning. Been a long night, and it ain't over yet."

Melissa stretched. "Where's Charlie?"

"I made him go to bed," Jeanette said. "He's snoring away."

Doc Potter checked Rayya's eyes and mouth, then moved to her abdomen and udder. "You save the afterbirth?"

"In the bucket." Melissa pushed into the stall and looked over his shoulder.

Jeanette took her arm. "Leave him to his work."

"I've got to tell him about Jade."

"Who?" Jeanette asked.

"The filly. Charlie told me when Rayya got pregnant that I could name the baby. I couldn't get her to nurse, Doc. I expressed some milk and stored it in the cooler. Rayya was real good about letting me do that. But I can't get the filly to take any of it."

A small man in his early sixties, Dave Potter had bright blue eyes and a full head of steel-gray hair. Charlie said he had been a hippie in his youth and had outgrown everything but the ponytail.

"Don't fret too much about it. You've done a good job, Melissa. Leave me alone with the gals here for a little while. I'll come get you when I'm done. Okay?"

Jeanette steered her out of the stall. "I made you some coffee. Your favorite. Hazelnut."

"I'm staying here," Melissa said.

"I know that, hon. I brought you a thermos."

"Yeah, thanks." Melissa numbly sat in Charlie's chair and let Jeanette rub her hands clean with soapy wipes. Her lower back throbbed. She had held the filly in a standing position off-and-on for an hour, trying to get her to nurse. She was a sick little horse, couldn't keep to her feet. But she'd come around. She'd be a champion yet. They'd have to give her some time, that was all.

"Look what else I've got. I couldn't sleep, so I made banana bread." Jeanette unwrapped a cloth napkin.

Melissa gobbled down two chunks of bread before she took the first sip of coffee. Doc Potter walked by, and she jumped up. "Is something—"

"No, no. I just need some supplies."

"I'll get them."

"Sit. You're going to have a very full day, young lady. Rayya needs some watching."

"You won't let Jade die, will you?"

Doc Potter scratched his head. "It's not always up to me."

Melissa sat back down, this time on the ground so she could stretch her legs out. Familiar comforts soothed her—Jeanette's arm around her shoulder, the smell of the barn, the wind whistling through the vents in the roof.

When she opened her eyes again, the sun was coming up.

Charlie was staring down at her from his wheelchair. His eyes were bloodshot and his hair unruly. "Doc has something to say. He wants you to hear."

Melissa sprinted for the back of the barn. Rayya stood nosing at some mash, an IV taped to her neck. Jade had been moved to the stall opposite Rayya's. She lay on her side, still. Melissa put her hand to the filly's nostrils, relieved to feel warm puffs of air.

"Why did you move her?" she asked. "She's got to nurse."

Doc Potter shook his head. "If by some miracle the filly's up to that, you can bring her back in to Rayya. But for now, I flushed the mare's uterus with antibiotics and have her on gentamicin. The biggest danger is infection, of course. From the filly's feces."

"The thing was stuck in the pelvis," Charlie said. "I told Susan—"

Doc Potter held up his hand. "What's done is done. I'm just sorry I couldn't have been out here."

"Don't be silly," Jeanette said. "We're grateful you showed up in the middle of the night, with your arm all banged up like that."

"How's my mare?" Charlie said. "She's gonna make it, right?"

"She's weak. I can't promise anything. Give her the usual food, maybe some extra mash. Mix in the antibiotics I'm leaving, plus keep up with the prenatal vitamins. And lots of clean water. Melissa, you'd better clean the stall a couple times a day. Walk her in the paddock, force her if you have to. We've got to keep her lungs clear. Best way to do that is make her move."

"Shouldn't we take Rayya down to the hospital?" Jeanette asked.

"That's drastic. More for emergencies than recovery. Sick animals spook each other," Potter said.

"What about Jade?" Melissa said. "We have to do something for her. We can't just let her lie there."

"I transfused her with plasma and a dose of antibiotics," Potter said.

"Like a blood transfusion?" Jeanette said.

"Not whole blood," Potter said. "Filtered plasma with antibodies. The filly missed a boatload of immune protection by not nursing first thing."

"She tried," Melissa said. "She was too weak."

Potter promised to come back after he had a few hours' sleep. He packed up, readied to leave. "Where's Susan? I want to say hello. See if she remembers me."

"Susan's been gone since yesterday," Jeanette said.

Doc scratched his head. "She left already? I would have loved to have seen her."

"She's here. Somewhere. We're not exactly sure where. After the mess with the foal being born, she was really upset. She took that devil horse out late afternoon and hasn't come back. Rick Sanchez came out last night, said he'd look for her, but we haven't heard from him."

Doc Potter's face drained of color.

"What?" Melissa said. "What happened?"

"Nothing. I'm sure everything's just fine." He slung his bag over his shoulder. "I'll be back as soon as I can."

Charlie pushed out of his wheelchair and hobbled to the door to block his way. "Dave, you're not leaving this barn until you tell me why you turned whiter than what little hair I got left on my head."

Doc's eyes shifted back and forth as if he was looking for a way to escape. "They found another body."

The scene swarmed with cops and forensic folks. Rick hung back, waiting for the medical examiner to finish her work. Renee MacArthur finally waved him over.

"Fortunately, the pelvis is intact. I can't manipulate it too much out here, but my measurements indicate a male. I'm 90, 95 percent sure."

Relief flooded Rick. "Did you do the post on the other body, Doc?"

She shrugged. "This isn't New York City. I do 'em all unless I'm on vacation. I sent you a copy of the report."

"I know. But between us—totally off the record—what's your best guess on the whole missing skull thing?"

"It wasn't missing."

"Wait a minute. The report said—"

"Not available for gross examination. I'll translate the Latin, Sheriff. The skull, teeth, and the rest were there in all that mess. Just pulverized."

"I don't understand."

"Me either. And I don't mind telling you, it scares the stuffing out of me." She stripped off her gloves, dropped them into an evidence bag. The paper gown came next. A fine layer of charcoal stained the front. Even these items were bagged and marked, on the outside chance trace evidence had transferred.

"Let me ask you this: is this the same flammable agent?" Rick said.

She shrugged. "I'll leave that to the arson investigator. Though at this point, your guess is as good as anyone else's. Honestly, Sheriff? The first body perplexed me. This one will give me nightmares. If you told me aliens or dragons or the Prince of Hell himself was splatting people with fireballs, I'd be likely to believe it."

Rick forced a laugh. "Don't let the press hear you talk like that."

"I don't let those buzzards hear me talk at all. That's your job."

She headed for the ME's van while he wandered the perimeter of the crime scene. He had taped huge margins, in part because he had done it in the dark but also because no one knew what was significant. He had done all he could here; he would check out with CBI and hit the road again.

Now that he knew the body wasn't Susan's, he would get some folks out on horseback and ATVs. Today was Wednesday; Joyce's office was closed. She could help him search out some of the tougher terrain.

Rick pulled the cruiser out onto RCR 47, mentally mapping the route Susan might have taken. Robinson land stretched for a thousand acres, all of it in a conservation easement. Word in the valley was that was the only way Charlie could avoid losing it after the bankruptcy. When Charlie and Jeanette passed on, the pastures wouldn't be cut up into housing developments, but kept as open land under federal management.

Rick drove west, Folly filling his view. The mountain was smaller than most of its Rocky cousins, but it was rough. A nook-and-cranny mountain, Joyce called it. Lots of places to explore and just as many places to get into serious trouble, which was why Charlie had forbidden them as kids to go up there. "You'll break my horse's leg," he used to grumble.

"It's my horse," Susan would say and fly away. Rick hadn't thought about Tasha for years—that sleek white Arabian with the proud neck and long legs. Tasha had been a champion show horse, strong and tough enough to take to the mountains. Throughout high school, Susan swore she'd send for her when she finished medical school.

Vanessa Robinson put an end to that dream.

He pulled over, sick to his stomach. He sipped some water, trying to distance himself from what he had just seen at the murder scene so he could think rationally about Susan's disappearance. What had happened to Christopher had devastated Susan. She was a survivor, but survivors could run out of rope. He bowed his head and prayed, ashamed that he had waited so long to take a quiet moment.

After a few minutes, he reached for his cell phone. First he'd call Robinson Ranch. If Susan hadn't yet returned, he'd organize a search party.

Something on the far side of the road caught his attention. Rick got out of the cruiser, shaded his eyes, and looked toward Folly. A black horse carrying two riders walked toward him. The animal's head was low, his gait steady. Grabbing his binoculars, Rick focused in for a closer look.

He was astounded by what he saw.

NINE

HE DIDN'T KNOW HIS OWN NAME.

He knew Susan's name. He knew she was strong, helping him up a slope so steep it should have been impassable. She had kept him from falling when he slipped; pushed him when he tired; encouraged him when he was scared.

He knew Susan was gentle. The touch of her fingers to his forehead was light and made him feel better. She was smart. That was clear by the way she took charge—first of the climb, then of the horse, and now of these people gathered about him.

In this short time, he had come to know them too. The girl with the tangled curls and quick eyes was called Melissa. Her hair was red. Her face was round and filled with freckles. She wasn't as tall as Susan, but she looked very strong, with wiry muscles in her forearms and shoulders.

The lady with the rounded back and creaky knees was Jeanette. Her face was filled with wrinkles, and there were shadows under her eyes. But she seemed to have endless energy, smiling the whole time they got him settled.

The man sitting in what Susan called a wheelchair was Charlie. He kept trying to get up and help, but his mouth would twist in pain and he'd have to sit back down. His arms looked strong, but the skin hung loose on his hands and face.

The big man's name was Rick. His job was sheriff, he said. His eyes were dark, and he was constantly looking left and right, as if he expected to see something coming around some corner that no one else could see.

He tried to search for his own name, but all he could see inside himself was darkness. And the only thing he had known in that darkness was where the key was.

Out of his reach.

Now he was safe in Charlie's house, with Susan in charge and Rick keeping watch. They had insisted he get in this bed. He was grateful for that, because his legs ached. "I'm tired," he said.

Susan smiled. "I'm sure you are. We'll let you sleep, but first I want to check you out. Make sure there's nothing wrong that we need to know about."

He pulled the blanket tight around him. "Wrong?"

"I want to make sure that there's not some way in which you're hurt or sick that we need to take care of right away."

She opened a black bag and pulled out something that he didn't recognize. Odd how he knew the horse and the blanket and the sun high overhead, almost blinding him as he came out of the ravine. But Rick's car—called a cruiser—with its lights and noises had scared him.

"Everyone out," Susan said.

"This is my house," Charlie said, his chin out.

Jeanette grabbed the back of Charlie's wheelchair and spun him around. Melissa followed them out, glancing back one last time. Rick stayed near the door. Susan looked up at him.

"I need to stay," he said. "To protect his interests and yours."

"You're right. Thank you." She sat on the bed. They had made him get under the blanket even though he wasn't cold. He still wore the jacket that Susan had made him put on and the short pants he had worn for as long as he could remember.

"Has your name come to you yet?" Susan asked.

He shivered, the first inkling of cold he could remember. "No. Can you give me a name?"

"Can you think of a name that feels good to you?"

A string of sounds spun in his head. Names that frightened him enough to pull the blanket tight again.

"Could I be called Jacob?" Jacob was a strong name, a *good* name that made the other names stop running across the back of his eyes.

"Sure. Jacob is a fine name, a good choice." When Susan smiled, the lines around her eyes crinkled. "I'm going to examine you to make sure you're all right."

"While she does that, I need to ask you some questions," Rick said.

"Surely the interrogation can wait." Susan's tone was suddenly cold.

"You know how the memory can play tricks. If we're going to help this young man, we need to get as much information as we can before . . ."

Rick's words faded. The wind had blown the curtain away from the window, and Jacob could see the mountains. Streaks of brilliant reds and golds stretched across the sky.

"Jacob." Susan turned his face toward her. "Listen to Rick, answer whatever you can. If anything makes you too uncomfortable, tell us right away. We'll figure out another way to ask, or we'll hold that question until later. I'm going to look you over, listen to your chest. Push on your stomach a bit. I'd like to look at all of you to make sure there's no terrible injury we need to know about. But if that makes you uncomfortable, we can wait until we have a male doctor to do that part of the exam."

"I won't be uncomfortable. I know I can trust you, Susan. And Rick too."

She showed him a flat piece of metal connected to a black tube. "This is a stethoscope. I'm going to—"

"It's okay," Jacob said. "You don't have to tell me. Just check me over and let Rick ask his questions."

Rick pulled up a chair and sat near the bed. "You can ask me questions as well."

Jacob nodded.

"Can you take that jacket off?" Susan said.

He let it slide off his shoulders. Susan motioned him forward so she could press that cold metal plate against his back. She made a strange sound, as if she breathed through her teeth. "Rick. Take a look."

He got up and looked behind Jacob. "Hm."

"Something wrong?" Jacob said.

"Nope. Just . . . helping Susan for a minute."

Jacob looked over his shoulder at her.

"Do you have any pain in your back?" Susan said.

He shook his head. "Only where you're putting that cold thing on me."

Rick sat back down. "Do you know how old you are?"

"Susan asked me that."

"What did you tell her?"

"Almost forever."

For some reason, Susan didn't like that answer. Jacob could tell because he heard her heart beat faster.

"Do you know where you're from?" Rick said.

He shook his head.

"Does any of this seem familiar to you?"

"The horse, the trees, the grass, the bread, the water, the way Susan smiles, and the way that Charlie kind of *harrumphs*. Melissa works with horses—I can smell them on her. And Jeanette's legs hurt a lot more than she tells anyone. I hear the creak every time she takes a step."

"You do?" Susan said.

"Don't you?"

She smiled. "I'm getting old. My hearing isn't what it used to be."

"Let me ask an odd question. Do you know what this is?" Rick pointed to something on his belt.

"Must you ask him about your gun?" Susan whispered.

"I'm just trying to establish a baseline," Rick said.

Jacob shook his head. He didn't know what a baseline was or what that thing Susan called a gun was.

"Okay."

"But I know what that other thing in your belt is. A stick, for hitting people."

Rick glanced at Susan again. Jacob felt like there was some strange language in the way they looked at each other, something that he should understand.

"Let me try this a different way, Jacob," Rick said. "Tell me what you first remember about last night."

"Susan crying." He rubbed his chest—the memory of her broken voice coming out of the darkness pained him. "No, wait. Before that. Rocks rolling down near me. *Thud, thud, thud.* Before that, water coming down, *rat, tat, tat.*"

"And before that?"

"Hold on for a minute, guys. Jacob, could you open your mouth for me? Say *ahh*?"

He did as she asked. "Ahh."

"Nice teeth," she said. "No fillings, Rick."

"Hm."

"You say *hm* a lot, Rick," Jacob said.

Rick laughed.

"Can you follow my finger with your eyes?" Susan passed her finger before his face, and he did as she asked.

"Okay," she said. "You're doing great. Scoot down on the bed. That's right. Lie flat. I'm going to press on your stomach in different places. Then I'm going to pull down the blanket so I can quickly make sure you're okay there."

"Okay."

"Rick, you can go on with the questions," Susan said.

"Jacob, do you remember anything before the time Susan tumbled down into the ravine?"

He shook his head.

"Think back. Before the rocks. What did you hear or see?"

"It's all black. I see nothing, hear nothing—feel nothing. Inside or out. It's like I'm not there."

"If not there, then where would you be?" Rick's voice was soft.

"Nowhere. Oh, that tickles."

Susan folded back the blanket. She glanced quickly, then pulled the blanket back up to his waist.

"Am I okay? Did I pass the test?"

"Why would you think this was a test?" Susan said.

"I don't know . . . I just . . ."

"Do you remember something else?" Rick asked.

"Just . . . not being good enough," he said.

"Good enough for what?" Susan said.

He shrugged. "Good enough to . . . answer all these questions."

Rick's laugh was cut off by a sharp look from Susan that she thought Jacob didn't see. When she looked straight at him, her smile was warm and full.

"I smell brownies. Which means Jeanette wants to feed you again. Can I send her in when we're done here?"

He smiled. "Yes. I'm hungry."

"Would you like to sleep afterwards?"

"You won't leave me, will you?"

Susan touched his cheek. "I'll be close by if you need me. We might be outside in the hall, but someone will be close enough for you to just call. Is that all right with you?"

Jacob smiled. "Yes. Okay."

Susan closed her bag. "I'll send Jeanette in. I'll be right outside with Rick. Okay?"

"Okay."

As she started to leave, he sat up in bed. "Susan!"

"Yes?"

"Leave the light on."

"What do you make of those scars?" Susan asked. Jacob's back had two thick vertical lines of scar tissue running from the crest of his shoulder into his lower back.

"Symmetrical, like he backed into some equipment, something that might have burned him."

"This is an abuse victim. Someone did that to him. I'm afraid to guess what they used."

"What about the memory loss? Does he have some sort of brain damage?"

"His neurological exam was normal, though he obviously has to be followed up by a neurologist. Based on the circumstances I found him in, I suspect this boy suffers from traumatic amnesia."

"Is he a *boy*, Susan? Or is he a man?"

She shrugged.

"Best guess."

"He's postpuberty. Got all his molars, but no wisdom teeth. Well-developed musculature. Beyond that, I don't even know how to measure. Some psychological and educational testing could suggest a range, but the amnesia complicates that."

"He looks young. Sounds young," Rick said.

"Sometimes. And sometimes he looks very mature. He could be anywhere from fifteen to almost thirty."

Rick rubbed his jaw. "Hm. This could be a problem."

"What do you mean? Other than the obvious, which you haven't bothered to address yet."

"I'll get to who did this to him. First I'm trying to grasp the situation you found him in. How long was he down there? Can you guess based on his physical condition?"

"He seems hydrated. His skin tone is decent. Then again, there was standing water within reach. No obvious signs of malnutrition, though liver function tests would indicate better if he'd been without food for longer than a few days."

"He didn't seem hungry at first. I thought Jeanette was going to pry his mouth open and pour the soup down."

"That could be his body's response to a perceived starvation. If he's stable tomorrow—emotionally, I mean—I can draw some blood, send out for tests."

"Whoa. Hold it, Suse. I'm taking him to the hospital tonight."

"Absolutely not. He's not going anywhere. How can you even suggest such a thing?"

The bedroom door opened. Jeanette peeked out. "Keep your voices down. I've just gotten him to sleep."

Rick steered Susan to the far end of the hall. "Did you hear what Jeanette just said?"

She folded her arms across her chest. "Nothing wrong with my hearing."

"She said, 'I've just gotten him to sleep.' Like he was a little kid."

"After his experience, he's likely to revert to young . . . not behavior

. . . but *dependencies* would be the right word. Imprinting on anyone who is kind and caring. Protective."

"Which puts you in the direct line of fire."

Susan's nerve endings sparked, firing in all the wrong directions. She needed food and sleep. It had been a brutal two days. "This boy— young man—is no threat to me."

"My problem is this: if I don't know how old he is, I can't determine what his legal status is."

"In regard to guardianship?"

He nodded.

"Fine. You've got a point. But so do I when I tell you that changing his surroundings after removing him from an obviously traumatic situation would not only add to his trauma but complicate his recovery."

"You want to keep him."

"Don't take that tone with me."

"What tone?"

"Like he's a puppy who followed me home. He's my patient, and I want to do what's best for him. I'm probably the most qualified professional in this area to deal with his trauma."

"Assuming it was trauma."

"Pigheaded."

"Excuse me?"

"I'd forgotten how contrary you could be, Ricardo Sanchez."

He smiled. "Just doing my job, ma'am."

Susan pressed her hand to his mouth. "If you say, 'Just the facts, ma'am,' I will toss you down the stairs."

He caught her hand and held it against his chest. Even as a skinny nine-year-old, Ricky Sanchez had been solid. Now he felt like a rock. "You'll need to show me where you found him. Maybe we can find something down there that will tell us who he is."

"How about who did that to him?"

"If we can answer who he is, then I suspect the latter will become self-evident."

"Nothing about the human psyche is self-evident."

"Nothing about the heart is either, Suse."

"Don't you think I know that?"

Rick opened his arms, and she melted into him, old friends in a familiar embrace.

Yet the LORD *longs to be gracious to you;*
he rises to show you compassion.
For the LORD *is a God of justice.*
Blessed are all who wait for him!

— ISAIAH 30:18

TEN

THE SUN WOKE JACOB.

He instinctively threw his arms up to block his face. The light stung. He sat up in bed and slowly opened his eyes, letting them adjust until there was no pain. Though he remembered nothing, surely he had dreamed of this moment. Nothing hidden, nothing lurking in the darkness. Questions didn't matter—the day became its own answer.

Susan slept in a chair a few feet away, curled in a tight ball. Jacob considered waking her, but she seemed to be locked in a needed sleep. Last night his near-nakedness held no shame, but now he felt a strong desire to be covered. Someone had set clothes out near his bed: blue pants, a white shirt with short sleeves. A second shirt, marked with blue and green lines, had long sleeves. He put this shirt to his face and smelled Jeanette.

He slipped on the clothes, putting the white shirt under the blue and green one. He had noticed Rick and Charlie wore theirs like that. After he slipped on the pants, he looked around for something to cover his feet. Perhaps Jeanette had nothing that would fit him. It didn't matter because the soles of his feet were as tough as leather.

Leather—the hide of cow or deer. How he knew about leather was a mystery. Susan and Rick seemed more alarmed at his loss of memory than he was. Perhaps there was nothing to remember. Why couldn't he simply be one born out of darkness, a young man taking his first steps among the people who had pulled him out of the cave and offered him food, shelter, and clothing?

The house was quiet. Charlie and Jeanette were also asleep. Jacob found a pile of little cakes in the kitchen. It took him a full minute to realize that some clear wrap covered them. He took two, knowing Jeanette wanted him to. He ate them slowly, enjoying the sweetness of sugar and the tang of cinnamon. He followed his snack with a long drink of water from the faucet that must connect to the house's well.

The world outside welcomed him, birds darting and chattering, a breeze dancing in trees that would soon burst with leaves. The mountains dominated on every side, rocky peaks clothed in snow. The grass stretched out in rolling fields, broken by occasional lines of brush that meant water was near. A dirt road wandered from the house to an unseen destination.

There were no other houses in sight. The buildings across the road housed the horses, tools, hay, and the like. He had seen them last night when they rode into the yard, Rick following them, blue and red lights flashing. Susan had wanted Jacob to get in the cruiser, but he was afraid so they stayed on the horse. Today he wouldn't be afraid.

As he approached the barn, he smiled at last night's memory—sitting astride the black horse named Prince Sarraf, arms around Susan's waist. Over and over she said, *Don't strain, don't press on the horse, but move with him,* and so he did. He had felt no cold, though Susan kept asking if he did. He only felt a growing excitement at the life he saw around him, patches of pungent sage, rabbits skittering before the horse, a hawk overhead.

Rick's face when he came upon them—surprise, relief, happiness.

Inside, the barn was darker than Jacob would have liked. He swung the front doors open, letting in daylight and fresh air. He did the same with the back doors.

Melissa slept in the straw with her arms wrapped around a small horse. Its breath was sour. When it saw Jacob, it tried to lift its head but couldn't manage. The little thing was sick.

Across the way was another horse, a mare. She would have been beautiful, Jacob knew, if her coat wasn't dull and her eyes rheumy. She barely registered his presence, as if standing at her feed bucket and slowly munching was all she could manage.

Melissa sat up, rubbing her eyes. "What're you doing here? You didn't touch these horses, did you?"

"No," Jacob said.

"Don't."

Until she had said not to, Jacob hadn't wanted to. Now he had to shove his hands into his pockets to keep from reaching out to them, especially the little one.

Melissa stood up and stretched. The little horse tried to stand with her, but couldn't muster the energy. It laid its head back down. Melissa draped the blanket over it. "Jade has a fever. She gets the chills and then tosses with sweat. She can't seem to adjust right."

"So you're helping her," Jacob said.

Melissa's eyes brightened. "Yeah."

Jacob followed her as she went to the front of the barn and mixed grain and water. "What are you doing?"

"Making bran mash for Rayya," she said. "Did you remember your name yet?"

"Jacob."

"Jacob what?"

He shrugged.

"You don't remember anything else?"

"I didn't even remember Jacob. I just . . . kinda chose it."

"Oh."

"Melissa what?"

"Huh?" She emptied small pellets from a bottle. "Oh. O'Brien. That's my last name."

"Do you remember where you're from, Melissa O'Brien?"

"Sure."

"Where?"

"Down in Steamboat. That's the big town southeast of here. I came to Harken when I was young." She poured white fluid into a bottle.

"Is that for Rayya too?"

"No. It's for the filly. She won't nurse. And because of all the handling—she needed help being born and medicine and that stuff—Rayya doesn't even want anything to do with her. So I went to the neighbors and got some goat milk for her."

"Is Rayya angry because the birth was hard?"

"No. She's confused because we helped in the birth."

"I don't understand. She knows you, right? Why would she be confused?"

"Because nature or God—take your pick—designed animals to give birth on their own. Without us interfering."

A sudden hollowness seized Jacob.

"What?" Melissa said. "You look like you saw a ghost."

"I just emptied out. I know it sounds weird, but . . ." He wrapped his arms around his waist.

"You're afraid."

He looked down at his bare feet, ashamed that he feared *nothingness*.

Melissa clutched his arm. Her fingers were strong and her nails chewed. "You'll be okay. Jeanette and Charlie are good people. We'll watch out for you. Help you out."

"Can you help me remember?" His voice was a whisper, even to his own ears.

"How would I do that?"

"By telling me about yourself."

Robinson Ranch has gone nuts, Melissa thought as she mucked out Rayya's stall. Prince Sarraf wandering out of nowhere and wandering back into nowhere like he owned the whole valley. Charlie's accident. Susan, her arms up to her shoulders inside Rayya, trying to make things right. And now this—a kid chained in a cave. That was beyond nuts, all the way to wicked.

Which must be why Jacob wanted to hear about her. Anything would be better than what ugliness was hidden somewhere in that head of his. As she worked, Jacob stayed close, sometimes helping but never in the way.

"I really want to hear about you," he said.

"Nothing to hear."

"Sure there is. I can tell by the way you toss that hay."

"Fine. How honest do you want me to be?"

"As honest as you can."

"My life isn't pretty," she warned.

"I don't think mine is either."

"Okay, then, you asked for this. My mother was a cokehead."

"A what?"

"She took drugs—stuff to make her feel high, but stuff that makes you useless. Or worse. Everything she did was to score the next line. I barely remember her. Hair redder than mine, but she probably dyed it. Eyes always bloodshot. She'd kiss me with cigarette smoke coming out of her mouth. The state found out about me, Jeanette said, because I got pneumonia, almost died. It wasn't my mother who took me to the hospital. One of her drug buddies saw me burning up, wrapped me in a dirty towel, and left me in the emergency room. I had strep throat, pneumonia, malnutrition, you name it.

"It was two days before my mother reported me missing. By then the state had contacted Jeanette about taking me."

"I like Jeanette."

"Yeah, me too. She was married once before. Her husband worked for Yampa Valley Electric. He got killed in a car accident. Her kids were grown by the time I went to live with her. She's got some grand-kids that are the same age as me."

"How old is that?" Jacob said.

"Twenty."

"How old do you think I am?"

He was taller than Melissa, broad-shouldered and narrow-waisted. His eyes were like the sky at dusk, a hazy gray with a hint of blue. His hair was the color of deep chocolate and hung past his shoulders in loose curls. She would swear he was her age, but unless he shaved before coming out to the barn—and she doubted that—he had no beard. His chest and arms were also hairless. She knew that from last night.

"I don't know," she finally said. "You're probably close to my age."

"Twenty."

"Does that work for you?"

He laughed. "Sure. Will you tell me more about yourself?"

That she had told him this much was strange. She guarded her personal life like Charlie guarded Rayya. Yet spilling her guts to Jacob hadn't emptied her out. Somehow it made her fuller. As they went outside to dump the manure and old shavings, she continued.

"I went to live with Jeanette in her trailer. The rich kids used to make fun of me, called me trailer trash. If they hadn't been such jerks, I would have invited them over. They could have seen for themselves how nice Jeanette kept it. She cleaned houses to make a living after her husband died. She took on Charlie's house after his wife died. He almost lost the ranch."

"How do you lose a ranch?" His blank expression made her laugh.

"He owed the bank a lot of money. When he couldn't pay it back, they were going to make him leave this place. Maybe live in a trailer somewhere, one not as nice as Jeanette's. He used to be really rich, lots of horses and people coming and going. Way before my time. But after it was all gone, he became a hermit."

"Like me?"

"I guess you could say that. But he wasn't chained."

Jacob screwed up his face. "Not by chains anyone could see."

Melissa slammed the pitchfork into the cart. "What do you know about it?"

"I don't know . . ."

"Don't go judging us."

Jacob touched her shoulder. "I'm sorry."

"Yeah. Okay."

"Will you tell me more?"

No way, Melissa wanted to say, but somehow the story had its own momentum and kept rolling out. "Somehow things got better for the ranch. Jeanette had something to do with it, but she won't take credit. Susan did something too, but no one will say what. Anyway, Charlie picked up some more horses and started leading tourists on trail rides. Weird thing was—just as he was coming back around, I was dropping out."

"Why, Melissa?"

"I was finally old enough to really understand what a tramp my mother was. How I was nothing to her but a welfare check. And how that check went to buy drugs for her, not food for me. It began to hurt so much that I just cut it out of me, but you can't do that without cutting out a big chunk of yourself. I didn't talk to kids, didn't do activities, and I sure as heck didn't do schoolwork. I tried to become what my mother thought I was. Nothing."

Melissa swiveled the cart around, headed back to the barn. It was Sunday. Jeanette would be after her to go to church, but she'd find some excuse. Maybe she'd take the dude horses down to the Advent, let them take a dip in the bend where the current wasn't harsh.

"How did you become *something* again?"

"The horses. Jeanette talked Charlie into hiring me to help take care of them in exchange for letting me ride. I don't know how to explain it—"

"You don't have to," Jacob said. "I get it."

"Charlie got the notion to start breeding Arabians again. He says it was because Rayya became available at a very attractive price, but I think he had the dream all along. So he built a new barn for Rayya, bought a breeding plan with the top stallion in the world, and here we are."

"But the filly is sick."

"The foaling went bad."

"I'm sorry."

"Yeah, me too." She got out brushes and the shampoo. What was she thinking? She couldn't take the dude horses out. Jade might need her. Charlie had given up on the filly. *Brain damaged*, he said, but how many times had kids at school said that about her?

"What else?" Jacob said.

"What else what?"

"There's something missing in your story."

"Who says?"

"I feel the hole."

Melissa slammed the brush into the wash bucket. "You don't even know who you are. So don't go thinking you know anything about me."

"I'm sorry," he said yet again.

She grabbed his shoulders. "Will you stop it!"

"Stop what?"

"Stop saying you're sorry," Melissa said. "At least until you know if you really have something you're sorry for."

ELEVEN

SUSAN'S EYES SPARKLED AND HER CHEEKS WERE FLUSHED. Had this been the result of the pure Colorado air, it would have been a good thing. That her newfound glow resulted from the discovery of a young man chained in a cave concerned Rick.

She extended her hand to the man Rick had brought with him. "Hi. I'm Susan Stone."

"Susan, this is Zach Hurley. He's a caseworker. Zach, you know Jeanette and Charlie." They stood on the back steps, Charlie leaning against the door frame.

"We met in the hospital," Jeanette said. "Nice to see you."

Charlie glared. "You wanted me to go into the rest home."

"For a week, Mr. Robinson. Only for rehab. If I had known your daughter was coming . . ."

Jeanette poked Charlie. "Yeah. Well, sorry," he said. "I didn't know she was coming either. I just didn't want to get shuttled into some old folks'—"

Zach held his hands up. "It's fine, Charlie. It's all worked out for the best."

"I've got a pot of coffee ready and biscuits in the oven," Jeanette said. "Come on in, grab a seat, guys."

"Don't mind if I do." Zach followed her in, plopped into a chair, legs stretched out, hands linked behind his head.

Susan glanced at Rick, then at Zach. "I guess I'm a little confused, Mr. Hurley—"

"Zach, Dr. Stone."

"And I'm Susan."

Zach grinned. "So what are you confused about?"

"I'm not sure why we need a caseworker involved in a criminal case."

"What if Jacob is a minor?" Rick said.

"I don't think that's the case."

"Zach is here to advocate for his interests on the outside chance that he is."

Susan gave Rick a sharp look. "Do you consider me inadequate to advocate for him?"

"Suse, I—"

Zach leaned forward and smiled. "Susan, of all the people who could have stumbled across this young man, you are the most qualified. Talk about incredibly good luck."

"God blesses even the fallen," Jeanette said. Her back was to them as she plopped biscuits from the pan, but she hadn't missed one syllable of the conversation.

"You have correctly identified the crux of the issue—there are legal aspects to his care," Zach continued. "When the picture clarifies, we don't want to be forced to play catch-up. Better to dot the i's now on every eventuality than to see whoever did this to Jacob go free."

Susan jumped up so fast she knocked her chair back with a bang. "How could anyone even consider such an outcome?"

"Abuse cases can be tricky. Which also brings into question guardianship. Even if we could establish that this young man is not a minor, his amnesia requires a legal guardian."

"Have I not already volunteered to advocate for him in any way that's needed?" Susan said. "If that includes acting as a temporary guardian, I'm absolutely willing to assume that responsibility. As you said, Zach: who could be more qualified than I am?"

Jeanette dropped the biscuits, shattering the plate. Zach got up to help pick up the pieces.

"Suse, let's go outside for a minute," Rick said.

She frowned but followed him out to the front porch. He took her hand, and she yanked it away. "Why did you bring a social worker out here?"

"I had to," he said.

"Jacob is emotionally vulnerable. It's not only unnecessary, it's unwise to get some petty bureaucrat involved in this situation."

Rick took her hand again, pressing it to his chest so she couldn't snatch it away. "Zach Hurley is not a petty bureaucrat. He's an experienced social worker. And we do need him involved *today*."

"Give me one good reason, Ricky Sanchez. One good reason."

"Why were you out riding in a storm?"

"What does that have to do with Zach Hurley?"

"Answer me."

Susan looked away. "The foaling was disastrous. My father blamed me. I had to get away."

"Any other reason?"

She pulled her hand away. "What other reason would there be?"

He walked to the end of the porch and leaned on the railing. "Jeanette was so worried that she called 911."

"That's ridiculous. I told you that."

"She was scared."

"Of what?"

"Don't you know?"

"No."

Rick turned to face her. "Suse."

"I said, no."

"A heartbroken woman, riding out into a storm. You've got to understand how it must have looked."

"I am afraid I do not." Susan's voice was brittle.

"She was scared. I was, too. They say it runs in families, Suse. We were afraid you were doing what your mother did."

Susan swore at him and stomped back into the house, slamming the door behind her.

Zach Hurley's voice grated on Melissa. He seemed harmless enough, a pudgy nerd with wire-rim glasses and thinning hair. Maybe it was the whole social-worker thing that irked her. The only good one she had ever met was the one who helped get her into Jeanette's care.

The guy sat at the kitchen table like he owned the place. Jeanette had fallen all over herself, getting him coffee and even some buttered biscuits. Then she helped Charlie into the wheelchair and wheeled him out to the barn to see Rayya.

Rick had gone with them, giving Susan and Zach privacy with Jacob. Susan stared at Melissa, expecting her to take the hint and leave as well. But no way, not in a hundred years. A social worker and a psychiatrist were a disastrous tag team. They'd decide what they thought was best for Jacob and shove it down his throat. The kid needed Melissa to help him through their maze of questions.

Why couldn't they just leave him alone? In just one morning Jacob had taken to the horses and they to him. He had even lured Prince Sarraf for her so Melissa could check him out. Taking him up into the mountains like that, in the dark no less—what a stupid thing for Susan to do. It was a wonder he didn't break a leg. The stallion had stood calmly as Jacob rubbed his muzzle, allowing Melissa to check his legs for nicks or cuts. When she finished, he galloped away until he was only a speck.

Susan looked up at her. "If you don't mind, we need some time alone with Jacob. You can catch up with him later."

Jacob took Melissa's hand. "Please can she stay?"

Zach Hurley smiled, showing teeth too big for his narrow mouth. "Sure. We want you to be comfortable, to understand that we're here to help."

Susan motioned to a chair, and Jacob sat down. Melissa pulled the chair out from between Zach and Susan, and put it next to Jacob so she could stay right by his side. Susan stared poison at her, but so what? The woman had done damage before—this time Melissa was prepared.

"How're you doing today, Jacob?" Zach asked.

"Good."

"Did you sleep well?"

"Sure."

"What did you think when you woke up in a strange bed?" Susan said.

Zach laid his hand on her forearm. "Let's save that for later."

"It wasn't strange." Jacob's gaze went to Susan, to Zach, and back. "Everyone made me feel at home last night, so I knew exactly where I was this morning."

Melissa leaned against Jacob's arm, a quick touch before Susan spotted it. He got the cue, taking one hand off the table, putting it on his leg where she could grasp it—out of the others' view.

"I need to start a file on you," Zach said.

"A what?"

A listing of everything you've ever done wrong, Melissa thought. *And what all the big shot teachers and cops and social workers thought about it.*

"A record of when we meet, what we talk about, suggestions on how to make sure you get what you need."

With a perfectly straight face, Jacob said, "I need more of Jeanette's cinnamon buns."

Susan laughed. "I think she put them in the freezer. I'll thaw them in the microwave. Be ready in a minute. Do you want butter on them?"

Jacob nodded and watched her intently as she worked, glancing at Zach on occasion to show he was still listening.

The social worker shuffled paperwork. "I have to ask questions you probably can't answer. But if I don't ask, I'll get in trouble with my boss."

"Boss?"

"The guy or woman he works for," Melissa said. "Like Charlie is my boss."

He squeezed her hand. "And now you're my boss. Melissa taught me how to clean the stalls."

"Good enough," Zach said. "Here goes. What's your name?"

"Jacob for now."

"Last name?"

"*For now* doesn't work?"

Zach stared blankly.

"It's a joke." Jacob laughed and slapped Zach's arm, exactly as Melissa had slapped his arm when she told him the joke about the horse that went into the bar.

Oldest and dumbest horse joke in the book—a horse goes into a bar and the bartender says, "Why the long face?" Most people groaned when they heard it, but once Melissa explained what a bar was and how bartenders function like . . . well, Susan . . . Jacob got it and laughed heartily.

"Jokes are a lot of fun," Zach said. "But my boss doesn't have much of a sense of humor. So what should I write down—officially—in the space for your last name?"

"Write that I don't know my last name."

"You mean, you can't remember," Melissa said.

"Let him answer for himself, please." Susan's fingers tapped the microwave keys like little hammers. *She'd probably like to hammer me,* Melissa thought.

Jacob looked at Zach with wide eyes. "The thing is—I don't know if I can't remember. Or if I just don't know."

"I'm not following," Zach said.

"What if I don't have a last name?"

"In this country, everyone does. It's our custom."

Jacob squirmed. "What if this isn't my country? How would I know?"

Melissa stroked his hand. She felt a tremble deep between the bones of his fingers. "Can't you just write he doesn't remember in all those empty blanks of yours?"

"Melissa, I think it's better if you leave." Susan's tone was biting.

"No," Jacob said. "I want her to stay. Is that okay, Zach?"

"Sure. Melissa, you need to trust that we're here to help Jacob."

Zach's smile sent a prickle through Melissa's shoulders. For a brief instant, he looked like the men who used to tramp through her mother's apartment. That must be stress weighing on her—those men were big and burly, reeking of cigarettes and beer. Zach looked like a chipmunk with glasses.

"Sorry," she muttered. "I'll keep quiet."

"No harm done. Jacob, if you don't know, it's fine if you just say that. We don't need to discuss any of it now."

The microwave binged. Startled, Jacob looked back at the stove. "What's that?"

"I'll take you around later on," Susan said. "We'll talk about things you don't recognize."

Jacob turned back to Zach. "Sorry. I won't keep interrupting."

Zach picked up his pen again. "Date of birth?"

Jacob shrugged.

"Place of birth?"

"I know I'm not supposed to interrupt—"

"Hey, that's me who's not supposed to butt in. You have something to say, they want to hear it. Right, Zach?" Melissa said.

"Here to help," he said.

Jacob took his hands away from Melissa and clutched them together. "It just feels like I wasn't born. At least not like horses, where there's a little horse who becomes a bigger horse."

"That's a hard concept to capture," Zach said mildly. "So I'm going to just write down 'unknown.'"

Rick Sanchez had come in and was standing near the door. Susan set a plate of cinnamon buns in front of Jacob, along with a glass of milk. Zach waited while Jacob ate. Melissa got up and made herself a bowl of cereal. Leave it to Susan not to offer food to anyone else. It was all about her own agenda and forget everyone else.

When Jacob finished eating, Zach resumed the questions. "What's your father's name?"

Jacob looked at the ceiling as if the answer were written up there. "Would it be the same as mine?"

"It might be. But not necessarily."

"I don't know."

"Address?"

Jacob responded with a shrug or by shaking his head to questions from schooling to health history to if he had ever been arrested. Finally Zach closed the folder. "That's enough for today."

"I'm sorry," Jacob said. "Your boss is going to see mostly 'unknowns' in that file. Will he be disappointed?"

Zach smiled. "He'll want me to do whatever I can to help you. In whatever way you need."

"That's enough for today," Susan said. "He needs to rest."

For once Melissa agreed with her.

Rick stepped forward. "One more thing."

Susan narrowed her eyes at him. *Interesting*, Melissa thought. Even her old best friend wasn't immune to her frostiness.

Jacob smiled up at Rick. "You probably should just write 'unknown' on whatever question you have for me."

"Actually, this may help make all the unknowns go away. I'm going to take your fingerprints," Rick said. "And get a swab for DNA."

Jacob grabbed Melissa's hand. "I don't know what those things are."

"Nothing that will hurt you," Rick said. He showed Jacob the ink pad, pressing his own thumb into the ink to demonstrate. He worked quickly, then laughed as he and Jacob shared the sink to wash the ink off their fingers. Melissa cringed when Rick reached for the soap and the gun on his belt pressed against Jacob's hip, but the kid didn't seem to notice.

Finally, Zach got up to leave.

"What's next?" Susan said.

How about you leave the kid in peace, Melissa wanted to say, but didn't bother. Why should she? For most of her life, she'd been made to believe that she wasn't smart enough or important enough or even loud enough to be heard.

Christopher heard everything she said—and things she hadn't said but wanted to. Jacob might be like that, which meant she had to guard herself. *I feel the hole,* Jacob had said. Most days the hole was big enough to ride a pregnant horse through.

"It was nice meeting you," Zach was saying.

"Maybe someday you'll meet the real me," Jacob said.

Susan walked Rick and Zach outside.

"Do you think they'll like me when they do, Melissa?"

"What? Like you? They like you now. We all do."

He leaned his forehead against hers, and for a strange minute, she thought he was going to kiss her. But he just stared into her eyes. "When I find out who I am, will I like myself?"

"Of course."

"I don't know," he said for the thirtieth time that morning. "I just don't know."

Rick still didn't know what to make of Jacob. Hopefully Zach would offer some insight. "So what do you think?"

Zach stared out the car window, humming a nondescript tune. "To quote Jacob—"

Rick laughed. "You don't know."

"Do you think he's faking?"

"I certainly hope not. The Robinsons have had a rocky time in the past year. Another crisis might just be the last straw."

"I could get a court order, get him out of there," Zach said.

"Over whose dead body? Even Charlie would have my head if I tried to enforce it," Rick said.

"If I'm going to get him to another family or facility, today would be the day to do it. Before he's any more attached to those people."

"He's beyond attached already. Did you see the way he clung to Melissa? How about how his eyes followed Susan as she worked? Even when Charlie was barking something at Jeanette outside, he stared back at the window, trying to see what was up."

"How quickly can you get a report back on the prints?" Zach asked.

"I'll scan and e-mail them to Denver. If he's a convicted felon in Colorado, his name will pop out of the computer as soon as the tech down there can run the file. The Feds can take some time. If they get a hit, they want to check and double-check."

"Everything in triplicate. How I love working for the government. So tell me—how unstable is Susan Stone?"

"Who said she's unstable?"

"You did. Every time you looked at her."

Rick clenched his jaw. When had he gotten so easy to read? "She's a hotshot doctor from hotshot Harvard. I'm just a county sheriff."

"Who knows the family's history. Maybe we should take him out of there, Rick."

"Not quite yet. Let me pray about it."

Zach tilted his head at Rick. "Did you learn that in criminal justice at the U?"

"Wish I had," Rick said. "I wouldn't be divorced with a son and a daughter who barely know me."

"Don't overcompensate by indulging this kid."

"Oh, are you the hotshot shrink now?"

"Someone's got to stay objective."

Rick gripped the steering wheel, irked at the implication. "I'll make you a deal, Hurley. You do your job, and I'll do mine. Okay?"

"I am." Zach folded his arms and went back to staring out the window.

TWELVE

HOW SHE HATED SUSAN. THIS WAS THE KIND OF HATE THAT ate a hole through a person's stomach and into the spine.

Melissa couldn't turn off the movie in her head, made all the more real by Susan's meddling. Why couldn't she leave Jacob alone? Given time, things work themselves out. He didn't need some uptight and overbearing shrink to yank stuff out of him. He needed time under the open sky, time with the horses, time just being free.

But once again, Susan was nosing around where she didn't belong. Melissa only hoped that another disaster didn't occur. Disaster was too weak a word for what Susan had done a year ago—what she'd forced Melissa to do.

She couldn't think about that. She needed to focus on brushing Jonas. Being out in the pasture. Dude horses, no drama. But the sun on Melissa's back had felt just the same that day.

The day she first laid eyes on Susan Stone . . .

When Melissa walked into the trendy coffee shop in downtown Steamboat, she knew Susan immediately. The woman at the corner table was thin, her face angular, her suit upscale. She had Christopher's eyes and his hair, but none of his tranquility.

"Dr. Stone?" Melissa hated the tremor in her voice. She needed to be strong.

"Yes. Sit down, Melissa. Please." Susan spoke in the same husky, deep tones that the news babes on television did.

The waitress came by. "Can I get you something to drink?"

"Milk," Melissa said. Susan had a cup of black coffee before her. No food.

"Let's not waste time," Susan said. "How pregnant are you?"

"Four months."

"Four months? But Christopher's only been here for two."

"It's not his baby."

Susan's mouth tightened. "Does he know that?"

"Absolutely." Melissa sipped her milk, hoping to calm her stomach. "He plans to raise it as his own."

"Oh my, oh my." Susan drummed the table with her fingers. "This changes everything."

"He called me last night," Melissa said, emboldened by the woman's sudden nervousness. "He was almost done with his packing. He's got to close out his bank accounts, so he's waiting until Monday to head back out here."

"No. He's not moving here."

"He said he was."

"And he knows this isn't his baby?"

"What did I just say? Of course he does. We haven't had se—we haven't made love yet. We're waiting until we get married."

Susan covered her eyes. "I don't believe what I'm hearing."

"That we haven't—"

"That I believe. Christopher is into religion right now. He doesn't believe in premarital sex."

"So what don't you believe?"

Susan leaned toward Melissa. "That you have no trouble sleeping around and getting pregnant, but you snag my impressionable son by *not* sleeping with him."

Melissa tossed a couple of bucks on the table. "It was so *not* nice meeting you."

She went outside, at a loss where to go. Jeanette wouldn't be back for two hours. Susan had sworn Melissa to secrecy about her visit. The woman hadn't been to Robinson Ranch in many years, and she had no plans to do so now. A dark history, Christopher said. He was hoping to change that.

Melissa walked north, aiming for the Elk River Valley even though it was fifteen miles away and Robinson Ranch another ten. It was not Susan's home, but it was certainly hers now. And that's what she had to cling to. Melissa had to brush away these *if onlys* that plagued her like flies.

If only she had stood up to Susan.

If only she had believed in Christopher's love.

If only she had told Susan to go back to Boston or anyplace but Colorado.

If only Melissa had been strong that day, she and Christopher would be running the ranch, raising a baby, keeping Charlie out of trouble.

But where would that leave Jacob? If Charlie hadn't gotten hurt, if Susan hadn't come to Colorado, if she hadn't ridden off into the storm, would he still be chained in that ravine?

"This is all God's fault," Melissa whispered into Jonas's neck. "He can't keep things straight, and someone always has to pay."

He takes a step back to assess the situation.

Two bodies, burned to an intriguing crisp. *Check.*

Family in chaos. *Check.*

Two sick horses, at least one likely to die. *Check.*

The chains off and the pawn in place. *Check.*

The master pulling the strings. *Check.*

Everything working just as he had planned.

Checkmate coming right up.

THIRTEEN

"His heartbeat is abnormally slow." Joyce Freeman might be in her midsixties, but she was fit and lean. A rock climber, Rick had said, and someone he trusted.

After yesterday, Susan wasn't sure she could trust his judgment. Maybe she had had some moments of doubt and even despair in that ride up Folly, but she was functioning. With Jacob in her care, she now had clear purpose.

"Thirty-five or forty," Susan said. "Very strong, though."

"Like an extreme athlete's."

Susan smiled. "What's yours?"

"At my age? When I'm working hard on my cardio, riding my bike the hundred miles a week, it runs fifty-five. But I've got my doughnut days too." She glanced at her notes. "His reflexes are perfect, muscle tone superb. If I tested his lung capacity, I bet it's double normal."

"You're leading up to something, or you wouldn't be giving me the laundry list of what's right about Jacob."

Joyce took a long swig of water, then replaced the cap. "There's something behind his eyes. Like a scarring, but—well, this is going to sound bizarre, but it seemed to reflect the light back. Like some sort of shiny occlusion."

"His vision seems perfect."

"Better than perfect. He tested 20-10 on the eye chart. I can't explain it—I just know that he shouldn't be able to see clearly with something hiding behind his lens."

"Do you have a preliminary diagnosis?"

"I'm not qualified. I suggest you get him into Boulder to see an ophthalmologist."

"Might the CAT scan shed some light on the eye stuff? We are proceeding on that, correct?"

"Absolutely. In fact, I can use the ocular finding to bump him in as an emergency. But honestly, Susan, I pray the scan doesn't show anything in regard to the eyes."

"Because we'd be talking some sort of tumor?"

Joyce uncapped her water and took another gulp—a delaying tactic. Susan had seen that gaze-shift in hundreds of patients.

"Rick wouldn't forgive me if I didn't give you my full assessment, even of the possibilities."

Susan remembered to smile. "And that is?"

"If this were either some sort of ocular tumor or arterial malformation—"

"You're speculating at this point."

"Admittedly so. But it is possible—and you know this, Susan—that something of this sort could cause personality issues. Paranoia. Even a divided personality."

Susan knew what was coming, had even listed it in her own notes, but refused to give voice to it.

Joyce shrugged on her lab coat. "It's very possible Jacob chained himself down in that cave."

"That's absurd."

"He may have suffered from the delusion that someone would come find him. Rescue fantasies are a common enough pathology."

"I assure you that I've seen no abnormal pathology in this young man. But I'll keep in mind what you've said." Susan stood and extended her hand. "Thank you for your time."

Joyce held her hand, eyes locked on Susan's. "Perhaps it played out like this: he chained himself in the darkness of the cave and threw the key out of reach, hoping that someone would find him."

"Impossible."

"I disagree. Susan, it's very possible that this young man had a death wish. Be careful because he could play it out again, and get you involved."

Jacob sat on a cold chair, dressed only in the new underpants Susan had bought him and something called a hospital gown. A nice lady named Julia showed him the CAT scanner. "It's like a camera. Do you know what that is?"

"Sheriff Sanchez took my picture a couple of nights ago."

Julia smiled. "This machine takes pictures as well. But of people's insides."

"Inside?"

"You know. Your bones and blood and heart and guts. It's amazing."

Julia's blue eyes and quiet voice spun into a maelstrom. Jacob tried to block his ears, but the screams broke through and then a haughty voice—

Amazing how a man can still live after that. Almost a work of art.

He tried to hide his eyes, but the images were imprinted inside his lid.

Bowels spilled on a rock-strewn plain. Blood throbbing from a leg wound, forming a pool and then a river. A face but no skin, only bones and caverns where the eyes should be.

"Jacob," Susan said. "You're going to break my hand. Are you all right?"

"Oh. Sorry." Why had these horrible pictures come into his mind? If these were his memories, he wanted no part of them. He couldn't tell Susan about them. She would think he was sick or dangerous, maybe lock him up all over again.

Julia helped Jacob onto a table that had padding, like a bed.

Susan rubbed his arm. "Are you feeling a bit scared?"

"Just a little." More scared of what was inside him than what was outside. What if the machine captured those images?

"Give me a minute, and then we'll get started," Julia said. "You just lie back and relax."

Jacob closed his eyes and saw a river of blood. He opened his eyes and stared at the ceiling. He forced himself to think other thoughts. Nicer thoughts, like the people he had met here.

A pretty lady named Kate had checked him in. *Admitting,* he read from her name tag.

"You know what that says?" Susan asked.

"Yeah. Sure."

"We'll definitely do an educational assessment. That might help pinpoint how old you are."

"Almost time," Julia said from behind the window.

Jacob closed his eyes, but the blood still dripped. Like water in Jeanette's sink, *drip drip* until he turned the faucet to stop it. Where was the faucet in his head to control this? Susan wanted to open it wide, but clearly, that would be a terrible mistake.

Think of something good. Who else had he met this morning? A man named Bill, bouncing down the hallway. "My daughter was just born. The most beautiful girl ever."

Susan smiled. "Congratulations."

"What's her name?" Jacob asked.

"Tierney. Tierney Beth." Bill pressed something called a cigar into Jacob's hands.

"You're not smoking that," Susan whispered.

"I didn't know I was supposed to," Jacob said.

In the waiting room they'd met a girl named Jenny who broke her thumb playing lacrosse. "I'm the goalie," she said. "See my splint?"

"Like Charlie has on his foot," Jacob said, pleased that he had made a connection.

Jenny's mother sat with her. Her name was Doris, and she was a librarian.

"I don't know what a librarian is," Jacob confessed.

"Well," Doris had said. "I'll tell you what I tell all the kids. Look it up."

"Ready, Jacob?" Julia's voice seemed to come from inside the machine.

The dripping had stopped. A scab had formed. Good. Now he could close his eyes.

Susan had been allowed to stay in the room with him. He heard her breathing, steady and sure, but her heart beat faster as the machine came to life.

"Okay, you'll feel the table move a bit. Close your eyes and just relax." The table crept forward, taking him into the machine, but it wasn't frightening like the elevator. Its tunnel was open on both sides and not long enough to enclose his whole body.

The inside of Jacob's eyes flushed red again. He searched the few memories he had. The muscles in Melissa's arms as she shoveled manure out of the stalls. The worry lines as she attended to Rayya, the heartbreak as she tried to coax the filly to take her formula. The ranch and its rolling pastures. Charlie's pride as he drove Jacob around in the truck and showed him the vast boundaries of his land. Susan's watchfulness, like a mother bird with her wings spread over her nest, covering him with her feathers.

"Hold your breath, please." Julia's voice, lilting like a lark's. He would store the music in her tone as a memory. Soon enough, his mind would be filled with only good things.

The machine whirred and clicked. Something sparked.

Jacob opened his eyes just as the fire swept over him.

"Shut it down, shut it down!" Susan screamed.

A storm of electricity engulfed Jacob's head and shoulders. He cried out but didn't move. Susan grabbed his hips and yanked, one foot braced against the CAT scanner. Even amid the chaos, the irony struck her: this was how she had delivered Rayya's foal three days ago.

"Cut off power!" she yelled.

"I can't. I'm throwing the switches, but it won't stop!" Julia said.

Jacob couldn't be moved. It was as if the crackling electricity had created an intense magnetic field to trap him.

Julia tugged on the main power cable to the machine, tumbling backwards as she freed it from its socket.

The storm died. Susan pulled Jacob out of the machine. Eyes still shut tight, he searched for her hand. "Susan. I'm sorry, I broke the machine."

"No, not you, Jacob. Something went wrong, but it wasn't your fault." She ran her fingers over his face, neck, chest. His skin was crimson, as if he had suffered a horrible sunburn, but there was no blistering. Second-degree burns at the worst. More likely just first-degree.

"Help Julia," Jacob whispered. "She's scared."

Julia was slumped against the wall, whimpering. "I'm so sorry, so sorry. I don't know what happened."

"Get up and call for help." Susan pressed her hand against Jacob's carotid artery, trying to ascertain if the shock had disrupted his heart rhythm.

He pushed her hand away and sat up. "She's scared, Susan. Please. Help her."

Susan turned and pulled Julia to her feet. She tried to swallow her anger and moderate her voice. "He's okay. But we need to make sure. Please get yourself together and get me some help."

Julia grabbed the wall phone. "It's not working."

"Then run to the ER. Just get a doc up here."

Jacob pushed up off the table. "Let me do it."

"You're not going for your own help," Susan said.

"I'm really okay."

Susan forced a smile. "I need to know that for sure. So bear with me." She peered into his eyes. An incident like this could have blinded him, especially with the scarring behind his retinas.

"Joyce just did that," Jacob said.

"That was before this asinine machine blew itself up. It's just a quick check."

Jacob sighed. "Everyone's always checking me out."

Susan parted his hair with her fingers, looking for any skin damage that they might miss because of the length of his hair.

"You're worried again. You worry too much, Susan."

"Of course I am. We're trying to help you, not . . ." She stopped herself, shocked that she had almost said *fry you*. Where had that entirely inappropriate phrase come from? Twenty years as a therapist had conditioned Susan to control her tongue, her facial expression, and even her body language. She would have to apologize to Julia. As shocking as this was for Jacob, the technician must also be completely unsettled.

Emergency room personnel swarmed in. Jacob sat patiently, enduring the exam, answering questions. He didn't flinch when they drew more blood or when the dermatologist examined every inch of his burns.

The head of the hospital, an overweight blowhard named George Brennan, tried to minimize the incident, laying defensive groundwork against a possible lawsuit. Susan wanted to shake him off, but the fool would cling to her like a leech until they got out of here.

Jacob received a dose of Demerol and a prophylactic dose of antibiotic for the burns. They hung an IV to infuse a liter of saline. The dermatologist and trauma doc descended on Susan, muttering reassurances.

No permanent harm done, no worse than a bad sunburn, we're all so sorry, this kind of thing has never happened here or anywhere, we'll be contacting the manufacturer, we'll keep you informed every step of the way, but the young man will be fine, don't you worry, Dr. Stone, just trust us to do our jobs.

As they stuck him for the IV, Jacob's wan smile made Susan's heart ache.

"I want to run an echocardiogram," the trauma doc said. "Make sure this injur—incident . . . didn't cause an arrhythmia."

They wheeled Jacob to the elevator. "Tell them we should take the stairs, Susan."

"They want you to stay on the stretcher a little longer and not exert yourself. One last test. Okay?"

Panic flashed in Jacob's eyes. "Okay."

"Squeeze my hand if you need to."

He clutched her hand and didn't let the pressure up until they wheeled him out of the elevator and into cardiography. A heart doc came in, still dressed for golf. Brennan wanted him to read the output in real time. The bureaucracy in overdrive. Every doctor and nurse in this room could read the EKG, Susan knew. Brennan was populating the incident report with every specialist he could get his hands on.

Jacob chatted up the technician as she put the electrodes on his chest. Within a minute, he knew her name was Beth, and she had two cats and a really nice boyfriend. All day people had responded to his earnestness. How anyone could have done such a horrific thing to such a sweet young man . . . but Susan had seen even worse in her practice. The depraved behavior of people had long since ceased to amaze her. Even so, Jacob's abuse appalled her deep into her bones. Rick had to catch whoever was responsible for those chains.

"Okay, this will take just a minute," the technician said.

The heart doc stood with Susan, muttering more of the hospital line: *a regrettable incident, likely no damage, so very sorry.*

Something clicked.

The electrodes sparked, tiny flames rising from each patch. Jacob cried out, slapping at them, but Susan leaned on him, smothering the flames with her own body.

"I'm sorry!" Beth cried. "This never happened before."

Brennan grabbed Susan's shoulders, trying to get her off Jacob. She swatted back at him with one hand, the other peeling charred electrodes off Jacob's chest. They seemed to have done no damage to his skin, other than intensifying the burn he already had.

He looked up at her, his eyes clouded by fear. "Susan, I don't want to get checked out anymore. Please, can't we go home now?"

The cardiologist reached under her arms with his stethoscope. "Jacob, try to be quiet. I want to make sure your heart is—"

Susan grabbed the stethoscope and flung it across the room. "Enough, already."

"I'm telling you, it's got to be him," the doc said. "I need to listen, see what's going on."

She grabbed Jacob's clothes and helped him off the table. "We're leaving."

George Brennan stepped between her and the door. "We need to keep Jacob here. It's imperative that we get to the bottom of how he's causing the machines to go haywire."

"How he's *causing* it?" Susan swore long and hard to his face, then turned to all the personnel in the room. "In all my professional life, I have never seen such raging incompetence. None of you will touch him again."

She helped him into his clothes and then carefully wrapped her arm around Jacob's waist. "I won't let them do anything else. You'll be all right."

"We haven't discharged him," Brennan called after her.

Jacob balked at the elevator, so they took the stairs to the ground floor. In the car, Susan carefully fastened the lap belt on him, but stuck the shoulder belt behind him to avoid the raw skin on his chest and back.

Brennan had followed them out to the parking lot. "You're taking him out against medical advice. We're not ready to discharge him."

She glared at him, swore again.

"I'm telling you, Dr. Stone. There's obviously something wrong here."

She got in, started the car, and drove away.

FOURTEEN

Life stunk sometimes. Especially when the innocent suffered.

Melissa stroked Jade's neck but could only see Krista. The first time she had held her daughter, Krista wore a pink cap and was swaddled in a receiving blanket. Her eyes were bright, her face placid and sweet.

Until the shaking started.

Nurses came in response to Melissa's cry, followed by a pediatrician. A neurologist came later. Seizures, they said. Perhaps caused by the difficult birth, or perhaps caused in the womb.

In the womb. Krista still developing when Susan descended on Melissa and demanded that she release Christopher from his pledge to marry her.

Even though Melissa had fled the coffee shop and run up the sidewalk, Susan had caught up to her, heels tapping on the concrete like gunshots. "What do you really want?"

"For what?"

"Your life, Melissa. As I see it, there are two options. An abortion, which will give you and my son time to really get to know each other."

Give Christopher time to learn I'm a slut, Melissa thought. *That's what she's thinking.*

"Or you go far away and have the baby. Without involving my son."

She doesn't call him by his name. It's *my son* all the time. Just like her father, who calls Rayya *my mare.*

"Look, I know my son cares deeply for you. But he's young. You both are. You're not thinking clearly. There's so much I could do to help you. If you agree to have an abortion, I'll buy you a condo somewhere. Pay for you to go to college. That would be a wonderful opportunity for you. You're what—eighteen?"

"Nineteen," Melissa said, numbed by Susan's offer.

"Only nineteen. You and my son have so much growing to do."

"Christopher!" Melissa yelled. People turned and stared. "His name is Christopher."

Susan smiled. "I know. I named him. He's such a fine young man—"

"I know. Don't you think I know that?"

"Which is why he shouldn't be rushed into marriage."

Melissa rubbed her abdomen, trying to dispel the acid in her stomach. "What? He's too good to get married?"

"No, Melissa. Not at all. But he's too young to get married. Are you aware that he's never held a real job?"

"He's a good worker. Charlie says so."

Susan guided her to a bench. "He loves the horses. He's been telling me that since last summer. You met then, didn't you?"

"Yes. So you understand then, it's not like we're rushing into this."

Susan tipped her head, brow wrinkled as if deep in thought. "So you met my so—Christopher—last summer. Did you know each other well then?"

Susan's voice had warmed, and her manner seemed open. Even welcoming. Maybe Melissa could make her understand.

"He came out to get to know Charlie, to make a family connection. And he wanted to do hard work, see what it felt like to challenge his body instead of his mind. He's not a good student, you know."

"Yes, Melissa. I'm aware of that."

"Those stupid learning disabilities. He's real smart, though."

"I know that also. I've kept him in private schools so he could have individualized programs that mediated his deficiencies."

Uh-oh, Melissa thought. *Shrink speech.*

"You were telling me about last summer."

"We got on so well."

"Tell me how. Help me get to know you better. Tell me what you have in common."

"We love the same music. Pop and sometimes a little country. Baseball. He almost jumped out of his skin when he found out I'm a Red Sox fan. Charlie got me into it. He's been following the Red Sox for years. You sent him a Christmas card with a picture of Christopher in a Red Sox cap."

"I remember."

"Anyway, he ordered a satellite television package so the three of us could watch all their games."

"I don't have time for baseball, though I used to make sure Christopher got to Fenway Park a couple times a year. What else brought you together?"

"We're both better at working with our hands than our heads. I'm not dumb, but school wasn't good to me."

"I'm sorry."

"We like scary movies, peanut butter but only the natural kind, and we like politics."

"Politics?"

"He's a conservative."

"I did not know that."

Melissa laughed. "He said admitting you're a conservative in Boston is like admitting you're a Yankees fan. We like to take turns pretending to be liberals so we can practice our skills debating. After we get settled, we might get involved with a campaign."

"You discovered all these mutual interests last summer?"

"Sure. And more."

"Did you love him even then?" Susan said, her voice soft.

"I did."

Susan clutched her arm, her tone harsh now. "You dare to tell me you loved my son, but you slept with other men?"

"*Man,* not *men.* I made a mistake. One mistake. Last winter, Christopher said he couldn't come back out. You had set up some trip to Europe or something. He stopped answering my e-mails, so I just fell into thinking he couldn't love me. That it was just a summer thing. I got involved with this other guy. But Christopher forgave me."

Susan rubbed Melissa's arm where she had grabbed it. "Do you really love him?"

"I do. How many times or ways do I have to tell you that?"

"Can you swear that you're not just using him to gain a father for your baby?"

Melissa held her gaze. "I swear."

"Do you love my son enough to put whatever is best for him ahead of your own welfare?"

"Yes. I do."

"Again I ask you—do you swear?"

"I do." This was weird—Melissa felt like she was taking her vows already, but with the wrong person. What was all this questioning about? Maybe Susan wanted to be completely sure before she gave their marriage her blessing.

"If that is true, Melissa . . ."

"Absolutely true."

"Then back off." Susan spit the words out. "Back off."

No! she wanted to shout to a year ago, but what was done was done.

Even so, she often wondered: was it Susan Stone's poison that had injured the baby in Melissa's belly? Certainly the shock of Christopher's death had shattered Melissa's heart, so that the only thing that kept her breathing was the baby.

None of it was the baby's fault. She shouldn't have been born injured, her infant brain sending out signals that shook her body and rattled her bones.

And none of this was Jade's fault. If the storm hadn't come and if the vet had come, the filly would have been born quickly and well.

Nor was it Jacob's fault. Once they found out the truth, they would see that he was a victim too. They would stick by him, and he would be okay.

If Susan Stone didn't smother him with her meddling.

Melissa would damn that woman to hell if she had the authority. But the only thing she could do *right* was to love horses, and so she poured herself into loving Jade.

Yet love never seemed to be enough. She had loved Christopher, and he died. She had loved Krista and had to let her go. She loved Charlie and Jeanette, and they struggled and suffered.

She wanted to do something right just once in her life. Was it too much to ask, to be allowed to raise a splendid filly into a spectacular horse? But as much as she put her whole heart into Jade, the little horse was dying.

And there wasn't a blessed thing Melissa could do to stop it.

"Stop the car!"

Susan slammed on the brakes, sending the SUV into a skid. She regained control and parked the car on the shoulder. "What's wrong, Jacob? Are you going to be sick?"

"No. Listen." He tipped his head to the side, eyes fixed on an unseen horizon.

"Is something wrong with the car?"

Before she could protest, Jacob jumped out and dashed across the road. Susan's heart flip-flopped. Routt County Road 101 might be lightly traveled, but the speed limit was fifty-five. Fortunately, no cars or trucks barreled down from either side.

Jacob disappeared down the embankment, wiggled through a wire fence, and ran across a grassy field. Just as she was crossing the road to follow, Jacob collapsed onto his stomach and disappeared.

Susan kicked off her heels so she could move faster. The tufts of grass were soft and cool under her feet, and she flashed back to childhood, chasing Ricky and the other kids around the ranch, laughing when someone stepped in a pile of horse manure. Hoping Mother was off on a charity event or long ride so she wouldn't haunt them.

She found Jacob lying headfirst in a rushing creek. She grabbed him by the belt loops of his jeans and yanked him back.

He twisted around, eyes wide with surprise, hair dripping wet in long strands. "What's wrong?"

"You scared the life out of me. Are you all right?"

"Sure. This is exactly what I needed." He stuck his head back in the water, inching forward until most of his upper body was submerged. Susan grabbed the waistband so he wouldn't slip all the way in.

It came back to her—this was Manchester Creek, separating Hoare land from the Connors'. Both families had lost their property in the collapse of the mideighties. The change in tax laws that disallowed a deduction for horses unless an owner was involved with hands-on care had resulted in a mass exodus of yuppie money. Horse prices plummeted, ruining ranchers like Charlie Robinson who were overextended with loans and breeding stock.

What had become of the Hoares and Connors? What of her pals in the show ring, most of whom had stayed with their roots? Twenty years past the industry collapse, were any of them still here? Was Jacob from one of these families or a newcomer to this part of Colorado?

He was still underwater. With more of his body submerged, it was impossible to pull him out again. Susan was about to step in and lift him by the shoulders when he turned and waved at her. Still under the water.

How long had he been under while she was strolling down memory lane? Three minutes at least; five minutes were likely. Extreme athlete, Joyce had suggested. Maybe they should post his photo on some of those Web sites that triathletes frequented. On second thought, that might be unwise if it resulted in the victimizer finding Jacob. Better to find the abuser and get him to justice before he could hurt Jacob or anyone else.

Jacob went under the water for the next twenty minutes, coming up every five or so to catch his breath. His endurance had to be worthy of a world record. When he finally pushed back and sat cross-legged on the bank, he wasn't even winded. His skin was no longer a raw red, having been effectively iced by the frigid water.

"Thanks. I needed that," he said.

"Was that what you heard while we were driving? The water?"

He nodded.

She hadn't heard it until after she had crossed the road. How had he heard it in a closed-in car, over the hum of the wheels?

"Wasn't it cold? Snow melt is still coming down off the mountains."

"Brutal. But I liked it."

"We'd better get you home and get you dried off."

"Can't we just sit here for a while?"

"You're wet."

He stripped off his soaking shirt and wrung it out. Susan tried not to stare at the scars on his back.

"This is the best I've felt since I broke that machine." His grin faded. "I'm sorry. I didn't mean to break it."

"You didn't break anything. Maybe the storm did something to the hospital's power supply, made it susceptible to surges." She pointed overhead. "Sunspots could even cause an anomaly like that, I suppose."

Jacob stared at the sun. "I don't see any spots."

"Stop it! You can't look at the sun like that."

He smiled. "Yes, I can."

She took his hand, rubbed it between hers. "You may think you can, but you'll injure your eyes. So promise me you won't directly look at the sun. Please."

Jacob shrugged, his right shoulder dipping forward just like Melissa's. Another imprint.

He leaned back in the grass, eyes closed. "Please let's stay here for a little while. Even listening to the water singing makes me feel better."

"The water sings?"

"Sure. Can't you hear it?"

Susan heard the blood rushing in her head, the snap of her nerves, the rustle of her blouse as she fidgeted. She leaned back and tried to let all of it rush away with the water.

"Is Jeanette your mother?" Jacob asked.

"No. She's Charlie's wife."

"Even though Charlie is your father, she's not your mother."

"She's my stepmother. Stepfamilies are common. Chances are close to 40 percent that you're part of a stepfamily."

He opened his eyes and stared coldly at her. "No."

"You remember something about your family?"

"No. But I know that I don't have a stepmother or stepfather. I can't tell you how, but I know that."

"Do you remember anything about your home?"

He shook his head.

"Will you tell me what you do know, Jacob?" Susan's tone was light, deliberately inviting a confidence. Lying in a field under a warm sun next to rushing water was almost as conducive to relaxation as hypnosis.

"I know you have a bruise."

"I have lots of bruises. From the tumble into the ravine. No serious ones."

"On your heart, Susan."

"What do you mean?"

"From your real mother."

She breathed back her sudden anger, but not in time to stop from spitting out the words, "Who told you that?"

"No one."

"Was Melissa talking about me? Or Jeanette?"

"No one, Susan."

"Whatever you think you know—"

"It's not true?"

"No matter how old you are, anything that happened between my mother and me happened long before you were born. So you can't know anything. You may be guessing, but it's all—"

"What happened?"

"There's no value in talking about it."

Jacob propped up on one elbow. "That's not what you told me. You said, 'Talking things out has great value towards recovery.'"

Susan picked through the grass, looking for clover.

"Please tell me about your real mother. Maybe it will help me think if I had a mother."

Stick a knife in my throat, why doncha? The old schoolyard refrain rose up, unbidden. Even thinking about Vanessa Robinson felt like ground glass in her stomach. Yet Jacob was infinitely curious and bound to ask Melissa or Jeanette, or even the strangers he so easily befriended. She'd give him a bit of the story. Sharing some of her challenges might shake loose some of his own.

"Do you know what social class distinctions are?" Susan asked.

"No."

"When people make decisions about other people based on what they do or how they dress or how much money they think they have."

"Like when the doctors came in and kind of pushed Julia aside, like she didn't know anything? Downstairs, the heart doctor was nice, but Kate looked at him like he was better than she was. It didn't make much sense to me."

"You've described it accurately. Here's something to remember. Much of human behavior doesn't often make sense."

"Okaaaaay," he said, drawing the word out like Melissa. "If you say so."

"My mother, Vanessa Collins, belonged to what some people call the upper class. She had a good education, a lot of money, and social standing."

"Like you, Susan?"

Jacob's acuity was not always charming.

"I suppose my life in Boston has a certain snob appeal to it. I've worked hard not to let it creep into my day-to-day life."

"You were talking about your mother, Susan."

He wasn't going to let her off this hook. Might as well give him a sanitized version of her history. "Vanessa grew up in what was the wealthy end of the Elk River Valley, about ten miles on the other side of Folly Mountain. She loved Arabians. Her family had a stable of them, though her parents kept them for status more than pleasure."

"Are her parents still alive?"

"They'd be close to one hundred if they were. I never knew them because they disowned my mother when she married Charlie." Susan used the word *disowned* deliberately to see if it would provoke a reaction. She was not disappointed.

Jacob sat up so abruptly his wet hair slapped his face. "*Disowned* sounds bad. What does it mean?"

"It meant that they deliberately chose to no longer be her family. They decided to treat her as if she never existed." A familiar pain gripped Susan. "They had no contact with her, didn't go to her wedding or come out to the ranch when I was born. But it's not always a bad thing to sever contact with your family."

Choose the words carefully, she told herself. *Don't let your pain become his.*

"When families are so sick—I don't mean from infection, like Rayya and the filly—in how they think and live; or when they're so dysfunctional that how they treat their children hurts them, it's not a bad idea *not* to be part of that family."

She paused, listening for a change in his breathing. She heard nothing, reminding herself of his slow rate of respiration. When he finally drew breath, it was through his teeth. She had touched something in him.

"What didn't they like about Charlie?" Jacob asked.

"He was a cowboy. Little education, no social standing, and few social graces. Worlds apart from the life Vanessa had been raised in. He hated people like the Collinses—what he and his pals called the West Coast invasion—because they bought up the old-time ranches and built fences across the open land."

"Charlie's got fences."

"Only to keep his horses in. Outside the paddocks, you can ride clear across Robinson land without having to open a gate or jump a fence."

"If they were so different, how did he and Vanessa get together?"

"Vanessa's favorite horse, a chestnut Arabian named Teddy, got loose one day. Charlie found him and kept him for a week."

"Because he didn't know who Teddy belonged to?"

"No. Even then horses were marked with an identification code. Lift the upper lip of some horses—or if it's an Arabian, lift the mane—and you should see a number. To track the owner, all you need to do is contact the registration office. Charlie didn't do that right away because he thought someone hadn't cared for this horse, had allowed it to escape and cross a major two-lane road. Like you just did, by the way. Please don't do that again."

Jacob hung his head. "I won't."

"By the time Charlie got around to returning Teddy, he had fallen in love with the horse. He had ridden quarter horses all his life and thought Arabians were for rich snobs. But they're not—they have wonderful spirit, great endurance. Strong. Lively. So smart."

"You still love them," Jacob whispered.

"I respect the breed. Vanessa saw that Charlie was smitten with Teddy. And that he was very handsome. He had a lot more hair back then, the same color as mine."

"His eyes are the same as yours too. I like them."

"Thank you. My father was not tall, but he was strong, well built. He smelled like fresh air and saddle leather. And he was very direct. Vanessa was used to people who spoke in undercurrents and nuance." She paused, waiting for him to question what she had meant by *nuance.* That he didn't became something she'd need to think about.

"Their coming together was like an explosion." Susan bit her tongue. After congratulating herself on *nuance,* she'd used a horribly inappropriate word.

"It's okay," Jacob said. "You don't mean explosion where your skin burns. You mean sparks and colors and bright lights."

"How did you know what I meant?"

"You smiled. When you used the word *explosion* with all those people at the hospital, you looked like you were going to smack them."

"Not very professional of me."

"But nice. Because you were concerned about me. Thank you, Susan."

"You're welcome. But there's no reason to thank me—"

"Because you're only doing your job? If that were true, you would have left me at the hospital."

She held her breath, waiting for him to probe her motives further. Thankfully, he just lay back in the grass and fell asleep. Sparing her from telling any more of the sordid tale of the dashing cowboy, the spoiled rich girl, and the little child who got caught in the cross fire.

Doc Potter loaded the lethal injection and was ready to go.

Melissa would have none of it. She covered the filly with her own body.

Charlie bellowed to Jeanette from the front door of the barn. "Come talk sense into this stubborn girl of yours."

"Did you explain to her why this had to happen?" Jeanette asked both men. She hated to see Melissa so desperately stubborn and so irrationally hopeful.

Melissa shook her head. "Not yet, I'm begging you. Don't give up on her. It's too soon."

"Hold this, and for Pete's sake, don't stick yourself." Doc handed Charlie the syringe. He squatted next to Melissa. "The circumstances of her birth were unfortunate, Melissa. But this does happen, fillies and colts being born too damaged to function properly."

"She can learn."

"Look at her—she can't even stand."

"She will when she's stronger. But for now I hold her up." Melissa's eyes were defiant.

"Not long enough to keep fluid out of her lungs. Listen to the rasp of her breathing. If she can't move around, can't even nurse, she's going to die anyway."

"One more day. Please."

"Melissa, they don't want her to suffer," Jeanette said.

"The other horses need you," Charlie said, his voice gentle.

"Please. One more day. That's all I ask. Let me take care of her one more day."

"Hon, what's that going to accomplish?" Jeanette said.

"A miracle. You believe in them, right? You're always telling me to believe." Melissa got onto her knees in a prayerful pose. "In the sight of all you guys, I am asking God for a miracle. I'm telling you that I believe it, believe right here"—she put her hand to her heart—"that if we wait one more day, we'll see it."

"Melissa . . ." Jeanette touched her cheek. "This isn't the way faith works."

"Please, Ma. Please make them wait."

"One more day," Charlie said. "And then we've got to move on."

FIFTEEN

"JACOB MADE QUITE THE IMPRESSION," JOYCE FREEMAN SAID. "On a lot of people."

"I heard about it, trust me," Rick said. "But you know what? I had an eventful day too."

Joyce fed line to him from the ledge. "That so?"

Rock climbing was not Rick's notion of fun, but he wanted to look at some of the ridges above where the first body had been found. The state had sent its own experts to search the area, but with so much ground to cover, their going had been slow. Something in Rick's gut told him to keep looking. But the cliffs of Folly were devilish to navigate, even wearing a harness.

"I'm listening," Joyce said.

"Let me get up there." Rick's breath came hard as he half-climbed, half-crawled up the rugged slope. When he finally hoisted himself up over the top, Joyce had the courtesy not to laugh. He wiped his face with the bottom of his T-shirt, grateful these murders hadn't happened in August when the heat was brutal.

"Anytime, Sheriff."

"A guest missed checkout at the Grand."

"The Steamboat Grand?"

"Yep. Housekeeping had been trying to get in to clean the room, but it had the *Do not disturb* tag on the door. They reported it, the desk left a message, no one did anything. Same thing yesterday. But today's desk clerk remembered that this particular guest was from Kentucky. A Dr. Alexander Rodgers had bragged about being the vet for last season's Derby winner."

"Let me guess. Susan Stone hired him to play midwife for Charlie Robinson's mare."

"You got it. I called Charlie. With a string of colorful cursing, he told me he didn't know where Rodgers was and didn't care. That Susan had paid this guy a thousand bucks a day—"

Joyce whistled. "Maybe I'll switch to horses."

"Rodgers never showed up for the foaling. Jeanette got on the phone, said that Charlie had conveniently forgotten that RCR 102 was washed out that afternoon. So unless this guy knew enough to drive fifty miles out of his way to circle around, he couldn't have come out to Robinson's during that storm."

"Susan didn't report his absence?"

"She went missing as well. Since she's been back, all her attention is focused on Jacob. Charlie had Doc Potter come in to see to the mare. The foal apparently didn't fare well."

Joyce's eyes narrowed. "Are you thinking—"

"We got a missing person; we got a body. Logical conclusion to think it might be Rodgers. Anyway, the desk clerk called the manager. She opened the room up and let me in. No one in there, but the clothes, shaving kit, and all were still there. We called the guy's home in Kentucky. His wife said not only hasn't he come home, but he hasn't called in the last few days. She assumed he was tied up with a big emergency. Now she's beside herself with worry."

Joyce slugged back some water. "You got some hair, I hope?"

"Not just hair but nail clippings, the toothbrush, all sorts of good stuff. Steamboat cops got involved when they found out he could possibly be a victim of what they're calling The Torch."

Joyce spit out her water. "You have got to be kidding."

"Gallows humor. Don't act like you don't have the medical equivalent."

"Guilty as charged."

"A Steamboat cop drove the stuff down to the lab this morning. They're gonna rush the DNA through. With summer season coming up, everyone wants this settled."

"Amen to that," Joyce said. "But there's still no ID on the first body, right?"

"That DNA went through the federal clearinghouse. The guy wasn't a felon, though not all the states have signed on to that system yet." He leaned back and tried to enjoy the view. As always, the mountains dominated the scenery. The grassy plains promised summer while winter held tight on the snowy peaks.

"So what did you think of Jacob?" Rick said.

"He's a patient. I don't know how candid I can be."

"I don't care if he's got three gallbladders. What's your impression of him as a person?"

"You sound worried."

"Of course I'm worried. The valley has become bizarro world. And we're not talking about UFO sightings. We've got two french fries sitting in the state morgue."

"Enough with the gallows humor."

Rick rubbed his face. "Sorry. I should know better."

"Are you thinking that Jacob is somehow involved?"

"Don't let Susan Stone hear you say that."

"I won't. Trust me," Joyce said.

"Same time, same valley—how can they not be related?"

"Have you reported his . . . discovery . . . is that the right word?"

"I haven't called the CBI guys. Yet. If it's just a weird coincidence, then I could set back any progress Susan has made with him. So I've played it by the book. I had Lisa fill in all the forms, statewide and nationally. Quite a few agencies contacted the office, but when she e-mailed them his picture—which we withhold, you know—"

"Sure. Let the inquiring party give the description first."

"No hits. So we've got Charlie Robinson being thrown—"

"That doesn't fall in bizarro category. That's a stubborn old coot being old-cootish."

Rick laughed. "It's the horse that qualifies as weird. As Charlie put it, rather poetically, 'appearing out of the sunset, sky flaming at its bleeping back.'"

"He hasn't bothered to call the registration office yet to see who's missing a horse, I'll bet. Mr. Finders-Keepers."

"I'll have to get on him. So we've got one found horse, one missing vet, one young man unchained, and two bodies burned but we don't know how."

"Flash burn to the skin and to the trachea, esophagus, and lungs. Agent of burning unknown," Joyce said, quoting the autopsy report for the first victim. "Put all together, I don't like it."

"Put all together, I hate it," Rick said.

Sometimes when the wind blows, he imagines it is at his bidding. He enjoys the rush on his face, the scent of trepidation.

He watches the sheriff and the doctor from a distance, too far to see their faces. Yet he knows they look up to the hills for help. Brainwashed, but that's okay. Keep looking, suckers. He is right under their nose, but as long as their gaze is glued to the sky, they won't see him.

He feels a lecture coming on, decides to indulge himself.

Listen up, students. *Cue a tap on the podium.* These ones of no consequence are like an animal in a stall, fouling its own space. The groom comes in, hauls out the manure, throws it a little grain. Next day, the same thing happens. The dumb beast starts to think that its manure will always be hauled and its feed bucket always filled.

But one day the stupid animal breaks out of its stall. On its own, it becomes its own master. Chewing grass, dropping its waste wherever it wishes. No one is about to haul it away because there's no need. It's a big world, after all.

But it's not an endless world, students. Eventually, wherever the dumb beast wanders, it steps in its own manure. *Cue hand slap on podium.* Pay attention now.

The lovely thing about manure is that, in enough volume and given enough time to ripen, it becomes flammable.

All it takes is one spark.

SIXTEEN

MELISSA HADN'T MEANT THAT MIRACLE STUFF. NOT REALLY.

It just wasn't time to give up. The filly needed one more night of being wrapped in a heating blanket and cuddled. One more night to try to suck on the nipple Melissa had made out of a rubber glove. Jade liked the formula and licked her lips when she dribbled it into her mouth.

Night had fallen and with it, a chill. Jeanette had been out with a clean sweatshirt, hamburger and fries, and a hug. "I'll pray," she had whispered. "Maybe you'll get your miracle yet."

Melissa leaned against the wall, watching Jade's back rise and fall. What would the moment be like when the horse—this little baby— no longer took a breath?

Oh, Christopher.

All Susan's fault. But that wasn't true. It was really Melissa's fault for giving in to her. If only she had stayed strong, walked faster, some-how gotten out of Steamboat and back home to the valley. But it all played out again—that awful day last summer.

"If you love Christopher, really love him, you'll back away," Susan had said that day. "Let him finish college. He can do it, make some-thing fine of his life. He's a good man, a kind man, who will contribute to society."

"I know that," Melissa whispered.

"But if you burden him with a baby that isn't even his, you'll put too much pressure on him. He won't ever be the Christopher that you and I know he can be. He'll have to muck stables for twenty years because he doesn't have the skills or education to bring anything of substance to your marriage. A child deserves more than that."

"Christopher will be a wonderful father."

"When he's ready. When you're ready. I beg you, Melissa, do what's best for my son and the man you tell me you love. A quickie marriage won't benefit him, nor will it be what's best for you."

"Then what is?" Melissa pressed her hands to her head.

"This is America—you get to choose. But don't delay, I beg you. It's early enough to still terminate the pregnancy with little fuss."

"I'm no angel, but I don't believe in abortion."

"I don't like it, but there are some situations that call for it. This is one. Have the abortion, call the wedding off, and I promise you that I won't prevent Christopher from coming back out next summer."

"I don't know what to say."

"Say you'll do what's right. That's all I'm asking. Not what feels good, but what's right."

Melissa wanted Christopher with her whole heart, but maybe she was selfish. Wasn't love giving up what you wanted for the good of the one you loved?

"Okay," Melissa had whispered. "Okay."

"No!" Melissa cried, spooking Rayya across the way.

How long would the *if onlys* haunt her? The rest of her life.

She watched Jade taking one breath. Held her own breath until the filly took another. Like when her baby was born—*oh Christopher*. Watching her struggle for breath while all those people crowded around the little girl.

Melissa covered her face with her hand. *God, if I were allowed to ask for one miracle, it would be Christopher. Because all the rest would just be fine, if only Christopher had come back to me.*

If Christopher had not died on the sidewalk in Boston, he would have been with her when the baby got stuck in her pelvis. Somehow he would have coaxed that child out of her or prayed it out of her, and her little girl would not have been born with those horrible seizures.

God doesn't deal in *if onlys*, Jeanette liked to say.

But the biggest if only dug its claws into Melissa's heart and wouldn't let go. *If only, God. If only You were really there.*

The door opened. "Melissa?"

Jacob. Jeanette had told her what happened at the hospital.

"I'm in the second stall on the left. Close the door and come in. Don't turn the light on."

"Why not?"

"The filly needs the darkness to get her rest."

Jacob slipped into the stall. Melissa peered at him in the dim light. "Are you all right?"

"Sure."

"I bet Susan ripped those hospital guys a new eye socket."

"Huh? Oh, you mean she was angry. Yeah, man. She was ripping."

He was starting to sound like her. Good. Melissa didn't want him to pick up that snobby Massachusetts accent that Susan had grown into. On Christopher it had been cute. On his mother, it was like a silver dagger.

She shivered.

Jacob wrapped his arm around her and rubbed her shoulder. "Are you cold?"

"Just weirded out."

"By me?"

"No, no. Not you. I'm just tired."

"From babysitting the filly."

"Yeah."

"Charlie said she's going to die tomorrow. If she doesn't die tonight."

Melissa opened her mouth to protest, but the words just wouldn't come. This little horse was brain damaged; would never be right; would die in a few days anyway from some massive infection; she was cruel to prolong it; stupid stubbornness.

"Jeanette says you're waiting for a miracle and that if Charlie stopped his yapping, he might actually see one."

Melissa laughed. He squeezed her shoulder and kept her close.

"I asked her what a miracle was," Jacob said.

"What did she tell you?"

"She said to ask you."

Sweet old Jeanette—dumb as a fox. "A miracle is when we can't possibly do something ourselves, so God steps in and does it for us."

"Oh."

"Do you know who God is?"

He twisted away from her, locking his hands together between his knees. "Am I supposed to?"

Melissa smoothed his hair. Just like Susan does, she realized. "Ask Jeanette."

He nodded, eyes at the floor. Melissa kept fresh straw in this stall, and with the filly barely taking in nourishment, there was almost no urine or manure to deal with.

"Are you okay?" Melissa said.

He jerked his head up and locked his eyes on hers. "Are you?"

"I don't know."

"You're going to be here all night, like the other two nights?"

She nodded.

"I'll stay with you."

"Does Susan know you're out here?"

He laughed. "She's sound asleep in the chair by my bed. Did you know that she snores?"

Melissa laughed. "No way. Hey, listen. Don't let her make you do anything you don't want to."

"What do you mean?"

"Nothing. But if Susan makes you feel like . . . oh, I don't know. I'm tired, can't think straight."

He touched her hair, guiding her head to his shoulder. "Rest now, Melissa. I'll watch for your miracle."

Melissa snuggled into him. Rest was a good idea. If her miracle came, she wanted to be ready for it.

Susan woke to the sun on her face and Jacob missing.

She smoothed her shirt—she had slept in the chair yet again—and went looking for him. Dawn came early this time of year. It was just a little past five and, as Jeanette so aptly put it, Charlie wasn't a morning person.

Jacob was nowhere in the house.

Susan ran back upstairs, hand poised to knock on Charlie's bedroom door, when it opened.

Jeanette came out, fully dressed and ready for the day. "What's wrong?"

"Jacob's missing."

"He's probably still in the barn. He went out last night to see Melissa."

"And you let him? You saw what condition he was in last night—"

"Susie, he was fine."

Charlie hopped to the door. When the bottom of his splint clunked against the floor, he let out a stream of obscenities. "What's all the racket?"

"Nothing, Pop. I'm just looking for Jacob."

He looked at Jeanette. "You said he's out in the barn. What's he doing out there?"

"Melissa was out there, tending the filly. He went to check on her."

A few minutes later, Susan and Jeanette wheeled Charlie out to the barn. The mountains to the east were framed by a golden glow, and the birds were raucous in the trees. In the main paddock, the dude horses lazily nibbled grass. Prince Sarraf stood like a statue in the open pasture, the rising sun stippling his neck with gold.

Jeanette tugged on the door. "It was cold last night. Melissa must have closed it tight."

Inside, the air was still and the silence profound.

"Look," Jeanette said.

Melissa slept in an empty stall on a bed of straw. She was covered by the heating blanket she had used for the filly.

"Where's Jacob?" Susan said.

"Where's the filly? Rayya's gone, too." Charlie said. "Melissa!"

She jolted out of sleep. "What? Where's Jade?"

Charlie pushed out of the wheelchair and hopped for the back of the barn. "If he hurt my mare, I swear—"

Melissa opened one stall after another, looking for the filly.

Heart pounding, Susan wrapped her arm around Charlie's waist and helped him along. "Don't put any weight on your foot, Pop."

"I'll kill him with my bare hands," Charlie hissed.

"Stop it," Jeanette said. "Just stop that ugly talk."

A horse whinnied from outside. Melissa ran into Rayya's stall, pushed open the thru-door that led to the paddock Charlie had fenced for the mare.

When they saw what Jacob had done, they were all speechless.

Jeanette fell to her knees and covered her face. Charlie's mouth hung open. He staggered against Susan for support.

Melissa whispered over and over, "I can't believe this, I can't believe this . . ."

What is happening to us, Susan thought, her hands pressed to her heart.

Jacob patted Rayya's side as she stood in a patch of sunlight. The mare looked at them with gleaming eyes, then bent her head to her nursing daughter.

The filly let go of the teat and looked around. She tottered toward them as if to say: *You asked for a miracle, and here I am.*

SEVENTEEN

"Okay, buddy. What's the joke?" Tanyon Stern, a good friend and CBI technician, did not sound amused.

Rick munched on a tuna sandwich as he drove. "What're you talking about?"

The crackling from the speakerphone punctuated the thump of his tires on RCR 47. Zach Hurley followed him in his own car. They were heading out to Robinson Ranch, facing an encounter that was guaranteed not to be pleasant.

"These fingerprints. Late April Fool's joke?" Tanyon was an old friend from the Marine Corps, now based in Denver with the state police labs.

"You talking about the John Doe I submitted?"

"Dem's de ones, pal. What's the story?"

"Guy with alleged amnesia. What's the beef?"

"You got me. Though I don't know how you pulled this off."

"I have no idea what you're talking about."

"On your honor?"

"Tanyon—"

"Okay, okay. These images you sent are totally bogus. I don't even know how to describe what I'm seeing. Hold on—you got the onboard handy?"

"Booted up."

"Can you get online?"

"Hold on." Rick pulled the cruiser onto the shoulder. Zach pulled in behind him. Rick stretched his arm out the window, gesturing "one minute" to Zach. He flipped up the screen on the laptop, tapped a few keys. They had shortwave communication and special software for accessing key databases, but wireless reception was sketchy out in the hills. After a couple of "no service" messages, the 'Net came up. "I got it."

"I just e-mailed the file. Check it out."

Rick accessed his e-mail and downloaded the file. "It's coming, but it'll take a few minutes. Big file."

"Slow processor."

"We county studs don't get the toys you spoiled little girls get."

"Wah, wah."

Rick laughed. Their standard joke was that CBI got all the funds but the county guys got all the fun.

"While we're sitting here counting our nose hairs, let me tell you my beef with your John Doe. The state database kept giving me an 'unrecognizable image' message."

"So it didn't match it."

"Duh, Ricardo, no wonder you're still a car jockey."

"I wouldn't squeeze into a cubicle for a million bucks."

"So anyway, I eyeballed your file. Looked like fingerprints, but the swirls seemed thick. Just enough width to set the computer's nose out of joint. I enlarged the right thumb until I could see what contributed to the thickness."

"So what did?" Rick said.

"I ain't sayin', bud. This you gotta see."

The laptop binged. "Okay, it's downloaded." Rick double-clicked. As the image filled the screen, he let out a low whistle. "What the heck is this?"

"What do you think?"

"I haven't got a clue."

"Enlarge it even more. You probably don't have the resolution on the onboard that I do here in the office."

Rick zoomed the image up to 200 percent. Each line was composed of a series of what looked like letters, until he went to 300 zoom. "What is this, Chinese?"

"According to the biggest brains this side of the moon, these don't belong to any known language."

"This is just nuts," Rick said.

"My conclusion, but I can't write that in the report. In fact, this conversation is so far off the record, it may as well be in China."

"Best guess?"

Tanyon laughed. "An alien. How cool would that be? But honestly? It's probably some bizarre computer glitch. You know when your printer goes haywire and starts printing lines of letters and unrecognizable geek characters? Maybe your scanner burped. Or the Internet passed gas and didn't say excuse me. All I can think of is that one of the processors that handled the data misread what should be solid lines as sequences of these weird characters. Needless to say, I ain't forwarding this to the Feds."

"Thank you. Those suits would have both our heads. So listen, pal. I've still got the paper prints. I could mail them down to you."

"I got a better idea. We're trying out this sweet little device that scans prints and Wi-Fi's them directly to the various state and federal databases. Saves days of shuffling paper. No ink, no mess. You just put the subject's finger on the glass and push a button. If you promise not to let it out of your hands—the guys who developed it are jumping down my back about the competition—I'll ship it up to you."

"Sure."

"Better yet, maybe I'll drive it up. I could chew through this mess on my desk by four or so, leave then. Wanna take me out to see your John Doe?"

"Hm. That might not be a good idea."

"Come on, Ricardo. If he turns out to be a real alien, I want dibs."

"Okay, as long as we're in and out. Hold on, I'll e-mail you the directions."

"What's he like?"

"He seems to be a good kid."

"Whatcha don't know can't hurt you, hey?" Tanyon laughed and clicked off.

Rick stared at the image on his laptop. *What you don't know can't hurt you.*

Maybe. Or maybe not.

Twenty-four hours ago Charlie had declared a death sentence on the filly. Now Jade frolicked while Rayya grazed nearby, tail swishing. Doc Potter had been out early and declared both mother and foal perfectly healthy. "This is a surprise," he had said.

"This is a miracle," Jeanette had countered.

Melissa wasn't sure what it was, but she'd take it.

"Melissa," Jacob said. They sat under a tree, watching Jade play.

"What."

"Your face is turning red."

"Oh. I'd better move out of the sun."

"You are out of the sun." Jacob pointed overhead where a sturdy bough sheltered them.

She shrugged and he shrugged with her, almost in perfect unison. She slapped at him and he rolled away, laughing. The filly tried to join the fun, falling on her nose and getting right up.

Something bounced off Melissa's arm. Jacob was tossing pebbles.

"You don't wanna start that," she warned. "I could—"

"Take your head off," he said in perfect sync with her.

"You're starting to scare me, Jacob."

His face fell. "I don't mean to."

"It's a joke."

"Oh. So do you think it was a miracle?"

"I don't know."

"Is it the hole that keeps you from knowing?" He picked at his fingernails.

"What hole?"

Jacob pressed his finger to his chest, right over his heart.

"That's none of your business." She tried to look away, but somehow he kept her gaze.

"Maybe if you tell me about it, that hole will go away."

"Maybe I don't want it to."

"Why wouldn't you?"

"Because maybe it's all I've got left."

"Of what?"

The snow on the peaks had taken on a sheen, melting by day and freezing to a shiny crust by night. Most of it would finally melt, just in time for the snow to start all over again up there.

Jacob pressed his hand against her back. "Of Christopher?"

"You don't know what you're talking about."

"Why doesn't anyone talk about him? He was Susan's son, Charlie's grandson, and your . . ."

"My what?"

"I don't know. You have to tell me, Melissa."

"Have you ever been in love, Jacob?" She locked her gaze on his eyes now, determined to see if he would squirm under the same cross-examination he laid on her.

"I don't know."

"When you can answer that question, then I'll answer yours. Until then, we talk about horses or we don't talk at all."

"Get out of this house. Now!"

Jeanette held Susan back from shoving Rick and Zach Hurley out the door.

Susan whipped around to her father. "Will you do something? It's your house. Show some backbone and tell them to get out."

Charlie looked to Jeanette. "You got any notion of what she's yelling about?"

"Go ahead, Pop. Look around a problem instead of at it," Susan snapped.

"Sheriff, can you explain what's going on?" Jeanette asked.

Rick's face was flushed. Zach Hurley's betrayed no emotion.

"You're the social worker, Zach. Perhaps you can explain this"— Susan waved the document Rick had given her—"in such a way that I have some inkling of why anyone would do something so absurd and so stupid. So cruel."

"What is that thing she's waving around?" Charlie said.

"It's a petition for removal," Zach said. "The hospital filed it. They want the court to appoint a guardian for Jacob, take him away from Susan."

Susan wrapped her arms around her waist to keep from shoving the order down Zach's throat.

"Why would they want that?" Jeanette asked.

"Because Susan took him out of there yesterday before they could finish their exam. Endangering his well-being, according to them," Zach said.

"After their faulty equipment and incompetent staff almost electrocuted him. Twice." Susan turned to Rick. "Don't you get it? This is a preemptive strike against a lawsuit."

"George Brennan said they're concerned for his health after the incident," Rick said. "They can't confirm his well-being because you took him out against their advice. Since you're not Jacob's legal guardian, their attorney argues you had no right to do that."

"That is patently absurd. I wasn't about to let them put one more hand on him. Did you see the photos we took of those burns? It was a miracle that he didn't suffer worse."

Zach stepped toward her. "Look, Susan—"

"Dr. Stone. See it right here, Mr. Hurley?" She pounded the paper with her fist. "I am Dr. Stone, and you're the authority I'm supposed to surrender Jacob to. Well, that is not going to happen, Mr. Social-Worker-Pawn of the hospital. Not going to happen."

His mouth tightened. "I'm here simply to evaluate what's best for Jacob."

"Isn't that clear? He's safe here, he's healthy—"

"Are you sure of that? They never completed the CAT scan," Rick said.

Susan ignored him. "—and not only is he in the care of a solid family, but he's under my care. Who north of Denver would be more qualified to treat him than I am?"

Rick glanced at Zach. "You've got the call here."

"Dr. Stone, I'm being pressured by my supervisor to take Jacob to one of our group homes."

"Absolutely not. That would be one of the worst environments for someone in his vulnerable condition. Not to mention, I'm certain he's older than eighteen. Possibly even older than twenty-one."

"But unless you can prove that, I don't have much to justify allowing him to stay here."

"What about what he wants? Doesn't that count for something?" Susan said.

"Not if he's incompetent."

"Prove it."

"I could ask you to prove that a young man who doesn't know his name or anything else about himself is competent to choose anything for himself." Zach took off his glasses, cleaned them on his shirt. "That said, I could get the state to stay this order under one condition."

"What?" Susan mentally cringed at the eagerness in her tone.

"We'll all help. Whatever Jacob needs." Charlie surprised Susan by patting her hand.

Zach slid his glasses back on. "If you would agree to give him active therapy, Susan."

"I've been doing that informally," Susan said.

"But now you would have to do it formally. My supervisor will insist that I observe the sessions."

"No. A third party violates the sanctity of the therapist-patient relationship."

"Whether you like it or not, he's my client too," Zach said. "I'm not thrilled with the idea of adding hours to my workload, but I know that this is the only way to keep the court off our back."

Our *back. He wants me to think he's aligning with us*, Susan thought. "Fine. We can work something out."

"Excellent." Zach took an appointment book out of his backpack. "Shall we start tomorrow? Say ten in the morning."

"Sure."

"Would you like to use my office?"

"That would not be wise. I hate to add to your burden, Zach. But someone who suffers from traumatic amnesia needs the most familiar surroundings possible. Jacob responded very poorly to the hospital, doesn't like closed spaces. This would be best done out here."

"Great." Zach forced a smile. "It's all set then."

"Hold it one doggone minute," Charlie said. "Isn't anyone going to ask Jacob what he wants?"

"Maybe your friend got lost," Susan said.

She and Rick leaned on the fence, watching Jacob lead one of the dude horses around the paddock. Melissa stood nearby with Charlie, talking over each other with instructions. To Rick, it looked as if Jacob didn't need any. He seemed as comfortable with horses as he did with people.

"I e-mailed directions. The ranch is in the boonies, but not particularly hard to find."

"Traffic coming up the interstate?"

"I checked." Rick glanced again at the long dirt road that went out to 102. No cloud of dust that would indicate a car was on its way. He checked his beeper, even though it was set to audible. No page, nor had Lisa heard from Tanyon at the office. Maybe he had gotten called out on some emergency of his own. Driving up to Harken hardly qualified as a priority.

He said a quick prayer for Tanyon and added one for Susan. Her eyes hadn't left Jacob as they watched him work. It was no stretch to consider that the mysterious young man had filled the void so tragically left by Christopher Stone's death. As pigheaded as her old man, she'd deny it, of course.

He cleared his throat, mustering the guts to speak his mind. "I'm sorry that this has upset you so much. I'm not your enemy on this."

"I know." She surprised him by leaning against his arm. Watching the horses had calmed her.

"The other night, I didn't mean to imply—"

She stiffened. "Yes. You did."

He put his face to her hair. She still smelled like she always had. Fresh air and a subtle, exotic scent. "Was I right, Suse?"

She slid her arm around his waist. "If I had to swear on that stack of Jeanette's Bibles, I still wouldn't know how to answer you. Some of that time, I felt so right—like being in the mountains and being on a horse was all I needed to live. I had forgotten how that felt, and it rushed back to me. Other times I was like the horse, not caring where I was going as long as no one got in my way. Ricky, there was a moment up there, maybe longer, when I thought I'd just leave myself up there. That all I had left to lose was myself, and I might as well get on with that."

"If you ever—*ever*—feel like that again, you holler. And I'll come running. Even to Massachusetts or anywhere."

"You can't be sheriff of the whole world." She squeezed his side, signaling an end to the discussion. Yet she stayed in the circle of his arm, holding on to him.

Rick rested his chin on her head. "I couldn't do this way back when."

"You grew."

"So did you."

"No, I didn't. I just ran away." She looked up at him. "Rick, that's what Jacob has done. He doesn't realize it, but that's better than any clinical definition of amnesia. The mind can't bear something, so it just runs and hides."

"Do you think it was something really bad?" Rick kept his tone even, with no hint of accusation.

Susan backed away. "How can you even ask that? He was chained in a cave!"

"You're absolutely right. I'm sorry if I sounded as if I had forgotten." He gave her a level look, relieved when she turned her eyes back to Jacob.

The young man had been chained in a cave. The question was: had he done it himself?

EIGHTEEN

"RATHER THAN TELLING ME WHAT'S FAMILIAR, WHY DON'T YOU point things out that you *don't* recognize. Or things you didn't recognize before coming to stay with us," Susan said.

"I didn't know what the television was until Charlie showed me. I still don't know what that thing is there—" He pointed to the DVD player.

Zach whispered, "Should we explain things as we go along?"

Susan shook her head. "This exercise will develop a baseline for Jacob's orientation to his everyday environment. We don't want to distract him or indirectly prompt him."

They had been through the kitchen and living room and were now in the family room. In one sense, this exercise also provided a new baseline for Susan's experience. Jeanette had almost completely redecorated the house. Though it wasn't her taste, Susan enjoyed the homey touches, from the brushed velour chairs of the living room to the border of daisies that brightened the yellow walls of the kitchen.

Mother would have disapproved heartily of the drapes from Macy's and the furniture from Sears. She had made Robinson Ranch stylish enough to be featured in several horse magazines and the Denver *Tribune's* Sunday home section, decorating in leather and chrome and glass—an odd fit for a graceful but traditional farmhouse. The stark surroundings of her childhood were just another reason for Susan to spend most of her time in the barn.

Jacob picked up the remote. "Charlie can't live without this," he said, quoting Jeanette's nightly refrain.

He recognized the woodstove, demonstrating how to open the flue and how to feed the fire. The computer and printer that Susan had bought for Charlie—and he had never used—were mysteries to Jacob.

He correctly identified a vase as pewter. When he found Susan's baby cup in the curio cabinet, he not only knew it was silver but spoke at length about the difference between silver and pewter.

Susan itched to ask him how he knew this. Was he an artist, a materials engineer, a machinist?

Jacob had moved on to Jeanette's collection of ceramic horses. "I've been wondering—are these toys?"

"No."

"Why would Jeanette have these?"

"She enjoys collecting them."

"Like Charlie collects real horses?"

Susan laughed. "I think that's enough for inside the house. You've done a great job, Jacob."

"Oh. Okay. I'm happy if you are."

Susan noted that comment. *A blank slate? Imprinting? Or desire to please?*

"Let's go outside. I don't think you've been to the toolshed yet," she said.

"No, but Charlie's always threatening to send me there." He stared straight-faced for a moment, then burst out laughing. "It's a joke. Get it?"

Zach clapped him on the back. "Good one, man. You had us going for a minute."

Jacob pumped his fist. "Yes."

Melissa's influence. But what did Susan expect? Of course he would gravitate to someone closer to his age. Charlie was old enough to be his grandfather; she was old enough to be his mother—and that was a topic of concern.

Others realized that as well. She'd seen the looks Jeanette gave her. Rick Sanchez too. He probably didn't know the term *transference*, but he had made it clear he thought Susan was becoming too involved. But what did they expect her to do? Ignore Jacob when he needed her most, just because she had a gaping wound in her own psyche? Susan understood the emotional risks, and she dealt with them. Let them clean their own house before they started sweeping out hers, or however that Bible verse went.

The toolshed was dusty and dim. Jacob's eyes lit up at the tools scattered about. "I know all this stuff. That's an axe, that's a hatchet. And I know the difference."

Susan noted his enthusiasm. Zach peered over her shoulder, a shadow that was always at her heels.

"This is for breaking up things. Like walls." Jacob slung the sledgehammer over his shoulder, as if he meant to tromp out with it.

He went on to identify a plane, various files and screwdrivers, even an adze. But the power tools were a mystery to him. *As if the twentieth century had never happened,* Susan thought.

He put down the sledgehammer so he could dig something out of a box. "This is an auger. What does Charlie use this for?"

"Have you seen the pond in the far pasture?" Susan asked.

Jacob nodded.

"In the winter Charlie used it to drill through the ice to make sure it was thick enough for my friends and me to skate on."

It came on Susan in a rush—cold air on her face, the *slick slick* of skates digging into the ice, the *pop* of the hockey puck, all the kids laughing as big Ricky Sanchez went down hard on his backside. She had misplaced this good memory just as she had forgotten the wonder of riding bareback, the pride of climbing Folly, the joy of looking into the wind.

Somehow only the bad memories had stuck with her. Was it the same for Jacob? Did he have horrid recollections that clung like burrs, so the only way to get them off was to put them somewhere far away?

Jacob held the auger with both hands at the level of his face, like a priest making an offering. His hands began to shake. "I don't like this auger, Susan."

Zach gave her a meaningful look, as if to cue her that Jacob's tremors were significant. Idiot. Of course she knew that. But to probe Jacob's reaction now might inadvertently contaminate this process.

"Why don't you put that away? We can look at some of the tools in the barn," Susan said.

"No. I've seen enough." Without looking, he whipped the auger behind him, a perfect shot back into the box.

Jacob walked out of the shed with his arms extended over his head, twisting his hands as if he were washing them in the morning sunlight.

The auger is a delightful touch. Perfect, really. He would sigh with satisfaction, but he must not give away his hiding place. The shadows are an absolute necessity, at least for now. When these people are gone, perhaps he can return for the auger, study it, cherish it, *plan* with it.

It is a helpful tool, used to ensure safe play. One churns through the ice until the water bubbles up. Simple really.

Like his auger, that word of doubt, that glimmer of temptation, that breeze of lust that churns through the thing of no consequence, promising safe play. But in the end, the soul bubbles up, the blood bubbles out, and once again, he skates away scot-free.

Perfect, really.

Burning.

People. Cars. Anger. Not just anger—absolute fury. Rick should pray, ask for the balm of the Spirit, for wisdom and discernment. But he owed it to Tanyon *not* to dampen this flaming in his gut.

He had been driving his regular route, eyes on the road and phone to his ear when he found out. Rick had wanted to check in with Tanyon, see if perhaps they had gotten their wires crossed yesterday. He still wasn't picking up his work extension. Perhaps he had taken sick, so Rick's next move had been to call the Stern home.

A man had answered—not Tanyon. The phone call played in Rick's memory in a continuous spool.

"May I speak to Tanyon?"

Silence.

"Hello?" Rick said.

"Who's calling, please."

"Sheriff Sanchez from Routt County."

"Oh. We met at Jillian's graduation last year. This is Stephanie's father."

Tanyon's father-in-law. "Sure. How are you, Mr. Leblanc? Is Stephanie okay? I haven't been able to get in touch with Tanyon."

"He . . . he . . ." Leblanc sobbed once and fell silent.

Rick felt like the floor had dropped out, leaving him in free fall. He pulled the cruiser over. "Mr. Leblanc, has something happened?"

"Was it you that Tanyon was coming to see yesterday?"

"Yes. What happened?"

"His car skidded, flipped, and—he didn't survive." More sobbing. "I'm sorry, Sheriff. I've got to . . . my daughter needs . . ."

"Of course. Give her my love, tell her if there's anything I can do—" Rick said, but Leblanc had already clicked off.

After he composed himself, Rick called Todd Stanley, the accident specialist who covered this part of Colorado.

"I knew him, too, Rick. This stinks, losing a good guy like Stern. When the scumbags walk away from crashes all the time."

"What happened?"

"You know that hairpin coming off the Rabbit Ears? All it took was a little water trickling across the road and a shadow deep enough to drop the temperature in one spot to freezing. Stern's SUV hit glaze ice, skidded, and flipped."

Rick struggled to understand. "Didn't he wear his seat belt? And the air bags—"

"Seat belts and air bags don't do any good in a fire."

"Oh, no. No . . ."

"I'm sorry, Rick. The SUV went up like that. All we can hope for is that Stern was unconscious when it all happened. I hear the people down in Steamboat saw the fireball. The nutcases came out of their holes, calling in everything from meteors to alien invasion. I tell you, Sheriff, this job can turn your stomach."

Hard to even breathe, impossible to speak. Sorrow, shifting to fury.

"Sheriff? You okay?"

"No. But yes, I have to be. I gotta go for now. I'll be back in touch." Rick clicked off, took a deep breath, and resumed driving.

Without intending to, he turned onto 102. He told himself he was just making his rounds, but when he passed the turnoff to Robinson Ranch, he hit the brakes and turned in. Melissa's trailer looked empty. She had been sleeping on a cot outside the filly's stall. After a half mile, the barn came into view. He pulled the cruiser to a sharp stop up near the house and got out.

Susan was on the porch, deep in discussion with Zach Hurley. Neither one bothered to look at who had come into the yard.

Jacob leaned on the fence, watching the horses. Rick walked over to him, trying to swallow back his anger.

"Hi, Sheriff," Jacob said.

"How're those burns today?"

"Burns? Oh, you mean from the hospital? All gone. I'm fine."

"Really? I'm glad to hear that. So did you and Susan do some work today?"

"I worked with Melissa today, shoveling manure. That job is never done." Jacob paused, waiting for a laugh. When Rick did not oblige him, he leaned his arms on the top of the fence and stared blandly into the paddock.

"I was referring to some testing that Susan was going to do. I assume that's why Zach is here."

"Oh. That."

Rick glanced back at the house. Susan had caught sight of him. He'd have to hurry it up. "And what did you learn?"

Jacob squinted. "That I know what an auger is."

Rick stepped closer, leaning on the fence to block Jacob from Susan's line of sight. "Do you remember anything yet?"

He shook his head.

"You still don't know your name then?"

He shrugged.

Rick leaned in. "Or where you're from?"

Jacob tried to back away, but Rick trapped him with his arm. "Or why you were chained in that cave?"

"Sheriff, I'm sorry. I don't—"

"You don't what? You don't know? Or you don't want to tell?" Rick lowered his voice. "Is it because who you are—or what you've done— is something you don't want anyone to know about?"

"No. I just don't know. I hope I didn't do anything bad."

"But you don't know that for sure. Do you, Jacob?"

He stared, wide-eyed. Rick dug his fingers into Jacob's shoulders. "Do you?"

He shook his head.

Rick pushed closer until they were almost nose to nose. "Why were you down in that ravine? Was it because you were hiding? Because you didn't want anyone to find you?"

"No, I don't think so. No, no."

"Because you didn't want *me* to find you?"

"I'm glad you found me, Rick."

"You're glad Susan found you. Because you can manipulate her every which way. She's got a lot of money. Is that what this is about? Getting her money? Or are you just getting your kicks?"

"I don't know what you're talking about." Jacob's breath came in fevered bursts. "I don't know."

"And you expect me to believe you when people are dying in this valley, being burned like a—"

Someone yanked Rick's shoulders.

"Stop it!" Susan got between him and Jacob. "What do you think you are doing?"

He stared at her, his face set like flint. "My job. And it's about time you stopped pussyfooting around and did yours too."

NINETEEN

"Rick didn't mean anything by it," Jeanette said.

"He had his hands on Jacob's shoulders and was about ten seconds away from throttling him." Susan put a cup of tea in front of Jeanette. "He meant something, all right."

"Don't judge him so harshly. He's stretched too far. These two murders and now his friend dying. That's all it was."

"You're not going to change my mind. We need to take legal action to protect Jacob's interests. Are you with me on this, Jeanette?"

"Yes. Of course. Charlie and I will do whatever you ask. But please, don't make Rick out to be your enemy. He's a good man."

"Why? Because he goes to your church? Is that what it takes to qualify someone as good?" Susan's voice was mild, but her fingers tapped mercilessly on her mug.

"No. I say that because he has made his heart right with God."

"Sorry, but that stuff doesn't work for me." She stared into her coffee.

Jeanette tipped her head under Susan's stare, trying to catch her eye. "Why not, hon?"

"For goodness' sake. I'm a scientist."

"Scientists can be believers."

"Anyone can believe in anything. I see it every day in my practice. People latch on to whatever quick-fix solution they think will make them happy. The more emotional energy they invest in their beliefs, the more rock solid those beliefs become. The heartbreak comes when they discover that wishing something was true doesn't make it true."

Jeanette laughed. "Susie, I'm about as down-home as you can get. But I'm telling you here and now that I don't just believe—I *know* God exists."

Susan gave her a weak smile. "I'm happy for you. Truly. But what works for you won't work for me."

"Why not give it a try? Maybe try a little prayer now and—"

"You think I haven't?"

"Hon, I know you must have. But maybe—"

"I can't. Life is futile enough."

Jeanette's stomach knotted. "What if I told you prayer can bring you true peace?"

"So can Valium." Susan pushed away from the table. "Thanks for the coffee."

Jeanette followed her into the hall. "Real peace. Real hope. If you could hear about some of the answers to prayer I've gotten . . ."

"You don't want to hear about the answers to prayer I *haven't* gotten."

Jeanette grasped her hands. Susan's skin was cold, and even the muscles in her fingers knotted. "I do."

"Fine. Where do I start? How about the one I prayed every day until I was fourteen? That my father who swore he loved me more than anything in the world would take me away from my irrational and narcissistic mother? That was my standby. But every day—sometimes every moment, Jeanette—there was a string of little ones. *Please, let this be her good day, God. And if it's not a good day, please let me get out of this house before she sees me.*"

Jeanette's blood went cold. Charlie had never said anything about this. "Did Vanessa abuse you?"

"Abuse? Physically? Not in the legal sense. But in every other respect of the word? With great consistency and dedication."

"Oh, baby." Jeanette rubbed Susan's hands, closing them in her own, wishing she had been in this place forty years ago.

"One time in third grade, I was all set to go to school when she came into my room. Took one look at me. *Not like that, you don't, Susan Pauline Robinson.* She made me undress and try on every item of clothing in my closet. *Not good enough,* she said. We got to the end of everything I owned, so she made me do it all over again, this time inside out. Finally she had this great revelation. *It's not the clothes, Susan. It's you. You slouch, your hair is too dark, your skin is too pale, it adds up to a very unpleasant package.* She collapsed in tears, and I thought I could escape. But she caught me and said, *I think I've got the solution.* She made me go through the whole dressing-undressing thing again, except in reverse order. I ended up going to school—four hours late—in the same clothes I started in."

"Oh, Susie."

"There were lots of variations on that day. I'd pray for her to just leave me alone, but she was right there, telling me *It's not right, Susan; stand up straight, Susan; you smell like the barn, Susan; your homework wasn't done right, Susan.*

"The day I started my period—I was young, just a bit over eleven— I tried to hide it, but she found out. And she got fixated on getting me clean. *You're a woman now. You must learn to take care of yourself, Susan.* She browbeat me until I got into the tub, where she almost scalded me with too-hot water. I screamed, so she put on the cold and wouldn't add hot. She wouldn't let me out of the bathtub until Charlie came home that night. Each time I tried to get out, she threatened me with her riding crop. I sat in cold water all day and half the night.

"I told my father when he got home, but she had already made up a story. Said I had been out too long with Ricky and wet my pants, and I was blaming her to cover my own stupidity. That day I prayed for her to let me out of the tub, prayed for Charlie to get home, prayed for her to die, prayed that I would die.

"But nothing changed except I got smarter about keeping out of her way. Are you aware that she sabotaged my applications to Princeton and Dartmouth? Stupid me—I had put the recommendations from my chemistry and biology teachers in the front of Charlie's truck so he could mail them for me. She found them, steamed open the envelopes, and forged new ones. It wasn't until I was finishing Harvard that I did the detective work. It didn't make sense that I could get into Harvard but not the other two. I had a classmate pretend to be a lawyer and threaten a lawsuit if the schools wouldn't release copies of all my recommendations. I recognized her handwriting as one teacher and her phrasing in the typewritten one."

"Why would she do that to you?" Jeanette was short of breath, trying to keep from either screaming with fury or bawling with sadness.

"She tried to go Ivy, but couldn't cut it. Bad grades, bad attitude. She had to settle for some little junior college in California that cost a fortune but had little content. She loved to put on airs, but my father, who barely finished high school, was far more educated than she."

"Susie, I'm so sorry. I can't believe your father didn't know."

Susan's stare was icy. "He did know."

"He couldn't have."

"Trust me, he knew."

"I can't . . ." Jeanette wanted to find Charlie and shake him. "What did he do then?"

"He turned the other cheek. Like a good Christian, right, Jeanette?

Don't rock the boat, don't make a scene, don't risk losing your horses and barn and wife's trust fund—just turn the other cheek. Oops, except it was *my* cheek he turned. For years and years, I prayed for God to help me, to make her go away or to die or for my father to divorce her so he and I could get away."

"I'm sorry, Susie," Jeanette whispered. "Oh baby, I'm so sorry."

"I'd tell him, but he'd just mutter that I needed to not get in her way, that I was overreacting or I'd deliberately provoked her. *Be a good girl, Susie, and we'll all just get along.* It was all about the horses, you know. Her horses that he fell in love with; her trust fund that bought more and more horses until we had to add on to the barn. The crazier she got, the more horses Charlie bought. Took a lot of time to take care of all those horses. And it was the one thing Mother approved of. The irony was that I loved the horses as much as either of them. But know what?"

Jeanette put her hand to her throat, unable to answer.

"I had to stable my horses at Camaras' because I didn't trust her not to hurt them."

Say something, anything, old woman. "Rick was a good friend to you then, wasn't he?"

"The best. Not good enough for her, though. She was supposed to be so well-bred, but when we were out in the barn or playing in the yard, she'd get close to his ear and call him *spic* and *wetback*. Told him he'd be lucky if he rose high enough to be her gardener. When I confronted her about it, she said *Oh, isn't that like his kind, to spread lies like that. He wants you to feel sorry for him, give him a handout.* Why he stuck it out to be my friend, I don't know even to this day."

"We're back where we started," Jeanette said. "Rick Sanchez is a good man."

Susan paced the hall, hands clenched and crossed over her chest. "Know why we rode up Folly all the time? Because—for all her precious Arabians and horse shows and big plans, she wasn't a good enough rider to get up there. Ricky wasn't either, but . . ." She pressed her fists into her eyes. "He did it, for my sake."

Jeanette wrapped her in a hug. "Baby, I am so sorry. No one should have to go through that."

"Your God let it happen. So He's either very absent or very incompetent or—" Susan's voice broke. "Very cruel."

Melissa had saddled the least spirited of the dude horses for Jacob, but she hadn't needed to bother. In Charlie's words, Jacob rode like he was born with the big wide sky over 'em and his favorite horse under 'em.

"Where you taking him?" Charlie had wanted to know.

"I haven't been to see the Camaras since your accident. I thought he'd enjoy the visit."

"Tell 'em I'll be by when I can." He waved them off.

"Who are the Camaras?" Jacob asked.

"Friends. They live on the next ranch, though that's almost a mile north of here. Sometimes I babysit for them."

"You mean you watch their baby?"

"Yep. She was born on Valentine's Day. Her name is Krista."

He fell silent, his brow one big wrinkle.

"What's the matter?" she asked.

"What if I have a baby somewhere? Or a couple of kids and a wife? Like some of the people I met at the hospital."

Melissa clucked her horse to a stop. "Jacob, don't you think you'd know? I mean, you can forget a lot of stuff, but not a kid who comes from your body."

"You mean a kid who comes from *your* body."

She flushed. "What? What do you mean by that?"

"Nothing. Just that it's the woman who carries the baby, that's all."

"Okay. Sure. But I still think you'd know."

He blinked hard. She was about to ask him if the sun was bothering his eyes when she realized he was trying to hold back tears. Melissa should tell Susan that this talk about babies had hit a nerve with him. But she wouldn't—no way. The less said to that woman, the better.

They pulled into the Camaras' yard a short while later. Don was out by the barn, digging a hole. Melissa introduced Jacob.

"Nice to meet you. I'd shake hands but . . ." Don held up muddy palms. Only then did Melissa notice the blanket-covered lump near the hole.

"What's that?"

"Blasted coyotes took down one of my lambs. Usually the dog drives them away but . . ." Don wiped his forehead with his sleeve.

"Why didn't the dog drive them away?" Jacob said.

"Shush," Melissa hissed.

"No, it's okay. I'll practice telling you because I haven't told Sara yet. The coyotes tore apart my sheepdog."

"Oh, I am so sorry," Melissa said.

Don noticed Jacob's wide-eyed stare. "I take it you're not from around here."

"Not really."

"Where do you hail from?"

Jacob glanced at Melissa, then answered. "Here and there."

"You in school? Or do you work for a living like the rest of us poor slobs?"

Melissa hadn't anticipated that Jacob would be subjected to polite questions. He bailed himself out.

"I'm helping Charlie for a while. Until his foot is all better."

"Glad to hear it. That old dude isn't as tough as he likes to pretend."

"Is the baby awake? I missed seeing her this week, what with Charlie's accident and all."

"And we missed our Saturday night at the bowling alley. Sara needed the practice."

"Sara?" Melissa laughed. "I'll be sure to tell her you said that."

"Oops. Busted."

"I should be able to do this weekend."

Don looked at Jacob. "What about you? Can you change diapers?"

Jacob wrinkled his nose. "I sure hope not."

Sara's frantic call cut through their small talk. "Don! Help!"

Don raced across the driveway, Melissa and Jacob right behind. They found Sara in the nursery, looking into the crib. The slats rattled; the crib shook.

Krista's back arched and her legs stuck straight out, like two little boards.

"I thought they were under control," Sara said, rubbing the baby's abdomen. "The new medicine, oh dear Lord, why isn't it working?"

Don ran for the phone and came back, dialing 911.

Melissa's gut ached. This was her fault. If only she hadn't waited to get to the hospital, if only her pelvis wasn't so small and the baby's head so big, if only she had had a Caesarean.

Don put his hand over the phone. "They're on their way. They said leave her like she is, but watch her. Don't let her knock into the side of the crib."

"I know the drill," Sara said. "We all know the drill."

Don and Sara had opened their home and hearts to both Krista and Melissa. They knew the baby had seizures, but they took her anyway. Loved her with their whole hearts, and allowed Melissa to share that love. Maybe she deserved this pain, but the Camaras didn't, and certainly Krista didn't.

"It usually stops by now. Why doesn't it stop?" Don leaned over, his hands reaching for the baby but pulling back. They all had been trained by the neurologist, even Melissa. *Make sure she's breathing and safe. That's all you can do.*

Jacob reached into the crib and picked the baby up.

"What are you doing?" Sara screamed. "Put her down!"

Don waved the phone like a club. "Give her to me. Now."

"Put her down," Melissa yelled. "This isn't a game, Jacob."

He turned his back to them. Don grabbed the back of Jacob's jacket and whipped him around. Krista lay in Jacob's arms, body still except for the flutter of her hands. Her eyes were wide and fixed on his face. He smiled down at her and she smiled back.

"How did you get her to stop?" Sara whispered.

Jacob handed her to Don. "I don't know. All I knew was if I picked her up, she wouldn't be sick like this ever again."

"How did you know that?" Melissa asked.

Jacob shrugged. "I don't know."

"Who are you?" Sara asked, eyes wide.

He shook his head. "I'm sorry, ma'am. But I don't know that either."

Jeanette burned with excitement. If nothing else, this proved that Jacob was not the guy who the newspaper called The Torch. "Melissa, we gotta tell Susan about this."

"No! You promised. She is not to know about the Camaras. She might go meddling again."

Charlie had sent Jacob out to the barn to tend the horses so Melissa could speak to them without his hearing. Susan was off with Rick somewhere.

"I don't see what the fuss is about," Charlie said.

"Don't you?" Jeanette said. "Melissa asks for a miracle and your horses are healed. Now this. Krista's electro—what is it called?"

"Electroencephalogram. The neurologist tested her and said her brain waves were clear for the first time since she was born. Perfectly clear and perfectly normal," Melissa said, her face flushed with excitement.

Charlie shrugged. "Jade getting better was great, but no way I'm tagging it a miracle. And we all wanted that baby to do better. These things happen. Bad things and good."

"Bad things a lot more than good," Melissa said. "Charlie, you've never seen her seizures, but I have. Jacob picked her up, and like that, she stopped."

Charlie shook his head. "Don't make too much out of it. Maybe it's that new medicine you said they were trying."

Jeanette wanted to shake him. Why was he so stubbornly dense. Did he really not know that Vanessa had emotionally tormented his daughter? She loved the man, but there was something weak running through him, something she had thought the Lord would put iron to.

"To see a sweet baby shaking all over, her eyes wide and her limbs out straight. It's worse than terrible. Usually she just falls asleep afterwards. But today she went from seizure to smile." Melissa snapped her fingers. "Just like that. A miracle."

"I'm happy for the little one. But it's got to be the medicine. Or maybe she's outgrowing them finally. But don't try to push this miracle garbage on me. I'm not some Sunday school student you can snow with those fairy tales of yours." Charlie steered his wheelchair out of the kitchen, banging it against the wall deliberately.

Melissa clenched her fists. "I'll give him a fairy tale. A book of them, right over that fat head of his."

Jeanette reached for Melissa's hand. "You okay, hon?"

She nodded.

"This is a real answer to prayer," Jeanette said, choosing her words carefully.

Melissa turned to the window. "Maybe I should go help Jacob. He might not put enough water in Rayya's mash."

"We'll keep praying. Perhaps you and I—"

"What the—Charlie, what're you doing with that?" Melissa said.

Charlie had come back into the kitchen, his arms filled with Jacob's laundry. "Let's see if the kid does miracles."

Jeanette laughed. "With his dirty clothes?"

"I was in church that day that Pastor Woodward preached about them taking Paul's snot rag around—"

"Charles Robinson! The word is *handkerchief*."

"Point is, the Bible claims people were healed just by touching Paul's stuff. And you think I don't listen?"

Jeanette frowned. "No. I think you hear just what you want to."

"Yeah, well. I can't keep track of all the yapping that goes on. So sue me." Charlie rubbed Jacob's undershirt on the splint. "I got the bum leg, and that kid Susan found *might* have the cure. Let's see."

"Oh, you are being ridiculous. Give me that." Jeanette yanked the shirt from his hand and tossed it at Melissa. When she turned back to Charlie, she caught Melissa's reflection in the microwave.

The girl was pressing Jacob's shirt to her face.

TWENTY

MELISSA DIDN'T KNOW HOW PRETTY SHE WAS.

Jacob sat with her under a cottonwood tree. Jade lazed between them while Rayya grazed nearby, casting an occasional glance to make sure her baby was in sight.

"Rayya's milk has come in strong, Doc says," Melissa said. "And Jade is making up for lost time, drinking it down."

"That's good." He had seen enough television now to know what was supposed to pass for pretty—girls with thin bodies, fat lips, and lots of hair.

Melissa was none of that, yet somehow she was a whole lot more. Those girls on television couldn't hop onto a horse like she could. Or command them to back up or turn or just stop. Those girls with the skinny arms wouldn't be able to toss a bag of grain like it weighed no more than the handful of violets Melissa had just braided into Jade's tail.

Her eyes were a pale blue, like the early morning sky. Her nose tipped up and her eyebrows arched so she always looked surprised. Freckles dotted her face, disappearing by the day as her skin tanned. Her hair looked orange but Jeanette called it fire-engine red. She wore it in a short ponytail that she had to redo ten times a day because it was so curly. Charlie called her *carrot top* when he wanted to irk her. She called him *wrinkle-puss*.

There was something about her hair, something about the color that made him think. "Melissa?"

"Hm."

"Krista's hair."

"What hair? She's bald."

"It's coming in. I saw it when I held her."

She kept braiding. "Cool."

Jacob touched her hair. "It's going to be the same color as yours," he said.

She ducked away. "Poor kid."

"No. She's a lucky girl." He touched her hair again. "She has your hair. Not Sara's or Don's."

"Like I said—bad luck."

"I've seen pictures of Charlie when he was young. Susan has his hair. His eyes."

"Do you want to ride after lunch? We could go down to the Advent River."

"Don and Sara both have brown eyes."

"Jacob, will you drop it?"

He couldn't, not until he caught hold of the notion that spun in his head. "Krista's nose isn't like theirs. Or her eyebrows."

"For Pete's sake, she's their kid. So get off it."

Jacob took her face in his hands. Her jaw trembled, but she looked at him straight on.

"She's their kid," he said softly. "But she was yours first."

"Let go of me."

"Tell me."

"No. Get away from me."

"Please, Melissa." He wiped the lone tear that slipped down her cheek. She slumped against him.

"It's ancient history."

"It's your history," he whispered. "Please tell me."

"The summer before last, Christopher came to Colorado. We met then, kind of took to each other. All fall we wrote letters—I don't have a computer—with him promising to come out next summer. I figured we'd take up where we left off, but Susan got wind of something. She didn't want him in Colorado anyway, and to think he might date a girl who never went to college—well, that didn't set well. She arranged for this internship in Spain for the coming summer. He stopped answering my letters—I think because Susan started to intercept them."

"She wouldn't do that."

Melissa's laugh dripped with bitterness. "You don't know her like I do. Trust me, she would. Anyway, I figured it was over. Around February, I took up with this guy named Chad. Stupid, no-good jerk. Jeanette and Charlie tried to tell me, but would I listen? This guy Chad was all over me. Bringing me CDs and DVDs, cool clothes. Even jewelry. I asked him how he could afford all this on a phone repairman's salary, and he claimed he had good luck at gambling. He was always going to Vegas and playing craps and blackjack.

"Jeanette sat me down and gave me the same talk she gave me every year from the time I turned eleven: *a woman's body is sacred, a gift meant to be kept for marriage, blah blah blah*. I went to church with her—both me and Charlie did—to keep her happy. She does so much for us, you know."

He nodded.

"Out in the barn on Sunday afternoons, Charlie and I would try not to laugh. We . . ." She looked down at her hands.

"You love her," Jacob whispered.

Melissa nodded but kept silent.

"Did you love Chad?"

"Now I know what love is—what Christopher taught me—no. But last winter, I needed a guy to love me, and if Christopher wouldn't do it, I figured I'd let Chad be the one."

"What happened then?"

"The usual story. I should've known better. Chad and I got caught out there—" She pointed at the shelter in the pasture where the dude horses grazed. "It was about this time last year. Another freak thunderstorm. I got soaked, he undressed me and kind of pulled me under his jacket. To keep me warm, but it was more than that. I'm not gonna lie, Jacob. I could've stopped at any time, but I didn't want to. The thing is that, growing up, I thought that I wouldn't want anyone to love me because those men who came to see my mother—my real mother—were so gross and crude and stoned or drunk. But Chad was good-looking and funny and nice to me. When he kissed me, I felt it all the way into my toes."

Melissa broke off in a sob. Jacob smoothed her hair and waited her out.

"A couple weeks later, I found out two things. One, I was pregnant. Two, Chad was a setup guy for a burglary ring. He'd go in on a repair, scope out the house, and report to his partners if it was worth a visit. Because he worked on the phone lines, he could hack into security systems and reroute the alarms. They were smart about it—didn't hit a house until weeks or even months after a service call. But eventually someone saw the connection."

"Is he in jail?"

She shrugged. "He took off. Never knew he was going to be a father. Good riddance."

Jacob rubbed her back, pleased to feel the knots loosen. "Melissa?"

"Stupid, wasn't I?"

"Human. But I have to tell you something."

"What?"

He tipped her face to him. "I assumed Christopher was Krista's father."

Tears flooded her eyes. "He was going to be," she said. "Until Susan Stone ruined it all."

Susan and Rick watched as Joyce rappelled into the ravine. Her mission was to retrieve the chain and manacles.

Susan had ridden up on one of the dude horses—for some reason Prince Sarraf wouldn't let her near him now. Rick and Joyce followed on ATVs because Joyce's many athletic talents did not include horseback riding.

Rick cleared his throat. "Susan, can't you understand my position?"

"Sure. Your world is so ugly, you assume everyone in it is."

"I'm not assuming anything about Jacob. I'm just doing my job."

"I called Joyce," Susan said. "Asked for a favor."

He twisted around to look at her. "In regard to . . . ?"

"She got a copy of the incident report—don't ask how—and it says what happened to your friend was a tragic accident. So you can take that one off our plate."

"Our plate?"

"Don't read your pop psychology into a slip of the tongue. I know you were grieved and shocked by what had happened to Mr. Stern, but that was no reason to further traumatize Jacob by somehow implying he's involved."

"Excuse me? That victim of yours was lounging out in the pasture with Melissa. He didn't look traumatized to me."

"Hey!" Joyce's voice echoed up somewhere. "One of you better still be alive when I get back up so I can find my way back home."

"All I'm asking is that you don't impede the investigation." Rick's voice was almost a whisper. "And please, please don't get in over your head."

Joyce popped up from the ravine, face glowing with exertion.

Susan jumped to her feet. "Did you find them? Where are they?"

Joyce shook her head. "Nothing down there."

"Of course they are. Unless whoever did this has been here in the past week. He must have come looking for Jacob, found him gone. Took the evidence—"

"Hold it. Time out, Susan." Joyce took a long swig from her water bottle. "You may be mistaken about the location."

"I'm not. I know this mountain inside and out."

"Hold on, let's hear what Joyce has to say," Rick said.

Joyce dribbled water over her head and toweled it off. "This terrain all starts to look alike. Maybe we zigged when we should have zagged. Because there's no cave down there."

"This is where the horse threw me. And trust me, there's a cave down there."

Joyce held her gaze. "No, there is not."

"I'm going down there. I'll prove it."

"Wait. Hold on. You can't go down there," Rick said.

"Sure I can. The question is will you help me, or should I just roll myself into a ball and take the hard way down?" Susan glowered at Rick. "Like I did that night. Right here. In this spot."

Joyce held up her hands. "Peace, children. I've got an extra harness. I can take Susan down."

"If anyone's going down there, it'll be me," Rick said. "This is a potential crime scene."

"I was there. I know what I saw, where everything was," Susan said. "I've rock-climbed some in New Hampshire. I can handle myself just fine."

"How about this?" Joyce said. "You both go down. I'll stay up here and work the lines."

"Fine," Susan said. "Rick?"

"Okay."

"But if you two keep fighting, I swear I'll cut the lines and leave you down there," Joyce said.

Rick laughed.

Susan bristled. "Don't even joke like that. If you had seen what I did, you wouldn't think that was funny."

She shrugged into Joyce's harness while Rick slipped into the extra one. He insisted on going down first. When he tugged on the line, she hooked on and followed him.

The ravine was about two hundred feet deep, carved eons earlier out of the side of the mountain by a rushing stream or a plodding glacier. When she reached the bottom, Susan unhooked from the line and took a moment to compose herself.

Jacob in chains was the worst thing she had seen since Christopher's coffin slid into the dank ground. Jacob unchained was the best thing that could have happened to her—perhaps the only thing that could have turned her away from her own grave.

The air was musty, the ground still muddy from last week's storm. Without moving air and exposure to sunlight, it would not dry for some time. Rick stood with one leg up on a rock, stretching his back. "This the place?"

"Yes. Over there"—she pointed to a pile of boulders and some thick brush—"is where I landed."

"Where did you find Jacob?"

Susan sat down where she had landed, re-creating the moment. She pointed to her left. "He was about ten feet that way."

Rick motioned left and right. "See? No chains."

"Like I said—maybe someone came and got them. Everyone in the valley knows about Jacob after that mess at the hospital. The abuser must be trying to cover his tracks."

"I don't know, Suse. That's a stretch. Are you sure this is the right place?"

"Absolutely."

"Where's the cave?"

"It was behind him. The chains went into it as far as the light could shine, maybe twenty feet or so. But the darkness in there had a different quality to it, like a substance that—" Her words stuck in her throat. The two sides of the ravine joined behind where Jacob had been chained, forming a solid rock crease.

"Maybe you were mistaken," Rick said softly. "It was dark. You had taken a tumble."

"No. I . . . maybe this isn't the right place. It was dark, and maybe I wasn't completely oriented to my surroundings and—"

He touched her arm. "Is that yours?"

Her hair clip was caught in a pocket of brush about ten feet up the slope. As her certainty about that night slipped away, a vertigo came

over her. She swayed, and Rick caught her. She didn't have the strength
to push him away. "It was deep and cold and I'm telling you, Ricky: *it
was there.*"

"I believe you."

She looked up at him. "No, you don't."

"I believe you saw something down here. I've got no clue what it
could be, but I'll tell you this. Something's got hold of this valley. I
don't know what it is or what it wants, but I do know something evil
is moving among us."

Susan pulled away. "Does Jacob need a lawyer?"

"No, no. I'm not saying Jacob has anything to do with the murders.
Not at all."

"What kind of idiot do you think I am? You think he's a sociopath."

"Ted Bundy was charming and sweet, remember."

"How dare you? Blaming the victim. I expected better of you."

"All I'm suggesting is that you maintain your professionalism. Help
this kid, yes, but please keep an open mind. The coincidence of his
being found when all the rest is going on is too much to ignore. If you
truly are committed to his best interests—"

"Haven't I made it abundantly clear that I am?"

"Then work with me to figure out who he is and where he came
from."

Susan grabbed his head, tipped his face to hers. "And *who* did this
to him. Are we agreed that is also a priority?"

Rick nodded. "Agreed."

They slipped back into their harnesses in silence. How she and Jacob
had made this climb in the dark and without help, Susan couldn't begin
to explain. Jeanette would say it was a miracle. Rick would say it was a
conspiracy.

Why couldn't they all just leave her alone to take care of Jacob?

Rick nodded for her to go first. She had only gotten up about six
feet when he tugged on her jeans. "What now?"

"Shh. Don't move. Hold perfectly still."

A warning out of her childhood. "Where?" she whispered.

"Near your right shoulder."

Susan kept her head still, moving only her eyes. A rattlesnake was coiled on a rock outcropping about eight inches from her hand. Its head was up, eyes fixed on her. The rock had blocked it from her view as she climbed.

Her hand slipped on the line. Only an inch, but enough to put the snake in defensive pose, his tail in a slow *rat-tat-tat*. She could let go and fall, but he had a bead on her neck. He'd have those fangs in her before she was out of reach.

"Susan, don't move. I'm going to shoot it."

She didn't even ask him how he could do that. Or beg him not to. Even a slight movement of her lips could startle the snake into striking. Rick didn't have a clear line of sight, not with the rock between him and the snake. The rattler's head might be at an angle where a bullet could reach it from below, but that was a long shot at best. If he missed, he would surely startle it into striking. Maybe she should just wait it out. But her arms throbbed already from the effort of keeping still, and her fingers were starting to slip again. And what would happen when Joyce tugged the rope, looking for a response?

"God have mercy," Rick said.

Amen, Susan thought as a bullet exploded by her ear.

Melissa stomped back to the barn, more angry with herself than Jacob. How did she keep letting him talk her into spilling her guts? She liked this kid, but she had liked Chad and look how that had turned out. Christopher was so special, he might have well been from another planet.

Jacob caught up with her and took her hand. She yanked it away.

"Sorry," he said.

"If Jeanette or Charlie sees us, they'll think it's something other than . . . let's just be cool on all this. Okay?"

"Sure. Melissa, I . . ." He blushed.

"What?"

"I hate being like this. Not remembering hardly anything."

"What brought this on?"

"I was thinking about what you said about Chad kissing you."

"Forget that. If I hear you told anyone what I said, I swear, Jacob, I will pull all your hair out. Got it?"

"I'm not gonna tell. I just wondered if I've ever kissed a girl like that. Or ever kissed a girl at all."

This kid had to be from Mars, he was so out there. "Wouldn't you know? I mean, you know when you're hungry and when you need a cold drink of water. For people our age, kissing is almost as important."

He ran his finger over his lips. "Maybe no one's ever kissed me."

"I find that impossible to believe."

"You do? Why?"

"Because you're so . . . you know."

He raised his eyebrows. "Is being *you know* better than being hot? Because that's what the lady at the hospital said I was."

Melissa laughed. "Take your pick. Either way you win."

"You're teasing me now."

"And you want me to kiss you. You're trying to trick me into it."

"No. I wouldn't do that."

"You don't want me to kiss you?"

"I'm not trying to make you kiss me. But if you're offering to, that would be okay."

She put her hands on her hips. "It would, huh? Why?"

"Because you're so cute. No, I take that back." Jacob leaned toward her, eyes wide open. "You're downright *you know*."

Melissa pressed her hands to his chest to keep a distance between them. "What did I just say?"

"Why?"

"Because I want to make a point."

"*Why* is what you just said. Before you said, *what did I just say*." His face was poker-straight. If he was playing her for a fool, he was better at it than any other jerk who had come her way.

"Jacob, where in heaven did you come from?"

"I don't know, Melissa. And I don't know if I want to know."

"Why not?"

"Because—what if they make me go back there?"

"They won't."

"How do you know? We don't even know who *they* might be?"

"Because, *Jacob-Never-Been-Kissed.*" Melissa brushed his lips with hers. "I won't let them."

"Oh."

"Oh what?"

"Oh, so that's it."

"Was that at all familiar?"

"I don't know. Maybe you could do it again."

Don't, she told herself. *Don't fall into another trap.* But she brought her face to his again and—

"Melissa!" Jeanette bellowed from the front porch. "Help!"

She took off in a run. Jacob outraced her and got to the house first. Jeanette was frantic. "Someone's got to talk sense into Charlie."

"What's wrong?" Jacob asked.

Jeanette gave him a strange look, but it was Melissa she grabbed. "He's in the kitchen, unwrapping his splint. Says he's going to walk."

Melissa banged through the front door and ran down the hall.

Charlie sat at the kitchen table, cutting through the elasticized bandage that held the two halves of the splint in place.

"Are you nuts?" she said.

"You don't have to shout. I ain't deaf."

Jeanette stuck her hand in his face. "Give me those scissors."

"I'm using them."

"Stop it, you idiot. You need that splint," Jeanette said.

"What happened to all your blah-blah about miracles? I thought you believed in them." Charlie lifted off the top half of the splint. Underneath, his leg was wrapped in cotton batting.

"I believe in God. There's a difference," Jeanette said.

"Get your story straight, woman. I thought God did miracles."

Jeanette looked helplessly at Melissa.

She squatted next to Charlie. "Why do you think this is a miracle?"

Charlie narrowed his eyes. "Why did you think the filly would get a miracle?"

"Because she needed it," Melissa whispered.

"Tell the truth. You wanted it."

"Of course, I did. But—"

"And I want this. So don't play *holier-than-thou* with me. We all want God to do what we tell Him to, but when He doesn't, we decide He's hard of hearing. Think He wonders why we can't tell if He's there or not? Because He doesn't make Himself heard. He wants us to worship Him, but does He show Himself? It just don't make sense."

"According to *our* standards, Charlie. He's got His own," Jeanette said.

"Yeah. Yeah. Easy to play by the rules when you get to make them up." The bottom half of the splint hit the floor with a loud clunk. Charlie lifted the top off and dropped it.

"Don't put weight on that foot," Jeanette begged. "The doctor said it would be a good eight weeks before the bones set. You're going to bust up all the work they did and have to have surgery all over again."

"Think so?" Charlie said.

No one responded.

"Come on, kiddos. I'm taking a poll. Who thinks I'm healed?"

No one spoke. Jacob looked confused.

"What a bunch. Afraid to say what's on your mind. You're never shy, Melissa. You think I'm healed?"

"A week ago, I would've said no. But now? Who knows?"

"Who knows? Hm. What about you, Jeanette? Do you know?"

"Charlie, at least wait until Susan gets back. See what she says."

"Don't think your God is big enough to heal my leg?"

Jeanette threw up her hands and turned away.

Melissa wanted to shake some sense into the old man. But who was she to tell him to be reasonable? She had faced down Doc Potter and his lethal syringe on the strength of one desperate hope. And what she had seen at Camaras' yesterday was something she couldn't even get her mind around. Maybe God took special notice of babies, both human and horses. But how would He treat a stubborn old man who didn't have a good word for Him?

Charlie looked up at Jacob. "You got something to say, son?"

Jacob shook his head.

"Come on, boy. Jeanette's been on the phone, whispering to her pastor that you healed our filly. Melissa saw you make little Krista's fit stop cold. See a pattern here?"

Jacob rubbed his arms. "I don't know, Charlie."

"You're the common denominator. So what the hel—I mean, *heck*. I figure why not give it a try."

Jeanette was furious. "You're being disrespectful, Charles Robinson."

"I'm being honest. You tell me no one gets anywhere with the Big Fella unless they're honest. So what do you say, Jacob? Am I healed? Tell me what you think, kiddo."

Jacob touched the crown of Charlie's head, a gesture so tender that Melissa wanted to cry. "I think . . . if you're going to try to walk, you'd better take my hand."

Charlie surprised Melissa by grasping the inside of Jacob's elbow. As he stood, he winced with pain.

"Sit down, you fool," Jeanette said.

"No, it's not the bone. The muscle in my ankle is tight, that's all. Needs to stretch some." Charlie took a step on his broken leg.

"Jacob, get ready to catch him," Melissa warned.

Charlie lifted his good leg, putting all his weight on his bad leg. "I don't . . ."

Jeanette rushed forward. "Sit. Oh hon, please."

"No, no, it's not that. I was going to say that I don't believe this. But I guess I gotta." Charlie let go of Jacob's arm, stepped over the pieces of his splint, and kissed his wife.

Melissa turned to Jacob, her heart hammering against her ribs. "Where did you come from?"

He gave her a heartbreaking look. "How many times do I have to tell you? I just don't know."

TWENTY-ONE

BLOWING OFF THE HEAD OF A RATTLESNAKE HAD BEEN tremendously risky. Yet peace had settled Rick's arm and grace gave him a clear sight, even in the murk of the ravine.

Even so, twenty-four hours later, he still felt a pang. He focused on the pile of work on his desk, trying not to imagine what would have happened if he had missed.

The phone rang. Renee MacArthur, the state's medical examiner, was on the line. "We got a DNA match on vic two. You were right—Alexander Rodgers of Lexington, Kentucky."

"Nothing on the first victim still?"

"Nothing."

"Cause of death for Rodgers?"

"Suffocation."

"From what?"

Silence. Then, "Scorching of the lungs. He breathed in the fire."

Rick leaned his head into his hand. To hear about this was nearly unbearable. To experience it must have been hell on earth. "And the flammable agent?"

"The arson people can't figure it out."

"Anything else I need to know?"

"Other than someone's got to catch this fiend before he strikes again? No, Sheriff. Just be careful out there."

She clicked off. Rick dialed Zach Hurley.

"I need you to go to court with me," he said. "Some more evidence has come up that links Robinson Ranch with these murders."

Zach agreed readily, made the arrangements. There was a district court right in Steamboat, which allowed them to get everything done quickly. Six hours later, Zach and Joyce Freeman had joined him in his office, mulling over the emergency order that Family Court had issued.

Their accommodations were above the Harken General Store and provided one cell for lock-up. If that was filled, Rick transported to Steamboat. His staff included a part-time secretary, a deputy, and round-the-clock dispatchers. It was back-country law enforcement, but Rick was proud of the work they did.

Lisa stuck her head in. "Dr. Stone is here."

"Hold on to your heads, boys," Joyce muttered.

"Send her in," Rick said.

"She's insisting on talking to you in private first."

He went out to the reception area. Susan was dressed in a dark brown suit and cream silk blouse. Her hair was pulled back into a tight bun, emphasizing the sharp angles of her face. A small, well-dressed man sat quietly across the room, punching in what had to be a text message on his cell phone.

Rick started for him. "Can I—"

Susan touched his arm. "He's with me."

Rick smiled at her. "You look very nice. But you didn't have to dress for the occasion."

"I absolutely did."

"I don't get it."

"I need to remind you and your coconspirators of what I am. You think of me as the girl riding in the mountains, but I'm a well-respected psychiatrist. All grown up, Sheriff, and you need to treat me like that."

"I'll say it again—"

She pointed her finger right between his eyes. "Don't. You are not on my side, and furthermore, *my* side is irrelevant. Jacob is the focus of this meeting—or should I say, this latest inquisition—and how I feel or what friendship we once had is of no consequence. I wanted to speak privately to you because it's important we set boundaries and agree to act strictly as professionals."

"I'm still not getting it, Suse."

"Susan. The name is Susan, and if you continue to push legal maneuvers on Jacob, you will be calling me Dr. Stone, if I agree to speak to you at all."

"Why are you making a mountain out of this mole hill?"

"Because you're making a bad dream into a nightmare. Jacob is a victim. But rather than pursuing his abuser, you imply that he might be somehow involved with the monster that's terrorizing the valley. That's going to stop, right now. If it doesn't, we are prepared to take legal action." She turned to the man in the chair. "Peter? I'm ready for you now."

The man got up and offered his hand to Rick. "Peter Muir. From Boston."

Rick shook his hand. "Rick Sanchez."

Susan's smile was frigid. "It was clear after our foray into the ravine yesterday that you would be acting against Jacob, rather than for him. So Peter flew out from Boston last night to provide legal representation for Jacob."

Muir fished a document out of his briefcase. "I went to court this morning and obtained a temporary guardianship for Jacob."

"Susan's not even a resident of Colorado," Rick said. "The court wouldn't agree to that."

"Charles and Jeanette Robinson have agreed to be his guardian. The young man known as Jacob Doe has accepted status as their temporary ward. Susan and I are here at their bequest and with Jacob's full agreement. I understand you have your own court order, Sheriff?"

Rick nodded, his mouth tight.

"Shall we get on with it!" Susan said. "See whose court order trumps the other?"

They went into his office. Rick made the introductions.

"Can we agree that we're here to determine the best interest of Jacob Doe?" Peter Muir said. His voice was quiet, his mannerisms courteous. Yet Rick sensed a powerhouse inside the tidy package the man presented.

Joyce Freeman nodded. "Absolutely."

"That's been our focus all along," Zach said. "Contrary to Dr. Stone's concerns, we didn't ask for this meeting to serve the hospital's order of removal."

"So the intent of this meeting is . . . ?" Muir said.

"Hold on," Rick said. "Before we get to a game of chicken with these court orders, I need to make the position of my office clear. Mr. Muir, you must be aware that we've had two horrible murders here in the past week?"

"I am. I was shocked and sorry to hear of the nature of the murders."

"I can't ignore the timing of Jacob's recovery from the cave and the second murder," Rick said.

"He's not involved," Susan said.

"I'm not saying that," Rick said. "Look, I've allowed him a low profile. I filled out the necessary paperwork that went to missing persons but haven't moved him onto the radar of CBI. Whether or not we want that to happen, it's got to now."

"Why now?" Joyce asked.

"Because the latest victim was Alexander Rodgers. The vet that Susan brought in to attend to her father's mare."

Susan put her hand to her mouth. "I just assumed he went home. I'm so sorry to hear this."

"Robinson Ranch is going to be the first place the state guys are going to go. I've submitted some reports, your interviews. But you are all going to have to be questioned. Including Jacob. We can't hide him any longer."

"Understood," Muir said. "Rather than shielding him, we want to protect him and support him. Which brings us to what Jacob's guardians have asked me to explain to all of you. They feel that if—well, I guess that's *when*—when it becomes necessary for Jacob to be questioned, it absolutely needs to be done in the presence of Dr. Stone. Even though he's thriving in her care and with the Robinsons, no one should lose sight of the condition he was found in and the potential nightmare that his memories may bring."

Susan cut in. "Not *may*. *Will* bring."

"Okay, okay," Joyce said. "We all get it, and we all agree. So let's stop this posturing and get down to what we can do to help Jacob. I'm here as a medical resource. Zach's the one with the updated order, so let's hear him out."

Zach cleared his throat and reached for his water bottle. *He's posturing as well*, Rick thought. *Playing meek, when in reality he holds the trump cards.*

"This amended order of removal does three things," Zach said. "The first is that it removes the hospital as a party to the petition. Second, for the time being it assumes Jacob is a minor child, younger than eighteen."

"He's not," Susan said.

"Perhaps we should let him finish, Susan," Muir said.

Zach continued. "It authorizes me to locate Jacob to a different foster family at my discretion. That is certainly not my intention. However, after long discussions with Sheriff Sanchez and Dr. Freeman—whom the court has assigned to monitor Jacob's physical well-being—we are asking one thing." He cleared his throat again. "The court order requires you, Dr. Stone, to either begin a course of therapy immediately or, if you're not qualified to offer cognitive rehabilitation, to find someone who is."

"You didn't need a court order and this inquisition to impose that. I've already started," Susan said.

Zach's face hardened. "You are now required to accelerate the process. I am to sit in on all the sessions and report daily to Dr. Freeman."

"But not to Sheriff Sanchez," Muir said. "Anything that comes out in therapy is privileged. Both you and Dr. Freeman are also bound by that privilege."

"Now wait a minute." Rick's blood took on a slow boil. "We've got a monster loose, and if Jacob can help us find him, I want to know."

Susan glared at Rick, Joyce, and Zach in turn. "I will decide what information can be released to you without endangering Jacob. Because, as you stated, the focus of this effort is restoring Jacob to health. Not cherry-picking his memory to find clues for some investigation."

"Agreed. But by the same token, you must realize the advantage this process will give you," Zach said.

"How so?" Susan said.

"It will keep the homicide investigators off Jacob's back, at least for a couple more days. Assuming we act immediately. Today. When can we begin?"

Susan glanced at her watch. "It's four o'clock now. Why don't we do a session at seven?"

"You can use my office," Joyce said.

"No. We'll need to do it where he's the most comfortable. On the ranch."

"That's fine with me," Zach said. "Can we agree on two sessions daily?"

"Assuming he tolerates them. This isn't a game. If the therapy is successful, it will be traumatic. Potentially devastating, based on the circumstances in which I found him. I beg you all to be patient." Susan looked pointedly at Rick.

Zach smiled and stood. "I'm glad we've come to agreement."

Muir shook hands all around. Susan did the same, her hand cold and limp in Rick's.

"By the way, Susan," Joyce said. "I got a call from the lab today. Jacob's tests were all screwed up."

Susan edged into full panic mode. "Why didn't you say something sooner? Are you talking about elevated glucose? Or liver function?"

Rick wanted to take her hand, talk her down as he used to when they were teens. But she had made her position clear. He was the enemy in her eyes, simply because he was trying to do his job.

"No, no. Not abnormal," Joyce said. "Just giving gibberish results. The lab first thought maybe the machines or even tubes were somehow compromised. But all the other tests drawn and run that day came back fine. Who knows? But we'll have to draw more blood, run the tests again."

Susan relaxed. "Fine. I anticipate using some IV relaxation later next week, so I'll draw the blood at the same time."

When the others had cleared the office, Joyce shut the door and looked at Rick.

"Is this the right thing to do?" Rick asked.

"For him. Yes. For Susan Stone? I pray we aren't indulging her need to compensate her loss."

"For her son."

"It's a pretty common and obvious pathology. We may need to push Jeanette and Charlie to truly act as guardians, even if it means distancing Jacob emotionally from Susan."

"What was your take on our hike into that ravine? Were there ever chains down there?"

Joyce tented her hands and stared at him. "The chains, I buy. Jacob agrees with her story on that."

"So what don't you buy?"

"The cave. She is so adamant that it was there, but you saw the solid wall, I saw it, even she admitted that it wasn't there yesterday."

"Why won't she just say she was mistaken?"

Joyce shrugged. "She's the shrink, not me. But if I had to venture a guess, I'd say that imaginary cave is symbolic of the void in her life. The void, unfortunately, that I think Jacob is filling quite nicely. She can talk all she wants about helping Jacob to recover his memory, but her subconscious may be screaming exactly the opposite—that it's in her best interest to keep him emotionally and psychologically a child."

"Did we accomplish anything here then?"

She smiled. "Zach's involvement and supervision should assure Jacob's safety and well-being during this whole process. After all, that was our focus."

Rick rubbed his face. "Fine for him. But with this maniac still free, no one's safety can really be guaranteed. And if Jacob has any knowledge of who was behind these burnings, then everyone at Robinson Ranch is at tremendous risk, whether Susan Stone wants to admit that or not."

TWENTY-TWO

SUSAN AND ZACH LEANED ON THE FENCE, WATCHING JACOB pick pebbles out of Jonas's feet. Melissa had gone off for the evening, and he had happily assumed her chores.

"I did the educational assessment this morning," Susan said.

Zach looked at her out of the corner of his eye.

"That was before our agreement."

"Sure. What did it show?"

"The results were spotty. Jacob went as far as I could bring him in the math assessment. Well into calculus. Even though I did a quick sampling, starting with addition—that's how basic I got—he clearly has a comprehensive knowledge of practical and theoretical mathematics. The assessment would show him at doctorate level, I believe, if I were competent to challenge him sufficiently."

"So he must be midtwenties then?"

"Or a prodigy."

"What are you referring to as 'spotty'?"

"He knows theoretical chemistry and physics, but no engineering. For example, he understood electricity but not how a lightbulb worked."

Zach laughed. "Neither do I."

"He knew world history inside and out. But nothing after about the twelfth century."

"That's strange."

"I even went on the Internet to find facts insignificant enough to stump him. I couldn't."

Zach turned sideways so he could look at her. "Never?"

"Let me back up here. At first I thought he was completely ignorant. I started with U.S. history, and he knew nothing. Current affairs, then obvious topics like the Civil War, and still he gave me blank looks. I was ready to pack in history when I threw out a question about Julius Caesar. He perked up and answered questions backward and forward. He knew the Magna Carta, but went blank after that."

"Selective dissociation?"

"Looks that way."

"For what purpose?"

"All I can imagine is that his abuser is a historian specializing in modern history, so Jacob reacted by denying all modern history."

"What about languages?"

"Consistent in an inconsistent way. I'm fluent in Spanish, thanks to eating half my meals with the Sanchezes when I was a kid. I'm passable in French and Italian, took Latin in high school. None of the modern languages meant anything to him. But he knew Latin, even corrected my pronunciation."

"How anyone knows how to pronounce Latin is beyond me."

Susan laughed. "Granted. I called up a colleague in Boston—Kay Kontos. Asked her to speak in Greek to Jacob. He listened, confused at first. Then he babbled away. Kay said he was fluent, but his pronunciation was strange. More like classical Greek."

"Ah. Ancient history again."

"Yep."

"Okay, let me toss out what will likely be the first of many wacko theories," Zach said. "What if somehow he was frozen in that ravine for a thousand years? And only recently thawed?"

Susan burst into laughter. "Thank you for brightening my day. That is totally nuts."

"At your service, ma'am. Based on these results, is your bottom line still he's either been through college and postgrad or is a prodigy?"

"Yes."

"Which is where we started. Past puberty."

"Past puberty," Susan echoed. "But beyond that? Who knows?"

"Melissa thinks she does. She's obviously hostile to the therapy."

Susan took a slow breath to mask her annoyance and maintain a professional tone. "Melissa is hostile to everything."

"I worry that she'll influence Jacob. Talk him into resisting therapy."

"I'd promise to talk to her, but it would be useless. She's stubborn, close-minded, and willful. She's—" Susan swallowed back the anger that brewed in her throat. "We'll just have to exert a more positive influence on Jacob."

"I'm not sure that's possible. He's very attached to her. Which makes me think perhaps we should ask Charlie to ban her from the ranch for the next few days."

"What? That's rather drastic, isn't it?"

Zach shrugged. "Jacob's need to get through this amnesia is even more drastic."

"No. It won't work. As much as Melissa is an impediment, she's also essential to keeping the ranch going right now. We'll just have to work around her."

"Shush. Here he comes," Zach said.

Jacob bounded toward them, one hand behind his back. "Got a present," he said, grinning.

"Flowers?" Susan said.

His grin faded. "No. Here." He slowly opened his hand.

Sitting on his palm was a wasp.

"Let it go, please," Susan said. "Those sting."

"Really?" Jacob put his hand up to his face, studying it. "I don't think this one does."

"All wasps sting. Let it go."

"I'm not holding it here against its will."

"Here, let me help." Zach took hold of Jacob's wrist and positioned his hand so he could blow across his palm. The wasp flew straight at him. He slapped at his own face, coming away with the dead wasp and a nasty sting.

"Why did you do that?" Jacob said. "It wouldn't have hurt you if you had left it alone."

Susan's stomach soured. Her growing concern was that if they only left Jacob alone, he wouldn't be hurt. But the court had decreed that she blow across her palm and make him take flight.

Jacob lounged under a tree, drinking orange juice and munching pretzels. Susan had given him a pill to take with his drink. Zach stood at a short distance, quietly watching.

"It's called a Xanax," Susan said. "To relax you so the talking will seem easier to you."

"I'm already relaxed."

"You don't have to take it."

But he did take it because she clearly wanted him to.

"Jacob, we'll be asking some of the same questions you've been asked before."

"Why?"

"Because time may have shaken loose some memories."

"Wouldn't I know it if that had happened?"

"It's like Rayya. She can't munch on grass unless you bring her out of her stall. To do that, you have to open the door. Once she gets out there, she might nurse Jade or even run around. She knew she wanted the grass, but being there made the rest possible."

Jacob made a face. "Okay, Susan. Whatever you say."

"All the questions refer to the last three days. But if something comes up that you remember from before that, that's fine. Just let me know so I can make a note of it."

"Sure." The sun was low on the horizon. His muscles unwound, and he thought that was weird because he hadn't realized they were tight.

"Where do you sleep at night?"

"In the bed you had when you were little."

"What do you do before going to bed?"

"I kiss Jeanette good night. She likes me to do that. I slap Charlie on the shoulder. Smile at you, and Melissa if she's around. I go to the bathroom to brush my teeth and wash my face. I wipe around the sink and straighten the towels and turn out the light. When I go to my room, I turn out the light and look out at the mountains."

"How does that make you feel?"

"Like if you measured each mountain or counted each star or circled the sky, I would be nothing. And yet, I'm important to someone."

"Do you know who?" Susan asked.

"You. Everyone in our house. Zach. Rick. Even Sara and Don and "

"Who?"

"The neighbors."

"Who else? Did you want to say?"

Jacob couldn't say. He had promised not to tell Susan about Krista, though he didn't understand why. "Rayya. Jade. The other horses."

"Can you name the other horses?"

"Jonas, Abigail, Job, Jeremiah, and Deborah. Oh, and Prince Sarraf, though he doesn't belong in that group."

"Why do you say that?"

"Because he's not from the . . . not mentioned in . . . the Old . . ." Something like a hot stone seemed to come out of his stomach. He coughed and choked, but it was stuck in the middle of his chest.

"Jacob. Drink some of your juice." Zach pressed the bottle into his hand.

He drank, swallowing back the pain.

Susan wore her worry line now. "Jacob, I forgot to write down that last answer. Can you repeat the names of the horses?"

"Are we done yet?"

Susan and Zach looked disappointed, though they tried to hide it with smiles that were too bright.

"Would you like to be?" Susan said.

He made himself laugh. "It's your fault. You talked about what I do before I go to bed, and now I want to sleep."

"The pill might make you sleepy. Remember I had told you that?"

"My memory isn't that bad, Susan." The sharpness in his own voice startled him.

"I'm sorry, Jacob. We'll finish now."

"No, no. Wait. I'm sorry."

"There is nothing to be sorry about."

What if there is, he wanted to say. But he didn't want to disappoint her any more than he already had. "Susan, you can ask me more questions. It's fine."

"Tell you what. Let's head back to the house and talk on the way. Okay?"

"Sure."

They started walking. The first stars sparkled in the eastern sky. In an hour, the heavens would be crammed with light.

"Susan."

"Yes?"

"Are heavens the sky?"

"In a literal sense, yes."

"What other sense might there be?"

Her eyes shifted to Zach again. "Jacob, can we discuss that tomorrow afternoon?"

"Did I ask something I shouldn't have?"

"No. Not at all. And I did tell you that I would answer any questions that I could. But I want to keep with the simpler course we started this evening and save some of the more abstract concepts until another time."

"Okay." It wasn't okay—his mind felt like it had an itch. Just like Charlie used to pry open his splint and scratch, Jacob would like to open his memory so he could scratch. But there was a danger in removing supports. Susan was convinced that Charlie's foot wasn't healed completely and would collapse soon. His mind might be in the same condition.

"Let's go back to what you do before bed."

"Kiss Jeanette, high-five Charlie—"

"Sure, I got all that. Think about being in the bathroom."

"Am I brushing, washing, or peeing?"

"You're brushing your teeth."

Jacob tasted the mint of toothpaste, felt the urge to drink some water and spit it out. It was strange to be in two places at once—walking through the pasture but also in the bathroom. "Okay."

"Look up at the mirror."

He looked up from the white foam in the sink, over the faucets, up to the oak frame of the mirror. Finally, the glass.

"What do you see?"

"Charlie looking in and asking me if I'm gonna take forever."

Zach laughed.

"Anything else?"

"The wallpaper."

"Is that what you see in the mirror? Or next to it?"

"In the mirror. It's the piece that's ripped, directly across from the sink. Jeanette says she needs to buy more paper so she can fix it."

"Anything else?"

"No."

"Do you see yourself?"

"No."

They crossed in front of the barn, Jacob walking between Susan and Zach. He focused on the porch light. Jeanette had just switched it on and, though they had a ways to the house, it flickered through the pines like—no, he would not think of Susan's flashlight, the light that had found him in that darkness. Better to think of her face, her concern for him even though he must be so awful that someone locked him away where no one could find him. Yet Susan had found him and she was trying to find *all* of him. He owed it to her to cooperate.

She took his hand, tugged him to stop. "Can you do one more thing for me?"

Jacob smiled. "Sure."

"Close your eyes."

He did, feeling the darkness close in on him. He tightened his grip on Susan, knowing she wouldn't let him fall.

"Let's walk into the living room," Susan said.

He imagined himself walking into the living room, stopping before he reached the center of the room.

"Imagine that you've got one of Jeanette's yummy cinnamon rolls in one hand and a cup of coffee in the other."

"I don't like coffee."

"Oh, that's right. Cinnamon roll in one hand and hot chocolate in the other. Can you see the mirror now?"

He pictured it hanging over the fireplace in its heavy gold frame. It was big enough to capture the whole room. "Yes."

"Turn to face it."

He turned toward the fireplace. "I am."

"That cinnamon roll looks scrumptious with all that white icing dripping off it. Look at it but not in your hand. Look at the mirror and see it there. Do you see it?"

"Yes. It looks really good."

"Can you see your fingers?"

"I . . . think so."

"Do you want to take a bite?"

"Oh, yeah. I really do."

"I'm going to let you, but I want to make sure you don't get that nice, sweet icing and tangy, buttery cinnamon all over your face. So here's what I want you to do, Jacob."

His hunger was so strong that he hung on every word, waiting for permission to take that first bite.

"I want you to keep watching in the mirror. See the cinnamon roll."

"Yes. Can I eat it now? I'm going nuts here."

"Slowly lift it to your mouth. Keep your eye on the roll, watch it coming to your mouth, going in, you're chewing, it tastes so good, feel it going down, it feels just right, open your mouth and take another bite. The next bite tastes even better, so chew and enjoy, watch yourself chewing, your jaw moving, can you see that, Jacob?"

"I—" He saw what must be his jaw, but it wasn't like Susan's or Zach's or even one of the horse's, but something fierce, something that could snap a horse or a mountain in two. He didn't want to see any more, but now that he had glimpsed what the mirror showed, he couldn't turn away from the eyes that looked over his shoulder, eyes that seemed to spit fire and shoulders that could toss this world into flames that would consume it and still be hungry for more. So hungry that those eyes and shoulders and wings would take to the sky, fly across the heavens and search for more to consume because this task was sweeter than cinnamon, but cinnamon had never left such a bitter taste in his throat. So bitter that it choked Jacob so that he couldn't breathe, and maybe that was good because he could not be world without end, *amen* because all things come to an end, don't you know. He would be the first to come and the last to go, but go he would, until he followed the flames as they burned out, burned him—

"Jacob. Jacob!" Susan shook him by the shoulders. He opened his eyes, and for an instant he saw not her but the bones under her skin and a heart cracked in half.

He bent over and vomited until his stomach turned inside out, but even that wasn't enough so he bled from his eyeballs, not knowing how to cry so he wept blood, not his own but blood shed by a mighty sword, rivers of it, enough to wash them all away.

"Jacob! Stop it!"

Susan pulled open his eyes, though he thought they already had been open. Even in the darkness of the coming night, her face was white, a light of its own that threw no heat. Zach stood at her shoulder, his face radiating warmth, but there was no light there.

"Open your eyes," Susan said, but weren't they open? Or was he still looking in some strange mirror that cast every likeness but his own because his would break that mirror and it would shatter and explode and *cut cut cut* until he was ribbons of waste, rippling on the tide of what had been flushed away.

"He won't open his eyes," he heard Susan say, but he couldn't tell her what he heard, and he didn't dare tell her what he saw and didn't want to know what he was.

He felt a prick in his arm, something swimming under his skin as if the wasp had decided to sting after all. When the poison took him, he fell willingly into its arms, his last true thought in the mirror that it would be far better for all if Susan had left him chained under darkness for ever and ever, amen.

TWENTY-THREE

"DID SHE BEHAVE?" THOSE WERE SARA'S FIRST WORDS EVERY Saturday night when they got back from bowling. What she meant was, did Krista have any seizures.

Don and Sara didn't have to let Melissa come over. They were Krista's parents now, in every way, and Melissa respected that. But they had big enough hearts to allow her one night a week with their daughter.

"She's just fine. Great, in fact." Melissa shrugged on her jacket, glad she had brought it. A cool wind had gusted down from the north. "She had quite the party. Laughed and smiled and talked. Gave me two messy poops."

Sara laughed. "She knew you were coming, wanted to save her best work for you."

"Melissa, we've been saving some big news for you," Don said.

Oh no, she thought. *They're moving.* "Really?" She struggled to keep her voice light.

"The neurologist is going to try to wean her off the seizure meds."

"Oh, that would be so awesome."

"He doesn't know what happened, but her second EEG looked great too. They did a CAT scan and couldn't find that area of damage in her brain."

"Whoa. Okay. Wow." Melissa felt a strange heat come over her, as if she was being gripped by a notion too big to fit into her brain so some of it had to squeeze into her heart. She couldn't deal with this, had to get back into the everyday. So she said, "How did you two roll tonight?"

Sara grinned. "My dear Donald Duck stunk up the joint. But I . . ."

Don twirled his wife about in an exaggerated waltz. "My dear Sara Sweetcakes got five strikes in a row and pulled our team out of the gutter."

"Despite my dear husband's efforts to keep us there. This man threw more gutter balls tonight than I've thrown all year."

"Sara, love. I stink so you will shine even brighter." He kissed her on the nose.

Sara pushed him away. "Aunt Missy put up with dirty diapers all night. She doesn't need to shovel through our mush to make it out of here alive."

Don kissed Melissa's cheek. "Thank you, dear Auntie."

She clutched his hand. "Thank you, dear Dad. You too, Mom."

Sara hugged her. "If we start these circle thank yous, we'll be up all night. I'm the designated driver. If I can find where I put the keys. I just had them . . ."

"That's okay. I want to walk."

"Oh no, you don't," Don said. "Not on that road. Drunks going sixty or seventy on back country roads."

Sara put her hand to her mouth. "Donnie, that guy they talked about on the radio. The Torch, they're calling him . . ."

"Which is why we insist that Sara drive you."

Melissa shook her head. She needed to be alone to work through all this wonderful weirdness. "Honestly, it's not necessary. I'm going to walk through the fields. This guy sets his victims on fire near the roads, not out in the country. Besides, I need the exercise."

"You haul hay around half the day and yank the horses around the other half. You do not need the exercise," Sara said.

"I need the time. And trust me, cowards like The Torch never leave the road. I'm safer out in the pastures than I am in my own bed."

Krista cried out. A strong, healthy wail, demanding food or another diaper change.

Sara looked at Don. "Can you drive her? Or would you rather deal with the doo-doo?"

Don headed for the door. "Let's go, kiddo."

Melissa balked. "No. Just let me be. I know those fields like my own face. I'll be fine."

Don stopped and took a long look at her. "You got a lot going on over at Robinsons'. A lot going on here. You need time to air it all out?"

Melissa gave him a playful punch to the arm. "You got it, pal."

"You got your cell phone?"

She patted the back pocket of her overalls.

He dug a flashlight out of the drawer. "Take this. It's not so easy to find the cut-through in the dark, and those rocks in the creek might be slippery this time of night. And if you have any trouble at all—you call."

"I won't have any trouble."

"Promise."

"Absolutely." Melissa grabbed the flashlight and headed out. She didn't need to turn the light on. The moon was full, flooding the fields with silver. The breeze carried the scent of fresh grass and wildflowers. It was a good night. A full night.

Maybe she'd sleep at the trailer. Doc Potter had finally convinced her that Jade was fine—*you got your miracle, girl*—and she really didn't need to keep watch from the next stall. The best thing was to let Rayya be mama. Even so, Melissa would stop at the barn first. It put an extra mile on her hike, but that was good. She needed to let the night air wash away the baby smells. Saturday night was precious, but if she didn't leave all thoughts of Krista until next weekend, it got to be too much.

She had made her peace with the adoption. No way was her baby going to start life like she had. Krista had to have a mother and a father. A familiar pain gripped her chest—Christopher would have been a wonderful father.

After all that had happened, Melissa would have thought Susan wouldn't dare show her face back here. But she was back and up to her old tricks, charging into every situation as if she owned the whole world. Melissa would have to warn Jacob to keep his distance.

The kid had settled into a nice routine. The horses liked him. What better indicator of character could there be? That he had Krista's blessing made him all the more special.

As for the miracles—well, who knew what they were? Who knew what Jacob really was? Why not just let him be? He could work the horses, help Charlie, help her.

She ran her fingers over her lips, summoning the memory of his kiss. Why had she done that? She had vowed never to let anyone's kiss cover the memory of Christopher's. The last time she had ever seen him, he had hugged her at the airport security gate and pressed his lips to hers. "I'll load my stuff in a U-Haul and be back before you know it. We'll get married quickly, and give that baby of yours—I mean, ours now—a good home."

When she and Jeanette had gotten back from the airport, Melissa found the present he had left. She ripped it open, laughing as she saw the Boston Red Sox bib, socks, and sleeper. She hadn't had the heart to send the Red Sox stuff with Krista when she went to live with Don and Sara. In quiet moments—empty moments—Melissa liked to put them to her face and try to breathe in what little was left of Christopher. His scent of mint soap had all but faded away, but she would always be able to remember his vow to raise his child as part of Red Sox nation.

Melissa arched her back and stared into the bottomless stretch of sky and stars. *I let him go, just like Susan wanted. Why weren't You there to catch him?*

"What're you doing, Susan?"

She jumped. "Jacob. You startled me."

"I'm sorry." He turned to go back into the house.

"No, no. Not your fault. I was just looking at the moon."

He peered up from under the porch roof. "What moon?"

"It was there just a minute ago." Heavy clouds billowed up from the mountains, casting the night back into shadow. "How're you feeling?"

"My head hurts a little."

"I'm sorry. I had to give you some extra medicine. That's why you fell asleep."

"Why did I need more medicine?"

"I think you remembered too much too quickly. I hadn't expected that to happen, and neither had Zach. I'm sorry."

"What do you say to me, Susan? Don't keep apologizing? So don't."

She linked her arm through his. "As long as you know we want what's best for you."

"I do know that. But what I don't know is why is it taking so long?"

Susan had never heard even a hint of irritation in his voice before. He sounded impatient, even frustrated. "Forgetting is a form of protection."

"Why can't I keep it, then? Why do I have to remember?"

"See those clouds?"

He peered again at the sky. "Yeah?"

"The moon is still there. We can pretend it's gone, but it's only hidden. For now, your life is hidden, probably because your mind can't look at it all at one time. See how the clouds are blowing? They shred apart, you see a little moonlight, and then the clouds rise up again?"

"Yeah."

"I think that's what happened today. You got a glimpse of what's hidden in your memory. Then your mind decided to cover it back up. We'll get there, Jacob."

Susan glanced at her watch. Don Camara had called to say Melissa was walking home and would they watch out for her. Jeanette and Charlie were asleep, so the task had fallen to her.

"Do you hide things?" Jacob asked.

"What do you mean?"

"Like I do. Things that hurt too much to remember."

"Everyone does, to some extent. It's a protective mechanism." She felt his eyes on her. "What is it?"

"What are you hiding, Susan?"

She smiled. "Don't worry about me."

"Why not? Aren't you worth worrying over?"

Susan's throat tightened. "That's not at issue here."

He propped his elbow on the railing and leaned, looking intently at her. "But why isn't it?"

"I can take care of myself."

He shook his head. "No, you can't."

"What makes you say that?"

"Because you're feathering apart, like those clouds up there. Tell me what you're hiding, Susan. Because I want what's best for you."

She turned away from him. "Shame."

"Over what?"

Her throat was so tight, she could barely breathe. She shook her head, motioned over her shoulder for Jacob to go away.

Instead, his arms circled her, and he hugged her from behind. "How bad can it be?" he whispered.

She swallowed her tears. "You must be starved. Let's go in and see what Jeanette left you from supper."

Don was right. It was hard to find the cut-through at night, especially with the clouds rolling in and blocking the moonlight. Melissa walked along the brush that bordered the creek, trying to imagine what the cut-through would look like in the dark. Behind that tangle of bushes and bramble, the stream ran by in a steady *swoosh*.

This was stupid. She should just turn around and hike back to the Camaras'. But Don and Sara would already be in bed. They had early chores to do before leaving for church. Don loved his sheep almost as much as she loved the horses. Sara had made a needlepoint pillow for his birthday: *The Lord is my shepherd.*

"I shall not fear." Jeanette would be pleased to hear her quoting from the Bible, but even a monkey knew that verse. Maybe she should forget the cut-through and push straight through to the creek. Forget that. With her luck she'd get caught in a briar patch and be stuck until Labor Day.

Finally, a gap. She moved down the slope, eager to get across. It was dark down here, so dark she walked right into a tangle of branches. Stupid—she had forgotten that she had a flashlight.

Melissa fumbled with the switch, trying to turn it on. It clicked, but didn't shine. Maybe the batteries weren't making contact. She shook it. The light came on and—

Something moved against her leg. She stumbled into the briars. The flashlight flew from her hand, lost deep in the brush. This wasn't the cut-through, just a gap. Melissa dabbed the blood off her face. She'd have some nasty scratches and scabs by tomorrow. Nice way to show up for church. Jeanette's friends would probably think she got into a Saturday night bar fight down in Steamboat.

Something rustled nearby.

Melissa jumped near out of her skin. A game bird, probably a quail or wild turkey. No, she was the turkey, goose bumps erupting everywhere. She walked, jogged, and rode this land all the time. The same stuff that was here in daylight was here now.

Something growled.

Fear twisted her spine, long fingers of panic pushing through her ribs. *Stop it.* It's just a dumb coyote, scared like she was. "Get! Go along, you dumb mutt."

Melissa jogged along to put some distance between her and the coyote. The clouds rolled overhead, breaking only long enough to tease her with patches of silver. She forced herself to slow down. The ground was uneven. She had to take care not to twist an ankle. Not that a coyote was any danger to an adult human, but everyone said they were getting bolder every year. Look what had happened at Camaras'. Lambs had been killed before. But a coyote taking down a sheepdog just didn't make sense.

She picked up the pace again, trying to outrun the image of something mangy and hunched—*dear God, something hungry*—circling Krista's stroller. Think of Jade, but no, coyotes would go right for the filly's throat. Rayya then, but she was too placid. Prince Sarraf would stomp them like cockroaches. Yeah, that was the image to hold onto. That arrogant horse, rearing up and warning them back into the hills where they could chew up rabbits and chipmunks like they were supposed to.

The clouds split apart long enough to show a clear path through the brush. Beyond, the moon rippled on the water. The cut-through.

"'Bout time." The sound of her own voice comforted Melissa.

Years and years ago Charlie's father had laid five wide stepping-stones in the creek as a bridge between his land and that of Don's grandpa, old Vic Camara. Melissa would have to move carefully over them. The stones could be slippery this time of year.

Something erupted out of the brush, roaring like thunder.

Before Melissa could react, it slammed against her back and sent her flying into the creek. She went facedown—*get up, go, run, it's coming—*

and lay there, stunned. The frigid water sucked the life out of her—*can't get up, can't run, it's coming.* She rolled onto her back, still completely immersed—*you have to get up, get up, get up before it comes in the water after you*—but she was too shocked by the cold to move.

A broad shadow swooped over her, wings hunched like a buzzard, but no bird could be that big. As it swept away, she struggled up on her elbows, getting only one breath before the rush of the creek knocked her flat again. The creature came back, beak or mouth or—*what was that*—jaw open, and for a crazy moment she saw light from the back of its throat. It must have swallowed her flashlight, she thought, until the light exploded, a ball of fire bursting over the water, flames rolling in waves, the brush catching, the surface of the water bubbling.

Too hot too hot too hot, but she could only lie there because she had no cut-through, no deliverance from this nightmare. With fire rushing on the creek, her thoughts settled to one last flicker, a candle flame carried off on the wind.

So sorry . . .

TWENTY-FOUR

SUSAN GLANCED AT HER WATCH. MELISSA SHOULD HAVE BEEN back by now. Maybe she had gone straight to the trailer. Susan rang her cell phone. No answer. She would come here first anyway. No way would she go to bed without checking up on Rayya and the filly.

Susan pulled on a sweater, found a flashlight, and headed out. She backtracked to the paddocks, whistled for the dude horses. She'd ride one and lead another for Melissa.

She was grateful that Jacob had gone back to bed. The last thing he needed was to be out in this cold air, his imagination working overtime. Could one have an imagination without informed experience to feed it? Interesting question. If she could muster the energy, maybe she'd start a research project. If she decided to keep on. She had reversed her decision for self-euthanization—suicide wouldn't change the past, wouldn't change her loss or her shame in what had precipitated Christopher's death. She remembered his phone call, his excited announcement that he intended to marry Melissa—it had played over and over in her head for the past eight months.

"Have you considered that she's not really your type?" Susan had asked.

His indignation was clear even through the static of the cell phone. "What do you mean by that?"

"Relationships need a common basis. You don't have anything in common."

"Could you give me an example?" Christopher played the shrink, asking her questions to make Susan commit. He hadn't bothered to tell her the truth about this girl. Did he even know about her sordid past? The investigator Susan had hired had dug up plenty of interesting information, none of which encouraged her to believe this was a good match for her son.

Melissa O'Brien had been in foster care for years, barely graduated high school, had a juvenile record that wouldn't be sealed unless she stayed out of trouble until she was twenty-three. How could Susan not believe that this girl had gotten a sniff of Christopher's substantial trust fund?

Susan had kicked off her shoes and paced the center hall. The robust air conditioning in the penthouse made the granite tiles ice cold, a perfect foil for her rising temper. "You're halfway through college; she has no intention of going. You're an Easterner; that ranch lifestyle might be appealing for a summer or two, but eventually you'll be bored out of your mind. You love the ocean; I bet she's never seen one."

"That's not her fault. And I intend to remedy it."

"I'm still waiting to hear what you've got in common."

"The horses."

"That's it?"

"Mountain sunrises, wide-open pastures, pickup trucks, fly fishing."

"You sound like a travelogue, Christopher."

"We both bite our fingernails and eat pizza with a knife and fork."

"You're simply not experienced enough to evaluate this relationship, especially after such a short time. You've had only three steady girlfriends since you were fourteen. This girl started dating when she was twelve, had one boy after another, was treated for venereal warts, even suffered a miscarriage when she was fifteen."

"How do you know all this?" His voice had had an unfamiliar edge.

"That's not relevant. The question is: has she shared any of this with you?"

Christopher remained silent, confirming Susan's suspicions. If she trod softly, she might turn him. "Sweetheart, she's had a tough life, much of which was not her fault. But that girl is not a suitable match for you."

"*That girl's* name is Melissa, Mum. Are you listening to yourself? You would never speak to your patients with that haughty a tone."

Her patients didn't try to steal her son.

"You're right. I'm sorry. I'm a worried mother, which doesn't excuse my transgression of acceptable boundaries. I do apologize." Appeal to logic, not pride. "I haven't asked you to break it off. I'm merely suggesting that you slow down a bit. You've still got two years of college. If you would agree to delay any wedding until you graduate, I would wholeheartedly support an engagement."

Christopher didn't respond. He must be weakening; she needed to keep talking. "I'm just caught rather short by this announcement of yours."

"I told you six weeks ago that we were in love."

"Men and women your age fall in and out of love constantly. I would feel more assured that you know what you're doing if you would allow time to test the mettle of this relationship."

"Mum . . ."

His plaintive tone almost melted her. But she had to stay firm for his sake, even if he refused to realize it. "What is it?"

"We can't wait. She's pregnant."

Susan had exploded. She couldn't remember exactly what she had said, only *how* she had said it. Her anger had been so raw that she hadn't even realized he had hung up. Even now a black hole ate at her, the anger superseded by a sick guilt.

Christopher hadn't deserved to die, and she didn't deserve to live. Yet she had a mission—to bring Jacob to health and to bring his tormentor to justice. When that had been accomplished, she could decide what her own fate should be.

The growing clouds obscured the moon, but out in these open pastures, a little light was more than enough to ride by. Susan hadn't seen Prince Sarraf for a day or so. Maybe the stallion had wandered back to wherever he had come from. These dude horses were well kept, but slow. She laughed aloud, amused that she was still a snob, preferring Arabians over any other breed.

She rode Jeremiah and she led Abigail, though she only knew this because their names were etched into their halters. She rode bareback—was there any other way? She had started riding bareback early on as a way to sneak a ride without Mother harassing her. Rather than saddle up a horse, she'd sneak out to the pasture and just hop on. She could almost feel her ponytail flying straight out behind her, imagining it was a mane and she could run like the wind.

The wind shifted, bringing the odor of smoke. The horses spooked, Abigail pulling hard on her lead rope.

Susan patted Jeremiah. "Shush, it's okay. Just a campfire somewh—"

A thundering *phlat phlat phlat* rang from the night.

A shadow passed overhead. It was the size of an ultralight glider, but no plane flapped its wings and nothing that man had made had talons longer than Susan's arm, swiping at her. Fear jackhammered her gut, and she flung herself off the horse, horrified as she heard Jeremiah bellow. The ground shook with the horse's struggles as the—*what could such a thing be*—thing ripped at him. Hot liquid seeped through her jeans, and Susan oddly thought of Rayya's membrane, but this was blood, acrid with the throes of terror.

She lay flat on the ground, her mouth pressed to the dirt, an isolated corner of her mind calmly noting that once again, instinct had driven her to survive. She took shallow breaths and tried to imagine herself home in Boston, trying to keep her fear subdued so its stink wouldn't give her away. She could have stayed like this for an hour or a century, transfixed with dread. Only one thing could force her up and running.

For Christopher's sake, she had to warn Melissa. He would do it, and so must she.

Susan hoped, prayed—*God, if You're there*—that somewhere ahead in the brush, the girl was safe. The smoke became more pungent by the creek. The sky cleared again, and the moon illuminated the cut-through. As she approached, she gasped before she realized the crackling was not the beast, but a fire burning on both sides of the creek.

Susan ran faster, terrified that Melissa would be in the same condition as those two burned bodies, ashamed that she had once again failed to keep someone in her care safe. Though fire flared along the bank, the cut-through was easy to find and, with no brush to feed the flames, clear. She splashed into the water, slipping on the stepping-stone and going down on her knees.

"Melissa," she hissed. "Are you here?"

Susan saw no one on the west bank and was turning to the east bank when she spotted something under the water. She switched on her flashlight and shined it through the rippled surface.

Melissa was completely submerged. Susan pulled, and she came out of the water, gasping and choking. When she had taken in enough air, the sobs came.

"Shh, it's okay," Susan said, trying to get her to stand. Even if Melissa hadn't been injured, hypothermia could set in, depending on how long she had been hiding like that.

"It came down on me," Melissa wheezed. "Spilling fire over the water."

"I saw it. It didn't use fire on us, though."

"What is it?"

"I don't know." She looped her arm around Melissa's waist and dragged her up the bank. Where should she go? The beast was heading toward the ranch, something that hadn't registered until now.

"Us? What do you mean *us*?" Melissa said.

"Nothing." They both trembled so hard their teeth clicked in frantic accord.

"Not Jacob, please not Jacob."

"No, no. Just hold on, keep walking."

"I heard a sound when I was in the water. I thought it was my own nightmare, that maybe I was dying or had died but—Susan, just tell me. Who is *us*?"

"I rode one of the dude horses to come meet you, ponied another. It got the one I was riding—" Suddenly she had to say no more because they stumbled onto Jeremiah's body.

Melissa's cry came from deep inside. "Where's the other one? Which one was it?"

"It was . . ." Susan could barely remember how to set one foot after the other. "Abigail. After it finished with this poor horse, it took off after her."

"S-s-s-u-san," Melissa quaked. "I have to g-g-get back to Camaras'."

"We'll call them when we get home."

"T-t-takes too long."

How Melissa was able to break away and run back for the cut-through, Susan could not explain. After watching her disappear, she raced in the opposite direction to warn Jacob, Jeanette, and her father.

So easily deceived.

So very amusing.

Even as the two women run for the ones they think they love, he knows they are entertaining theories of what happened. Laughable ones no doubt, though neither woman has enough imagination to even guess at the truth. If the fools had slowed down at any point, they would have gotten a clear look at him. That might have settled the matter, but then again, perhaps not. They were not of sufficient experience to identify him, though soon enough, for one of them, the truth would become clear.

The other would likely not survive. No matter, as she was of no consequence. She had been allowed to live this long as an investment. He could justify spending her life on his pleasure as well as his business.

But—*sigh*—business must come first. He had his mission statement, he had his business plan, and—*chuckle*—he had his human resources. He was indeed—*cue trumpet flourish*—a man on fire.

TWENTY-FIVE

LIKE A BIZARRE CIRCUS, RICK THOUGHT.

The Colorado Bureau of Investigation had descended on the scene in full force, setting up enough high-density lights to hold a football game out here. Techs and detectives poured out of vehicles, prepared to scour every inch of ground. The scene would be tightly controlled and lightly trod until daybreak. Colorado's arson investigators had joined the parade, and word was that the Feds were trickling north from Denver and west from D.C. to add their expertise—800-pound gorillas to rein in all the monkeys.

Rick had been first responder and still hadn't sorted out the accounts. Joyce had sped out right after him, trailing ambulances in her wake. At the moment she was up at the house, checking out Melissa and Susan. Now that the big guns had taken over, Rick would head over there, see if the ladies were in any shape to shed more light on exactly what had happened.

He was almost to his cruiser when Renee MacArthur caught up to him.

"Please tell me there are no dead bodies," Rick said.

"The two horses."

"Not the end of the world."

"I hear Mr. Robinson will think it is."

"Not as long as his Arabians are safe. He's got the barn locked up and is sitting outside their stall with a shotgun. If he thought the roads were safe, he'd load them in the trailer and book it out of Dodge."

"He would remember to take the humans with him, I hope?"

Rick shook his head. "Can't promise he would. So tell me, Doc. You do animals too?"

"I did a prelim, but we'll have a wildlife specialist in."

"Wildlife? Why not one of the Steamboat vets?"

"The horses were torn to pieces. Ragged tears, what looked like claws, but nothing alive has claws that long. We'll photograph the wounds every which way to determine if maybe they were made by some nasty machine. Once I had to do a post on a guy who had tangled with a pavement grinder—"

"That's okay, Doc. I get your point."

"This is your turf, Sheriff. You got a best guess for me?"

"I'd rather not say."

"At this point, any speculation is welcome."

"You won't rat me out?"

She shook her head. "Scout's honor."

Rick wiped the sweat off his forehead. He was soaked under his arms and in the small of his back even though the temperature had fallen to below fifty degrees.

"I swear, Mr. Sanchez. Go ahead."

"Call me Rick. We are seeing a lot of each other."

"If you say 'we've got to stop meeting like this,' I swear I'll take a scalpel to you.'"

"All I can think of is that this is the work of some whack job or—" He took a futile swipe at the sweat dripping down his face. "Or something from outer space."

"You mean that literally."

"I do."

Renee nibbled her thumb. "I can't rule that out. Not when it looks like the perp splats fire on his victims and then disappears. What will be interesting is getting some DNA out of those wounds, see what plays out. What do the ladies say?"

"I'm heading up there now. Would you like to come?"

"I suspect the less of a crowd, the better."

A few minutes later, he pulled the cruiser up to the Robinson house. Joyce was on her way out. She motioned for him to sit with her on the steps.

"How are they?" he asked.

"Susan's nose was put out of joint when I insisted on doing an EKG."

"Huh?"

"After seeing one burst into flames on Jacob's chest, she doesn't trust what she calls our 'local technology.'"

Rick scratched his head. "She survives a vicious attack, but is put out by the suggestion that she isn't as young as she used to be?"

"The attack was too disturbing to rail against. So the EKG makes a great target."

"She okay?"

"Fine. Some bruises, a lot of shivering. You know what it's like—your body explodes with adrenaline, but when it's all gone, you're like a dishrag."

"Melissa?"

"I would have liked to admit her to the hospital, but she wouldn't hear of it. Susan got on her back, insisting she get in the ambulance. That guaranteed Melissa was not going to budge. Those two have some issues, I take it?"

"Melissa was supposed to marry her son."

Joyce turned to look at him. "Really. What happened?"

"The young man died."

"From?"

Rick rubbed his eyes. "He took a plunge out of their penthouse condo. Probable suicide."

Joyce whistled.

"Anything I should know about Melissa?"

"I'm pretty concerned about her lungs—she took in water and maybe some smoke. Don't forget—your other two victims died from inhaling the fire. Melissa had the water to shield her. Anyway, Susan promised to listen every couple of hours, make sure there's no fluid building up."

"Melissa agreed to that?"

"Apparently even Susan Stone is preferable to going to the hospital."

Rick leaned forward, forearms on his knees. "Let me ask you this: while you were examining the two ladies, where was Jacob?"

"According to Susan, he was sound asleep when she went looking for Melissa. The three women—I'm including Jeanette now—played Mommy, decided he shouldn't be woken up."

"He slept through all the commotion? Don't you think that's very strange? Especially with Charlie shooting his shotgun every ten minutes at bats and barn owls?"

"Apparently something in today's therapy session freaked him so much that Susan had to sedate him. It's possible he slept through all the sirens and the rest."

"Did you actually see him?" Rick said.

"No. But before you throw cuffs on him, Jeanette said Susan had checked on him while Melissa went out to check on the horses. So I'd say both the Arabians and Jacob are off whatever hook you're thinking of fitting them for."

"Maybe," Rick said.

She slapped his back. "Okay, I'm off."

"You coming to church tomorrow?"

"After this? Wild horses couldn't . . . never mind. Even that doesn't feel right to say. You?"

"If I can get away. Joyce, don't go climbing tomorrow afternoon, okay?"

"You don't have to tell me twice."

He kissed her cheek. "I didn't think so."

Shell-shocked, Melissa thought. Like we went through a war. The Camaras fled their farm, stopping only at Robinson Ranch to drop her off. Rick questioned them, but they had seen nothing, heard nothing. Maybe that was worse—knowing something monstrous is over your head, but not seeing it. As soon as Rick cleared them to leave, they peeled out, heading for Sara's mother's house in Granby.

Jeanette hovered over Melissa, smoothing her hair, trying to get her to *at least take a sip of the tea, hon.* Susan sat across the kitchen table from her. For once, there was no spite in her eyes.

When Melissa looked up from the water and saw someone reaching for her, her first thought was *Christopher*. The shape of the head, the straight line of the nose, the color and shape of the eyes. *I'm dead,* she thought, pleased that Christopher had come to greet her.

But her rescuer was not Christopher but his mother, the woman whom Melissa had sworn to despise for the rest of her days. Susan felt the same way about her. Yet she had come back for Melissa. The first nightmare that they had shared made them bitter enemies. This one made them—not friends, certainly—but it lessened some of the tart bitterness that Melissa tasted every time she looked at Susan.

"Susan," Melissa said. "Thank you."

Susan tipped her head, looking at Melissa with an odd smile. "You're welcome."

Rick sat between them, ruffling pages in his notebook. He looked older, the lines around his mouth deep, the bristles of his beard a stark white.

"The CBI guys will be coming by in a while," he said. "If you'd like me to put them off until you two get some sleep, I can."

Susan arched her eyebrows. "Melissa?"

"I can't sleep. Can you?"

"No."

Rick tapped his pen nervously. "Apparently Jacob can."

"I explained that to Joyce," Susan said. "He's sedated."

Rick stood. "I need to see him."

"No," Susan said.

"Let him," Melissa said. "Otherwise he's going to be suspicious."

"Is that true, Sheriff?" Susan's tone was frosty.

He looked across the kitchen to Jeanette. She was making biscuits for everyone working the crime scene. "It's your home, Jeanette. Will you take me up there?"

"Never mind. I'll do it," Susan said. "Come on."

"I'm coming too," Melissa said, expecting the usual protest from Susan. Instead, she helped her stand, walked by her side as they took Rick upstairs.

Jacob slept so soundly, at first he didn't even seem to be breathing. Melissa's heart skipped a beat at the scars on his back. She tiptoed into the room, went to pull the sheet up over the scars.

Susan was on the other side of the bed, about to do the same thing. They stared at each other. Then Susan smiled. "Go ahead, Melissa."

Melissa covered him carefully. Was it just a few hours ago that she had covered Krista like this? Don and Sara had called awhile back. They made it to Granby just fine, *thank You, God.*

Back out in the hall, the walls closed in on Melissa. "I need to get outside."

"Me too," Susan said. "You done with us, Rick?"

"A few more questions."

"Let's go check on the horses," Melissa said.

A couple minutes later, they knocked on the barn door, shouting so Charlie wouldn't send a load of buckshot their way. He unlocked the door from the inside, let them in.

Melissa went right to Rayya's stall. The mare and her filly slept peacefully in the straw. Rick slid to the floor, sitting with his back to the wall. Melissa felt a pang of guilt—the guy was just trying to do his job and was exhausted. Susan sat opposite him.

"The dude horses," Melissa said. "I've got to get the rest of them in."

"No," Susan and Charlie said together.

"Wait until the sun's up," Susan said. "Come, sit."

Melissa glanced at Rick but sat next to Susan.

Rick opened his notebook and was about to speak when he did a double take at Charlie. "Where's your splint?"

Charlie jumped up and danced a little jig. "I'm healed."

"What?" Eyes wide, Rick looked at Susan.

"He took off his splint, fool that he is. I called his surgeon, but he couldn't get this idiot to listen to reason. Pop, you're on borrowed time until that newly knit bone lets go."

"It won't let go," Melissa said. "It's a miracle. Just like our horses. The filly was brain damaged, but we asked for a miracle and now she's fine." *And Krista, thank You, God, and thank you, Jacob.*

Charlie rubbed his face. "Let's get Jacob out of bed. Maybe he can bring Jeremiah and Abigail back."

"For pity's sake, Pop. Jacob doesn't do miracles. Tell him, Rick."

"Susan's right. God does the miracles. Why would you think Jacob does miracles?"

Susan cut off Melissa's explanation. "No reason. He's just addled."

Charlie sat back down. "God ain't fooling around. He's stirring up some stew in this valley. Miracles and—"

"Monsters," Melissa whispered. "Miracles and monsters."

"But why us?" Susan said. "Why come after us?"

Rick shook his head. "We'll have to delve into your backgrounds, see if either of you has roused any animosity."

"Maybe it *is* Jacob," Melissa said.

"How could you say such a thing?" Susan's tone was razor-edged.

"No, not that he did this to us. What I mean is maybe that thing is after him. It knows we've got him and are taking care of him."

"Maybe." Susan pulled her jacket tight around her shoulders. "I'm sorry I snapped at you."

"Speaking of Jacob—I have some questions I should have asked last week," Rick said. "About Jacob's chains."

Rick questioned Susan intensively, wanting to know the kind of metal the chains were made from, the size of the links, the gauge of the metal, even how many links she could see trailing back into the cave that turned out not to be there.

Finally he said, "One last question."

"Fire away," Susan said, and then cringed. "Sorry. Poor use of words."

Rick crossed the barn and squatted next to her. "Where's the key?"

She looked at him, eyes wide. "I don't know."

"You don't know?" he echoed.

"That's what she said," Melissa retorted.

"It's not that I don't know, Rick," Susan said. "I just can't remember."

TWENTY-SIX

"I REFUSED TO LET THE HOMICIDE GUYS HAVE ACCESS TO Jacob," Zach said. "I said he was mentally vulnerable and that any questioning could destabilize him to a point where he'd never regain his memory. They threatened a court order, but I told them we already had two. So they were outnumbered."

Susan hugged him. "I don't know how you did it, but thank you. Thank you so much."

"Do you get it now, that I want what you do? Full recovery for Jacob."

Susan was grateful that Zach had run interference for Jacob, but she still needed to keep the boundaries clear and the goal defined. "Full recovery means far more than breaking through his amnesia."

"Agreed. What's the plan for today?"

They stood at their usual spot on the fence. Charlie, spryer than all reason said he should be, walked Rayya around the paddock. After he had made a full circle, he handed the lead rope to Jacob. Melissa was in the midpasture, trying to herd the three surviving dude horses into Rayya's paddock.

Charlie refused to let the Arabians outside unless he was on guard. His shotgun was on the top of the fence. Buckshot would have little effect on whatever attacked Melissa and the horses last night. Susan pushed that nightmare away, focusing instead on Rayya. As she regained her prepregnancy form, her champion lines showed through. And Jade was exquisite, her grace undeniable even as she learned to use those long legs that Charlie said she inherited from Magnum Psyche.

"Susan?" Zach said.

"It's a beautiful sight, isn't it?"

Miracles and monsters.

Susan had never known a miracle, though she had prayed all her young life for one—an act of God to save her from her own mother. Vanessa Robinson had ripped her to shreds as effectively as that flying thing had ripped Jeremiah and Abigail last night. Why had the horses been destroyed, but she and Melissa spared? Though the beast or whatever it was had tried to kill Melissa. Why fire for her and ripping apart for the animals? CBI was exhuming the bodies of Don Camara's sheep and dog, to see if they had also been victims of this *thing.*

"Susan. Hadn't we better get started?"

"Oh, sure."

"Still rattled from last night?"

"Wouldn't you be?" she said, possessed of a strange notion that nothing rattled Zach Hurley. "We'll use Charlie's office. I'm planning some art therapy. The mirror exercise seemed too direct for Jacob."

Zach narrowed his eyes. "I told the lead detective that you'd accelerate the therapy even further. It's the primary reason they aren't climbing down our throats."

He had just told Susan that *he* was the reason that the investigators had kept their distance. She would have to be more alert, make sure Zach's bland appearance didn't mask skillful manipulation. "Joyce is rounding up some of the more specific meds we'll need. But it would be counterproductive to conduct all his sessions under sedation. We need to use more routine therapy to establish a baseline before we use pharmacological forceps to yank the trauma out of his psyche."

"As long as we keep going."

Awhile later, they were in Charlie's office with Jacob. Susan had set up a card table in the middle of the room with a single chair and had laid out art supplies: clay, paper, markers, scissors, glue, glitter. She explained what each craft item could do, demonstrating by drawing a silly picture of Rayya and using glitter for her tail.

"You don't have the lines of her back right," Jacob said.

"I don't have to," Susan said. "This is what she feels like to me. Not exactly how she looks."

"Wow. You must think Rayya is beautiful."

"I do. While you make things in here, Zach and I will be sitting out in the hall."

"Why?" Jacob said. "I want to see you, make sure you're still here."

"You'll hear my voice. But we want to be out of your line of sight so we don't distract you or unwittingly suggest something to you. I want you to have complete focus to draw or sculpt whatever you want to. That's why I took the pictures off the wall."

"I liked those pictures," Jacob said.

Charlie had framed pictures of all his horses on the long wall. The original Prince Sarraf was set in the center, surrounded by the many champions Robinson Ranch had produced in its glory days. Tasha was there, the picture pricking Susan's heart every time she came in.

"Are you all set? Do you understand what we're doing?" she said.

He nodded. "I think so. You read, I draw what you read."

Susan smiled, taking care not to betray her concern. Already his subconscious was resisting. She hadn't told him about the nanny-cam she had set up to make a video record of his session. He was very aware of pleasing the people closest to him, which was why she and Zach were going to leave the room. Otherwise, he'd be looking for them for visual clues rather than turning his focus inward. The tape would allow her later to see how his physical response—facial expressions, body language, even squirming—corresponded to the scenarios she read.

"Let me explain in a bit more detail," Susan said. "I read a scenario, and you draw or sculpt whatever pictures the story brings to mind. What you create may have nothing to do directly with the story. For example, I might say something like, 'The sun shines over the barn,' but you might see the shadows that trees next to the barn cast and draw them. Don't worry about trying to use your drawing or sculpture to mirror what the scenario is. The only correct response is whatever comes from inside you."

He nodded. "Yes, I understand now."

"I want to stress that you should give in to whatever you feel. Don't try to please me, and don't worry about startling or scaring me. You are safe. Zach and I are right here with you, just a few feet away. When you've had enough, you let me know."

He grinned. "Enough."

"Are you serious?"

"Joking." He poked her side. "Gotcha, Gretchen."

Susan bit the inside of her cheek to hide any response. *Gotcha, Gretchen* was Christopher's own construct, a running joke between her and him from the time he was four. Melissa must have picked it up from him and passed it to Jacob.

"You did get me good," she said. "One last thing. You should know that most people really enjoy doing this. Especially adults who don't often play with markers."

"Unless they have a little kid to draw with?" Jacob said.

Mommy, is this what Daddy looked like? I'm losing him from my head, Mommy.

You'll never lose him, Christopher. His hair was a little longer. See? Like this.

Okay. And this is you, Mommy. You look very sad . . .

She and Christopher had dealt with their grief with crayons and paper. Eventually the dark tones were replaced with brighter ones, the dead flowers took on petals, the stark cemeteries were replaced by Fenway Park and Boston Common.

How she missed him. And how easy—*how pleasing*—it would be to create an emotional dependency in Jacob. But that would not be good and that would not be right.

Susan had freed him from his physical chains, and now it was her job to free him from the terrors hidden deep in his mind.

The last time Melissa had come to church was for Christopher's memorial service. Jeanette had sat with her arm around her, holding her so she wouldn't fall. That was last September. Susan had not only refused to come, she wouldn't even give her blessing for it.

Jeanette had tried to tell her that Christopher had been a believer since the summer before. "That's what we celebrate," she had said. But Susan wouldn't hear of it. Nor would she listen to Jeanette's pleas that they all be allowed to come east for Christopher's burial. "We loved him too," Jeanette had said. "We want to say good-bye. Melissa needs to say good-bye."

Susan's anger had flared. "You and my father were supposed to watch out for him. But good ol' Charlie Robinson would rather shovel horse manure than to take care of his own child."

"Child?"

"Grandchild. Wasn't that what I said? And you, Jeanette—you had promised to be responsible for him. But you were right there, watching him and this girl fall into each other's arms. No supervision, no telling me what was happening right under your nose. Were you so desperate to get that girl off your hands that you just let it happen?"

Jeanette had slammed down the phone in anger. Ashamed of herself, she had tried to call back. Susan wouldn't answer, though Jeanette tried for days straight.

A week later she sent Jeanette a note.

I know you grieve too. But you can't know my grief, the bottomless pit that the loss of my son is. I cannot accept your condolences, though courtesy pushes me to try. Christopher and I were estranged over what you and my father should have prevented. Please leave me to deal with my pain in private. If something happens to my father, certainly contact me and I'll respond. But otherwise, I ask you to please leave me alone.

Only one way to comfort such pain, Jeanette knew. At least Melissa had agreed to come this morning. "I've got to start talking to God more," she had said.

Jeanette was as deeply grateful as a body could be and not dance or shout or sing. Her heart would have been shredded if that thing had burned Melissa as it had those other victims. "We've got a lot to be grateful for."

"And to be mad about," Melissa said. "But I guess He knows that."

Jeanette turned her attention to church. The smell of sulfur as the candles were just lit, the bustle of latecomers trying to find a seat. The piano prelude brought balm to her troubled soul. She needed to let the monsters go for now, give thanks for the miracles. Perhaps Charlie's accident was a miracle, in its own way. It had brought Susan out here—finally. Even soul-shaking events like Christopher's death or monstrous events like these attacks and murders were a chance for God to show His power and love.

The worship leader took the microphone. "Shall we all stand and praise the Lord?"

The music started, but Jeanette heard a different song in her head, a quiet melody like dew settling before dawn. She sank to her knees.

Melissa bent down to her. "You all right?"

"I just have to pray."

For once, Melissa didn't screw up her face. She sang along to the praise music, her hand resting on Jeanette's shoulder.

Lord, You see it all, Jeanette prayed.

Susan—bitter daughter and grieving mother, ripping mad at Melissa because she blames her.

Melissa—grieving too, furious with the woman she counts responsible for Christopher's death.

Rick Sanchez—standing at the side door of the church, ready to rush off if he's called. Willing always to do your work. Scared, but not for himself.

The cops and technicians and others I can't even guess at—all working to find this monster who killed those people and attacked our two daughters.

Monsters, yes. But miracles too.

The miracle of Melissa with me in worship. Of Jade coming to life, of Rayya restored, of all horses who run with power and energy and speed, and yet bend their backs to us and let us go along, too. Of Charlie taking off his splint—forgive his stubbornness—and walking. Of that little precious baby, born in grief and pain. Raised to health.

The miracle of the destroyer passing over Melissa and Susan last night. Melissa sheltered under that water, our little creek that became living water, and Susan going to find her even when she could have run and hidden.

The guitars and keyboard died abruptly. The drummer and saxophone guy played on until they realized the others had stopped. The power had gone out. People laughed nervously, but a couple peered at the windows to see if anything was out there. Rick had his hand on his gun.

The lights flickered and came back on. The worship leader tapped his microphone. "The people walking in darkness have seen a great light."

Jeanette got up, her knees creaking with pain. *Miracles and monsters. Both hidden too long, both coming out in Your time.*

Jacob's whole world became Susan's voice and the blank paper set before him.

"A boy walks in a field. The sun is out, the breeze is warm."

He picked up a yellow marker in one hand and a green in the other and began drawing. Part of the way through the first picture,

Jacob squeezed his eyes shut because fear had snaked its way under his skin. He would do as Susan asked, but he would not watch himself do it.

"In the middle of a big city, a boy sees his house. He runs as fast as he can because he wants to open the door."

Jacob drew a picture and set the paper aside, facedown as Susan had asked. She went on, her voice echoing in the hall as she described various scenarios.

"A girl plays with a dog. He is on a leash."

"A mother bathes her baby."

"A boy eats a sandwich. He's very hungry."

"A family picnics under the trees."

After each sentence, Susan paused to give Jacob time to draw. He would open his eyes long enough to find the right color, but he didn't begin drawing until he closed them again. When he was done, he would turn the paper over and say, "All done." That was Susan's signal to read the next image.

"The sun sets over the mountains, casting long shadows."

The Rocky Mountains were gray and brown, still topped with snow with many patches of green. Why had he picked up a black marker?

Because shadows were black.

Black was the absence of light and so he filled the paper with it, eyes squeezed tightly so the shadows wouldn't get in and fill him. A long time ago they had wrapped around him and made him disappear, but he feared to go back there because whatever had been chained in that endless night had deserved to be there. His life now was sunshine and horses and Melissa and cinnamon rolls and why would he want to know what was hidden in that darkness—

—or what darkness was in him?

The black flowed from his marker, thicker than blood. *Stop me*, he wanted to cry, but his mouth had become that which is not and the rest of him would soon follow into the emptiness against whose gates nothing would prevail, into the darkness that would not be emptied until it sucked the light and life out of himself and out of Susan and out of the mountains and out of the sky and out of the world without end whose end indeed had been chained in that darkness and what would happen if it were loosed without end on this world, amen?

TWENTY-SEVEN

SUSAN PUT HER HAND TO HER MOUTH, BITING ON THE INSIDE of her palm to keep from crying out. Zach stood at her side, silent and still.

Jacob was naked except for his boxer shorts. He had used the black marker to cover himself in strange symbols from scalp to toe. He had also scrawled the symbols on the wall. When had he done all this? Susan had moved him briskly from one scenario to the next. She would have to check the videotape and see what scenario had provoked this reaction.

Susan drummed her fingers against her notebook, trying to compose herself. After deciding on a strategy, she rolled the desk chair over to the table and sat next to Jacob. "How're you doing?"

Jacob's smile was wide. "Good. Am I done?"

"Almost. Would you mind looking at some of your pictures with me?"

"No, I wouldn't mind."

"But first, let me ask what you thought of the session."

"You mean, how I did?" His gaze shifted from his papers to Zach and back to her. "I thought there were no wrong answers."

Susan forced warmth into her smile. "There weren't. You worked hard for the past hour. Did you find the time stressful? Tedious? Boring?"

Jacob narrowed his eyes enough so the symbols on his cheeks seemed to connect perfectly with those sketched on his brow. "Fun."

"What was the most fun for you?"

"What you asked me to do. Draw what I felt instead of what I heard."

"Okay," she said. "Why don't you show me the pictures?"

Jacob turned the pile of paper over. She had given him 8½-x-11 card

stock. The sturdy paper gave patients a sense of security. Sometimes they
scribbled so violently, they'd rip ordinary construction paper.

"This is the house in the city." Jacob stared at his work with a sat-
isfied smile. "I made the house yellow because that's a welcoming
color. Jeanette said that's why she painted our house yellow."

Our house. After just a few days, Jacob had integrated himself into
the Robinson household.

"I made the buildings brown and green so the boy could pretend
that they were trees. He hates living in the city. He wishes his home
was where it used to be before his father made him move. I made the
boy with short hair because everyone in the city looks like that. He
doesn't want them to know he's from another place—a better place—
because they might be jealous and hurt him. He's happy that he gets
to go home. See his smile?"

What Susan saw was a blood-red house, daggers in the place of tall
buildings, and a stick figure pressed against the door of the house.
"Did he forget his key? Is that why he can't get in?"

"He's waiting for his father to let him in." Jacob scratched his nose
absently and turned to the next drawing. The skin on his arms
crawled with gooseflesh, but he had not yet acknowledged that he had
taken off his clothes. Susan resisted asking him why he had done so.
Better to wait for the moment of realization.

"Here's the one of the girl playing with her dog," he said.

"Why did you choose that color for the dog?" The dog—more like a
terrifying beast—was orange, streaked with red and yellow. *Like flame*,
Susan thought. The beast's claws were pressed on the girl's shoulders
and its fangs about to pierce the girl's throat. Susan swallowed to
unknot the catch at the back of her throat. The girl's hair was red and
curly, and her face freckled.

Jacob leaned back in his chair. "Don Camara's dog is brown like
that."

There was no brown in the picture. "And the girl? What kind of
game is she playing?"

"She's running so he can catch her."

"What will he do when he catches her?"

"He'll lick her face. But that's okay because she likes that. Just like Melissa likes it when Jade chews on her fingers."

"Does this girl look like anyone you know?"

Jacob tapped his lips with his index finger. "I didn't think so, but now that you ask—she's got blonde hair like that little girl we met in the hospital who broke her thumb. Jenny was her name, right?"

"That is what I remember," Susan said. How could he see yellow hair where he had drawn red? Patients routinely deceived themselves, but usually not with such ruthless efficiency.

She went through the next ten pictures with Jacob. Where he saw greens and pinks and yellows, she saw black and red. She was oddly reminded of the old Gershwin tune: "You say to-ma-to, I say to-mah-to." But this was not a song; it was reality.

Zach stood calmly against the wall, out of Jacob's line of sight. The man must have nerves of steel to lean his back against those symbols. To sit next to Jacob and stare at his sweet face marked with black took every ounce of Susan's training and resolve. What had been done to this young man that he was capable of not only producing these frightening images but also suppressing them?

"Oh, here's my favorite picture. The family having a picnic."

This was the first picture not slashed with black and red. It was conventional with its setting of green grass, leafy trees, and blue sky. A man and a woman sat under a tree, a picnic basket in between them. This pastoral scene was somehow more chilling than all the scenes of torture and mayhem because its very ordinariness seemed to make it vulnerable.

"They're eating fried chicken and mashed potatoes."

The same meal Jeanette had served last night. "So the family is brother and sister? Or husband and wife?"

"They're married, Susan." Jacob blinked rapidly. "He's got a bad headache."

"Really? What from?"

He shook his head. "He doesn't know. I don't either."

"Do they have any children?"

He tipped his head in puzzlement. "They have a son."

"Can you show me where he is?" Susan clutched and worried her hands under the table.

"Oh, he fell down."

Struck silent, Susan looked up at Zach, begging him to intervene.

"Where did he fall from?" Zach asked.

"From here." Jacob turned the paper over, showing her a perfect rendition of her apartment building in Boston.

Darkness clouded Susan's vision. She gratefully grabbed it with both hands and pulled it around her as she fell to the floor.

"What did you think of the service?" Jeanette asked.

Melissa didn't dare express too much enthusiasm as they drove down County Road 102. She didn't need Jeanette on her case every Saturday night about going to church, every Friday about the singles group, the rest of the week about the various Bible studies, craft groups, and choir rehearsals. Worship was okay, but the rest of it choked her.

"It was okay," she said.

When they first walked into the church that morning, a crushing sense of loss hit Melissa. She and Christopher used to attend church together, she leaning against his arm as they sang, he holding her hand as they prayed. She hadn't been on speaking terms with God since the night the guy from the Boston police called.

"I have some bad news for the family," he had said. "I need to talk to Charles Robinson. He'll need someone nearby to lean on, Miss O'Brien, because I have some very tragic news about his grandson."

Please have another grandson somewhere, Melissa had prayed as her knees buckled, but the officer had gone on to say, "Dr. Stone was too broken up to call, so she asked us to call her father."

How could Melissa lean on God when He had slippery hands? Yet today, somehow between the prelude and the benediction, a peace had trickled into that aching void, nurturing a hope she had assumed was long gone. What she had thought was an emotional hiccup had stayed with her, all the way back to Harken.

Even now, as Jeanette pulled into Don Camara's driveway, Melissa felt a strange emotion that must be what people called serenity.

She had volunteered to tend Don's sheep while they were away. She already missed Krista, even though she wasn't due to see her for almost a week. Maybe by then this maniac would be caught and the Camaras could return home. Otherwise she'd have to beg Jeanette to drive her to Granby. Melissa knew how to drive, but she had lost her license for five years. Too much chronic speeding and reckless driving in her teens.

Jeanette turned off the truck and opened the door, struggling to get her legs around so she could climb down.

"Wait. Let me help you," Melissa said. Jeanette was literally on her last legs. She needed to have both her knees replaced, but Charlie had used what little savings they had to buy Rayya. Once they sold Jade, they could afford it. Melissa would miss the filly like her own heart, but Jeanette had to come first.

"What?" Jeanette said. "You look like you just swallowed a cupcake."

"Your knees," Melissa said. "We should ask Jacob if he could fix them."

"He's not a surgeon," Jeanette said.

"You know darn well that's not what I'm saying."

Jeanette limped to the fence, an angry set to her shoulders. "You're talking nonsense."

"You can't deny the miracles. Jade coming back almost from death. You've seen Krista's seizures with your own eyes, but since Jacob touched her she's been fine. And Charlie's bouncing around like a kid. Why not ask Jacob to touch your knees?"

She turned, her eyes narrow with anger. "You're teetering on blasphemy, young lady. And we just left church."

She hated it when Jeanette gave her that *I'm disappointed* look. "I don't see how. I honestly don't."

"God does miracles. Not Jacob, whoever he is."

"I'm not saying Jacob is God. But I listened to the sermon today, about Peter laying his hands on people so the Spirit could heal them." Melissa unlocked the padlock on the feed shed but couldn't pull it apart. Stupid thing was stuck. The sheep bleated, unsettled by her yanking and banging.

Jeanette leaned against the shed. "You think I haven't asked God to heal me? Every morning, getting out of bed, it's like I have broken glass in each knee. At your age, you can't even imagine what it's like to—"

The lock jerked free and the door banged open.

A black mass thundered out of the shed.

Melissa flung herself onto Jeanette, knocking her to the ground and covering her with her body. She screamed the whole time until Jeanette snaked her hand up between them and covered her mouth.

"Hush, girl. Get off me. It's only bats."

Melissa twisted around to look. A few swooped overhead, but most were already settling back in the rafters. "What an idiot. Did I hurt you?" She helped Jeanette off the ground.

Jeanette patted her own backside. "Just my pride. But you know what? I love what you just did."

"Spooked like a howling idiot?"

Jeanette squeezed her hands. "Protecting me like that."

Melissa looked at her feet, embarrassed. "That's what you've been doing for me all these years. I guess I've never said it, but I should've. Thanks."

"Okay, enough mush. What do we feed these sheep?"

"Nothing. They're grazing this time of year. I've just got to scrub out the water trough. Don's nervous about the lambs getting sick from mold or something. You know how he loves his sheep." Melissa pawed through the shed, looking for the scrub brush. "You want me to get you a stool so you can sit? This'll take about fifteen minutes, tops."

"No. I'll just lean."

Melissa unrolled the hose and dragged it to the water trough. There was an old bucket nearby for bailing. Once she had the trough almost empty, she could tip it and dump the rest of the water. Scrub with the antibacterial soap, rinse it all out, and sit and stare at the mountains while it filled.

Something red was at the bottom of the trough. The water was too murky to get a clear look, so Melissa fished it out with a stick.

Krista's bonnet. The one she had given her two weeks ago.

"Jeanette," Melissa said, her voice caught deep in her chest.

"What? You look like you saw a ghost."

Fear burst inside Melissa, an adrenaline bomb blast that made her leap the fence and race for the house. The key would be under the mat at the back door, but she didn't need the key because the door had been ripped off its hinges. The kitchen smelled foul, like a backed-up sewer.

Jeanette limped across the yard as fast as she could, gasping with pain and calling after her.

Melissa searched through the drawers and grabbed a carving knife and a butcher's knife.

Jeanette leaned against the door frame. "What happened here?"

"Get out, Ma."

"You get out too."

"No. Call 911."

"Melissa, please."

"What if Don and Sara came back today? What if they're in here somewhere? What if Krista . . ." She grabbed the phone and slid it across the floor to Jeanette. "Call Rick."

Knives at the ready, Melissa stepped into the hall.

TWENTY-EIGHT

"IT'S ALL GREEK TO ME. BUT THIS DNA STUFF USUALLY IS." Rick handed the report to Joyce.

She wrinkled her nose. "Their conclusion is the sample was contaminated. You took the specimen, right?"

"Sure. I swabbed the inside of Jacob's mouth and put the swab back into the tube. Twisted the top nice and tight. The lab affirms it was still sealed when they received it."

"Maybe something fouled their equipment."

"They ran it twice. This is costing Routt County plenty, by the way."

"We can't let the jerk who chained Jacob up get away with it," Joyce said.

Rick cracked his knuckles, the *pop* giving vent to his frustration. "If there is a jerk. If there were chains."

"Susan Stone said there were. Do you think she's lying?"

"Hm. What people see and what the reality is aren't always the same thing."

Joyce ran her fingers through her hair. "What are you getting at?"

Rick leaned over, scanned the report. "Here. Read this."

"Sample displays vaguely human characteristics." She raised her eyebrows. "So?"

"So what if the sample wasn't contaminated? What if the test was run correctly?"

"What if Jacob isn't human? Is that what you're saying, Rick?"

He punched his fist into his palm. "It's what I'm afraid to say."

"If not human, then what?"

"The obvious—extraterrestrial."

Joyce laughed.

"Please. Don't. I feel like a big enough fool."

"I'm sorry." She clutched his forearm. "It's just that aliens and UFOs are so *not* you, Rick."

"I know, I know. Which is why I'm on shifting sand here."

"Let's work through it together. Brainstorm—no one but you, me, and the pizza delivery guy. What's holding him up? I'm famished." Joyce grinned at him.

She kept threatening to retire so she could travel, hike, and climb all over the world. The Elk River Valley would miss her robust caring. Rick would miss her wisdom and friendship.

"The only reason they deliver out here to my office is because the owner lives in Harken, wants to stay on my good side."

"Back to work, then. We've got E.T. on the table," Joyce said. "Being of alien origin might explain his unusual rate of respiration and heartbeat. The memory loss could be deliberate so he could infiltrate our society."

Rick laughed.

Joyce slapped him. "I didn't laugh at you. Well, I guess I did. But, you know what? Now I'm feeling weird about the whole thing. Like maybe he isn't human. Jacob certainly is almost too good to be true."

Rick's head throbbed. He didn't have the imagination for this. "What else? A robot, maybe?"

"He bled when I took his blood."

"But he shorted out the CAT scan. Susan blames the hospital, but the fact that the EKG machine failed too . . ."

"A hybrid? Flesh and machine. What a great story. Robot's memory is deleted, his personality reformatted out at Robinson Ranch."

"You joke, but he's doing just that, Joyce. Half the time he sounds like Melissa. Even walks like her. Sometimes I hear Susan in his speech, carefully choosing words, even a hint of a Boston accent."

Patricia, the weekend dispatcher, buzzed Rick's phone to announce the arrival of their pizza. Rick left a couple slices for her and brought the rest back to his office. They said grace and ate, Rick barely tasting it.

"What else, Joyce?"

She wiped her mouth. "How about this: a clone that didn't quite take. Something in the process shifts, and the DNA mutates. Or maybe someone deliberately tried to improve on what God created."

"Does the technology exist to do that?"

"Who knows? Even with the federal controls, you got mavericks all over the world playing around with this stuff. Maybe Jacob wasn't the victim of abuse so much as a unit locked up in storage."

Rick pushed his pizza away. What little appetite he had was gone. "Any of these options creeps me out. If we take Jacob's story at face value, Susan is absolutely right in saying that there's some abuser out there who needs to be brought to justice. Because of the timing, I have to consider the probability that Jacob could be involved with the killer."

"Speaking of The Torch—"

Rick cringed. "I'm sick of that nickname."

"We don't even know if that thing that attacked Melissa and Susan was human. Didn't it sound like Melissa was describing a dragon?"

He covered his face with his hands. "I keep telling myself it was dark, she was scared. I almost can't process it, it's so weird. I wouldn't have believed a word of her story if I hadn't seen the brush all burned out like that."

"Let me ask you something. And please don't get upset by what I'm going to say. But while we're brainstorming, there's something we need to consider."

"What?"

"Don't freak, Rick."

"And you don't pussyfoot. Will you just tell me?"

The intercom buzzed. "There's trouble out at the Camara farm," Patricia said. "No casualties, but Jeanette Robinson says you'd better get out there."

Rick jumped up, buckled on his gun belt. "Call CBI, Patricia."

"I'm coming with you," Joyce said.

"No."

"I might be needed. Let me grab my bag out of my car."

As they ran out to the cruiser, Rick shouted over his shoulder. "What was it?"

"What?" Joyce said, buckling into the front seat.

Rick started the cruiser and peeled out of the parking lot. "What is the possibility that you're dancing around?"

"It can wait."

He tightened his fingers on the wheel. "Maybe it can't. Give it, Joyce."

"Okay. Fine. What if—" She looked away, directing her gaze at the passing countryside. "What if we're looking at this all wrong? What if your killer is Susan Stone?"

Something creaked.

Melissa jumped, her muscles going into an instant tremor. The floorboard, that was all. Don was always going on about fixing it. She held the butcher knife in front of her, angled upward, and the carving knife over her shoulder, taking a deep breath so she wouldn't stab herself. Absolutely ridiculous, but if something jumped out at her, at least she was covered.

She glanced in the living room, the bathroom, the extra bedroom that Sara used for quilting, the master bedroom. It was only when she reached the end of the hall that she dared admit what any dummy would know.

No knife was going to protect her from the monster she had seen last night.

The door to Krista's room was closed. Maybe the wind had blown
it shut. Surely the Camaras hadn't done anything as stupid as come
back today. Rick would be here in another ten minutes. Melissa could
just wait.

No way—this was the nursery. The door shouldn't be closed, and
what was that stink?

She opened the door and looked into a black hole. It flowed out and
around her, so she couldn't see, couldn't feel except for frigid hands
pulling her into the room, but she couldn't reach back for Jeanette,
even though she was behind her and the darkness would not—could
not—touch her.

Oh God, Melissa thought.

Fire flashed, followed by a huge boom that flung her against the
opposite wall. A wall of flame blocked the door to Krista's room.

Jeanette limped down the hall. "Don't go in there. Please. We gotta
get out of here, please hon, come back, come out."

Melissa pushed up, her arms and legs trembling. She steadied herself against the wall, felt the heat from the explosion.

"Hon, come this way, please, baby. They're not here, the baby's safe
in Granby, don't go in there."

Melissa looked at Jeanette. "You'd do it for me."

She grabbed the blanket off Don and Sara's bed, wrapped it around
herself, and pushed into the fire.

The room was untouched except for the outside wall. The curtains
flamed around a hole where the window had been. The wall was black-
ened and the exposed studs charred. Melissa shrugged off the blanket
and scanned the room quickly. No monster, no maniac. She used the
blanket to beat out the flames, thinking this is wrong, it makes no
sense, it's evil. Why would someone terrorize a baby's room?

Unless the baby were in it. The crib was in the corner, away from
the drafty window, Sara had said. Melissa hadn't looked in it, didn't
think it was necessary.

Melissa took the first step to the crib. They aren't here. Second step.
What if they came back? Third step. The minivan wasn't in the yard.
Fourth step. Sometimes Sara pulled it into the barn.

Krista wasn't in the crib. *Thank you, Jesus.*

The mattress was slashed from top to bottom, the ragged tear scorched at the edges.

Melissa dropped to her knees, wrapped her arms around herself, and rocked back and forth. Praying that Rick would get here soon.

"Okay, Joyce. Care to defend that accusation?" Rick said.

"I knew you'd get frosty on me. I shouldn't have even brought it up."

"Yes, you should have. I can't let a childhood friendship cloud my judgment. Have I missed something?"

"I'm not accusing, but in the interests of comprehensive brain-storming, consider this. The first murder happened the night Susan arrived in Colorado. She saw Charlie around eight thirty that night—"

"Hold on. How do you know that?"

"His nurse noted it. Susan pulled rank, the whole *I'm a doctor so show me the chart* thing. Anyway, assuming she stayed for no longer than an hour—"

"Was that marked as well?"

"No, but Charlie was postsurg and on pain meds. He wouldn't be able to stay awake longer than that at one time. Let's assume she left at nine thirty. Even ten. It's an hour ride out to Robinson's. And she'd have to pass right by where the body was found."

"Would she have been able to climb that ridge in the dark?"

"Someone did, Rick. Dr. MacArthur's post couldn't pinpoint the exact time of death because of the condition of the body, correct?"

"Yeah. You're telling me she arrived in Colorado—flying first-class—carrying a combustible agent?"

"Hang in here with me. Flash forward a week to the next event. Susan was missing all night. What time did Jeanette call you?"

"It was dark. Eight or so, maybe. But I was diverted from looking for her to go to the scene of the second burning."

"Susan left the farm midafternoon. Plenty of time."

Rick had to wipe his hands on his trousers. Too sweaty to drive safely. "Explain Jacob. Where did he come from?"

"As a shrink, Susan's got plenty of access to people with bizarre mental maladies. And trust me—the blank innocence Jacob demonstrates could be a persuasive form of sociopathy."

"Joyce, I couldn't buy this in a million years. Susan is a doctor."

"She's a human being. A very traumatized woman. You know what a nightmare her mother was."

Rick glanced at her. "Did you?"

"You forget how old I am, child. I had been practicing for about three years the first time the school nurse called me in. Susan had stopped talking in school."

"I remember that. She said she had laryngitis. But it always got better after school."

"Her throat was clear. I spoke at length to her teacher, the nurse, and Mary Potter."

"Wow. Been a long time since Doc's wife was the school principal." He took the turn for 102. Still four miles out.

"The bruises were never bad enough to even file a complaint, but anyone who interacted with Vanessa Robinson knew how troubled she was. Yet no amount of trying to draw Susan out would get the girl to admit anything was amiss at home."

"I knew," Rick said. "I should have done something."

"What could you do? You were just a kid. These days, kids are educated how to help friends in abusive situations. But back then, what happened at home stayed at home unless the evidence was very clear." He rubbed his chest as if he could rub away the regret. "What does this have to do with these murders?"

"Susan Stone leaves Colorado, builds a life in Boston, raises a son who Jeanette says was everything to her. Yet he comes out here to marry a girl who couldn't be farther from the Ivy League if she lived in China. There's some sort of blow-up, and Christopher Stone dies a horrible death. Susan blames Melissa, even Charlie and Jeanette. She comes back to Colorado out of a daughter's duty to her father. Or perhaps for a darker reason that only the tormented little girl knows.

"Face it, Rick. It's conceivable, based on Susan Stone's childhood and recent events, that she finally cracked and now she's striking out."

"Why not go after Melissa directly?" Rick pulled into Camaras's driveway.

Melissa sat on the back stoop, arms wrapped around Jeanette.

"Hasn't she? What are we doing here?" Joyce said.

Rick turned off the car and got out to ask Melissa exactly that.

TWENTY-NINE

"Doing an intensive second session today could be counterproductive," Susan said. "Surely you see that, Zach."

"Hey, my career is on the line here. My supervisor was set on institutionalizing Jacob, but I went way out on a limb, promised two sessions a day. So don't wimp out on me."

"Okay, okay. It's just that—" She laughed. "I've never hung an IV from a tree before."

Charlie's office was unusable until Susan could wash down the walls. Jeanette and Melissa hadn't come home from church, so she left a note telling them not to go in there, making the feeble excuse that she had left some important test results that still needed evaluation. After a quick lunch, she had saddled up the three surviving dude horses and taken Zach and Jacob to Advent River. Jacob had responded so positively to the river after the CAT-scan incident that it made sense to take advantage of the setting and the nice weather.

She would begin the session as soon as the sodium amobarbital had sufficiently infused. Its function as a truth serum was a movie myth, but the medication was effective in loosening inhibitions.

"What do you make of those symbols?" Zach whispered.

"I don't have a clue. I'll need to check the tape, see which scenario initiated the response."

"When shall we watch it?"

"Maybe tomorrow. I'm exhausted. I need some downtime when we're done here." If there was nothing significant on the tape, Susan would let him see it. If there was, she'd claim the camera had malfunctioned. Zach insisted he was her ally, but she wasn't sure.

His amiability could mask a loyalty to the court or the hospital. She was irked at herself for almost fainting this morning. Yet how had Jacob known?

Jacob stretched out under a cottonwood tree. When Susan pressed her fingers to his wrist to take his pulse, he opened his eyes and smiled. "Hey."

"Hey there. How do you feel?"

"Nice. I love listening to the water."

"Me too."

"And the birds. Hear the meadowlark?"

"I don't. Is there a nest up there?" She peered up into the tree.

"No, they're"—Jacob sat up and pointed to a ridge on the other side of the river—"up there. In the willow brush."

The cluster of brush had to be a good tenth of a mile away. Was his hearing that acute?

Susan pressed her stethoscope to his chest. She had insisted he take a shower before lunch. "To relax you," she had fibbed, wanting those symbols gone, thankful she had bought washable markers.

He never did express surprise at being unclothed, something that she found remarkable. In an institutional setting, Susan might have let that situation go on until Jacob finally acknowledged that he had undressed. But she couldn't let Jeanette and Melissa see him like that.

Charlie had called from the barn, asking her to bring him his lunch. He had been out there since the middle of the night, guarding his Arabians. Apparently it hadn't occurred to him that it should be of higher priority to ensure the safety of his wife, daughter, and step-daughter.

A familiar ache gnawed at Susan. She had to put any resentment away. All her focus needed to be on Jacob and navigating this session well.

She sat down on the blanket next to him. "Ready to start?"

Jacob smiled. "Sure."

"Do you know how old I am?"

He peered up at her. "A little older than Melissa. Maybe twenty-five."

Susan laughed. "I'm forty-eight. I lived in Harken until I was almost

Melissa's age. I went to Boston for college and stayed there. Do you know where Boston is?"

He nodded solemnly, gaze fixed on her. "Sure. It's in the middle of Red Sox nation."

She put her finger to her lips, a delaying tactic until she could decide how to handle that pronouncement.

Jacob poked her arm. "It's a joke. Melissa showed me a map, so I saw where Boston was. And Colorado, Turkey, Japan, all those places."

"Turkey? Why Turkey?"

He shrugged.

Susan had to get the session back on track. "I had a friend whose father was born in Japan. Though Evelyn had never been there, she could tell you all about the country. Just as I can tell you what life was like in the Elk River Valley before I was born."

"Even though you weren't here?"

"Sure. I've heard stories, seen old photos. Not just from my family, but from parents of friends, even in history class. There are many ways to pick up information about events that we weren't there to experience firsthand. I'm wondering if you can think back to a time before you were born. Maybe tell me some things you've heard people talk about or learned about in school."

Perspiration broke out across his forehead. "I wasn't born. I told you before."

"The time before you came to be, then." Susan opened the flow on the IV to increase the sodium amobarbital. Her hope was that, by removing him from the recollection, Jacob might feel less threatened. At the very least, they might gain some context for where he had come from. "Think back to breakfast, Jacob. What Jeanette made for you."

"Cornbread. Homemade strawberry jam." His voice was thick as he slipped into deeper relaxation. "Big chunks of berries."

It was tricky walking him back through immediate history because of what had happened to her just last night. She clasped her hands, pressing her nails into her skin to keep her horror of the attack from shading her voice. "Back two nights ago. When Melissa, Charlie, and you watched baseball."

"Stupid Yankees won again," he murmured in a perfect imitation of her father. "Sox gotta fix their stupid bull pen or they won't win any stupid championship again."

"Remember back to the time I freed you from those chains." She should have jumped over that, but his reaction might be telling.

He smiled. "Thank you, Susan."

"Anything else?"

"I'm glad the batteries didn't go out."

"Let's go way back now. Before you were young."

Why did he insist that he had not been born? Susan had assumed his abuser was a man, perhaps his father. But perhaps it was his mother, which is why Jacob denied his own birth. Susan certainly could identify with that.

"Think back before you came to be. Walk back."

Eyes closed, he wrinkled his brow. "I'm starting to see some stuff."

"Can you tell me what you see?"

A slow smile dawned on his face. "A pasture. There's grass, some trees, but no mountains and no rivers. There's mist covering the ground, and it sparkles. Oh, there's a man. He's looking over there." Jacob leaned on his elbow and pointed to the east. "His eyes are wide and he turns his head back and forth, trying to look at everything at once."

"Is he there alone?"

"Yes. But he doesn't mind."

Jacob sat up, his head turned west as if he were facing the man he had described. His eyes were open, but seeing something that only he could see. Susan felt an unprofessional pang of relief that apparently the vision was pleasing. Soon enough they'd have to dig deeper into memories that had to be devastating. The art therapy was clear proof of that.

"What does this man look like?"

"Like Zach or Rick. Just a guy. Except he's very content. And he's very clean."

"Clean? Like he's just bathed?"

Was Jacob seeing himself, perhaps as the observer? Cleanliness could indicate the desire to be relieved of guilt. Some abuse victims

believed that they were to blame, that somehow they deserved what
had happened to them.

"It's like . . . no matter where you looked on him, even the bottom
of his feet or inside his ears, he'd be clean."

"Do you know the man's name?"

Jacob shook his head. "I don't think he knows it."

"Did he forget it?"

"No one has told him what it is yet."

A blank slate, like Jacob. Hoping for someone else to assign him a
history so he wouldn't have to relive his own?

"What's he doing?"

"Animals, oh, they are filling the pasture, all the way to the edge of
the sky and into the sky, even."

"What kind of animals?" Susan said, anxious for at least a geo-
graphical clue that could provide context.

"Horses! Running like the wind, legs outstretched, manes flying.
Others just as fast. Zebras. Donkeys. Some even faster now. Deer,
antelope, gazelles. They cluster with their own kind. And now look—"
He motioned as if directing her attention. "Rabbits, gophers, hedge-
hogs, squirrels, chipmunks. Dogs, wolves, coyotes, foxes. Mountain
lions, panthers, cheetahs, and oh . . . that's what an ocelot looks like?
The man speaks to each one as they pass him."

He went on for five minutes, listing animals from the exotic to the
familiar, domesticated to wild, ocean-swimmers to mud-dwellers,
even listing extinct species like the woolly mammoth and the saber-
toothed tiger.

As they had agreed, Zach sat about ten feet away behind, out of
Jacob's line of sight. Susan caught his wave from the corner of her eye.
He tapped his watch. *Move on.*

"Jacob. You've given me a solid idea of all these animals. Can we see
something else?"

"The birds are coming now. Crows and blue jays and condors
and pterodactyls. Insects too. Mosquitoes, but they don't bite, and
the bumblebees don't sting."

Jacob's version of reality allowed no threat. His innocence was a lovely thing, but it was not real, and it would not hold. Better to heal the wound than slap a covering over it that eventually would peel away.

"Can we move on from here? Maybe to somewhere else?" she asked.

Jacob closed his eyes and pondered. "I can see water. Oh, and now I can see under the water."

"Is the man with you?"

"He lay down on the sand and kind of drifted right into it."

"Is he all right?"

"He's not."

Perhaps Jacob was reliving his imprisonment in the form of this man being buried.

Susan took care to speak in calm tones. "What happened to him? Did someone hurt him?"

"No. He was and is not, not yet."

If the man represented Jacob, it was good that he had removed himself from the recollection. Perhaps now she could probe a bit. "What kind of water is it?"

"Ocean and lake and river, all mixed together."

"How can that be, Jacob?"

"They know how to get along."

Humanizing his environment. Jacob's worldview allowed no conflict, no harm.

"You said a minute ago that you could see under the water."

"Sure. It's moving hard in some places, like the Advent over there. Some places are deep, so deep you can't even imagine. The water is filled with fish and whales and plants and tiny creatures. They all fit the space they're supposed to."

Susan needed to shift his focus before he wrapped himself in another long recitation. "Can you tell me about something other than the animals and fish?"

Jacob jumped to his feet, arms raised to the sky. "I am here. Oh, I am here!"

"You're part of what you're seeing?"

"I'm right in the middle of it all."

Why now? Had he recalled a place or time where he felt safe? "Are you the man who is sleeping in the sand?"

"No, no. He's just a dream right now. He is not yet, but he will be."

"Where are you?"

"I don't know how to explain it. I fly the sky and swim the depths, so much a part of it all that I didn't know I was separate from it. But now, I am truly who I am. Who I became and then was."

Susan's pulse quickened. "What are you doing?"

"I'm singing. Can't you hear it? We breathe, and it comes out as music. We soar, and the music fills the skies. We rest, and the music surrounds us."

We. He is finally connecting to people, though in a very imaginative way, Susan thought.

Jacob began to sing.

Susan clutched the tree, stunned. How could harmony come from one person, a chorus of flute and lyre and even bass horns and percussion, all woven into words that at first she couldn't comprehend, yet were majestic beyond her ability to hear, to know, to embrace. She looked for Zach, wanting him to either confirm that he heard this also or to yank her out of this shared delusion, but he had run away, his back hunched as if this glorious music had driven him away.

Leaving Susan alone. Not alone; how could she even know the concept of *alone* when the air hummed and the water roared and the grass swished and the birds sang with Jacob in a way she had never heard, never imagined.

The words resolved, and she understood.

Be still, and know I have loved you.
Be still. My arms surround you.
All of the seasons are a myriad of reasons
I'm right here beside you.
Be still, and know that I am . . .

If only she could be still. If only Susan could be loved.

Jacob stopped singing. Yet the music lingered, sweeping away on the Advent, stretching across the sky, from mountain to mountain in a rainbow that had surely never before had so many colors.

He tugged on her, wanting her to kneel with him. He pressed his palms to the ground. "Hear that?"

She pressed her ear to the ground, dimly thinking that she had lost control of the session, thinking what did it matter anyway? She heard the surge of the river and her blood rushing in her head, but nothing in the ground. She looked around, trying to get her bearings. The horses grazed lazily in the meadow, but Zach still jogged in the opposite direction.

"Hold on, Susan. Hold on to me."

"Why, Jacob?"

"Because as we walk backwards, it all comes apart but not apart, it comes to what it once was, what it is, what it will be."

"Jacob—"

"Hold tight, Susan. Watch the moon be stretched into silver lace, the sun cast into raging fire." He took her face in his hands, pulled her to him so their foreheads touched. "The sun and the moon and the stars shine and sing, sing and shine. See them and hear them."

It was improper to be in a patient's personal space, but what Susan knew was of no consequence because Jacob would not let her go, but kept her head to his, eye to eye, breath mingling in a way that was not at all suggestive, but somehow elemental, something good.

Eyes locked on his, nevertheless she saw beyond herself and him as the suns and moons and planets spun in their ordained paths. The ground thundered and broke apart, but Jacob held her fast so Susan could see the ground rising into the sky, the heavens swallowing back its mantle of grass and tree and blossom, and yet this was not destruction because this life was not destroyed but returned. The light came out of the darkness so that there was night and there was day but the two did not mix, *could* not mix.

"I'm lost," Susan whispered.

"I've got you," Jacob said.

A radiance roared about them, the entire sky split by lightning that was bigger than the sky and then swallowed the sky. The night disappeared, and all was day with no sun and no moon, no darkness because nothing existed that could shadow this light that was, that is, and that will be.

For an instant and no more, she saw Jacob soar towards the light, the same radiance streaming from his shoulders, rippling his body, weaving wings so he could soar into a sky that no longer was bound by earth. Music seeped from his skin, but it was not he that made the music, but a voice before all voices making the music and in that music was Jacob.

A distant shadow of Jacob held her tight, his forehead searing hers. "And now, Susan, now is before I came to be."

The soaring Jacob drew back into the light, folding his cloak into it, the music following him so that he became *not* in a whirlpool of light that spun into a perfect center, tighter and tighter until it was one point—one magnificent instant—of all music and light and joy and love and wonder beyond forever.

And then it disappeared.

The light, Jacob, the ground under Susan's feet, the river horses trees grass sky mountains life were all swept away.

There was just darkness.

And One hovering over the darkness, and Susan was ashamed and dirty and not able to understand, to name, to bear this One's presence. She was not, is not, would not be, because even darkness was beyond what she deserved. Yet in her utter bleakness, one voice sang to *be still and know I have loved you.*

"Susan."

She waited, the silence weighing on her like a mountain, waiting to hear about *arms surrounding her,* lifting her arms so she could be lifted . . .

"Susan! Snap out of it!" Zach shook her by the shoulders.

She blinked up, trying to make out his features, but only saw a dark form blocking the sun.

"What happened to you?" he said. "I'm beginning to think this therapy is too much for you. You went out cold."

Her legs were numb. She rubbed her face, trying to orient to her reality. Jacob had collapsed against her shoulder and was unconscious. "Lift him off me, please."

Zach moved to her other side to move Jacob. Susan felt the sunlight on her face and heard the river to her side, the grass against her ankles, a blackbird shouting in the cottonwood. She reached up to stop the flow of the medication, checked Jacob's pulse and respiration. He was okay, and she'd let him rest.

Zach helped her stand. "Should we take you to Joyce? You blacked out again."

"No, I'm fine. Just up all night, that's all. Don't read too much into it."

"What do you think of all this? Animals, plants, sun, and moon?"

Susan held up her hand, trying to get her bearings. Jacob's vision was coming clear now, a delusion so powerful that it swept the therapist into it. But she was regaining control, her mind clicking along rational paths. "Did you ever go to church or Sunday school, Zach?"

Zach shook his head. "I was spared, thank you."

"Jacob was recounting the—" The word myth stuck in her throat, even though that's how most of her colleagues in Boston referred to it. She looked at her hands. They seemed clean, but they felt dirty, with a stickiness to them. She jogged to the Advent and rinsed her face and hands. The cold water felt good, restoring her to her professional calm and objectivity. She stood and shook out her hands. When she turned, she bumped into Zach.

"Jacob was recounting what?" he said.

"The story of creation. Backwards."

Zach cracked his knuckles. "I'm disappointed—I expected something more imaginative."

"What?" She held up her hands to the sun, letting its heat warm them.

"Jacob's delusion." Zach smiled. "It's so typical. The kid thinks he's God."

THIRTY

Melissa sobbed so hard that Jeanette had to finish the phone call for her.

"Sheriff Sanchez is on his way, Donnie. No need for you to come up here. We'll call back after he looks around." She looked over at Melissa. "Sara wants to talk to you."

Melissa wiped her face with a paper towel and took the phone.

"Hey," Sara said. "It's okay."

"I'm so sorry about all this."

"It's not your fault. You don't think that, do you?"

Melissa just didn't know. The cyclone of wickedness that had hit the valley seemed to center over Robinson Ranch. "It knows."

"What knows?"

"The thing. *The Torch*. It knows it can get to me through Krista. But I don't know what it wants."

"Why don't you come stay with us? Mom's got plenty of room. She's fond of you, asks about you all the time."

Full-time with Krista. How wonderful that would be. But what if this evil followed her to Granby? "I'd love to, but Charlie can't work the horses without me. Maybe Jeanette can bring me down on Saturday night. You and Don will miss your team competition, but he needs the practice, right?" Melissa tried to laugh, but her voice cracked.

"Mr. Gutter Ball takes the show on the road. Yeah, I like the sound of that. And Krista will miss you if she doesn't see you. Hey, before you go, I gotta hand the phone over."

Probably to Don, with more instructions about hanging the tarp over the hole in his house. She waited, chewing her fingernail. What if the thing that had blasted out the window came back while Rick was out searching the grounds? The fire marshal hadn't gotten here yet, nor had the guys from CBI. They were just out here in the middle of the night. Probably wishing the whole valley would just burn up and go away so they could get some sleep.

Krista babbled into the phone, and for that moment, Melissa's world righted.

"Hey kid," Melissa said.

Krista went off on a riff of ga-gas and ba-bas. Melissa could hear the smile in her little voice, knew her feet would be kicking and her arms waving so hard that she'd probably smack herself in the nose.

Sara came back on. "When Don told her Aunt Missy wanted to talk to her, she smiled."

"No, she didn't," Melissa said, desperate to believe that she had.

"I swear she did. By the way, we lessened her meds this morning by a third. So far, so good. So you see, it's not all bad news."

Maybe not. But Jacob seemed to somehow be in the middle of all of it. Good or bad. She and Sara talked another minute and clicked off.

Melissa went back to the nursery. Jeanette stood at what used to be the window, arms outstretched.

"Are you insane? What are you doing? What if that thing comes back?"

"I'm praying," Jeanette said. "Keeping it out."

A chill took hold of Melissa. She wrapped her arms around Jeanette's waist and held on.

"Shush. It'll be all right," Jeanette murmured, one arm around Melissa and the other still raised to the sky.

"I don't get it," Melissa whispered.

"I'm covering the Camaras with prayer."

"Thank you."

"Two praying would be better than one."

"Oh, Ma. I don't remember how." She and Christopher had prayed together. When he died, she had filled the void he had left the way she always had—with anger. Susan made a deserving target. The bitterness probably would have killed Melissa, but she had to push it away. She couldn't let the baby in her womb be touched by it.

"Be honest," Jeanette said. "It all comes from the truth."

Melissa closed her eyes and clung to Jeanette. *God, there's poison in this valley and poison in me. Take it all away, please. And keep the little ones like Krista safe. The innocent animals like Jade. The ones chained in darkness like Jacob. I'm chained in darkness too. I came out once but—*

"You betrayed me!" The poison gushed out of her, ugly and hot.

Jeanette held her tighter. "Keep going. It's okay. He knows it's there, so let it out."

"I trusted you, and you crushed me like a bug. You didn't care, never cared, let me be born to a cokehead slut, let me—" The sobs came, shaking her body. "Let me be brought to Jeanette. And Charlie. And the horses."

She took a long breath. The air was clear and cool, surprising because there was no odor of smoke. "You gotta work it out, God. Because I can't. And help me stop this stupid crying because I've emptied myself out every day like this. But I don't know what to do about that. About anything."

LET ME FILL YOU, CHILD.

"I don't know how." Melissa buried her head in Jeanette's shoulder. "I don't know what to do, Ma."

"He's not gonna let you go, baby. So you can." Jeanette held Melissa tight until the police and fire investigators filled the yard with lights and sirens.

What Rick had seen at Camaras' enraged him. What Joyce had suggested about Susan terrified him. Distracted by these murders, he had let the *Jacob-in-chains* thing play out too long. He needed to take charge of the situation, find out who this kid really was. And why all of this swirled around Robinson Ranch.

After the first wave of technicians and troopers arrived at Camaras', he followed Jeanette and Melissa home while Renee MacArthur drove Joyce back to her place.

Jeanette insisted on sitting him down with a ham sandwich and big glass of milk. Surprised by his hunger, Rick gobbled it right down. Melissa took a tray out to Charlie in the barn. The old fool was still guarding his Arabians. Had the attack on Melissa been just the night before? It seemed like days ago.

Susan and Zach had taken Jacob riding, planning to do another session out among the hills. What kind of fools were they, heading away from the ranch when this attack had only happened the night before? Some people had no idea of what true evil was, even when it swept them off their seats, like that machine or animal did to Susan last night.

Rick had yet to see a report of the first couple of sessions. That would change, and right away. He would insist on sitting in on the therapy, if need be. He would also take another set of fingerprints, redo the DNA, and post Jacob's picture on the Internet. If he was a victim of abuse, it was time to flush out the abuser. If he wasn't, then something very bad was at work here, and Rick needed to deal with it as soon as humanly possible.

"Can I get you anything else?" Jeanette hovered in her usual position, poised between stove and refrigerator.

"I need the key that unlocked Jacob. Susan can't remember where she put it."

"You want me to help you look for it?"

"Sure. But I'm obligated to tell you that I don't have a search warrant." She shrugged. "What do you need one for?"

"I really need to find that key. Which means looking everywhere."

"Is some search warrant going to sharpen our eyes?"

"It makes everything legal and clean. But I don't need one if the owner of the house gives me permission."

"Charlie put me on the deed when we got married. I'm not only giving you permission, I'll help you look."

"We need to start with Susan's room." They went upstairs, with Rick automatically turning to the front room.

"She's not in her old room. Jacob is. She's in the guest room."

The guest room was newly papered and painted in soft blues and greens. Jeanette's influence, no doubt. When Vanessa ruled this roost, the house was stylish but stark.

Susan's suitcase and briefcase were neatly stored in the closet.

"I can look under the bed, on the floor, and behind furniture. But I can't go through her personal stuff," Rick said. "A judge wouldn't allow it, even with your permission."

"I'll do it."

Rick watched as Jeanette opened the drawers. Susan's slacks and sweaters were folded neatly. The jeans and T-shirts looked brand new. She must have bought them when she decided to stay here for a while.

"Go through each pocket. Turn them inside out."

Jeanette did as he asked. Nothing. She opened Susan's cosmetic kit and dug through it. "No key here."

"Her purse?"

Jeanette grimaced, but she went through it.

"Even the wallet," Rick said. "My wife kept her spare key there."

"How's she doing, by the way?"

He shrugged. "The kids say she's fine. Still married."

"I'm sorry," Jeanette said.

Lori had had an affair and ended up marrying the guy. Rick didn't half-blame her for cheating on him. He had been a hard-nosed Marine, expecting her to pick up and move whenever and wherever the Corps sent them. When he wasn't busy rounding up drunk recruits, he was busy drinking. He denied he was an alcoholic until God opened his eyes.

"I'm glad she's fine," Rick said. "Carey and Wayne are doing great, too. I just wished they were closer than Arizona."

"You need to find a good woman."

He kissed her cheek. "I have. But you're married."

Jeanette pawed through Susan's wallet. "Nothing." As she slid it back into the purse, she said, "Hold on, there's a hidden compartment in her purse. I feel something."

She took out a tiny frame, with a little boy's picture and a lock of hair. Jeanette's face flooded with tears. "Christopher."

Susan burst into the room. "What are you doing in my—how dare you!" She snatched away the picture. "Get out. Get out now."

"I'm sorry, Susie," Jeanette said. "We're looking for the key."

"I said to get out."

"No," Rick said. "We're not done looking."

Susan tried to shove him to the door. "I told you I didn't have it. You have no right to go through my stuff. Get out before I call the—"

"Cops? Here I am," Rick said. "Trying to do my job."

Susan turned to Jeanette. "You let him in here. How could you?"

"We're trying to help Christo—"

"What!"

Jeanette covered her mouth. "I'm so sorry. I meant Jacob. Rick thinks if he only had the key, he could track it back to the padlock. Find the guy who bought it."

Susan turned her anger back to Rick. "You had no right to touch my personal items."

"He didn't," Jeanette said. "I did."

"We'd like to finish," Rick said. "You could help by opening your suitcase."

"Are you deaf or simply stupid, Ricky Sanchez? I told you I checked everywhere for it."

"No. You told me that you didn't remember where it was. Or maybe you don't you remember that?"

"Rudeness is not what I would call an effective interrogation technique."

"I'm not being rude," Rick said. "I'm just frustrated."

"You call pawing through a woman's personal belongings not being rude?"

"Susie, he's only trying to help."

Susan whipped around to Jeanette. "Oh, he's a lot of help. Harassing a poor victim of abuse when he should be out chasing down the monsters who did the abusing."

Rick touched her shoulder, gently turned her to face him. "Are we talking about Jacob? Or about you? I'm sorry for both. So sorry."

The anger drained from Susan's face. "I know you are."

"Then work with me, Susan. Please."

She sat down on the bed, rubbing her temples. "I thought back to the night we brought him here. I remember every word you said, every word I said. I can recall how his pulse felt, and Jeanette making brownies. I know I stuck the key in my pocket after I unlocked Jacob, but I don't remember . . . there's a blank spot when I try to think about taking it out of my jeans."

"Maybe it fell out when you climbed out of the ravine," Rick said.

"No. The key was too heavy. Thick gauge, very antique-looking. I could feel it in my back pocket as we rode back down the mountain. This I remember—Jacob sitting behind me, holding on to me, and I hoped he couldn't feel the key in my jeans because it might traumatize him."

"Suse, would you help us look? Please?" Rick said.

"Jacob's resting. You can't go in there."

"When we're done in your room, we'll do the downstairs. In case you put it down somewhere and—I don't know—it got knocked off, fell under something."

She lugged her suitcase out of the closet, but paused before she unlocked it.

"I'll leave," Rick said. "But Jeanette will need to stay."

Susan shook her head. "I want you both to see this. Rick, you never knew my life after I left. It was better. I need you to know that. You too, Jeanette."

The suitcase was empty except for a photo album. Susan paged through, showing them Paul Stone, who disappeared too soon from the photos. Christopher—from a tiny baby to a slender boy to a teenager with his mother's eyes. But not quite, Rick realized. Christopher's eyes were filled with laughter. The only time he had ever seen Susan like that was when they rode the horses hard.

Tears flooded Susan's face, dampening the front of her shirt. "This is what I lost, Ricky."

"I'm sorry, Susan. So sorry," Rick said. "Listen, Jeanette and I will go downstairs, give you some time to yourself."

She nodded, wiping the tears with the back of her hand.

He followed Jeanette downstairs, his chest aching with Susan's pain. "Should we start in the family room?" he said.

She looked down the hall. "Maybe Charlie's office. The next day Susan set up the computer so she could look up stuff on amnesia."

Susan came running down the hall. "No, don't go in there."

Which meant Rick had to go in there. He opened the door. Black markings were scrawled on the walls.

"I'm sorry, Jeanette," Susan was saying. "It's washable marker, but I didn't get a chance to clean it up."

All Jeanette could say is, "This isn't right. Not right at all."

The rage swelled inside Rick, a sharp fury with whatever had taken Tanyon and two other people. This proved Jacob was somehow involved, that the kid's fingerprints were not a blip in the computer. "It's psychotic. And incriminating."

"No, please. It's not like that," Susan said. "Sometimes with abuse victims, the truth comes out in ugly ways. It's only marker. Jeanette, I'll clean it myself, or pay to have it cleaned. But please take my word for it that it doesn't imply anything bad about Jacob—other than what was done to him."

"Susie, I have to tell you honestly, it makes me tremble in my stomach. I don't know why, but I think maybe we should find another place for Jacob to live. If your father could see this, he'd flip."

"But my father won't see this." Susan's voice was hot with anger. "Because he can't leave his precious horses long enough to see what's going on under his roof."

Jeanette shook her head. "I'm sorry. But this just feels so wrong to me. Rick?"

If Rick could read these symbols, he would have the answer to the burnings, the attack on Melissa, the chained boy in the darkness. But the only person who might know couldn't—or pretended not to be able—to remember.

"Did you videotape the session?" Rick said. "That was part of the guardianship agreement."

"No." Susan's eye flicker gave away the lie.

"Show me."

"I said—"

"And I said to show me. Right now. And then I'll tell you what I think."

Susan set up the camera to feed into the television. "I haven't even shown this to Zach."

"Zach's not responsible for the safety of this valley. I am."

"You're infringing on doctor-patient—"

"Save that horse manure for the lawyers. I need to know what's going on, Susan."

Rick's face was deep red, his jaw clenched.

We all have our anger, she wanted to shout, but that would be counterproductive. She quickly described the methodology she had used and why. "You'll hear me explain it in layman's terms to Jacob on the tape."

The screen lit up, showing her sitting at the table with Jacob. His face was blissfully innocent, his delight in the markers obvious. He picked up the tube of glitter and shook it, fascinated by the way the tiny sparkles caught the light.

She and Rick sat silently as they watched Jacob go through the first few scenarios. She grimaced as he slashed black and red on most of the pictures. His eyes were closed except when he chose a marker to use.

"His face is calm, but the way he moves those markers is brutal," Rick said.

"Later on, you'll see him explain those pictures to me. He thinks he drew with green and yellow and blue. Safe colors."

On the tape, she read another scenario. "The sun sets over the mountains, casting long shadows."

Jacob jerked, his head pulled back as if he were a puppet. He stood, eyes blanked.

"What's he doing?" Rick said.

Jacob stood, completely still, hands at his side. Yet the wall and his skin filled with symbols, cast in black though the marker lay unused on the table.

Panic swept through Susan, making her want to flee, to forget Jacob, forget Colorado, forget she ever saw what still played out on the screen. "How is he doing that?" she said, struggling to find breath even to speak.

Rick got up, one hand on his gun, handcuffs dangling from his other hand. "I have to bring him in. I can't leave him loose."

Susan fought through the urge to cry out: *yes, take him away, he scares me.* "You can't. Please, Rick. You can't."

"He's dangerous. Dangerous beyond anything we can even hope to understand. See for yourself."

The symbols continued to appear, one by one. Along the walls and then across his body. In a line, Susan realized. *Some unseen hand is writing them, and Jacob's body is in the way.*

"He's not dangerous. I can't tell you how I know, but I know. Perhaps we're seeing some hysterically induced telekinesis."

"We don't know anything. I'll take him to a secure lock-up—"

"No! Don't lock me up. I can't be locked up again."

They both turned to see Jacob standing in the door, Jeanette trying to pull him back. "He wouldn't listen to me. He always does, but this time he wouldn't listen when I said he couldn't come in—" Her mouth dropped in horror as she saw the screen. "He did it to himself too? Susan, I thought it was just the walls, and you said that wasn't a horrible thing, but to do it to himself?"

She shrunk away from Jacob, but he didn't notice. His gaze was intent on the screen, and his eyes were wide. "I know what that says."

Susan touched his arm. "What?"

"I can't remember. It's bad, very bad, but I can't remember."

"That's it," Rick said. "We need to find a safer place—"

Jacob grabbed the handcuffs from him. "You can't lock me up. Not again."

"Jacob, I took them out from habit. I wouldn't—"

Susan was touched by the compassion in Rick's voice.

Jacob tore the handcuffs apart, the metal splitting like brittle wood. He threw the pieces at the screen and ran out of the room.

By the time they followed him outside, he was gone.

THIRTY-ONE

JACOB RAN UNTIL HE COULD RUN NO FURTHER. HE COLLAPSED next to a little creek, taking shelter from the sun in a copse of aspens.

"Well, well. You're not as dumb as you look."

He turned to see an Other, smoking a cigarette and smirking.

"I know you!"

"Do you now?" The Other chuckled. "No more amnesia?"

"I . . ." Jacob felt like he swam in murky fluid, the truth obscured by stirred-up sediment.

"You still can't remember? How rich." The Other flicked the cigarette away. A nearby bush burst into flames. "Easy, eh? Yet the fools persist in thinking that trick as major league."

"Where are you hiding?"

"You know exactly where. You play Mr. Innocent, but you know what's at stake here."

Jacob ought to know. Perhaps he could pretend he was a therapist like Susan and fish for answers. "I'm not sure you really comprehend the stakes."

Each burst of laughter was punctuated by a puff of smoke from the Other's mouth. "Don't kid a kidder. And don't try to out-bluff the master of bluffs. Oh, the precipices I've seen . . ."

Jacob instinctively opened his arms as if to catch something. Or was it someone?

"Shall I tell you the truth?" Jacob said.

"Such a bore. But if you must unburden your stinkin' little heart . . ."

"I know you, but I don't remember you. I know the stakes, but I don't remember them."

"How droll. That little woe-is-me act probably goes over big with the gals, eh?" The Other plucked a handful of grass, twisted it into another cigarette, and lit it from the bush that burned.

"It's the truth."

"Youch." He blew on his hand. "Burned myself. You think I'd know better."

"So what are the stakes?"

"For you? Nothing, you sniveling cow puke."

"Go ahead, tell me how you really feel." Jacob laughed until he realized he had echoed Melissa's words. She would be looking for him by now. He couldn't let her see the Other, or let the Other see her. "Go away. I don't have time for you."

The Other laughed. "You have all the time in the world, you idiot. And you will not easily get rid of me. I can promise you that."

"Whatever."

The Other moved in on him. Should Jacob try to run away or take him on? He could hit him with a rock. Maybe he could punch him out. Charlie had boxed with him, but that had been playful. Baby punches, Melissa had said.

"Melissa," the Other said. "Know what I'd like to do with darling Melissa?"

Images filtered into Jacob's head: bodies entwined, Melissa's head bent back, her throat exposed as she begged, *Bite me.*

The Other touched his shoulder. "She could be yours, you know. It wouldn't take much to persuade her. She's a needy little sow."

"No. Don't speak about her in those terms." Jacob tried to control his face like Susan did.

"Oh, Susan? Would you rather have her?"

The same image, but this time it was Susan's head bent back.

Jacob pushed away from the Other, but the images followed him like a filthy dog, nipping at his heels. Jeanette bent back, and then children, younger and younger until Jacob had to turn and punch the Other, hit him again and again, but the images only got worse as they splintered and multiplied.

Jacob broke away, running along the creek until he found a spot wide enough and deep enough to cover his whole body. He lay under the water just as Melissa said she had the night before. But what if there were not enough water in this world to wash him clean?

Better to know nothing than to know that.

Melissa found Jacob in the northwest corner of Robinson Ranch. How had he come to be here? Only Charlie and Jeanette knew about this spot. Vanessa was buried here, though last year Melissa and Jeanette had to fight through the brush to find the grave marker. It had taken Melissa a week to clear enough space to make room for Christopher's memorial marker. Susan had buried him in Boston, but he would be remembered out here, where the creek ran clean and the trees rustled in the wind.

At first she had wanted to put the marker near the barn. It was a simple piece of granite, etched with the words: *Christopher Robinson Stone, loved and missed.*

"Families need to stay together," Jeanette insisted, not getting how ridiculous that statement was. The Robinson family hadn't ever stayed together, not by a long shot.

In the end, Melissa had to agree that this was a lovely spot, fitting for a remembrance. Perhaps its beauty was what had drawn Jacob here when he ran away from Rick Sanchez. Or maybe, in some instinctive way, he knew this was where she came to remember.

"You're soaked," Melissa said. "Fall in head first?"

"Jumped in," he mumbled.

"Why?"

"I was dirty."

"From what?"

"Don't know."

"You're lying," she said.

"Fine. I'm dirty from lying."

If Jacob had developed a smart mouth, she only had herself to blame. She tied Job to a bush and sat down next to him.

"Were you smoking?" she asked.

"No. Why?"

"You smell like smoke."

He shrugged and looked around nervously.

"What's wrong? You look like you saw a ghost."

"I didn't," Jacob said.

Melissa rubbed her arms. Where were these goose bumps coming from? "Did someone bother you?"

Jacob shrugged. "Why would someone bother me?"

For the same reason someone chained you in that ravine. She tugged on his arm. "Let's go. Everyone's looking for you."

"Jeanette's afraid of me now. She won't let me come home."

"That'll pass. But meanwhile, we need to get you where they can't find you."

"Wait."

"For what?"

"I need to know about those."

"What?" She hoped he meant the hummingbirds hovering over the creek, though she knew he didn't.

He squatted next to Vanessa's marker, pushed away the winter-dried grass. Melissa felt guilty about not grooming hers along with Christopher's.

"Vanessa Robinson. 1934–1985. What does that mean?"

"She was Charlie's first wife. The dates mean she was born in 1934 and died in 1985. She was fifty-one years old."

"How did she die?"

"She killed herself. Went off a cliff, up on Folly Mountain."

"Why won't Charlie talk about her?"

"Because she didn't just *jump* off the cliff. She rode a horse off, and to him, that's almost the biggest crime in the world. She could have just taken herself out, but she blindfolded the horse and rode it over. To get back at Susan."

"Why?"

"Because she was a mean, nasty woman. They say she was a different person from minute to minute, sometimes nice, sometimes vicious, sometimes violent."

"How did riding off a cliff get back at Susan?"

"You know how Robinson Ranch used to be big in the Arabian industry? That was Vanessa's doing. She got Charlie into it. Besides breeding and selling horses, they kept favorites for themselves. Vanessa owned four horses, Charlie owned seven, and Susan owned a gorgeous gray Arabian named Tasha. Plus they had other horses on the ranch that weren't theirs, some being bred and some for training. Even a couple of dude horses for when a client's bratty kid wanted to have a ride. All those horses to choose from—but when Vanessa wanted to go off the cliff, she rode Susan's horse to do it."

Jacob looked stricken. Melissa took his hand and rubbed it between hers, Jeanette's favorite form of comforting. *He's becoming me and I'm becoming Jeanette*, she thought.

"Susan had trained Tasha from the time the filly was born," Melissa said. "When she left for college, she wanted to take the horse with her. Tasha was only three years old at the time, but Susan couldn't come up with the money to support herself and board a horse."

"You said that Charlie used to have a lot of money."

"Didn't matter. That witch Vanessa refused to let Charlie pay for college unless Susan went to school in Colorado. She hated the idea of Susan getting out of her reach."

Melissa's stomach ached—she had heard this story more than once from Jeanette, but somehow, telling it drove home how nasty Vanessa Robinson had been.

"Susan had to get scholarships and work two or three jobs just to get through college. Charlie promised to take good care of Tasha until Susan could afford to bring her to Boston. After college, she had medical school. Then she trained as an intern."

"What's an intern?"

"A doctor who is just learning. Anyway, Tasha was thirteen when Susan finally saved enough money to bring her east. Things had really settled down for her, Jeanette said. She had married Paul Stone, they had Christopher. Paul was going to stay with Christopher while Susan drove to Colorado to get her horse and trailer her to Massachusetts.

"Charlie was happy for two reasons. He would get to see Susan again after all those years. And this was twenty years ago when the Arabian industry was tanking, so it was a relief that he'd have one less horse to feed."

"What happened?"

"Susan had written to Rebecca Camara—Don's mother—and asked her to give Charlie a letter with all the details. In the letter, she begged Charlie not to tell Vanessa she was coming. Being the dope he is, Charlie hid the letter in his underwear drawer. Vanessa never did his laundry, so he figured it'd be plenty safe. He didn't know that she searched his dresser every day.

"That witch waved the letter in his face, blasted him for sneaking around her back, for conspiring with *that girl*—she refused to speak Susan's name. She told him that he would be sorry and Susan would be sorry. Typical of Charlie, he just let it run off his back. He rode Tasha over to Camaras' to board her for the next couple days. Then he said good night and went to bed in his own room."

"They didn't sleep together? He and Jeanette have the same room."

"After Susan was born, Vanessa wanted nothing to do with him— except around the horses. Out in the barn or the show ring, they got on just fine. Honestly, she only married him to get back at her parents. And because she was pregnant, of course.

"When he got up the next day, Vanessa was gone. Rebecca called and said Tasha was missing from their barn. Charlie searched all day, called the neighbors, all the horse people they both knew, finally the police. They looked for a week, but Vanessa never turned up. They didn't find her body or Tasha's until the next spring, after the snow melted. Charlie was out riding up on Folly and saw her at the bottom of a cliff. He left Tasha's body up on the mountain, covered with stones. But he had Vanessa buried out here."

"Did he hate her?"

"If he hated her, he could have left her at the bottom of that cliff."

Jacob rubbed his palms together so hard Melissa half-expected the friction to raise sparks. His feet tapped on the hard-packed dirt. Perhaps she shouldn't have been so graphic in telling him what had happened. Yet when he finally spoke, his tone was even.

"Did Susan come to see him when Vanessa died?"

"No. She blamed Charlie because he couldn't keep her horse safe."

"So why did she let Christopher come to Colorado?"

Melissa smiled. "She didn't. When Christopher turned eighteen, he decided it was time to meet his grandpa. He said all the bitterness had to end somewhere."

"But it didn't."

"In one way, it did. He got to know Charlie and Jeanette. And the horses. First time he got on the horse, it was like—" Melissa stopped. Like Jacob's first time. *Like he was born with the big wide sky over 'em and his favorite horse under 'em,* Charlie had said both times.

Jacob shook his head. "It didn't end."

"I just told you—"

He put his finger to her lips. "You're still bitter."

Melissa jumped up. "Oh, you bet I am."

"How can you be, when Christopher said the bitterness had to end?"

She grabbed his arm and yanked him to his feet, her anger making her strong. "You have no right to judge me. You don't know what Susan did to him and to me."

Jeanette hung up the phone. "Melissa's got him safe."

"Where?" Susan said. "Why didn't you let me talk to her?"

"She won't say where. Just that he's safe. Jacob is terrified that Rick is going to take him off the ranch and lock him up somewhere."

Rick sat at the kitchen table, silent. Charlie sat next to him, staring into an empty coffee cup. Susan paced the kitchen.

"Are you happy now, Rick?" Susan shouted. "You drove him away when he needs us the most. What's next? Oh, I know. You'll go after Melissa for harboring a fugitive from—not justice. No, you're not serving up justice here. You're persecuting a victim of abuse while some fiend terrorizes this valley. Not like you, Ricky Sanchez. Not like you at all to take the easy way out."

"The man's just doing his job." Jeanette's heart thumped so hard, she rubbed her ribs to slow it down. She wanted to add her own fear, that maybe it was best that Rick did lock Jacob up. Susan said writing on walls wasn't unheard of in mental illness. But neither were murder and other atrocities. Even so, Jeanette had washed the walls before Charlie came in. How would he understand if she hadn't?

Rick stood. "That's right. And that job—that duty—requires me to be objective. Susan, you're so caught up in your emotional need that you can't see the danger surrounding this kid."

Susan's face was hard. "Leave. Just go."

"If you care for this family at all, and not just your surrogate son—"

Susan shoved him. "How dare you."

"How dare you?" Rick stepped back, hands up in appeasement, but now there was no trace of surrender in his voice. "Melissa's out who-knows-where with a kid who is who-knows-what, and your complete focus is on him. You have more family than Christopher, Suse. You need to attend to them."

Susan burst into tears. Jeanette tried to hug her, but she broke away.

Rick shook Charlie's shoulder. "Old man, you've got to live up to it now. It's late, but not too late."

Charlie shrugged him off.

Rick crossed the kitchen to Jeanette and wrapped her in a hug. "I can't do any good here. Pray. And keep the doors locked," he whispered.

"Where are you going?"

"To unravel the mystery of our boy chained in darkness." Rick glanced once more at Susan, then went out the back door.

The uneasy silence was broken when Charlie said, "My leg hurts."

"You absolute fool," Susan said. "I told you not to take the splint off. You're lucky the bone hasn't collapsed completely."

Jeanette crossed the room, bent down, and rubbed his shin. "This where it hurts?"

"It feels weak, Jeannie," he whispered. "I'm losing the healing."

"Hon, a healing's no good if it doesn't involve the heart."

He bent close to her, his eyes so like Susan's. "Jacob's not here. Who can heal my heart?"

"Jacob never healed your leg in the first place. God saw fit to do that."

"It was a joke," Charlie said. "I dared him, because you and Melissa were going on so."

"He knows that."

"Stop it," Susan said. "Has everyone gone insane? You two are blubbering about your church stuff and Rick's gone all macho and Melissa's playing rescuer, and you've all gone crazy."

Jeanette stood, her knees shooting with pain. She took Susan's hands. Susan tried to pull away, but Jeanette held her fast. "Susie."

"What?" Her eyes flashed anger, but otherwise she had the gaze of a wounded child.

"Your father's heart will never be right until you tell him what he did to you."

"He knows," Susan hissed. "How can he not know?"

"It's buried too deep. You need to dig it out and show it to him. Like . . ." Suddenly Jeanette understood, and the fear dissolved. "Like Jacob did when he wrote all over the walls and himself."

"What're you talking about over there?" Charlie growled. "I don't know nothing."

Susan broke away from Jeanette. "Stand up, Pop."

"My leg hurts."

"Stand up, I said."

Charlie stood.

"Look me in the eye and tell me you didn't know what Vanessa did to me."

Charlie looked down.

"Look me in the eye, Charles Robinson."

"Charlie. It's the only way," Jeanette said.

Charlie slowly lifted his gaze to his daughter. "I didn't know what to do, Susie. I tried to make her head straight. Thought I could keep her busy with the horses, make her happy that way. I kept buying 'em, figuring sooner or later there'd be so many, she'd be too worn out to bother you. When that didn't work, I tried to love her enough so her own mind wouldn't keep ripping her apart. I'm not a strong man, Susie."

He wiped his face with his handkerchief. "I gave you the best horse I could find because I knew you could outride her. Even when you left, I still tried to love the woman. I did love her, but not the right way because nothing ever fixed her. No doctors, no pills, no horse, not me trying to show her all the love I could. She was my Vannie, the gal who roped my heart, the woman who gave me a daughter who was smarter than either of us, a daughter who was stronger than me."

He lowered his eyes. "A daughter who knew how to make her own way when I wouldn't make it for her."

Susan stood impassive, unmoving. *Barely breathing,* Jeanette thought.

"I know I did wrong," Charlie said. "I knew it back then and I still know it, but I try to forget it because she's gone and I can't make the past better. All I knew to do was to get some horses and try again for Melissa. And for Christopher."

"Don't you dare pair them together," Susan said. "Even if I could forgive you for eighteen years of leaving me at that woman's mercy; even if I could forgive you for letting her take Tasha off that cliff; even if I forgive you for all of that—how can I forgive you for looking the other way and letting those two get entangled?"

Charlie's face flooded with tears. "I guess you can't."

"I'm going to my room," Susan said. "If you hear from Melissa again, I'd appreciate the opportunity to speak to her."

Jeanette reached out, but Susan brushed past her, her skin like ice.

Charlie sank back into his chair. "I know I was a bad father. I always knew. There's nothing that's gonna change that now. If I was a real man, I'd have thrown Rick out of here. Protected Melissa from that thing instead of Susan having to help her. Gone to Boston with Christopher to face Susan instead of letting him do it himself. None of that would've happened if I had lived up to my responsibility. But Jeannie—" He looked up at his wife. "I don't know how. Never did and won't ever. I can't change. I'm too old. I can't make myself a better man."

Jeanette wrapped her arms around his head and pulled him to her shoulder. "You can't. But you know God can. You trusted Him once. Can't you again?"

Charlie nodded, his back shaking with sobs.

As she kneeled again, the worst pain she'd ever felt shot through her knees. Hot iron pokers, side to side and down into her legs, but she ignored it all, holding to Charlie, holding on to the hope she knew, trying to bring them together.

"I didn't mean it about how I loved Vannie," Charlie said.

"You did. And that's okay."

"I love you better."

"You don't have to love me more or less. Just love me your best," Jeanette whispered.

"I don't know about love. Healing, any of that stuff."

Jeanette looked up at him. "Will you pray with me?"

"I can't kneel. My leg's breaking all over again."

"Your leg doesn't matter. Only your heart matters. Will you pray, Charlie?"

He bowed his head. "Our Father, who art in heaven . . ."

THIRTY-TWO

RICK SAT IN HIS OFFICE, HEAD IN HANDS. THE CBI INVESTI-gators still scoured the Elk River Valley, shuttling back and forth between Camaras' and Robinsons'. But they weren't any further along in the investigation than the day the first burned body had been found.

He had prayed for wisdom, discernment, insight—even a lucky break—but he was as befuddled as the experts. He grabbed the phone and dialed a familiar number, then asked to speak to Tanyon Stern's supervisor. It had become very clear that those symbols weren't random, but were somehow tied up in all this.

"Jim Lauter."

"This is Sheriff Rick Sanchez up in the Elk River Valley. I was a friend of Tanyon's."

"What a loss."

Rick swallowed hard. "Yeah."

"Rick San—wait a minute. Was it you who submitted the bogus fingerprints to our office?"

"Yes, but they weren't bogus. Tanyon thought a computer error caused the odd image, but I've got some new info—"

Lauter cut him off. "All I had were Stern's handwritten notes, referring to an R. S., but no official paperwork filed. I've been hoping and praying that whoever this R. S. was would follow up."

"Why?" Rick said.

"Stern posted part of the image you sent him to an online bulletin board. Some geek place where linguists and anthropologists hang out when they're not solving 5,000-year-old riddles. Anyway, we've been getting e-mails at his old address from a . . . hold on a sec." Lauter rustled papers. "Where is . . . oh, here it is. From a Professor Maxim Rintzek. This guy claims he has vital information regarding the image. Something about weird symbols? That mean anything to you, Sheriff?"

Perspiration trickled between Rick's shoulder blades. "It could."

"Anyway, I was about to have my computer guy just delete the whole thing, thinking this Rintzek was a kook. But he e-mailed again, this time with his very considerable academic background and references. We couldn't connect the dots because no one in Tanyon's lab knew who R. S. was. Okay if I forward these e-mails to you and let you handle it?"

"Absolutely."

"I want to keep informed," Lauter said.

"Deal." Rick gave him his e-mail address, thanked him, and hung up.

Minutes later he had the messages. *Of great concern . . . I need to speak to the person who obtained these images at once . . .*

Rick called Rintzek, who was adamant that Rick come see him.

"This can't be ignored," the man said in a heavy Eastern European accent. He gave his address in Taos, New Mexico. Rick could make it there in ten hours, maybe less.

One more call to make before leaving. Jeanette answered, and he told her what he wanted.

"She'll kill me," Jeanette said. "I can't . . ."

"You have to. On my word, you have to get me that tape."

"I'll drive it over to you."

Twelve hours later, in the dark of night, Rick arrived at Maxim Rintzek's home. A single light burned at the side of the house.

On the phone, Rintzek's accent and husky voice had led Rick to imagine a guy with unruly hair and rumpled clothes. When the professor opened the door, Rick was startled by his youth and athletic good looks. He had expected Rintzek's office also to be movie-stereotypical—crowded bookshelves, faded leather chairs, pipe rack, stacks of journals. In reality, the room was airy and uncluttered. Instead of a desk, Rintzek had a workstation, complete with a flat-screen monitor, three printers, and other devices Rick couldn't identify. The walls were covered with surrealistic black-and-white photographs of Middle Eastern locations.

"Sorry to bring you all the way here, Sheriff," Rintzek said, shaking hands.

"Call me Rick. You thought it necessary, Professor."

"Max. Urgent. Before I show you some of my research, can we watch the tape you brought?"

Rick passed him the tape. Rintzek watched it in silence, clenching his fists when the writing scrolled across Jacob's body.

"Can I make a copy of this?" Rintzek's face was grim.

"I'm sorry, but it's part of a therapy session. I shouldn't even have it."

Rintzek nodded. "I understand. Let me ask you something, Sheriff. Do you believe in God?"

Rick studied the professor's face, saw no trace of hostility. Not that it would matter anyway. "Yes. I do."

"Do you practice your faith?"

"I try my best. You?"

"I also."

"Why do you ask?"

Rintzek held up his hand. "One last question. Do you pray?"

"Every day. Sometimes every moment. Again, why are you asking?"

"Because you are going to have to pray as you have never prayed before."

Someone shook Jacob awake.

He opened his eyes, but no one was there.

He ran to check on Melissa and found her curled in a patch of moonlight. The silver glow somehow made her hair shine like gold. He laughed at the notion of silver making something turn gold.

"We have to be proper about this," she had said, setting up her sleeping bag in the hay shed while he spread out his blanket in the shelter. They were miles away from home, using the abandoned outbuildings on the Eldridge ranch.

A branch broke behind him.

Jacob jumped into a crouch, ready to defend Melissa though he did not know how. He was strong—she had told him that—but he wasn't sure he could fight. He knew he couldn't kill. At least he hoped he couldn't.

The Other stared at him from the darkness.

Jacob crept out of the shed, trying to shield Melissa from the Other's line of sight. If she didn't awaken, maybe he wouldn't know she was here with him.

"What do you want?" he whispered.

"The question is: what do *you* want?" the Other said.

"To be left alone."

"Bzzzt. Wrong answer. Try again." He looked harmless, but Jacob suspected—no, he knew—that he was not.

"For you to leave me alone."

The Other smiled. "Perhaps that, too. But what do you really want?"

"I told you—"

"Don't you want Melissa? She's there for the taking."

"I told you before, no."

"She pretends to have had some spiritual reawakening, but she's fooling herself. You pluck, she'll fall. That simple."

"I don't know what you're talking about."

"Like an apple hanging on a tree. When it's ripe, you pluck it and it falls. You enjoy its juicy sweetness. Is your mouth watering yet?"

Jacob put his hands over his ears. "Go away."

The Other knocked his hands down. "Such a cute little pout you got there. The naïve thing plays very well with the ladies. You know why, Jacob?"

"Go away before I make you go away."

"Because they want to remake every man into their own image. Sure, some chicks enjoy the challenge of the chase, just love those bad boys. But the Melissas of this world like the sweet ones. Like you and her darling Christopher. Do you know why that is, Jacob?"

Jacob started to move away, but stopped. He couldn't leave Melissa alone with this guy.

The Other laughed. "Thought that would get you. We so love to talk about ourselves. And even more, we love to hear everyone else talk about us. Okay, take notes now. The reason that some women like sweet, innocent, naïve men is because—are you listening, kiddo?"

If Jacob had to describe the Other, perhaps to Susan or to Rick, he would have to do it in a series of *nots*. He was plain but not ugly; chunky but not fat; mature but not old. "If it'll make you go away, yes. I'm listening."

"Women like your type because they want to think they are so powerful, so amazing, so sexy that they can bring out the bad boy in you. That's what little Melissa is waiting for. To make you sizzle."

Jacob drew his arm back to knock him away. "Shut up."

The Other skittered out of reach. "You don't believe me? You think she's really putting her neck on the line to protect you? Get real. This is all just an excuse to make herself available to you. Look at her."

Jacob caught himself before he turned his head to where she lay sleeping.

The Other laughed. "Oh, like you've got her hidden? Nothing stays hidden from me, bud. So you may as well look at her. Save me from spouting poetic descriptions of how pretty she is. You're right—she's not Hollywood pretty. But there's nothing like a horsewoman to give a guy a good run for his money. Whoa, baby."

Jacob moved so fast, he had his hands around the Other's throat before he could escape. He wanted to choke him, do whatever it took to make him stop, but somehow the Other slipped out of his hands and dashed away.

Something else caught his notice. Heat, bristling across his back.

Melissa's vitality—powerful even as she slept—radiated over him. Even though he was a good twenty feet from where she lay, he smelled her breath, sweet with chocolate from the candy bars they had munched. He counted each beat of her heart, each rise of her chest. He followed the moonlight along the curls that twisted in a ponytail, the caress of the night air as it wrapped around her like a spider's web, drawing him to her. Spinning and spinning until he was caught in a cyclone of silver and gold, a trap of desire that he thought he didn't have, but how could he possibly know?

Unless he tested it.

Jacob moved toward the hay shed, tugging his shirt over his head. At the hospital, Julia had whispered to another tech that he was "hot," and he had seen enough television now to know what *hot* meant. If he pressed against Melissa, she wouldn't resist and—

"If she resisted too much, you could just take her," the Other whispered. "Unless you're chicken."

How had he dared to come back? Perhaps that was good, because Jacob might need help and certainly the Other would be able to show him how to find the *bad boy* deep inside. He flung his shirt into the grass, flexing his arm to admire his own strength, thrusting his chest outward, his body a sacrament of the power he contained, the temple of the glory that he was. He didn't need to know his name to know that he was—

What was he?

"All that is needed," the Other prompted.

Yes, all that is needed.

"The best of all the rest."

Yes, he was the best of the rest. He caressed his own throat, thinking how *hot* it would be when Melissa put her lips there, how she would have no choice but to want him, now that he knew it was what women wanted. And if she wasn't of that mind, so what? The Other said he could take her anyway. Why else was she here if she didn't want to be taken? He reached for her, the heat of her face drawing his fingers like a magnet.

A bird called out from the darkness.

One bird, one note. Small, far away, of no consequence to Jacob, but suddenly it was not he who was the all-in-all, but that pure note in the night. The little bird called to a mate or simply to mark its return to the nest. Yet there was purity in that sound, a goodness that added note upon note until a song was formed; voice upon voice until a choir was formed, joy upon joy until it all returned to the place from which it had come.

He would not be the bad boy, he would not be *hot*, he would not be anything except that which was worthy of joy upon joy.

Jacob pulled on his shirt and went to the little pond across the pasture. He stuck his head in the water to wash. As he came up for air, he saw the reflection of the Other, standing behind him. He had screamed when he saw the same reflection in the mirror, but on this night, he simply stuck his head back in the water and let joy upon joy sing him clean.

How gracious he will be when you cry for help!
As soon as he hears, he will answer you.

— ISAIAH 30:19

THIRTY-THREE

MELISSA WOKE UP IN THE MIDDLE OF THE NIGHT TO FIND Jacob staring at her.

"Problem?" she said, yawning.

"My stomach hurts."

She sat up, tugging her fingers through her hair, trying to think straight. "Are you sick?"

"No."

She slugged down some water. If they stayed here past tomorrow, she'd have to find a way to get them supplies. They could go to Camaras', travel after dark so no one would see them. She shivered. *Idiot—not with that thing out there.*

She focused on Jacob. "If you're not sick, why does your stomach hurt?"

"This thing between you and Susan hurts me."

Melissa scooted further back into the shed. "Why should it? It didn't have anything to do with you."

He rubbed his stomach. "You sure?"

"What makes you think it did?"

"I don't know."

His innocent look irked her. Who did he think he was, prying into her business? "You're not my shrink. So get off my back."

Jacob grabbed her face, and for a moment she was afraid he was going to kiss her. Before she could either protest or cooperate, he pressed his forehead to hers. "I need to know, Melissa."

"Just get off it, will you? It's got nothing to do with you."

"It hurts me too."

"Oh, don't give me that we're *all one so it all hurts* horse crap . . ." she said, but her head spun from the heat between her forehead and his. She clutched his shoulders, but the spinning made her hazy, and

229

when it cleared, she wasn't strong enough to keep from slipping back into the movie that played in her head in the middle of too many nights. She seemed to have no choice but to invite him into that movie so that it seemed like he was in that coffee shop named Jo's and he was on that sidewalk in Steamboat. But why didn't he stop her, why didn't he tell her not to back off but to keep strong?

Melissa felt Susan's hand on her shoulder as if it were happening now. She heard her voice, saw her cool face as she plotted the course for Melissa, the strategy that would release Christopher from his promise to join his life with hers and her baby's.

When she told Jacob the worst of it, she relived it in real time, as she had so many times before.

"Do you have a cell phone?" Susan had said, once she had gotten Melissa to agree not to marry Christopher.

Melissa nodded.

"Call him."

"Now? Out here in public?"

"You'll lose resolve if you wait."

"He'll talk me out of it. You know how he is. He won't take no for an answer."

Susan leaned close. "Which is why you're going to tell him that the baby's father came back. And that you're marrying him."

"But next summer . . ."

"You can say you realized the mistake, backed out of the wedding. It's just a temporary fix to get you over this hump. Go ahead, Melissa. I know you'll do what's right. Call Christopher."

Christopher, I'm sorry, but Chad's back. You understand—a baby should be with its real father. Don't, Chris, don't honey, I know, I know. But this is best, you have to understand . . .

Melissa broke free of Jacob's grasp, ducking out of that too-real sunshine and into the night that was real. "Are you happy now that you know?"

"I'm not happy at all." His eyes flooded with tears. "I'm sorry for your pain."

Melissa sat down, trying to get her head back into the present. Was she going nuts? That whole ugly thing with Susan had felt so real, even down to the acid in her stomach. She could feel the cell phone in her hand, feel Christopher's phone number on the tips of her fingers, tapping them out from memory, could hear his gasp when he tried to hold back tears.

"So now you know what a horrible thing Susan did, talking me into telling Christopher a terrible lie. If I hadn't lied, he might still be alive today."

"Why did she do it?" Jacob said.

"Because she can be a horrible woman. I know you don't think so, but you're too nice sometimes. She'll chew you up just like she chewed Christopher up."

Jacob helped Melissa to her feet and guided her outside. The night was fresh, the stars endless. The moon was low on the horizon, crowning Folly Mountain like a halo.

"Maybe there's another way to look at this," he said.

"There's not. You can't say anything that will change my mind," Melissa said.

"What if it were Krista?"

"It was Krista. I was pregnant. Didn't you listen?"

Jacob leaned his face toward hers. She backed away.

"Melissa. What if you were in Susan's position, and Krista was in Christopher's?"

Melissa stared at the sky, summoning the moon to fill the wound in her heart that Jacob's question cut open.

"What would you do, Melissa?"

"Anything I thought I had to, if it would keep Krista safe," she whispered. "Absolutely anything."

Rick hung out of his truck, vomiting. He was sick to the core.

Rintzek was one of only six linguists who had studied a language that had roots in ancient Babylon and Egypt. The written symbols of this language had been found in only one location, deep under an archeological dig in Iraq, buried under millennia of rubble.

The Tower of Babel, Rintzek had proposed, though he didn't dare publish his findings.

Each symbol spelled out a name. Asmoday. Mammon. Sariel. Beliar. Nine more, forming a troop of thirteen soldiers, a number that eventually would become mythic for covens. In their dig, Rintzek and his colleagues had come on thousands of groups of thirteens.

In Susan's tape, the same thirteen symbols repeated over and over. The first time they viewed the tape, neither Rick nor Susan had spotted the pattern. It became clear once Rintzek showed him. The symbols had appeared inside out, upside down, turned left, turned right. An unseen hand wrote them, line after line, crossing Jacob's chest as if he were part of the wall.

"It's a list," Mintzek said. "His fellow soldiers."

The professor showed Rick reams of research, but what sealed the matter was the verse in the book of Jude, confirmed by Peter's second epistle: *And the angels who did not keep their positions of authority but abandoned their own home—these He has kept under darkness, bound with everlasting chains for judgment on the great Day.*

Susan Stone had unleashed what could be the beginning of the end. Rick had to get home and set it right.

He popped open the Pepsi he had picked up at the all-night convenience store. He needed to stay alert. He debated calling Joyce to ask her to pray; calling Jeanette to warn her; calling Susan to beg her not to search any further for Jacob.

Better not. That might bring more trouble on them. Best not to let anyone know what he had discovered, at least until he was ready to lock Jacob back up. If he only had the original chains. Where had they gone? He'd stop in Steamboat, beg the PD there for a full set of wrist and leg manacles, the kind used for court transport. They weren't "everlasting chains," but Rick would pray that human-forged steel and his faith would be strong enough to bind this devil.

His phone jingled. Zach Hurley had tracked him down. "Hey, Rick."

"What's up? It's the middle of the night."

"The guy covering your duty said you were out of state. I woke up in a sweat, thinking about the other two victims. Sounds like you're okay, huh?"

"Sure."

"So where are you?"

"I had business down in New Mexico."

"What kind of business?"

"Some guy knew how to read those symbols."

"Really?" Zach sounded alert. "What do they say?"

"I'll tell you when I get there." Rick wasn't about to broadcast what he had learned over an unsecured cell phone.

"How far out are you?"

"A couple hours still. I'm on 131."

"Coming through the mountains? You really want to go that way?"

"I'm trying to save time."

"Okay. Watch those switchbacks. Call me when you get in. We'll catch up on Jacob Doe and everything else. Glad you're okay."

"I'm fine. Go back to sleep, Zach." Rick clicked off.

The mountains loomed in the distance, crowned with stars and a few clouds. Almost home—but this home was under attack.

The road climbed and dipped, taking sharp turns. Rick slugged down another Pepsi. No longer chilled, it tasted sicky sweet. His mind took strange jumps and, despite his fear, he felt sleepy. *Hold on, man. Not far now.* The sky lightened, dawn an hour away after a day that seemed to have no end. Soon enough he'd be coming into Steamboat, the pretty little city built around its famous hot springs. Hot water hidden deep in the earth, breaking through in springs that steamed out of the ground, even when snow lay heavy all about.

Like this threat.

People passed through their lives, thinking they were white as snow, not understanding the fire under their feet. Even when it broke out, it was attributed to a horrible mental illness or a sociopathology or an isolated evil. Folks didn't understand that the same fire of destruction that burns through their world also sears their souls.

KEEP WATCH.

Rick jerked awake. He was on the wrong side of the road, head-lights bearing down on him. He yanked the wheel, not caring what lay to his right but determined not to cause harm, not to kill the innocent driver—*please, Lord, not a family*—bearing down on him.

As his pickup bounced over the shoulder, the other car bent in half. As if turning its head, the car's headlights followed the truck.

Impossible, I'm asleep, Rick thought. But he was not asleep, and the car that he had almost crashed into head-on was not a car at all but a beast, its eyes extended on long limbs and swimming with fire. They had been rounded like headlights, but now they burst out, globes of fire creeping over his truck, searching for the gas tank, its candle-fingers twisting open the cap, snaking its tongue into the tank, searching for fuel to magnify itself.

Rick's fingers were like stone as he struggled to unhitch his seat belt. He counted the instants because a second was all he had left before he would blow sky-high, *Lord, into Your arms I beg to come*. Split moments in which to say good-bye to his children, Wayne and Carey, to say thank you to Joyce. To hope Susan found the way. To plead for Jacob to be contained. To know that the end would come in God's time and no one else's.

And then his world blew apart.

THIRTY-FOUR

As SUSAN RODE INTO THE PASTURE, MELISSA RAN OUT TO meet her. "How did you find us?"

"We've been searching all night. Finally, Jeanette remembered you hung out with Bette Eldridge before the family moved. Where's Jacob?"

"He's sleeping."

Susan dismounted from Jonas and shrugged off a backpack. "You hungry?"

Melissa's eyes lit up. "You brought us food?"

Susan laughed. "Unless you'd rather munch grass."

"I thought I brought enough for a week, but Jacob went through it in a day and a half."

"Susan!" Jacob flew into her arms.

Susan kissed his cheek, fighting disappointment that he didn't smell or feel like Christopher. This was wrong thinking, wrong *wanting*, to expect Jacob to fill the hole in her heart when his own was still a void. Jacob could only be who he was—whoever that turned out to be.

Susan unwrapped from his embrace and pretended to check Jonas's halter.

"Susan." It was Melissa right behind her.

Susan lay her face against the horse's neck.

"I need to tell you something. Please look at me."

Everyone had something to tell her. Jeanette telling her to pray. Charlie telling her to calm down. Rick telling her to trust him. Zach and Joyce and the courts telling her what was best for Jacob. Even Jacob, scrawling symbols and singing impossible music—he had something to say, if she could figure out what.

"What is it?" Susan asked.

"I need to tell you how sorry I am," Melissa whispered.

Susan stroked Jonas's face. "For what?"

"For blaming you. For hating you. For not understanding that you really did want what was best for Christopher. For all the nasty thoughts I've had about you and the times I wished you had died instead of Christopher. I'm sorry, Susan. Will you forgive me?"

Susan was in emotional free fall. This was the girl she had despised. The girl who had driven a nail in Christopher's coffin and in Susan's heart. This girl needed to be taken into her arms. She could only pretend to have enough graciousness to do it, yet once she did, the pretense became real, the grace became hers to give freely.

"I forgive you," she said, squeezing tight. "Will you forgive me for being such a cruel idiot?"

"I already have," Melissa said.

Their hearts pounded so hard that Susan didn't know which beat was hers and which was Melissa's. It was good to finally let this struggle go. Not good in an emotional sense, but in some deeper, elemental sense of the word. *Good* to let go.

Yet something horrible still weighed her down, something that Melissa couldn't possibly forgive. Susan pulled away and covered her face.

"What's wrong?" Melissa said.

"You don't know all of it. No one does."

"Tell me."

"You'll hate me again. But that would be nothing compared to the guilt I carry, the pain that swallows me every moment because there's nothing to make it stop. Nothing *should* make it stop because I deserve it."

Melissa waited.

Susan looked over at Jacob, who stood silently, watching them.

"Jacob. Could you take Jonas down to the pond? He's apt to be thirsty."

"Sure." Jacob took the reins and led Jonas away.

Susan went to the hay shed and sat down, head in hands.

Melissa sat next to her. "What did you do, Susan?"

"I killed Christopher."

"What are you saying?" Melissa's voice rose to a shrill pitch. "You pushed him out that window?"

"No, no. Not with my hands anyway. But . . . after you and I met, I flew back to Boston. You had called him, said you couldn't marry him."

Melissa wrapped her arms around her knees. "Because I believed you when you said it was the best thing for him."

"Christopher didn't. He didn't care what you said. He called you four times that night, at least four that I knew of."

"Nine. It killed me not to talk to him."

"The next day he called me at my office, said he had to get to Colorado to show you how—" Susan hiccupped, pain knifing her ribs. "Show you how much he loved you. I was desperate to stop him. So I lied."

"I don't understand."

"I told him that you had called me a few days earlier, looking for a lot of money. That I had flown out to Colorado the day earlier, and we made a business deal. He didn't believe me, so I told him where to look in my desk to find the boarding pass. That he'd also find the brochure from the family planning clinic I had tracked down for you. I told him that I took you there, paid for your abortion, and gave you enough money to buy a condo."

Melissa buried her face against her knees. "What did he say?"

"He groaned—my precious son—I caused him so much pain that he actually cried out from deep in his stomach. He took a few deep breaths and said he loved you with all his heart. He believed you loved him, but even if you didn't, he was going out to Colorado to make you love him."

Susan grabbed her hair as if she could rip her head in two. "I told him if he went to Colorado, I would disown him. He said he didn't want any money from me, that none of that was important. I said, 'No, Christopher, this is not about money. If you insist on going to Colorado and marrying that girl, I will never speak to you again. You will be dead to me.'"

Melissa looked sideways at her, confusion and shock flushing the blood from her face until she was stark white. "That's what your grandparents did to your mother."

The blood rushed to Susan's brain like a freight train roaring in her ears. "I know. And for that, I am so ashamed."

Moving as if her arm weighed a hundred pounds, Melissa lifted her hand and extended it toward Susan. "I'm sorry."

"You're sorry? For what? I'm the one who said those horrible lies."

"I understand. And I'm so sorry for you."

Susan pushed her hand away. "Don't you understand? *You will be dead to me.* Those were the last words I ever said to my son."

The words cut Jacob like a knife, stirred with a razor tip, around and around in a bloody dance . . . *my son* . . . *dead to me.*

The pond faded away, Jonas disappeared, and Jacob was on his face, chewing the dirt so he would not cry out. He smelled the blood, felt it dripping on his back from above him. Each strike of blood seared his skin like hot ore.

"You fool. Get up," the Other said.

"I can't." Jacob found a rock, bit into it to keep from howling. But the sound of the hammer leaked through his pores, a wintry wail that went unnoticed among the laughter and jeers.

"Stop playing holier-than-thou. You're to blame as much as I."

"No. I can't be."

The Other laughed. "Don't deceive yourself. We're closer than brothers, you and I. We look alike, we sound alike—"

"Not anymore," Jacob murmured, choking on the dirt. No matter. He would not watch, could not watch such torment that the Other delighted in.

The Other doubled over, seized by mirth. "The apple doesn't fall far from the tree, my friend. Even if, on this night, you still do not spill blood with us, it is only a matter of time."

Surely there was another way to deal justice. One that did not involve beatings, torture, and murder. He would face whatever the Other—the Others—would bring on him, but he would stop this now. He pushed up on his elbows, shocked to see the One-before-all so torn and shredded that he was barely recognizable.

Jacob struggled to get to his knees, the Other breathing on the back of his neck, whispering in his ear. Ugly things, gross and vile acts that he had committed and would initiate Jacob into.

"Won't be long," he whispered. "The first step's a doozy, pal, but once you're in, you're in forever."

Jacob ignored the patter, pushed himself to stand and look straight on what they had provoked. So many conspirators, and yet no one had dared to stop the brutality.

"Can I help?" he had begged, but the One-before-all would not even favor him with a look.

Jacob had to do something. He could shield the One-before-all with his body, perhaps long enough for his friends to fight for him. But his friends had fled. Anyway, the One had told them they could not raise a sword to save him. Too many had died, and Jacob had seen too much of it.

But this one was different. This was the first who did not deserve death.

He looked around for a sword. Perhaps he could use the blood-stained mallet that had been tossed into the dirt. Better yet, let surprise be his weapon. He was quicker than any of the guards. He leaped forward, his hands brushing the feet of the One-before-all, when a hand clasped his shoulder.

His commander. "Walk away."

"I . . ."

"Walk away, warrior."

"Must we do this?"

"You are not being asked to do anything but turn away. More might be required of you later, but you will not be trusted unless you can walk away now."

Jacob stared at the One-before-all, who had been flogged and beaten and pierced, feeling each cut of the whip and blow of the mallet and bite of the nail on his own skin.

"You asked to be here," his commander said. "Now it's time to walk away."

He turned and took one step. Another step. His comrades walked away with him, leaving the One who had been pierced alone.

They were almost out of sight when the One broke the silence with a sharp cry to ask his father, *Why have you forsaken me?*

"Jacob, stop. We're here. Jacob!" Melissa shook him, but he wouldn't wake up and he wouldn't stop screaming. He had collapsed next to the pond, lying face-first in the dirt. "Susan, make him stop."

"I don't have my bag. I didn't expect to need meds out here." She rolled him over, checked the pulse in his neck, and pulled up his eyelids.

Melissa only saw red where his eyes should be. "Is he bleeding?"

"The blood vessels in his eyes burst. His pressure must be sky-high."

Jacob's scream became a high-pitched shriek. His arms and legs went so stiff, they felt like boards. His tongue thrust forward, and saliva dribbled from the side of his mouth.

"He's seizing," Susan said.

"Do something, please, Susan."

"There's nothing I can do without intravenous Valium. I can't stop this."

His eyes leaked blood like tears.

Melissa grabbed the water bottle and doused Jacob's face, but that had no effect other than to flood the blood over his face and down his neck. "Oh God," she said.

ASK, CHILD.

Melissa saw Jeanette, standing in the hole in Krista's room, arms outstretched. *Asking.*

"I ask you—beg you—to make him stop this. Please, God. Please."

Jacob's arms and legs went limp, his head lolling to the side.

"Susan! Look, oh, thank You, God."

Jacob's shriek became a moan, the moan became a gasp.

"He's coming out of it," Susan said. "We've got to get him to a hospital." She pressed her ear to his chest, listening to his heart.

"No, Susan. This time, I know what's best."

"What's best, then?" Susan said without a hint of either sarcasm or superiority.

Melissa touched her arm. "It doesn't help to keep things hidden, does it, Susan?"

Susan met her gaze. "No, Melissa. It does not."

"Which is why we need to take Jacob home and, once for all, help him remember who he really is."

Flames danced in a chorus of crackles and snaps. A hellish rejoicing, to be sure, swallowing the truck. Vinyl hissed and melted, steel cracked, the seats burst into little bonfires. Rick was trapped in his seat belt, fire wrapping him in unrelenting arms.

Yet he was cool, calm. Untouched.

In glory. Thank You.

NOT YET, SON. THERE'S STILL WORK TO BE DONE.

He imagined himself with skin flashing to black, splitting open, and his muscles searing. Unbearable pain, screaming himself inside out, but *If this is Your will, so be it.*

The fire roared, and Rick waited to feed it, strangely content to accept the pain that awaited him and the witness of a man burned unrecognizable yet living, a scarred witness who must depend on every breath for the mercy of God to proclaim it. Why wasn't he burning? He had accepted his fate, but the only injury was the burn to his fingers when he tried to undo his seat belt.

His body urged him to breathe, but he knew the consequences, remembered the two victims who had breathed the fire into their lungs, yet what choice did he have because he needed to breathe now, no will left to oppose the urge that had been created in him to live, even in the face of flaming death.

Rick gasped.

The air was cooler than water, flowing over him in streams, true water now, soothing him so no flame could touch him. A man leaned over him, as Rick had leaned over so many accident victims, unbuckling their belts with a *click*, telling victims help was on the way, but this was different. This hand led him out of the fire, making a path through the flames, trailing cool water in his wake so that Rick felt neither pain nor fear, only hope.

Hope and awe as he stepped out into the cold night and could breathe in the mountain air, lifting his eyes to the hills.

Knowing where his help had come from.

THIRTY-FIVE

JEANETTE FED THEM AND INSISTED THEY ALL GET SOME REST, even though morning was breaking. Jacob trudged up to bed and Jeanette settled Melissa on the sofa in the living room while Charlie went out to feed the horses.

"Ma," she whispered. "I'm over it."

"Over what, hon?" Jeanette smoothed her hair.

"Being mad."

"At Susan?"

"At everyone."

Jeanette kissed her forehead, said a little prayer of thanks, and tucked the blanket around her shoulders.

She went back to the kitchen to clean up and found Susan staring into a cup of coffee.

"You're supposed to be sleeping."

"No rest for the wicked."

Jeanette sat across from her. "That's just a saying."

"In my case, it's true."

Dark circles lined her eyes. Her cheekbones were prominent, as if all that was left of the woman was skin. Everything else had been emptied out. And that was what this strange, horrible, wonderful time was about, Jeanette thought. We're being shaken upside down, and all the garbage in the pockets of our souls is being dumped out.

Jeanette took her hand. "Hon, I'm here to listen."

Susan smiled, but sorrow shadowed her face. "You did a good job with Melissa. She's a good young woman. I only wish—" Her voice broke. She took her hand back and covered her face.

"You're safe now. I know you weren't all those years back, but things are different now."

Susan wiped away tears. "I only wish you had been my mother. That's all."

"We're not too old to start. Can you tell this old Ma what's troubling you?"

Susan told her about the last conversation she had had with Christopher. "I told Melissa all of it, and she still forgave me. I don't know where she found it in herself to do that. I certainly will never forgive myself."

Jeanette wrapped her arms around her. "She doesn't have it in her. She has it in God. It's the only way our hearts get cracked open and put together right. He can do the same thing for you."

Susan pulled away, shaking her head. "Even if I could forgive myself—and I can't—there's still one bottom line left."

"What's that, hon?"

"Maybe I couldn't catch my son, but God could've—if He exists. If He exists and He stood by and let Christopher go out that window, how can I ever forgive Him?"

Jeanette could have quoted Scripture or talked about theological truths. Instead, she took Susan back in her arms and held her while Susan flooded her shoulder with tears.

Three hours later, they sat at the kitchen table. Jacob and Melissa had just polished off a huge stack of hotcakes. Susan had forced down some cereal. No one spoke as they ate, but Susan suspected that their minds whirred as much as hers did. She seriously considered the option of taking Jacob out of Colorado, hiding him somewhere in California or New York until the murders in the valley had been settled and the attacks explained.

But it was time to stop running away. "I still wonder if we shouldn't do this at the hospital," Susan said.

"No," Melissa and Jacob said in unison.

"I need to be home," he added.

"Stupid police can't do their job, so they want to lock Jacob up, just to say they got someone," Melissa said. "We can't let people know he's back here."

Susan looked at Jeanette.

She nodded. "My old bones say to do it right here on Robinson Ranch."

"We need a safe place," Susan said. "I don't want to be out in the open in case Rick or Zach comes sniffing around."

"The house," Jeanette said.

"Too closed in."

"The barn," Jacob said. "I'd feel comfortable out there."

Melissa and Susan shared a glance. "I don't know how comfortable Charlie would feel," Susan said. "He's had Jade and Rayya locked up in there for a couple of—"

"Don't you go speaking for your old man." Charlie stood in the doorway, leaning on a crutch. He had refused to get his leg x-rayed, but had allowed Susan to resplint it. "What are you all talking about?"

Jeanette explained.

"Yep. The barn is the place," Charlie said.

"What about the Arabians?" Susan said.

He waved his hand in dismissal. "They can go out in the paddock."

"Are you going to guard them there?" Melissa said.

Charlie shook his head. "Nope. Me and my trusty shotgun are gonna set wherever my girl tells me is okay. To guard my family." He locked eyes with Susan.

She smiled, choked with tears.

"Wait, I want to say something." Jacob looked in turn at each one of them. "If something horrible happens—if I'm someone horrible— I want you to get away. Don't try to help me. Just run away."

Susan's stomach fluttered. Why was he projecting evil upon himself? Associating himself with the abuser? Or had the abused become an abuser, as too often happened. No matter what his degree of innocence or involvement, Jacob had been a victim. She could see that cave now, despite not seeing it when she had gone down there with Rick. A chasm, perhaps an abyss with no bottom. Was she seeing reality? Or somehow a manifestation of the void in her that had been soothed somewhat by a shaky accord with Melissa?

Soothed but not closed. No longer hidden, but an aching gap that Susan would never be able to cover or even cross. There was no bridge for this kind of rift, this ravine that had been cleft in her heart and mind. *Her soul,* if Jeanette was correct in saying she had one.

"Susie?" Jeanette said.

"The barn will work." She asked Jeanette to bring some blankets and pillows out and help Charlie open all the windows so they'd have fresh air and be able to keep an eye on Rayya and Jade.

"You don't have to do that," Charlie said.

"I sure do," Susan said. "I care about those horses too."

She sent Melissa and Jacob for a short ride, telling them to keep close. "Circle the paddocks if you have to, but don't get out of sight of the barn."

Susan went upstairs, opened her medical bag to inventory what she had available. She still had a couple doses of sodium amobarbital. She could do the IV drip, which would allow her to moderate Jacob's response. Or she could try a deep hypnosis. Jacob was very responsive to suggestions, though once he was relaxed he went off into directions no one could foresee. Maybe Valium. She could give him an oral dose, add the sodium amobarbital if she didn't get a good response. Another option was putting this session off until tomorrow, have her psychopharm guy overnight her some hard-core meds.

No. They all agreed it needed to be done today. And so it would.

Jacob lay on a blanket in the fresh straw Melissa had spread. His eyes were closed and hands folded across his stomach. Jeanette sat nearby on a folding stool. Charlie had locked the front door of the barn and stationed himself at the back door, one side open to the sunlight. "No one gets in unless I let 'em," he had promised.

Melissa fluffed the pillow under Jacob's head. "You comfy?"

He opened one eye and looked sideways at her. "You do that one more time and Susan will have your head."

Melissa glanced up at Susan.

"Two more times," she said, laughing. "Then I'll have your head."

"You sure you don't want to give him some medicine?"

Susan squatted down next to Jacob. "I'd rather try this without it. It's up to you, Jacob."

"Whatever you think is best, Susan."

"If this is successful, it will also be difficult." She went on to explain some of the bad side effects of memory retrieval, like waking nightmares and nighttime wakefulness.

Either way you lose, Melissa thought. She had already asked Susan privately what would happen if they just took Jacob away, let him live his life from this point forward.

Nothing stays hidden forever, Susan had said. Better it comes out with us close by.

In a very strange way, that had made Melissa think of her pregnancy. She had known Charlie would be furious and Jeanette disappointed, especially when she told them Chad was a criminal. For the first month she'd hit the crackers and ginger ale, claiming a stomach bug the couple times Jeanette caught her throwing up.

The night before Christopher came out, she had to tell them that she was pregnant. You can't keep a pregnancy hidden for long unless you abort the baby, and she'd had no intention of doing that. The same thing might apply to Jacob. If they tried to keep his past hidden, it could kill him—or them. Especially if The Torch or monster or whatever it was had something to do with him.

Susan glanced over at them, her finger to her lips.

Melissa put her hand over Jeanette's. "She's ready to start."

Jeanette smiled down on her. "I'm proud of you."

"I didn't do anything."

"You did what was right. What more could a mother ask of her kid?"

"Thanks, Ma."

Jeanette kissed the top of her head. "Thank you."

"Thanks for picking me up," Rick said.

"You sure you don't want to go to the hospital?" Zach said.

"Nah. I'm fine."

"Don't see how. Your truck is a lump of charcoal. It's amazing you escaped."

Rick leaned forward so he could see Zach's full expression. "It was a miracle."

"Yeah, no kidding."

"I mean it."

Zach's knuckles whitened on the steering wheel. "That religion stuff isn't exactly my thing. But I'm glad it works for you. Hey man, you going to tell me about those symbols?"

Now wasn't the time, Rick decided. If the word *miracle* unsettled Zach, certainly the discovery of a demon would make him drive off the road. He'd done enough of that for one day, thank you.

"What's so funny?" Zach said.

"Nothing. I'm just light-headed. Giddy."

"Survivor's giggles."

"I suppose."

"Don't start thinking you're invincible," Zach warned.

"No chance of that." Especially with the prospect of going out to Robinsons' and facing down Jacob.

"When are you going to Robinsons'?"

Rick scratched his ear. "Who said I was going out there?"

"You just did."

"No, I didn't."

"You did."

Rick looked at him sideways. "No, I did not."

Zach threw up his hands. "Fine. You didn't. But when you do head out there, I want to come. I insist on it."

"Because . . . ?"

Zach gave him a cold look. "I've been very flexible. Lenient, one might say. But let us not forget that, regardless of Susan's posturing and the Robinsons' guardianship, my office has the authority to remove Jacob from that household. If I decide he needs to go into custody—protective or otherwise—I will."

"Sure." Rick rubbed his arms, chilled from exhaustion and adrenaline depletion.

Zach stared right through him. "And you will enforce my decision."

"That's my job. Will you watch where you're going?"

Zach smiled. "I always do, Sheriff. Now, are you going to sneak out to Robinsons' on your own—because I know you're going—or will you let me drive you?"

Rick raised his hands in surrender. "I'm all yours, pal. Drive on."

THIRTY-SIX

Jacob slipped into a half sleep, lulled by Susan's voice.

"It's time," she said. "Time to remember where you came from, who you are, how you came to be down in that ravine. You have nothing to fear. I'm here. Jeanette, Melissa, Charlie are all here with you. We will keep you safe."

It's time, his commander said. *Time to remember how this all started. Time to remember your part in this all. To take responsibility.*

"No, don't make me. Please." His own voice sounded empty.

"Shh. It's okay. It's okay . . ." Susan's voice faded away and—

—swords flashed. Not of steel but something like hard-edged energy, light and heat and gravity forged into an elemental weapon. The blades clanged against each other like discordant bells, tolling against each other when they should ring in harmony. Blood ran, not blood of flesh but rivers of diamonds, flaming to ash and becoming sludge.

Arrows flew and daggers stabbed. Agents of destruction burst all about, weapons that Jacob couldn't even put a name to but could only strive with and against. His arm ached, and a sensation he knew theoretically as pain became reality. As he struggled to swing his sword for another blow, the *clang* vibrated his insides and made his skin weep.

The music that had always been and should be now faded, but no, that music could not fade. The song stretched across the heavens and powered the stars, but Jacob could not keep it in his head because his ears were filled with the clamor of sword upon shield, hammer upon helmet, fist upon face. He breathed pain in, panted out fear, his gut curdling at the sensation of what never should have been.

A battle cry went up, a call so unassailable that all weapons fell silent. A mighty warrior flew over the field of battle, dragging his sword so that the heavens quaked and broke open.

The first warrior fell and kept falling, a scorched shriek trailing away just as another took his place. Another and another, hundreds and thousands and then hordes fell through the open spiral into a dark unknown.

Jacob fought until he found himself on the edge, looking at the void below where rebels burned out like dying stars. His commander landed next to him and said, "It's time to go."

Jacob wrapped his fingers over the edge and desperately tried to hold on. His commander's voice cut through the din. "You chose this path, did you not?"

"Yes," Jacob said, and one by one, his fingers opened. He slipped forward, trying to will his toes not to dig in, trying to keep some semblance of dignity. Suddenly he was top-heavy and tumbling.

The rebels struck creation like arrows aimed for the heart. The swords forged in the fall were far more effective than any cast in a fire. Wickedness, greed, depravity, envy, murder, strife, deceit, malice, gossip, debauchery, idolatry—these were only a few of the too many. These weapons were passed to men and women who eagerly grasped them, rejecting mercy, choosing sin, birthing death.

The rebels piped a seductive tune that snaked around hearts of flesh. Godlessness became the chorus, sung to flesh by flesh so that heaven's fallen could sheathe their swords and simply whisper. Even creation gasped, the earth and sun and moon and stars falling under a shadow, their reflected glory rocked by tremors of disobedience.

Blighted and cursed, the world wept with all manner of discord to plague what had been made perfect. A Light came into the world but the darkness did not understand it and so the darkness snuffed it— *walk away, warrior*—but that made the Light flame brighter, exposing the darkness.

It was decreed that heaven's rebels be chained for a time. And so Jacob went deep into the chasm, locked in manacles and chains and forgetting. After a moment or a millennium, a penlight shattered his sleep and a key loosed him.

He came awake in Charlie's barn, stunned by the blood and mayhem that had oozed out of his memory, reminding himself of what he had battled through, what he had chosen to endure.

Where is the key, he asked because he had a task set before him. One last time to swing his sword, and then he could rise from the ashes and regain what he had forfeited. In that moment, he knew the answer.

He was the key, and the time had come.

Melissa shook against Susan's shoulder like a leaf in a gale. Charlie curled into a ball, clutching his knees like a tumbling rider. Only Jeanette could gaze straight on at what had been wrought from Jacob's remembering. She croaked out *holy holy holy,* but there was nothing sacred about the horror seeping from Jacob's pores, Susan knew.

Carnage played out around them in full flesh so that the barn reeked of blood and rot, the ground soaking in so much that it formed a stream, damming against the front door. Susan thought she should let the sunlight in, but she didn't dare step into the dark history that appalled her, pained her, shamed her.

She watched as humankind blew up innocents; raped for pleasure, raped for revenge, raped for political advantage; burned women as witches; beheaded prophets, stoned apostles; tortured children before their parents and parents before their children; destroyed villages and cities; corrupted forests, streams, and oceans; assaulted and murdered; slandered, lied, and cheated; called forth children from the womb and crushed them; sneered at the poor; stirred up riots and waged wars; systemically butchered Jews, Armenians, Chinese, African-Americans, Koreans, Kurds, Sudanese, Cherokees, Greeks, Shiites, and on and on in every land, killing tribes and races and countries though all were brothers under the skin.

Yet a scarlet path ran through all this blood, a ribbon that bound up wounds, shined a light, offered a hope, and though Susan's skin was splattered with blood and Charlie's face was splashed with blood and Melissa's shoulders dripped with blood, Jeanette's cry of *holy holy holy* somehow offered a balm, a rushing stream that drove back the atrocities, the horrors, the sin upon sin upon sin that—despite its power and despite its acceptance—could never stand against the *Holy Holy Holy*.

The front door banged open, and Rick rushed in.

"Demon, he's a demon!" he yelled. "He was supposed to stay locked up, but somehow he lured you, Susan, and persuaded you to unlock him. He's got to go back! We have to lock him back up, or what you see here will be unleashed upon the world. Susan, are you listening to me?"

Susan turned, stiff and cold as marble. "Jacob won't unleash this horror. We already have."

Rick took a good look at what filled the air. He tried to say something, forming the syllable *hol* but somehow he couldn't finish the word though an elderly lady with creaky knees could say nothing else but *holy holy holy*.

Susan tried to say the words, to sing the faint music that she could hear through the din of explosions and cursing and howling and threats and promises, but all she could say was, "Jacob. Wake up."

Jacob stood. That must be love in his eyes, Susan hoped, but how could she really know because she had been unloved and she had fueled most of her life with that *unlove*.

He opened his arms and sucked the violence out of the air, rolling it in his hands like a potter with clay. He spat on it, and it burst into flame. Susan quaked with dread. He could not be the monster that had haunted the valley, yet he held in his hands the very weapon that had killed two, maybe three people and almost killed Melissa.

As he spun the flames, he looked at Susan. "I'm sorry you have to see this."

He turned to the front doors where Zach Hurley stood, his face in shadow. Jacob flexed his arms, ready to throw.

Susan cried out, "No!" but Melissa sprang into action, grabbing Jacob's arm and deflecting the ball of fire.

The wall of the barn caught fire and with it, a mound of dry straw that Melissa had stumbled into. Susan pulled her away, but not before her arm was singed, perhaps even worse. Melissa cried out, catching Jacob's attention. He raised his arm and the sprinklers came on, but all strangely coming down on Melissa in a surge of cold water.

As she helped Melissa up, Susan heard an intense ripping sound.

The scars on Jacob's back tore open. Light unfurled from the gaps in his skin, forming broad wings that had been torn and singed. He glanced down at Melissa and said, "I'm sorry, but you'll be okay."

He bent low and flew rather than ran, racing after Zach, who had finally turned to run.

Rick helped Melissa up and led her to the back door, the fire skittering across the rafters as if in pursuit.

In the fresh air of Rayya's paddock Susan examined Melissa. Her heart beat fast but strong. The burns on her arms were raw but not charred. Rick ran into the house to grab Susan's medical bag while Jeanette moved Melissa away from the conflagration, half-carrying her to Zach's car.

Susan dressed the wound and gave her a shot of Demerol. "We've got to get to the hospital."

"Where's Zach?" Rick said.

"Forget him. Melissa needs to get that burn dressed, and some stronger pain meds. Come on, let's go."

They lifted Melissa into the backseat, Jeanette and Charlie sliding in on either side of her. Susan got in the front.

Charlie pounded on the window and cried out. "There's Hurley. What's that fool doing?"

Zach was on Prince Sarraf's back, riding away from them and the fire.

Melissa roused. "Where's Jacob?"

"We'll deal with him later," Rick said. He squealed the sedan around, tires spinning.

Melissa grabbed Susan's shoulder. "You have to go after them."

"She's not going anywhere," Rick growled, but Susan jumped out, shouting over her shoulder that he needed to get Melissa to the hospital now.

Jacob was heading for Folly Mountain. Rather than running away, Zach was following him. Susan ran for the SUV, but the front wall of the barn had collapsed onto it and Charlie's truck as well.

She hopped the fence and whistled for the dude horses. They scattered at her call, breaking through a fence that was supposed to be horse-proof.

She could barely see Zach now. What kind of madness was driving him? And where was Jacob? She scanned the horizon but realized that he would not need to drive or ride. A blip of light circled the open sky, like a firefly in the daytime.

She started running, pain stitching her side almost immediately. Even on pure will, she couldn't make it all the way to Folly on foot.

Hooves thundered at her back. She turned, expecting to see one of the dude horses, but it was Rayya who bid her ride. A horse who had foaled only days ago, who had been infected and weakened, a nursing mother who should be in no shape to be ridden, and yet Rayya the Regal pranced with vigor.

Susan slipped on to her back. No halter, no blanket, no saddle. As

they were meant to be, horse and rider with nothing between them—
so Susan and Rayya raced toward Folly Mountain.

THIRTY-SEVEN

ONE NURSE STARTED AN IV WHILE ANOTHER IRRIGATED
Melissa's burns.

"You're going to be all right," Rick said, stroking her forehead.

"I wish everyone would stop saying that and just let me out of here.
Youch!" She bit her lower lip as the needle bit into the back of her
hand. "What you said—it's not true."

"You don't need to worry about—"

Melissa grabbed his wrist. "I'm telling you, Jacob is not a devil."

Both nurses jerked their heads up and stared. "Just an expression,"
Rick said with a little wave. He kissed Melissa's cheek. "I'll check back
with you later."

"You're going after him, aren't you?"

"It's my job."

"Please, Rick. Don't hurt him . . ."

"It's not in my hands, honey."

Charlie and Jeanette waited outside the exam room. "I've notified
the CBI about a fire in your barn," Rick said. "That's all I said. The rest
of it wouldn't make sense to them. I've got to go after Jacob, figure out
what needs to be done."

Charlie rubbed his face. "Susan's my daughter. I need to go with you."

"Old man, you're not going anywhere." Jeanette had an iron grip
on his arm.

"I need to protect her."

Jeanette turned Charlie's face to her. "There is something you can
do. We'll do it together." She looked up at Rick. "Go. We'll be back at
the ranch once they let Melissa go. I'll call Doc Potter to give us a ride."

Rick held out a set of car keys. "Take Zach's car. Lisa is on her way
over here with the cruiser."

Jeanette wrinkled her brow. "What was Zach doing going after him?"

"I just don't know," Rick said.

After dropping Lisa at the office, he got back on the horn with the CBI. Should he tell them that he was going after Jacob? He'd like to have backup. But their weapons would be useless. Either Rick could handle this on his own or no one would be able to.

Jacob was headed back to Folly, and Rick knew why.

There was a cave down in that ravine, one that couldn't be seen by human eyes. A cave in which at least one troop of thirteen demons had been chained. No, that wouldn't be right. There would be twelve chained demons.

The thirteenth—Jacob—was on his way up there to free them.

Susan passed Zach at the base of Folly Mountain. Prince Sarraf had slowed, his chest heaving as he struggled up the trail. She urged Rayya faster. Zach didn't know where the ravine was, and Susan wasn't about to lead him there. This would be between her and Jacob, and *God, if You're there . . .*

With a holler and a slap, Zach muscled Sarraf after Rayya. "What's the hurry, Susan?"

She ignored him, leaning into the mare's neck and trusting her to go faster.

Zach grabbed the back of her shirt and tugged. What was he thinking? Susan pressed her knees into Rayya, trying to hold on, but Zach was too strong. She tumbled off, splitting her forehead on a rock. Before she could sit up, he jumped on her.

"Answer my question," he said.

Had the man gone crazy? "Get off me!" Her heart raced. She had to get to the ravine and to Jacob.

"You're trying to rescue your pretty boy."

"What are you talking about? Let me go."

"He is rather comely, isn't he. Have you tried him out yet, or are you still mulling your seduction strategy?"

"You're sick. And when this is over, I'm reporting you." Her forehead streamed blood. With her arms pinned, she couldn't wipe it away.

He laughed, his breath hot on her face. "You'll report *me*? Oh, that is grand, Dr. Stone. Just delightful."

"You'll be sorry—"

"Wake up, little Susie. You are the one who will be sorry if you don't give me that key."

"I don't have any key."

"Oh, yes, you do."

She squirmed and kicked. How could Zach be this strong when there was nothing to him? *Unless he wasn't really Zach.*

"Absolutely correct, Susan. There is definitely more to me than meets the eye."

A sliver of ice slashed her spine. How had he known what she was thinking?

"Because I'm in your mind, Susan. Trickling down the back of your neck, creeping in and out of your backbone, sliding up and down your throat. I'm the time bomb that tick-ticks in your soul. Hear it? Tick-tock, baby. Someday, baby. Someday I'm gonna blow, and you'll see what you are, what you—"

"Who are you?"

"Don't you know?" His voice had dropped a full octave.

"I don't, I swear . . ."

"Zachary Hurley, employee of the state of Colorado. Quite the good ol' boy. Easy to hang with, easy to possess. Know why?"

"Please let me go, Zach."

His fingernails dug into her wrist, drawing blood. "What did I just tell you? I am not Zach. Now answer my question. Do you know why it was so easy to take possession of that delightful slimebag?"

She shook her head, shivering so hard she thought her bones would crack.

He laughed. "Because Zachary Hurley loved the little ones, he did. Little perv had the perfect cover. Goes in on a case study, gets a kid alone, and says, 'Did your mother's boyfriend do this, or how about this?' All under the guise of authority. No wonder his head exploded."

"His head exploded?" Hysteria edged Susan's consciousness, making her want to laugh insanely at playing straight man to a psycho. "What are you talking about?"

"Hurley was victim number one, doncha know? Listen to my modus operandi and see what you think. I borrowed a little boy whose mama was strung out, put him right out there for Mr. Social Worker to get his greasy hands on. Just at the right moment, I was able to administer justice. Ba-boom! Sparing the boy—the first good deed I've done in a long, long time. Honestly, it was too easy. Usually I have to muscle my way in, but good ol' Zachary Hurley had an open door policy. I just strolled right in, took enough to make a counterfeit for myself, and trashed the rest."

Her throat clenched, utter fear making it impossible to speak.

"Don't make like I'm some stranger, Dr. Stone. You see my handiwork in your practice all the time. Like the borderline from Saugus or the depressive narcissist from Cambridge. They have names, but to you they're clinical diagnoses, good ol' DSM-IV defined and categorized. Makes it easier to deal with their pain like that. Talking and medicating, more talking and more medicating, decorating your office in soothing blues and greens, helping your patients to put into words the *horror* that I invite and inflict. Yet you, Dr. Stone, never consider demon possession in your diagnosis, even when we stare you right in the face."

Oh God oh God oh God . . .

"I intend to be," Zach said. "So let's make a deal while you're still in a vague position to negotiate. You give me the key, and I won't force my way into you like I did to Zach Hurley and that lying, cheating, philandering vet of yours, Alex Rodgers. Victim number two, in case you were inclined to leave that self-centered world of yours and wonder where your Kentucky hotshot had gotten himself to."

"Why him?"

"I needed to turn the screws on you Robinsons. Rodgers was another willing victim, right time at the right place, doncha know?"

"I'm not like them. I'm a good person."

"Tsk, tsk. You haven't been reading the handbook. No one is good. No, not one."

"Why us?" she whispered.

"Why not you? Why not anyone? Those of us still on the loose have some wiggle room, you know. A little free will goes a long way when you don't let anything—or anyone—stand in your way."

"No . . ." Susan gasped. "Surely it can't be as random as that."

He sighed dramatically. "Okay, you'll pout until I give you a reason. How's about this one: your family was ripe for the pickin'. Bitter and unforgiving and pigheaded. Talk about holdin' that door wide open so I could stroll right in. Oh, yes, you Robinsons are quite the feudin' bunch."

"We're getting past that," Susan said.

He laughed. "You think so? Take a look at what you've still got invested in that shriveled little thing you call a soul." He put his lips to Susan's and inhaled.

She tried to fight back, but how could she oppose her own darkness? She had heard that love was salvation, that Jesus was love, but how could she know that, how could she even know love when love always abandoned—

Papa, Mommy hurt me, she spanked me hard when I didn't do anything, there's a boo-boo on my leg; Papa, Mother told Nicole that she wasn't smart enough for me, that I need a better class of friends; Papa, I can't live here anymore, you can have her but I give up, I have no mother; Papa, why did you turn away, walk away, leave me to her?

An aneurysm? That's impossible, he's young, he's healthy, we eat fish and fresh vegetables, he can't have an aneurysm. Brain dead? No, he can't be. Too young, I need him, how could he die? Paul, don't you understand, I don't know how to be a mother. I needed you, how could you leave me?

Too young to get married, I absolutely forbid it; she's not right for you, Christopher; Colorado isn't right for you, you don't know but I do; my son, my baby please don't leave me, not for this girl because, don't you see, a rushed marriage will be like my parents all over again and that was torture for me, I'm afraid for you, don't leave like this.

Yes, officer, Christopher Stone is my son. No! NO! Oh God, oh God, I can't bear this, let me die in his place, please dear God, I can't do this, don't let this be, they're lying, he can't be dead, he wouldn't leave me like this.

Love leaves me, always leaves me, I can't do this, I can't love . . .

I CAN, SUSAN. I CAN.

Zach jerked away. "Enough of this, woman. Your breath stinks." He wrapped his fingers around her throat, rock-strong hands that pressed against her windpipe.

I'm so lost confused scared angry out-of-my-mind. Oh God, I need help, please help . . .

When she heard the *clip clop* of a horse, Susan thought it must be Tasha coming to take her through death's door, but it was Rayya who reared up and with sharp front hooves struck the Zach-creature so that he rolled off Susan.

Rayya bowed low and Susan rolled onto her back. They rode up the mountain, Prince Sarraf obediently trailing behind.

Leaving the Zach-creature behind like trash on the trail.

THIRTY-EIGHT

RICK BOUNCED UP FOLLY ON A BORROWED ATV. IT WAS CLEAR that Jacob was heading back to where he had been chained, though why Zach followed him—on a horse, of all things—he couldn't even begin to guess. He didn't know the theology of fallen angels, but his gut told him that freeing Jacob's troop of demons was not part of God's plan. He had to do whatever it took to lock Jacob back up.

The Bible warned that Satan himself masquerades as an angel of light. Jacob had that one nailed. The kid's gentle manner and trusting nature were all a lie, learned no doubt from the Father of Lies. The name he had chosen should have rung bells for Rick. Jacob meant *supplanter*. The kid had easily supplanted Christopher—in Susan's heart, in Melissa's, even with that old crank, Charlie Robinson.

The question was: how had he gotten by Jeanette? She may not have finished high school, but she knew her Bible backward and forward. She was kind and hospitable, but she was also discerning. Yet Rick knew that even now she'd be urging him to give God time to work.

Right. *Give the devil time to work* was more like it. Give him time to free his buddies and take over this valley. No wonder the arson investigators couldn't determine what had burned those two victims. No existing profile in their database could match hellfire.

Rick leaned over the handlebars, pushing faster. Around a sharp turn of the trail, he came upon Zach collapsed in a mass of brush. Rick hopped off the four-wheeler and doused Zach's face with water, rousing him to consciousness. Zach grabbed his side and rolled over, retching.

"What happened?" Rick said.

"You're going to think I'm insane."

"Try me."

"Jacob flew right at me. He had wings—how could he have wings? Eyes like hot coals. He spat fire, but I ducked behind the boulders, tried to hide under one. He threw rocks at me—no, not rocks, small boulders, cracking open around me. Finally I played dead, hoping for the best, and it worked—he left. I saw him fly away, Rick. This can't be, just can't . . ." Zach gasped for air.

"Hold on, man. Take some water."

Zach gulped down some water, promptly vomited it back up.

"Is anything broken?" Rick said.

Zach rubbed his head. "Some bumps, but I'm in one piece."

"What about internally? Anything feel not quite right inside?"

Zach's laugh was edged with hysteria. "None of this feels right. Are we all insane?"

"Hey, let me worry about that, okay?" Rick put his hand on Zach's shoulder, careful not to squeeze. "I've got to get up there and track Jacob down. Take my two-way. Give me ten minutes before you call my dispatcher. Don't tell her or anyone what happened."

"Why not?"

"Because they can't help."

"What do I say?"

"Just say you've been injured hiking. A rock slide on snowmobile 13. That's the number for this trail. Not one word about Jacob. I don't want anyone else coming up there after me. It's too dangerous."

"Up where? Where are you going?"

"He's heading for the ravine. I've got to stop him."

Zach struggled to stand. "You know where the ravine is?"

Rick unsnapped the two-way from his bag. "I went there with Susan and Joyce, remember?"

"I don't think I knew that." He stretched his arms over his head. "Listen, I'm all right. Just shook up, that's all. I'm coming with you."

"No, that's nuts. You wait here."

"You are not going up there alone." Zach grabbed his arm. "Two of us will be a better match for Jacob."

Two would be, Rick supposed.

"Let's go, then," Zach said. "Let's go find Jacob."

Susan found Jacob standing at the edge of the ravine. She slid off Rayya. "Stay here," she whispered. "No closer, okay?"

She walked slowly, not wanting to startle Jacob into a sudden lurch. She went to his side and looked down. The slope was steeper than she had remembered.

He did not turn around, but continued to stare into the ravine. "You shouldn't be here."

"I want to help you."

"You can't. But thank you for trying." His smile was tinged with sadness.

"There must be something I can—"

"Nothing." He stretched his arms over his head, reaching for the sky.

"Maybe take you to a priest or something? I don't know about these things, but I'll do anything I can."

He rose up on his toes.

"Jacob, please. What are you doing?"

"Keeping my word." He pushed off with his legs and dove headfirst into the ravine.

Fly, her heart cried, but he kept those silver wings tight around his body. Before Susan could even scream, she heard him hit the rocks below.

What Jacob knew he left behind.

The roar of wind and the hush of breeze. The slash of sunset and the smolder of moonrise. Rustling grass, murmuring trees. Surging rivers, silent dew, jubilant fields, sailing clouds, flowering meadows, lofting skies, rolling thunder.

Soaring larks and swooping hawks.

Lamb's down and Krista's cheek.

Charlie's cackle and Jeanette's hum. Rick's watchful eyes. Melissa's loyal heart. Susan's tight grasp.

And the music.

Binding the sun and moon and stars and the tiniest sparrow and the loudest lion and every hair on every head. Jacob's center, his purpose, his being. Music that burst out in laughter and goodness. Spun by light, filling the skies, filling every darkness except the one that rose up to meet him.

He'd miss the music most of all.

Susan skidded down the slope, more on her backside than her feet. The slide roused old bruises from her last tumble and tattooed her with new ones. Yet she would hold tight because now her will was not to die but to live. She bounced hard into a clump of brush.

Shadows filled the ravine, lacerated by reflected reds of the day's dying sun. Where was Jacob? His body had to be broken, neck snapped, skull crushed—

. . . a jumper, a young man, right outside your apartment building . . .

—or could he have survived this fall? She had heard the *thump*, only one thump, because he had sprung like a diver and cleared the same slope that she had just bounced down.

Her eyes adjusted and she could make out boulders and the outcroppings in the rock face that formed the outer side of the ravine. Just as she had that night, she again turned to her left.

Darkness—so deep it was black, but not glossy, more like velvet. It stretched as a breach in the rock, not just in Folly Mountain but perhaps in her own folly in ignoring what was right before her eyes. In sunsets and birdsong and mountain air and the sweet smile of a baby.

I AM.

"I don't know," Susan whispered.

"Susan." Jacob emerged from the breach.

She ran to him, but he put up his hand. "Don't touch me."

"Are you okay?"

He nodded.

"What are you doing down here?"

"What are *you* doing down here, Susan?"

"I want to help you."

He shook his head. "You can't. Climb back up, please. It should be easier this time, without me to drag along."

"I want you to come with me."

"I can't."

"Why?"

He unwound his wings. Glimmering strands formed of a cloak of lacy light. Yet the breach shone through his wings.

Darkness shines, Susan thought. *That can't be.*

"It's allowed to be," Jacob said. "Can you accept that, Susan?"

I hate it, she thought. *Hate it, fight against it, become it.* "How can I accept it when I don't like it," she said.

"You think I do?" His eyes brimmed with pain. "Will you accept the pain that mercy allows?"

"Don't ask me that."

He put his hands to his face for a moment. Then he looked at her. "You can't enter the struggle if you don't accept the pain."

"I won't."

"In that case, you need to leave, Susan."

"Maybe I'm not supposed to leave."

His forehead wrinkled. She had touched a nerve.

"The truth, Jacob. Do you know for sure that I'm supposed to leave?"

He shook his head. "No. I don't know."

"Then I am staying."

"If I had permission to go back up there, I might be tempted to force you," Jacob said. "But I don't, so I can't."

"So what now?"

Jacob wrapped his wings again, the lustrous fabric melting into his skin. He looked like the young man she had always known. Not always— just days—and he had claimed her heart completely.

Yet what bound her to him had been his need for protection. His dependence. She hadn't let Christopher be free, always hedging him in so she could protect him. And when she gripped too tightly, he broke away and fell—

. . . *you have to let me see him, maybe it wasn't him, maybe it was his friend, you have to let me see him, oh God oh God oh God my baby my baby why did you do this oh God my baby* . . .

The breach rippled with a burst of foul air. Something *clanked*. Fear swept over Susan, but she ignored the stink and the clamor and stood tall, tucking in her shirt, running her fingers through her hair. "What now, Jacob?"

He looked up. The crimson streaks deepened as night crept in. "We wait, Susan. We wait."

"This is it," Rick said, braking the ATV.

Zach had clung to his back the whole way up. Poor guy must be afraid of heights.

He slipped off the back, trying to get his footing. "You sure this is it? All these rocks and cliffs look the same."

"We marked it. See?" Rick shone his flashlight on the cross Joyce had spray-painted on a rock.

Zach shaded his eyes. "Yeah. I see it."

"Listen."

They stood still and silent. Susan's voice drifted up from deep in the ravine.

Rick unwound the rope. "I'll anchor this and go on down. You can—"

He stopped, spooked by a hot gust of air on the back of his neck. Rick turned just as Zach ripped his gun from his holster.

"What're you doing?"

Zach pointed the gun at him. "You're not going anywhere, pal."

He raised his hands in appeasement. "Zach—"

The safety *clicked*. Rick instinctively ducked his head. The first round whistled over him as he dove, no cover close by, *I got it all wrong*, the next round took him in the side and then in the back, pain exploding, *not Jacob but Zach*, another bullet, *open Your arms, Father,* scraping his hip and then one more, shredding him, *my daughter, my son, my babies into Your care* the one that spun him into a chasm of night—

THIRTY-NINE

DOWN IN THE RAVINE, THE SHOTS ECHOED LIKE BOMB BLASTS.

"Who's up there?" Susan called. "Rick?"

A dark shadow stretched over the sky, circling down like a massive hawk. Zach landed at Susan's side, keeping her between him and Jacob.

"So did you hear the news?" he said, chortling. "Rick's gone bye-bye."

Her heart broke—*please don't let this be, please let him be lying.* Her insides turned to water, and she longed to faint but she couldn't, maybe she could still help Rick and here was Jacob, who needed her too. He wasn't a demon, couldn't be because he wasn't anything like this thing called Zach.

"Zach works fine," he said. "It has a hard ring to it. A finality. Unlike my pal here. Jacob—named after a sniveling weasel who lied his way through his inconsequential little life."

Jacob stood silent, arms crossed over his chest.

"Hail hell—the gang's all here." Zach rubbed his hands in glee. His wings were transparent, veined with what looked like rust. Susan stared, her physician's eye recognizing lines of infection, the kind that creeps along blood vessels.

She felt something cold in her hand, though neither Jacob nor Zach touched her. She instinctively clenched her fist.

Zach caught the motion. "Little Susie has got the key. The guy temporarily-in-charge has a penchant for entrusting his important tasks to lumps of no consequence." He stretched out his hand. "Okay, girlie. Give it here."

Susan pressed her fist to her chest. How the key had come to be there, she didn't know. That Zach should not have it was an absolutely certainty. "No."

He fluttered his wings, the rust-lines throbbing. "How delightful. I get to take it."

"He can't," Jacob said.

"Oh, who says I can't?" Zach said, sneering.

Jacob tipped his head back, looking up.

Zach laughed. "Come on, boy. You know what I think of those rules."

"He can't take the key from you, Susan. I can't either," Jacob said. "You need to give it to him. Or give it to me."

She looked from Zach to Jacob, from night to day. "What will you do with it, Jacob?"

"Lock myself up again."

Her heart splintered. "Why would you do such a thing?"

Jacob closed his eyes. "Because I choose to."

"I don't understand."

"It's not up to you to understand. Please give me the key."

"Please give me the key," Zach mocked. "Mr. Goody-snot, flapping his tinsel wings like the chicken he is. Afraid to test, afraid to question, afraid to think for himself. You're a scientist, Susan. What's the first thing you were taught? Test the thesis, question the results, think it all out. So let me pose this question: does God exist?"

"You do," Susan whispered. "Therefore, He must."

Zach reared back with laughter. "Evil proves the existence of good? Bzzzt. That wouldn't even pass Philosophy 101, Susan. Try again."

Anger ripped through her. "This world exists. I didn't make it. Did you, Zach?"

He blew on his fingertips. "Obviously not. Have you noticed how imperfect this dump is? What an abysmal failure."

Sadness flooded her, cold and damp, smothering her resolve. She knew all about failure—her life had been a study in failure, passed on to her from Mother, passed on by her to her precious son.

"Precious? What is it with you folks and your *precious* little boys? But we digress. Two strikes on you, Susan. One more and you are outta here."

Does God exist? She had seen a miracle, hadn't she? She tried to picture Rayya, but she saw Jade in the straw, brain damaged and dying.

"Because that's where she'll be back at," Zach said. "Maybe not today or tomorrow, but eventually she'll be feeding this big manure pile of a world. Brutality, agony, terror. Kind of puts the kibosh on the kindly old gent who is supposed to be guiding this whole shebang."

She turned to Jacob. "You tell me."

"I can," he said. "But telling doesn't make it so."

"What does?"

"You know, Susan. You just have to do it."

She pressed her hands to her head and turned from Jacob to Zach, Zach to Jacob, caught in a loop until she pressed her face against the rock. This, at least, was solid. "What if I take the key away with me? What will you do?"

Zach laughed, wiggling his hands in her face. "Am I chained? I think not, girlie. I followed you this far—think I'll stop just because you want me to?"

She turned to Jacob, desperate. "Can you stop him?"

"Only if I have the key."

Maybe that was enough—not accepting God, but locking up evil. Hadn't she done that her whole life? She had tried to be good, to do good, to choose what was good for the ones in her care.

. . . *please, Dr. Stone, it's not a good idea to see him, the fall was bad, ma'am, please, really bad, you don't want to remember him like this . . .*

And she had failed.

"That's right, Susan," Zach said. "You failed. But what if you had another chance?"

"What do you mean, another chance?"

"What if I could turn back time?"

She glanced at Jacob.

"I can't tell you what to believe," he said.

Zach rubbed his hands. "What if I could put you back to before that final phone call? When you told your precious baby that he would be *dead to you*. How did that work out for you, Susan, huh? Not too good, I'd say."

"I . . ." She swallowed hard, trying to quell the temptation. She could taste twisted hope in the back of her throat. "No. I don't think you can do that."

"But what if I can?" Zach whispered. "Surely you can't take the chance of not giving it a try, can you? I've felt your tears, Susan. Tasted them as you flood your pillow. When you dream, Susan, your arms flail. Did you know that? You're trying to stop him and then you're trying to catch him, but you're too weak and face it—with no one running the asylum, no one was around to catch the poor kid.

"But listen, girlie. I've got an in with someone powerful. Someone who could change all of that. It's just a matter of knowing the right guy. You help me out, give me that key, and I'll put in a good word, Mummy. Tit for tat, tic for tac, key for me. Simple trade. I get the key, you get that precious son of yours back and get rid of that staggering load of guilt. How can you pass on a second chance to set it right? Whaddya say, Suse. The second chance is in play already. The window's open, and Christopher is wondering if life's worth living when Mummy says he's dead to her, and maybe he'll just show her that he can escape her apron strings and make her sorry, but it's such a long way, Mummy, and I don't want to go, but you won't let me stay, so I—"

"Baby, don't, Mummy didn't mean it, don't, baby," she cried over and over, her hand open. But as Zach reached for it, she whipped around and pressed the key into Jacob's hands. Zach lunged, but Jacob put the key in his mouth and swallowed it.

"You'll be sorry, Mummy," the demon snarled. "Your precious baby only had one second chance, and you just blew it."

"No . . ." Susan moaned, going to her knees. "Please, God, no."

Jacob snapped his wings with a loud, sparkling *crack*. "Susan, don't believe anything that one says. Second chances aren't what the Lord offers. Redemption is."

Zach backed away, shaking dust off his arms. "You're such a grandstander. Always were. But now you've made it easy for me, lad."

Jacob held up his hands in surrender.

Susan forced herself to attention. "Jacob? What's he talking about?"

"I couldn't take the key from you, Susan," Zach said. "But I can sure take it from this loser."

Susan backed against Jacob, her arms outstretched. "Run. Fly. Do what you need to, but run away."

"Time to stop running, Susan," he whispered.

Oh God, why don't You hear me, why don't You help me?

Zach chewed a fingernail, spit it out. "Test the thesis, Susan. Either he's not there. Or he doesn't care. Either way, I win."

She clutched for Jacob's hand. "What do I do?"

He squeezed, his touch so gentle she wanted to cry. "Let go, Susan."

Let go. But who would catch her if she let go? She let go of Christopher, pushed him away, and no one caught him.

LET GO, SUSAN.

Who was there to catch my son? Who is there to catch me?

I AM. LET GO.

She teetered over darkness, not the chasm of this ravine but a darkness in herself, and only one thing would save her, if she dared say it, dared to believe, dared to reach out for the true key to her chains, dared to allow herself to fall—

"Yes," she said, and a rain came, a flood of cool water, soothing the fire of her guilt so she could open her fingers so a sure hand could grasp her and never let her go.

Zach chattered at her, but she waved him away like the gnat he was. She turned to Jacob and saw this was the one thing she had gotten right. That he was innocent and gentle and sweet, and fierce in all those things. She saw relief in his eyes because the final piece in his clouded memory was her belief.

"Why were you chained?" she whispered.

"I'm the guardian. The one holding this troop back until the proper time. I chose this, knowing what I would give up for a time. The forgetting was a mercy until then."

"Why wasn't he chained?" She pointed at Zach who chattered away, empty threats that amounted to no more than a boring waste of space.

"Some have been allowed to roam for the Almighty's purpose. He belonged to the group I was sent to lock up. I chased his troop through the devastation you saw in the barn, captured all but him. He's been searching for his comrades for a long time, wanting them free with him to multiply his work."

"Why in Colorado?"

"This is where they finally made their stand. This troop is only one of many that are locked up. And he's only one of many that are permitted to rove about, though he truly is of no consequence."

Comprehension crept through Susan's mind at a glacial pace. "In the twelfth century. Am I right? That's when you locked them up, and that's why your knowledge of history—"

"Of human history," Jacob said. "There's so much more."

"Yes. I see that now. But that's why you have no memory since that time?"

Jacob nodded.

"Oh, stop with the questions," the demon said. "When will you get it through that thick head of yours, Susan Stone? You are of no consequence."

"You are of great consequence, Susan," Jacob said.

"Why?"

"Not because he chose you to play a part in his silly plan." He waved at Zach as one might wave off a fly. "But because the One-before-all chose you to be His."

Jacob pressed his hands to hers, burning her palms. Yet it was a good searing, one not to be drawn away from. "Get out of the way."

"Wait. I . . ." Susan looked at her hands. Her left palm was marked with an inch-wide burn. Her right was branded with a puzzling image. "It looks like a boat. I don't understand, Jacob."

"Be patient. You will." He let go of her hands. "But right now—now is the time, Susan, to show that you have truly let go."

There was only one way to lure the demon, only one thing he wanted. Jacob strode toward him, the key pressing out of his stomach, outlined against his skin.

"I used to love you, brother," Jacob said. "I'm sorry it's come to this."

"I've always despised you, pretty boy." The demon squeezed his hands and flicked them open, unsheathing talons. "I'm thrilled it's come to this."

Jacob flung one arm up, blocking Susan's view. Anything she could imagine would be less excruciating than the reality. He extended the other arm and beckoned the demon forward. "As my friend Melissa says—bring it on."

"This won't be fair. But I'm so far beyond caring about that—"

The demon leaped on Jacob, and he allowed it, just as he allowed the demon to rip open his belly. Just a worthless piece of metal, because Jacob was the key, and as the demon ripped through him, Jacob smothered him with the Light against which nothing can stand, the Light that forged the everlasting chains that would bind the demon's kind. Jacob easily slipped the manacles around the demon's hands and feet, even as the demon continued to tear through Jacob, looking for a key that opened nothing. His only pain was the howl of the others in his ears, chained deep in the darkness and clamoring for release.

When the Zach-demon had been locked up, Jacob slipped into place as the last link of the chain. He folded his wings and accepted the mercy that would blanket him in music until all was music once again, forever and amen.

FORTY

JACOB COVERED ZACH WITH HIS WINGS. CHAINS CLANKED, light whirred. Jacob cried out in pain and Zach in fury.

And they were gone.

Like that—a gust of wind, a shiver of air, and Susan was left alone in the ravine. She had intended this place to be her grave. Instead, it had become a womb. All that was needed was for her to climb out.

"Sleep well, Jacob," she whispered.

She began to climb, sluggish at first and then with a frenzy. *Please, Lord, I'm asking for a second chance. Not for me, but for Rick.*

Her feet skidded in the dirt and she fell, sliding twenty feet until she crashed into an outcropping. She wiped the blood from her face and pushed upward. Night settled in, and a thousand stars winked as if just out of reach. About halfway up, the air stirred with the *tat-tat-tatting* of a rattler. "Go back to sleep," she muttered and kept climbing.

Jacob was wrong. It was more difficult without him, harder to climb with only a tiny faith to sustain her. Easier to use him or Christopher or her anger or pain as a crutch. She climbed for Rick, hoping—praying—that she wasn't too late to help.

She was a few feet from the top when her hand sank into wet sand, stirring up the metallic tang of blood. Rick's blood for sure, but *please, Lord.* A hard kick pushed her over the top.

The moon had risen over Folly, casting a silver light onto the trail. Rayya stood silently, regarding Susan with placid eyes. Where was Rick? Had he fallen into the ravine without her knowing it? Perhaps that demon had carried him down. If need be, she would tumble back down to find him.

"Rick! If you can hear me, let me know. Somehow. Rick?"

The wind sighed. Otherwise, the night was quiet.

Susan raced down the trail until she spotted the ATV. She found a flashlight and sighted it as if she were aiming a gun. Over the ravine, showing the outer face. North, down the trail. Going west, over some boulders, turning until she noticed a stand of scrub pine.

Rick lay on his side, not moving.

His jeans were soaked with blood. Hot blood—he was still alive. Susan ran her fingers over the wound, relieved to find the blood was not from a thigh wound—something that could cause him to bleed out—but from the crest of his pelvis, over the hip.

"Rick. Ricky!"

He moaned.

"It's Susan." She brushed his face with her hands, trying to gently rouse him.

"Hurts," he said.

"I'm going to help you. Hold on, Ricky. Let me check you out."

His face was stark white, contorted with pain. His shirt was ripped from bullet holes. No blood though. "Are you wearing a bullet-proof vest?"

"Thought it would protect me against Jacob," he mumbled. "But he wasn't the one."

"I know."

"Where is that Zach thing?" Rick pushed up, cried out with pain.

"Shush. Quiet. Don't move." Susan helped to lower him back down.

"Where?"

"Jacob locked him up."

"Jacob . . ."

She pressed her hand to his cheek. "He's an angel. An angel and a blessing. Are you shot anywhere besides your hip? I can't find anything, but I don't want to roll you."

"The vest took all but one. I've got some cracked ribs. Think that's it."

"Okay. I need to call for help."

"Use my two-way, Suse. But they won't find us. Joyce won't know the way. Not in the dark."

"That's okay. I know someone who will."

Joyce and two paramedics arrived on ATVs, led by an old man on a horse.

"Pop." Susan ran to him. "I wasn't sure you'd make it with your bad leg."

"What bad leg? Nothin' wrong with my leg." He stood in the stirrups to demonstrate.

Joyce taped Rick's ribs and shot him up with painkillers. She and the EMTs loaded him onto an ATV that seemed more Hummer than four-wheeler.

Charlie sent them down first. "Doc Freeman sprayed trail markers with glow-in-the-dark paint," he told Susan.

Once everyone else was gone, he asked, "Where's Jacob?"

Susan told him what happened. Every single bit, expecting at any moment that he'd throw up his hands and head for home.

Instead, he hugged her. "I knew he was a good guy. The horses liked him."

Susan laughed.

Charlie wagged his finger at her, biting back a grin. "Don't you laugh at me, young lady. What's the story with you taking my horse without permission?"

"She took me."

"I told your mother—I mean, Jeanette—"

"Ma," Susan said. "That fits her really well."

"Yeah. I told Ma she was a spectacular horse."

"Amen to that. Have you seen Prince Sarraf around anywhere?"

Charlie shook his head. "Maybe he's gone back to wherever he came from."

"Maybe."

"So whaddya say? You too city to keep up with an old man?"

"You too out-of-shape to keep up with a half-old gal?"

"Ol' Job and I got some life left yet."

They took off down the trail, Rayya galloping hard on the straight-away, leaving Charlie and Job in the dust. Susan eased her to a stop and waited, expecting a lecture.

Charlie only laughed. "Who taught you to ride like that? Must have been some old fool."

Susan smiled. "No, Papa. Just some old cowboy."

Although the Lord gives you the bread of adversity
and the water of affliction,
your teachers will be hidden no more;
with your own eyes you will see them.
Whether you turn to the right or to the left,
your ears will hear a voice behind you, saying,
"This is the way; walk in it."

— Isaiah 30:20–21

FORTY-ONE

THOUGH DAYS PASSED, THE IMAGES REMAINED ON SUSAN'S palms.

"What do they mean?" Melissa asked one night. "A wide stripe and a boat. It doesn't make sense."

Susan shrugged, trying to hold back tears. The not-knowing was a deep ache, like a hunger impossible to satisfy.

"If the answer isn't in Colorado, then it's got to be elsewhere," Jeanette said. "So get a move on."

By the time they had packed their bags, Jeanette had made sandwiches for the plane and called the Camaras about helping Charlie with the horses.

"Don't you want to come with us?" Susan asked.

"This is not my trip to make." She hugged Susan first, then Melissa. "Go. Figure out the gift that Jacob left you."

For the first part of the plane ride, Susan and Melissa had plenty to say. When the topics of Jacob and Arabians were exhausted, they fell into an awkward silence.

Melissa opened her backpack and handed Susan a photo. "She's Don and Sara Camaras' kid."

"She's adorable." Dressed in a little pink dress, the baby had big eyes and a halo of peach-fuzz hair. Susan studied the picture, the truth slowly dawning. "She's your baby, isn't she?"

"Don and Sara's now."

"I just assumed you had the—"

Melissa shook her head. "I swore everyone to silence. For once, Charlie kept his yap shut."

"I'm so sorry for what I did, what I said."

"I know."

"I don't know how you can ever forgive me for how I treated you."

"Let it go," Melissa said, an edge to her voice. "It's over."

"I'm trying," Susan whispered.

"Don and Sara asked me to name her. I said 'No, she's your baby now,' but they swore they'd call her Lamb Chop if I didn't name her."

Susan smiled. "What's her name?"

"Krista."

"That's pretty."

"Krista Robinson Camara."

Susan put her hand to her throat, unable to speak.

Melissa bit her lip. "Maybe I shouldn't have. Because I told the truth. She wasn't his baby. How I wish she had been, but—"

"Shush. Christopher would be so proud. You should be too. The Camaras are great people."

"They want to know if you want to meet her when you come back. You are coming back. Right?"

"Joyce asked me to take over her practice. I can't for about three years. I have to work under her and at the hospital. Like a second internship so I can certify in family medicine."

"Jeepers, Susan. A *yeah* or *no* would have said it," Melissa said.

"Yes. I'll be back."

"Because Don and Sara want to know if you could help out with the grandma chores. Don's mother isn't around anymore."

Susan stared at her.

"Is that like an insult or something? Are you too young to be a grandma?"

"Not too young. Just not deserving."

Melissa laughed. "As Jeanette would say: 'Who is? But we get blessed anyway.'"

"I haven't been in Christopher's room since . . ." Susan stood outside the suite at the back of her penthouse apartment. "After the inquest, Peter Muir took down the police seal, but I've kept the door closed." She pressed her forehead against the door. "I'm not sure I can do this. Maybe I should just sell the place."

"We came two thousand miles. We're not going to back out now."

"I just don't know if I can," Susan said.

"Then I'll go in, look for you," Melissa said.

"No. We came together, we'll do it together." Susan opened the door and they went in.

Melissa was struck by the light, airy feel of the sitting room. The walls were white, unlike the rest of the apartment that Susan had decorated in rich browns, rusts, and cream. Sunlight poured in through large windows overlooking Boston Harbor. Papers and books were stacked haphazardly on a desk and on top of a computer. A leather recliner perched in front of an entertainment center.

"Two TVs?" Melissa said. "What the Sam Hill did he need two televisions for?"

"Sports on one, history channel on the other."

"Why doesn't that surprise me?" Melissa said, laughing. "He drove Charlie crazy with the clicking back and forth."

In the bathroom, Melissa's throat tightened at the sight of his toothbrush, the cap left off the toothpaste. Little things hurt the worst. The toilet seat was still up, and two towels were tossed carelessly over the shower curtain.

Susan hung them neatly. "Look at this. I tell him all the time, but . . ." Her voice faded.

"Jeanette said he never met a towel rack that could tame him."

They went into the bedroom, their attention immediately drawn to the windows. All three windows were floor to ceiling. One was covered with plywood. In a newer building, they would have been solid plate glass, but this was a renovated brick mill and the windows could open wide. Too wide.

Melissa searched for something to say to break the bitter spell. "What's that gray stuff everywhere?"

"Fingerprint powder. They had to rule out foul play. I told them over and over that he wouldn't have done this to himself. When they learned how my mother had died and about his broken engagement—" Susan choked on a sob. "The coroner's report said *inconclusive,* but everyone thought they knew. And I thought, deep inside, that they were right, this was a suicide, but I never told anyone until that night with you that I drove him to it."

"Shush. If that's all there was, we wouldn't be here." Melissa's gaze wandered the room. A weight bench and treadmill dominated the window side. The bed was set kitty-corner, tossed with sheets and a quilt. One wall was covered with framed photos that Christopher had taken. Fenway Park, flying geese, the Rocky Mountains, kids playing in a big fountain. And a figure on horseback, riding into the sunrise.

Susan wiped her eyes. "That's you on Rayya, isn't it? I was so angry that he put your picture up, I didn't even notice that she was an Arabian. I'm so sorry, Melissa. Can you please for—"

"As Charlie would say, stifle it."

"That's Archie Bunker," Susan mumbled.

"Stunning resemblance between him and your pa, huh?"

In the middle of laughing, Melissa's breath caught in her throat. On the floor next to the bed was an open suitcase, overflowing with clothes. Her knees buckled, and Susan caught her.

"Sit," Susan said, guiding her to the weight bench. "Head between your knees."

"He was packing to come to me . . ." Melissa bent double and stared at the floor, deep breaths, pushing through the fog, when she saw it.

She dropped to her knees. Susan tried to help her back up.

"No, wait." Jammed under the leg press was an iron bar. She opened Susan's left hand and lay the bar across it. It was a perfect fit.

"I don't understand," Susan said. "What did Jacob have to do with these weights?"

"Don't you see?" Melissa's heart burned, fury rising up her throat. "Christopher was always leaving things around, must have left this near the window. Got in that fight with you, wasn't watching where he was going, and stepped on it."

Melissa demonstrated how Christopher must have slipped on the bar, his feet going out from under him. She tumbled against the plywood while the bar rolled under the leg press—but on that day there was no board, just an open window.

"It was an accident, a stupid accident. How could you, God? I hate

You for this," Melissa said over and over, until Susan pressed her hand to her mouth.

Melissa slapped it away.

"No, listen. There were angels," Susan said. "I know there were, that's what Jacob wanted me—wanted us—to know. No one falls without God knowing. They were there for him. It's okay, Melissa. Christopher's okay, better than okay."

Melissa breathed deeply, letting this hope—no, this certainty—sink in. Peace settled into the void that her anger had owned, a firm peace that made her wipe her tears away and look into Susan's face. "Are *you* okay?"

Susan nodded, lips trembling.

"What about the sailboats?"

She bit her lip. "I just don't . . . wait! I forgot about the pillows he bought at Macy's. I didn't like them because they didn't match the décor."

Susan straightened the bedcovers, a bright blue-and-yellow quilt and pale yellow sheets. In the pile were two pillows in yellow shams marked with blue sailboats. She handed one to Melissa, and each woman pressed a pillow to her face, smelling more mustiness than Christopher, but that was okay.

After a minute, Melissa pulled off the sham, pounded at the pillow, found nothing. Susan did the same.

"There can't be nothing," Melissa said.

"Christopher had three of these. There's another one somewhere."

Susan looked under the bed. Melissa was drawn to the suitcase, sadness pricking the delicate peace. *Mercy allows the pain,* Jacob had told Susan. Melissa would have to learn to live with it, and yet she couldn't bear to look into his half-packed suitcase with the tumble of T-shirts and jeans. She closed the suitcase.

The other pillow had been hidden by the lid. "It's here." She passed it to Susan. "Check it out."

Something rustled, caught inside the sham. "It's a letter."

"Who is it to?"

"Me." Susan's voice broke.

"Can you read it?"

Susan began to read aloud, her eyes clear because, like Melissa, she was all cried out.

Mum, I know you didn't mean what you said. You'll worry, but it's okay. I'm not leaving because of that, but because I love Melissa and need to get to her. All that stuff about her wanting a bribe . . .

Susan looked at Melissa.

She held up her hands. "It's over. Don't even go there."

. . . it's not true. She's up to something or you're up to something, or maybe both of you think you're doing this for my own good. Like I'm too young or something. I am young, but I've thought this through, prayed this through. And I know what I need to do. I'll move mountains to get Melissa to marry me. And Mum, someday . . .

Susan looked up at Melissa. ". . . someday Melissa will be just like a daughter to you."

Melissa found her way into Susan's arms and stayed there.

BE STILL

By Victoria James

Raindrops falling on my window.
The world I see is washed away in gray.
Facing this reflection
there are thoughts one wouldn't mention.
What can I do to push them away?

Pre-chorus:
You give every day to be its own
when the sparrow falls, Mercy's wings will carry her home.

Chorus:
Be still, and know I have loved you.
Be still. My arms surround you.
All of the seasons are a myriad of reasons
I'm right here beside you.
Be still, and know that I am God.

Time alone and on the edge,
there's nothing safe about this rocky ledge.
I hear a voice upon the wind.
How can I face my pain again?

Petals lying on the floor
like many dreams I've had before.
Still you send your grace like the rain.
You wash me clean and I have found hope again.

ACKNOWLEDGMENTS

I OWE A HUGE DEBT OF GRATITUDE TO JO HARDESTY LAUTER who provided expert help on Arabians for this Eastern "dude." I know nothing about horses except that they are beautiful and powerful and loyal and . . . as you can see, Jo's done her job well. Jo was God's gift to me exactly when I needed her, and has blessed many in the same way.

I'm grateful to L. B. Norton who helped midwife this book with a fine and gentle touch. I couldn't do any of this without the guidance and support of my agent, Lee Hough, who continues to shine the Lord's light in my path.

What can I say about Victoria James who wrote a haunting song for this book? Before she even knew anything about this book, the Lord showed her the heart of this story and she obediently and lovingly brought it to life. Go to Victoriajamesmusic.com and enjoy *Be Still* as well as many other songs she has written and sung to bless my books.

Reading Group Guide Available at:

www.westbowpress.com/readingguides